"COME NOW, YO[...]
OF WHAT IS ON M[...]

Lord, it wasn't longing she saw in him but something far more dangerous to her sensibilities. "How should I know? Reading your mind would be like trying to catch dandelion fluff."

With a catlike grace, he moved to where she sat. He leaned on her desk with both hands splayed palm down. He bent over, so close there was no escaping his essence. "It is not finished between us, *chère*."

For a moment, she was afraid he was about to kiss her and that she'd be helpless to stop him. "We were finished when I left."

"*Non*. That will happen only when we have the talk I spoke of."

He hovered over her, so close she could make out the subtle differences between his black pupils and those dark irises. A wide chasm opened low in her belly. Deep in that chasm, an indecent flame lit.

Also by Kathleen Bittner Roth

Celine

Alanna

Josette

Published by Kensington Publishing Corporation

Felice

Kathleen Bittner Roth

ZEBRA BOOKS
KENSINGTON PUBLISHING CORP.
www.kensingtonbooks.com

ZEBRA BOOKS are published by

Kensington Publishing Corp.
119 West 40th Street
New York, NY 10018

All Kensington titles, imprints, and distributed lines are available at special quantity discounts for bulk purchases for sales promotion, premiums, fund-raising, educational, or institutional use.

Special book excerpts or customized printings can also be created to fit specific needs. For details, write or phone the office of the Kensington Sales Manager: Attn.: Sales Department. Kensington Publishing Corp., 119 West 40th Street, New York, NY 10018. Phone: 1-800-221-2647.

Zebra and the Z logo Reg. U.S. Pat. & TM Off.

First Printing: May 2020
ISBN-13: 978-1-4201-4208-2
ISBN-10: 1-4201-4208-9

eISBN-13: 978-1-4201-4209-9 (eBook)
eISBN-10: 1-4201-4209-7 (eBook)

10 9 8 7 6 5 4 3 2 1

Printed in the United States of America

Chapter One

New Orleans, 1859

No matter how far Felicité Marielle Christiane Andrews traveled, her stubborn heart refused to abandon New Orleans.

As she stepped smartly off her family's clipper ship, *Celine*, onto the sun-bleached docks of New Orleans' Crescent Harbor, sweet nostalgia gripped her, moistening her eyes.

At her side, her fiancé, Mayhew Rutherford, Marquess of Ainsworth, wrinkled his nose, causing his mustache to twitch. "Pray don't linger, darling. This place reeks of fish."

"What were you expecting, the scent of roses along a waterfront?" Felice tilted her head and arched a brow. Then she looked away, a hint of a smile on her lips.

"Why, you little minx. I do believe you are flirting with me."

"Is it sweetening your ill-humored mood?"

His brown-eyed gaze slowly swept over her from head to toe. The corners of his mouth lifted and he gave her a wink. "It's hotter than Hades here as well. And to think we're barely into March."

She glanced at his fair-haired locks, darkened with perspiration and plastered against his forehead. "You might try putting your hat back on your head. The sun and all."

He swiped at the damp hair clinging to his brow and donned the beaver hat. With a scowl, he removed it again. Unintelligible grumblings erupted from his lips.

"Really, Ainsworth? You sound as if you've marbles tumbling about that sharp tongue of yours."

"Gads, you just called me Ainsworth." He pinched the bridge of his nose, then with a tilt of his head, cocked a brow at her. "I do believe I've managed to annoy you."

As mischief filled his eyes, he reached out and caressed her cheek with the back of his hand. "Do forgive me, darling. The combination of this sultry heat and the need to acquire my land legs has taken a ghastly toll on my usual charm and effervescence."

She laughed. His was a wicked wit that never failed to amuse her.

With a snap of his wrist, he flattened his beaver hat against his thigh, then wedged the bothersome thing under his arm and glanced about. "Any hope of locating a decent horse in these parts?"

"Not dockside, I would expect."

"A pity. After weeks at sea, a good ride would surely cure what ails me."

Felice studied the tall, handsome man beside her. Mayhew could charm the coat off the queen's back had he a mind to. Silently, she congratulated herself on landing one of the most eligible bachelors in the whole of England. Soon, he would make her a first-rate husband—provided her father gave his blessing—and provided that deplorable incident in Paris, along with its ensuing nightmare, remained her secret.

Fingers of guilt trailed a path down her spine, sending a flurry of goose bumps along her arms. What she wouldn't give if the saints above would kindly erase the dreadful memory. But blast it all, she wasn't about to let one miserable blunder that occurred three years ago ruin her chances of a decent married life.

Mayhew waved a hand in front of her face. "Hallo? Have I lost you somewhere in the ethers? Or are you quizzing that sharp little mind of yours for the location of a good equine?"

Snapping out of her reverie, she caught his curious gaze and quipped, "My *little* mind? Have you forgotten I can beat the stuffing out of you at chess? My brother keeps a fine stable, by the by. I'll see to the matter at once."

"Brilliant!" His entire countenance lit up while the dimple in his left cheek deepened.

She slipped her hand through the crook of his arm and started forward. "After a short jaunt in the saddle, not only will you be fit as a fiddle, you'll find New Orleans quite captivating. Especially the Vieux Carré."

"Ah, the French Quarter. Where the aristocrats originally settled, and where your late mother was born." He shot her another fetching grin. "See, pet, I do listen. And what makes a fiddle fit?"

"I'll ignore your last remark. See the building over there with my family's name etched in gold?"

"One would have to jolly well be blind to miss it."

"Therein lie the offices of the Andrews Shipping Company. My brother oversees the entire Gulf Coast and Caribbean lines from here and has been expecting our arrival, so unless I am mistaken, Michel's eyes should be fixed on us at this very moment."

Mayhew harrumphed. "Then why the devil isn't

Mee-shell, as you call him, out here to greet us? Has the heat fogged his brain, or do the natives hereabouts lack proper manners?"

"That wasn't amusing in the least."

"Wasn't meant to be."

"Truly, you *are* out of sorts. You'll find my brother's manners impeccable, by the by, but less rigid than those of you English. He's likely avoiding the blazing sun and waiting until we enter the offices to greet us. Come along."

As if on cue, the door opened wide. Michel stood at the entrance, a generous smile aimed at Felice. "It's about time you arrived, little sister."

A thrill shot through her at the sight of him, at the sound of his familiar soft, Southern drawl. Casting decorum aside, she shoved her parasol at her lady's companion and rushed to her brother's side. She threw her arms around him and blew a kiss on one cheek, then the other.

"Oh, Michel, it's so very good to see you! I am absolutely dying to meet your wife. Who would've thought you, a confirmed bachelor, would end up wed to a widow with six children?"

He set her at arm's length, his warm brown eyes glittering with amusement. "Soon to be seven."

"Oh my word!" She turned to Mayhew, who'd stepped forward. "I'd like you to meet Mayhew Rutherford, Marquess of Ainsworth." She smiled at her intended. "And soon to be my fiancé, once we make our way to Carlton Oaks for Papa's approval. Behind him is Mrs. Dawes, my traveling companion."

Michel reached out and shook Ainsworth's hand. "Good to finally meet you, sir." With a sweep of his arm, he bade them enter. "You'll find the air a bit cooler inside."

He turned to Felice's traveling companion. "Mrs. Dawes,

I do hope my sister gave you little reason to consider jumping ship in the middle of the Atlantic. Felice can be quite the spirited woman. As well as hardheaded. Has been all her life."

Felice poked her brother in the ribs. "Oh, you."

He laughed and sidestepped another jab.

Plump Mrs. Dawes, a sheen covering her red cheeks, swiped at a limp feather adorning a felt hat the color of mud and tucked a stray lock beneath the brim. "I've no complaints, sir. She's been kind to me, she has. And her pluck is far more agreeable than the dreadful young ladies I had the misfortune of serving previously."

Felice followed Michel's lead and stepped inside.

And nearly tripped over herself.

At the sight of the dark-haired, dark-eyed man standing in front of a waist-high table in the center of the large, whitewashed room, the breath she'd sucked in stuck in her windpipe.

René Thibodeaux!

The blasted, no-good Cajun who'd fractured her heart three years ago—and the sole reason she'd fled New Orleans—turned his head and settled his penetrating midnight gaze on her.

She didn't need an iced drink to prompt the chill that raced through her from head to toe. What the devil was *he* doing here? He was supposed to be overseeing their offices in Jamaica, and not scheduled to return until well after she'd departed Louisiana altogether. She'd taken great care to check and double-check the company schedule, had timed her visit to avoid him.

The moment hung suspended between them, only to expand as his feral gaze remained fixed on her. For the life of her, she could not look away from the man who'd once kissed her as if she meant everything in the world to him, only to discard her with appalling words that had cut to the bone.

She stuffed the sharp memory inside the knot in her throat and swallowed. The years, and apparently his elevated position in her family's business, had matured him in a way she couldn't quite define. His was a chiseled face, leaner and more defined than when she'd last seen him. Thick, shiny hair, black as a moonless night, hung near to his collar, framing that gloriously handsome visage. Crisply starched shirtsleeves, meticulously rolled at the cuffs, exposed the roped muscles of his forearms. A gold-embroidered silk waistcoat was draped over broad shoulders and fitted snug against a taut stomach. The expert tailoring of his trousers over long legs revealed a man in superb physical form—serving to further display someone she'd done her best to forget.

Despite his polish and refinement, an imperceptible shift took place in his demeanor, betraying the uncivilized, unreachable man lurking beneath the surface. He stood over an array of what appeared to be maritime maps, his gaze upon her so intense it could have been a physical touch.

This wouldn't do, gaping at him like an utter fool. Had her brain ceased to function as well as her lungs? Collecting herself, she managed to incline her head in a small gesture of greeting. "Monsieur Thibodeaux."

His all-pervading gaze never left hers. "Mademoiselle Andrews."

Two words. Two bloody words in that lyrical Cajun drawl rumbling low in his throat, and in one cruel instant, wicked memories she'd thought time had erased licked at every nerve she possessed.

Mayhew glanced at her, then at Thibodeaux and back again. His brow furrowed. "Felice?"

She forced a smile. "Forgive me, darling. Monsieur René Thibodeaux, allow me to introduce you to Mayhew Rutherford, the Marquess of Ainsworth. Lord Ainsworth has accompanied me from England for the purpose of asking my father for my hand in marriage."

"*Oui*. I am aware." An indecipherable keenness flared in René's eyes. "I review every passenger manifest and message that crosses my desk."

He stepped forward, his movements as sleek as a bayou panther's. Extending his hand to Ainsworth, René lifted his left brow. Felice knew that little quirk—a telltale sign he wasn't particularly pleased. The audacity of him, to boldly scrutinize the man she intended to marry.

Was that her imagination, or did a flicker of coldness form hard lines at the outer corners of Mayhew's eyes as the two clasped hands?

"We have iced lemonade with crushed mint if you are feeling overheated," René said.

Ainsworth's brow furrowed. "Iced, you say? How the devil does one come about such luxury in this morbid heat?"

"In winter, we ship large blocks of the stuff down the Mississippi from up north and store it in heavily insulated icehouses. I'll see to getting you a glass."

Her emotions at odds, she gave the men her back and faced the empty desk at the end of the room. "Where is Mr. Abbott? I've never known him to be absent from his position."

Michel's expression turned dour. "I'm afraid Abbott has taken seriously ill."

Her heart tripped. "Oh, dear. I must visit his bedside at once." She turned to Mayhew. "Mr. Abbott keeps the ledgers. He's been with the company from the beginning and is like an uncle to me."

Michel scrubbed a hand through his hair. "He's not taking visitors."

"Surely he'd see me."

Michel shook his head. "You know what a private person he can be. An attendant who looks after him stops by once a week to keep us apprised of his condition. He'll let us know when Abbott intends to return. In the meanwhile, you'll have to remain for as long as we may need you to manage the ledgers in his absence."

"Me?"

Ainsworth stepped forward. "Her? What the devil? Women of her ilk do not labor."

She knew the answer before she spoke, but objections worked past her lips nonetheless. "Surely you can find someone other than me to take his place for a few days? Can't Monsieur Thibodeaux fill in? It's imperative I go upriver to Papa."

Michel, ever the big brother, stepped forward and peered down his nose at her. "Besides the lurch Abbott's illness has left us in, we have three new ships due to anchor, which has caused Thibodeaux to delay a vital journey to Jamaica. As it is, he's overworked. We cannot spare a moment of his time to tend to the accounts."

Lord, this wouldn't do. She could hardly wait to exit the office in order to leave René behind, and here Michel was telling her to work alongside the man? But then, how could her brother possibly know what had occurred between René and her? "I am sorry, Michel. I am unavailable. Hire someone from town."

He cocked a brow and fisted his hands on his hips, his demeanor taking on a familiar sternness. "This isn't like you, Felice. You haven't even inquired as to the nature of Abbott's condition."

"Well . . . well," she sputtered. "I didn't think it a proper subject to discuss in mixed company."

"For your information, he has a heart condition and suffered a bout of apoplexy."

Her hand splayed over her heart. "Oh my, this *is* serious."

"He may not be able to return for a long while. He's the one who taught you everything you know about keeping the books for our company, and because you've inspected the ledgers in most of our offices around the world, there's no one better to take his place. I'm not asking you, Felice; I'm telling you to step in. It's not as if you have a pressing need to return to England."

Ainsworth stepped forward. "Impossible, Andrews. You heard Felice. We don't intend to remain in town for more than forty-eight hours. Besides, no future wife of mine will toil in an office—especially one alongside a dock teeming with stevedores and sailors. I don't care if this is the largest maritime operation in the world. I'll not have it."

Felice swore she heard a soft snort coming from behind her. Be damned if she'd turn around and acknowledge René's caustic response. Under any other circumstance, she'd have been the one to offer her services without hesitation. She'd always done all she could for the family business. And Michel was right—she'd spent more than two years traveling from one seaport office to another, scrutinizing the company ledgers. No one would be better suited to take Abbott's place; he was the one who'd trained her in this very office.

But to be confined in the same room with René? Hell's bells.

She narrowed her eyes at her brother. "The least you

could've done was ask me nicely, instead of demanding I do your bidding. You know how I deplore being ordered about."

Michel's stubborn scowl told her that not only would there be no backing down, there'd be no rephrasing his request. At least he'd be at his desk every day to act as a buffer between her and René. If she put her head down and tended to the accounts, she'd not have to utter a word to the man.

Beside Mr. Abbott's desk stood a glass-fronted bookcase. She caught René's reflection. With his back to her and his head down, he toiled on whatever lay before him. Nonetheless, he had to have heard every word spoken. Dear heavens, he must have known all along that she'd be in the office first thing in the morning—working right alongside him.

Saints help her.

Chapter Two

René stood at his worktable and stared at the map in front of him. Where the hell had he left off? Discreetly retrieving his handkerchief from his trouser pocket, he swiped at the moisture left by Ainsworth's clammy handshake.

By rights, René should be in Jamaica, not standing here with this familiar sensation of being an outsider in his gut. What he wouldn't give to have all three ships dock before nightfall. He'd be too busy inspecting one newly crafted vessel after the other to set foot inside the office. Once that was done, his brother would take over the office assignment, leaving René free to set sail for the islands without so much as a backward glance. Whatever the case, before his departure, he intended to try to make things right with Felice.

Maybe then he could get a decent night's sleep.

Christ, he needed to gather his wits about him, ignore her and Lord What's-his-name. He'd known before she stepped through the door that Michel intended to put her to work in Abbott's absence, so why had her arrival skewed his sensibilities?

He knew why, damn it.

She'd breezed in big as you please, only to come to a

dead halt when she'd set those spectacular onyx eyes on him. Her recovery had been swift enough, but there'd been no escaping the stunned look on her face—an expression that woke the devil inside him. Had it not been for Michel's presence in the room, René might've responded to her discomposure with something he damn well shouldn't have. Good thing her protective brother had followed her in and hadn't caught her ill-disguised response. God forbid the man should guess there had ever been anything between Felice and him.

Her voice.

That silken sound still had the bad habit of sliding under his skin and making an idiot of him. He swore he could smell the light scent that was hers alone—like magnolias at midnight.

Impossible.

He hadn't stood that close to her.

Christ, but he still found her intriguing. While she bore the demeanor of a woman who knew nothing of poverty or ugliness, she nonetheless seemed unaware of her unique allure. He'd once thought she must have been spoiled rotten. Not only had she enjoyed a privileged upbringing, she'd been the only female raised in a family of protective males—brothers, cousin, and doting father. The last thing he'd expected when he'd met the raven-haired beauty was a woman possessed of a keen wit and a no-nonsense air, one who easily held her own among her powerful kin. And if all that was not enough, she was also an heiress, wealthy beyond reason.

Quite the catch, this one.

And one who would forever be well beyond this Cajun's reach.

A pulse along his temple began to pound. He rubbed at the back of his neck. How in hell was he going to work alongside her and keep her brother from suspecting there had ever been anything between them? If Michel or any other of her male relatives knew René had nearly ruined her, he'd be out the door. He couldn't bear to give up this life he'd worked so hard to create. His position in the company was what had delivered him, the illegitimate son of a voodoo witch, out of the bayou shanty where he'd been born and raised and into a position of respectability he'd otherwise have no hope of achieving. If he were ever to lose his place in this revered company, he'd be rejected by the entire town before sundown. And so would his brother, who'd followed along in his footsteps.

He wasn't a particularly devout man, but now might be a good time to pray for those ships to arrive.

Just when he'd managed to tune out the conversation across the room, Felice's voice grew suddenly irritated, catching René's attention once again.

"What do you mean, I won't be residing with you while I'm in town?"

She wouldn't?

René turned his head enough to catch a glimpse of Michel looming over his sister, his voice growing gruffer by the moment. "You'll remain in the family town house."

"But I assumed Lord Ainsworth would board there."

He would?

"Dear sister, use a bit of common sense. With you laboring here in the office, and with no one at his disposal other than a single day servant, Lord Ainsworth would be bored silly. He'll be more comfortable sequestered in the manse with all it has to offer."

"What does that have to do with my not staying with you?"

"We'll get to that." Michel turned to Ainsworth. "Our company owns the largest home in the Garden District of

New Orleans. It is called Le Blanc House. It's situated two blocks from my residence. Our ships' captains bunk there. They've been known to be good company, by the way. Any one of them would likely relish the idea of poking around town with you while awaiting the next voyage. Also, the estate is managed by Thibodeaux's two cousins, one of whom happens to be the best cook in the city—if not all of Louisiana."

Ainsworth shoved his hands in his pockets and rocked back on his heels. He grinned at Felice. "Fancy that, darling."

Michel gave him a perfunctory nod. "I think you'll find yourself nicely situated."

He turned back to Felice. "As for boarding with me, my wife's children are a rowdy lot who have taken up every bedroom, nook, and cranny in my home. I doubt you'd find a moment's peace, let alone a decent spot on which to lay your head."

Felice narrowed her eyes at Michel. "What is it you are not telling me, brother?"

He snatched the chair in front of his desk, turned it backward and straddling it, hung his wrists over the back, and gave her a sardonic grin. "How very good it is to see you, dear sister. Suffice it to say that my newly acquired children entered my life as a rather unruly lot. I'm still in the process of"—he shrugged—"settling them in, so to speak."

René couldn't help his soft chuckle. "That's putting things mildly."

"I'll ignore your comments, Thibodeaux." Nonetheless, he shot René a mirthful glance.

Henri, the company's gangly, fifteen-year-old errand boy, who was in dire need of a decent haircut, scooted into the office, slapped a stack of papers on René's desk, and shoved his hair out of his eyes.

"Ah, Henri," René said, and continued speaking to the lad in French. "Kindly serve Mademoiselle Andrews and Lord Ainsworth a glass of iced lemonade, *s'il vous plaît*."

Michel craned his neck. "And then escort my sister and Lord Ainsworth to Le Blanc House, where his lordship will be residing during his stay in our town."

"*Oui, monsieur.*" Henri disappeared behind a closed door, shortly to reappear with two glasses of the iced thirst quencher on a silver tray.

"After Mademoiselle Andrews has taken the time to introduce his lordship to the staff and has given him a tour of the premises," Michel said, "kindly escort her and her companion to the family town house in the Vieux Carré. Also, have their luggage delivered. And ask Régine to prepare a Cajun dinner for . . . ah, six or seven persons. I'd like to dine at nine of the clock."

"*Oui, monsieur.*"

Michel addressed Ainsworth. "Ordinarily, I would host a dinner at Antoine's your first evening in the city. It happens to be the finest restaurant in the Quarter, but because Felice is eager to meet my wife, and because Brenna's present condition leaves her indisposed to public outings, I thought it best to take our meal at the manse. If you'd prefer to dine elsewhere with only the two of you, we can arrange that as well."

"I'm quite content with a private gathering. What say you, Felice?"

She glanced around the room before giving a silent nod.

Michel turned to René. "The number for dinner includes you and your brother. Where the devil is he anyway?"

René shrugged. "I am not my brother's keeper. Henri, leave word at Le Blanc House for Bastien to join us."

"*Oui, monsieur*," Henri shot over his shoulder as he raced out the door.

"Michel," Felice said. "Might Mayhew and I slip over to your stables and fetch a couple of your fabulous horses for a ride about town this afternoon?"

René chuckled. Michel glanced over his shoulder at him and mumbled under his breath.

Felice scowled. "What did you say?"

"Nothing worth hearing," Michel replied. "Except for a mare we use for the buggy—and she's kept under lock and key—all my equines, including that donkey you rescued some years back and passed over to me, are temporarily stabled at Le Blanc House. You're welcome to any of them."

"There's a story behind this, is there not?" Ainsworth asked.

Michel leaned back in his chair and blew out his breath. "It seems my newly acquired progeny helped themselves to my horses and set about blazing a trail throughout the city. The law didn't take kindly to their actions."

"Not to mention how many neighbors were appalled when the little darlings rode straight through open front doors and out the back," René added. He returned his attention to the maps, silently cursing the prospect of dining with the newly arrived couple. He swiped a hand across his weary eyes and attempted to focus once more on the maps set before him. Picking up his ruler and pen, he shut out the chatter behind him.

A shadow fell over the table.

Ainsworth.

"I say, old chap, are those sea currents you're plotting?"

"*Non*," René replied without looking up. "Nature has provided man with the currents already in place. I am merely creating routes for the three new ships we expect to reach port any day now." *Christ, leave me to my job. I'll have more than enough of your dubious company tonight.*

Ainsworth picked up René's pencil and set about examining it. "I say, old boy, this might be the most unique pen I've ever seen."

"It's a pencil. We use ink to trace over pencil sketches on the final chart."

Ainsworth flipped the gilded utensil about in his hand. One long finger tapped at the stone set in the top. "Ruby, is it?"

René nodded. A muscle twitched along his set jaw. Did the man feel entitled to do whatever he damn well pleased? The arrogant prick had about thirty seconds to let go of the pencil before he'd be divested of it. Perhaps a couple of fingers broken along the way would send a strong message to leave well enough alone. "*Oui*, a ruby."

"Where'd you get such a fine utensil, if you don't mind my asking?"

I do mind. "China. Had it made there."

Ainsworth slowed his flipping of the instrument. As he set it down, his shrewd gaze settled on René. "You like the finer things in life, I see."

"Should finer things suit me, then *oui*, I manage to get them."

Once again, Ainsworth placed his fingers on the pencil he'd set in front of René. Slowly, he rolled it back and forth. "As long as what suits you does not belong to someone else. I too prefer the finest that life has to offer. And when something is mine, I protect my property, even if it means drawing blood."

René met Ainsworth's eyes with a hard gaze of his own. Either the man was extraordinarily perceptive and hadn't missed the tension between René and Felice, or he was mighty insecure about her affections. Whatever his thinking, he was like a dog taking a piss to mark his territory. René gave a nod toward Felice, who was locked in conversation with Michel. "Mademoiselle Andrews, she is your fiancée, *oui*?"

"It will be official once her father gives his approval." Ainsworth arched a brow. "So, we are clear on certain points, my friend?"

Another kind of devil inside René raised his sleepy eyelids, one who'd fought dirtier battles than Ainsworth could ever imagine. Slowly and decisively, René collected his pencil, along with a stack of bills of lading Henri had deposited on the worktable. Before he turned to exit the office, he spoke quietly, his unflinching gaze still fixed on Ainsworth. "It is a wedding vow you will be taking, not a blood oath, *oui*?"

Chapter Three

The small, covered landau Felice rode in pulled up in front of Le Blanc House. The driver jumped from his perch, opened the door, and lowering the footstep, helped her from the conveyance. She adjusted her emerald necklace, smoothed the front of her matching silk gown, then paused long enough to take in the sight of a fancy, two-seater gig parked alongside hers.

She ran her gloved fingers over the gleaming black fender edged in gold. A carriage ride under the stars in this open-top jewel would've been just the thing. But leave it to her unduly protective brother to send a driver in a closed equipage outfitted with curtained windows too small to catch so much as one flickering firefly.

She turned to face Le Blanc House. The imposing, white-columned mansion, surrounded by an ornate, wrought-iron fence, took up half the city block. It was the largest and most magnificent home in the Garden District—or at least it had been when she'd departed New Orleans on the run.

Despite the balmy evening, a sudden chill overtook her. She rubbed her bare arms. Blast it all, the last thing she needed was to spend the evening in René's company. Working alongside him on the morrow would be torture enough. Had it not been for her curiosity regarding Michel's bride, she'd have found an excuse to beg off.

Thus far, little had turned out the way she'd anticipated. Her nemesis was not even supposed to be here. And now she was about to share a meal with the scalawag right here at Le Blanc House, where both he and his brother resided. She'd be required to sit at the same table for an entire evening and pretend to be happy as a lark. Lord have mercy should the vexatious man take a seat beside her.

She passed through the elaborate gate, hiked her skirts to her ankles, and climbed the few steps leading to the front entrance. Lifting the heavy brass lion's head, she let the knocker fall against the metal plate with a resounding bang.

One of the double doors set with beveled glass swung wide. Felice stared into the face of René's cousin, a dark-haired woman dressed in gray and white, the mansion's hostess. "Vivienne. So good to see you."

Ever the stoic one, Vivienne managed something akin to a smile. "Welcome, *mademoiselle*. The other guests are in the parlor. If you will follow me, *s'il vous plaît*."

"Of course." Felice entered the foyer only to trip over a pair of women's shoes.

"Pardon," Vivienne said, and set aside the embroidered slippers. "One of the guests left these behind."

"What a curious thing to do."

With no further explanation as to the mysterious guest or why someone would leave expensive footwear behind, Vivienne led Felice along the grand corridor.

As they passed the wide staircase leading to the second level, heat flushed Felice's cheeks. Three years ago, she'd been carried up those very steps and to a suite four doors down on the right—René's rooms. What had she been thinking? She hadn't been thinking, that's what. Lord, what would have come of her had he not suddenly stopped at the threshold and set her down. What if he hadn't suddenly turned on her and uttered those scurrilous words that had cut her to the quick and sent her flying from his arms . . . and away from New Orleans.

Her breath hitched.

She braced herself for whoever she might run into on her march to the parlor. But as she passed through the wide corridor, where gilt-framed oil paintings hung against damask-covered walls the color of an emerald-green forest, where lush flowers and a silver candelabrum topped a French side table, her only greeting was the savory aromas of a delicious meal to come.

"Régine must be busy preparing her marvelous Cajun fare," she said as they proceeded toward a faint buzz of voices.

Oh, dear.

She reached the open parlor doors and paused at the entrance. Vivienne deftly stepped aside and hastened down a corridor leading to the kitchen. No one appeared to notice Felice's arrival. Mayhew, his back to her, had the full attention of a golden-haired beauty wearing a low-cut gown of burnished silk. Michel and Bastien stood to the right of a blue velvet divan, deep in conversation. René, seated on a luxurious sofa, was chatting with a very pregnant woman.

Michel's wife.

Despite her expanded girth, Brenna was a striking woman. Much to Felice's surprise, a cloud of red curls framed her lovely face. For some reason, she'd imagined someone with dark hair. But then, Michel had never described Brenna's physical appearance in his letters, leaving Felice's imagination to fill in the blanks.

She glanced about the ornate room, bursting with

priceless goods from around the world. A French *étagère* stood against the far wall between two large windows hung with curtains matching the deep blue of the divan. An exquisite Chinese carpet covered the dark wood floor. A Greek bust on a pedestal filled one corner.

René glanced her way. His intense gaze pierced her skin and set every nerve in her body on edge. Brenna shifted her attention from René to follow his line of sight, then turned her head and said something to Michel.

"Felice." Michel strode to where she stood, blew a kiss on each cheek and, lifting a flute of champagne from a servant's tray, slipped the drink into Felice's hand.

"*Merci*," she said as she stepped into the room. Not giving a darn about appearances, she downed the drink. "I'll have another."

"Take care lest you become light-headed, little sister," he murmured as he handed her the second glass and reached for one for himself.

"I *always* take care, *dear* brother." Taking small sips of her drink, she matched the low volume of his voice. "Have you forgotten I am no longer a child to be ordered about? Oh wait . . . I am soon to enter into hard labor on your behalf, so it would be remiss of me if I failed to remind you that I came of age some three years ago. Hence, I do not require your unsolicited advice."

She took another sip of her champagne. "Never have, actually."

"Trying to goad me, are you?" Amusement settled in his eyes. "It's about time you arrived. I'm so famished, my stomach is ready to dine on my backbone."

"I lost track of the hour." In truth, she'd dawdled far too long over her hair. Mrs. Dawes, who'd grown more anxious at every passing moment, finally pulled the sides of Felice's hair back, affixed tortoiseshell combs behind each ear, and created a cascade of curls down her back.

Mayhew and Bastien Thibodeaux nearly collided making their way to where she stood. "Darling," Mayhew said, and deftly stepped in front of Bastien, who paused in midstep and cocked a brow at her.

Mayhew raised her gloved hand to his lips. His gaze dropped to the necklace at her throat. "Would you look at this beauty?"

Slipping a finger behind the large, square-cut emerald she wore on a finely wrought golden chain, he drew it away from her body for closer inspection. "Sink me if this isn't a rarity. I fear my family's jewels might do little to impress you once we are wed and they are at your disposal."

She nudged his hand away. "As long as a bauble complements my garment, it could be paste for all I care."

He winked at her, and the dimple in his left cheek deepened. "Nonetheless, you look stunning. As usual."

She grinned at him. "And you, as usual, are a hopeless flirt."

He chuckled.

Her peripheral vision caught sight of René. He rose from the divan and moved to where the golden-haired goddess stood. She slipped her hand through his arm and leaned close—intimately close—and either whispered in his ear or planted a kiss near it, Felice couldn't tell.

His mistress?

His wife?

Surely she'd have heard had he wed. Felice's heart had no business stalling in her chest. Nonetheless, the fickle thing did just that. She downed the champagne and, setting the empty flute on a side table, snatched a third from the servant's tray. "If you'll excuse me, I've yet to greet a dear friend or meet my new sister by marriage."

"Of course, love," Mayhew said, and struck up a conversation with Michel.

She extended her hand to René's brother. "Bastien, what a pleasant surprise. I'm puzzled, though. Unless I read the schedule wrong, I thought you'd departed London for Spain."

He leaned in and greeted her the French way, by blowing a kiss across each cheek. He addressed her in his native Cajun tongue. "*Non*. With three new ships due here all at once, I was ordered to return home."

He flashed her a grin, exposing even, white teeth against a closely cropped black beard—a beard so artfully clipped, he must take great care every morning to sculpt it just so. "Not that I find being dispatched back here a hardship."

Had he been clean-shaven, and had he been born with René's dark-as-sin eyes instead of his father's deep blue, the brothers could've passed for twins. And when it came to their questionable pasts, they did indeed mirror each other. So how could one brother have become a trusted friend, while the other scoundrel still managed to upend her world with a mere glance?

Truth be told, had she been attracted to Bastien in the same way his older brother once fascinated her, she'd have run from him as well. Gossip had it he was a very, very bad boy when it came to the fairer sex. But despite his wicked ways, women swooned over him—just as they fawned over his equally nefarious brother. Not that she gave a darn, but at thirty-four years of age, perhaps the elder Thibodeaux had at last decided to settle down with one woman.

"Come meet Brenna," Michel said. He took her hand and led her to the divan. "My wife is most anxious to meet you. She's not up to moving about or standing for any length of time. Or sitting in one place for very long, for that matter. Which is why I must insist on keeping the evening brief."

Thank the Heavens.

Felice took a seat on the divan next to Brenna and clasped her hand. A smattering of adorable freckles danced across the bridge of Brenna's nose and across her cheeks—pixie dust. Her rich, burgundy curls framed intelligent green eyes the color of Felice's necklace. Strength and fortitude were evident in the woman's stark gaze. Michel had wed no shrinking violet.

"I cannot tell you how much I've been looking forward to meeting you. Not only did you turn my elusive brother into a devoted family man, but having been raised by men, I am delighted to have acquired a sister through marriage."

Brenna winced. "If'n ye'll let go of me fat fingers, we can have us a wee chat. Hurts ta squeeze the swollen things. Stifles me thoughts, so it does."

"Oh my, I do apologize." Brenna's heavy Irish accent surprised Felice. Michel hadn't written that his wife was Irish, let alone a first-generation immigrant—she had to be a newcomer, what with that heavy, melodic lilt to her voice. He'd only mentioned that they'd met in Baton Rouge when he'd traveled there on business. Not that it mattered, she supposed, but wasn't it just like a man to leave out precious details when communicating with a sister?

"Michel penned more notes to me after wedding you than I received in all his years at university. After giving me brief news regarding the shipping business, every word referenced you, and how much he adored your children . . . well, *his* children now. I am most eager to meet them."

At the mention of her offspring, Brenna's countenance lit up as if a ray of sunshine had been cast upon her. She rested her clasped hands on her swollen belly. "They'd like that ye care enough to be meetin' them. It's plain to see why I don't get out much these days. Sure as yer born, ye'll find me at home, so do come to visit whenever ye can find the time. Did ye take notice of my shoes deposited at the front door?"

Felice glanced down at Brenna's pudgy toes peeking out from beneath her gown and laughed. "So those were your lovely slippers."

"Aye." Brenna glanced over Felice's shoulder at René and gave a nod. "He's the one encouraged me to cast off me shoes. Says the energy rising up from the earth flows straight into the babe. Strengthens the both of us, he says, so 'tis. I'll be holdin' on to the notion because goin' bare of foot keeps my miserable toes from being pinched."

Felice shot René a quick glance, then returned her attention to Brenna, but not before noting his impeccable attire, his incredible good looks—and the beautiful woman on his arm. "I do recall Monsieur Thibodeaux's sister telling me they'd been raised barefoot in the bayou for that very reason."

Brenna's brows knitted together. "Monsieur Thibodeaux, ye say? Oh, so 'tis René ye be referrin' to."

Apparently, he'd overheard the conversation. He moved to stand in front of them. The corners of his lips curved. The golden-haired woman on his arm fixed Felice with a steady, doe-eyed gaze.

"We have not met, Miss Andrews. I am Mrs. Worth."

A widow.

Of course.

The Thibodeaux brothers chased skirts, but never as far as the altar. How well Felice knew this. The woman was not from around here. Her soft Southern drawl, with its elongated vowels, spoke of someone from the Carolinas, or perhaps the Virginias.

René must have serious intentions toward this woman. Else why bring her to a private dinner?

Dash it all, what did she care? She scanned the room for the servant with the tray of champagne. At the quick turn of her head, dizziness gripped her.

Enough of the bubbly!

The dinner bell rang. And not a moment too soon. Michel helped his wife to her feet. At the sight of Brenna's girth, Felice nearly gasped. *Good heavens, could there be more than one babe in there?*

Reading her expression, Michel shot her a wry grin. "As I said, I do apologize for having to keep the evening rather brief, but as you can see, my lovely wife's capacities are severely limited. Shall we?"

"We could easily have dined in your home," Felice said.

Brenna lifted her chin. "And miss out on some of the finest cookin' in town? Nay."

Felice slipped her hand through Brenna's other arm and gave it a squeeze. "Then onward we go, because I am also looking forward to Régine's legendary fare."

Michel led the group to the smaller of two dining rooms, this one more intimate than the larger one, which seated well over fifty people. French chairs upholstered in a deep rose velvet surrounded a round table covered in a white lace cloth. A bold trompe l'oeil of green ivy and colorful spring flowers covered the walls.

Platters of Cajun food appeared, filling the air with the

redolent aromas she'd known growing up. Everyone began chatting at once. Her stomach rumbled, but no one could've heard over the din that had erupted. Baskets of hot, fresh-baked bread were set on the table, along with tureens of brown jambalaya, two kinds of shrimp gumbo, and several bottles of French wine.

"See here, Mayhew." Felice lifted the lid from a vessel of steaming jambalaya and spooned a ladleful into her dish. "With this kind of local feast, tradition calls for casual dining, so there'll be no servants to fill your plate. And take note—some of this might be a bit spicy for your English palate."

Ainsworth glanced around the table in obvious surprise as everyone but Mrs. Worth eagerly helped themselves. Then, with a shrug, he collected himself and reached for the crockery. He heaped his bowl full of the aromatic stew thick with chicken, andouille sausage and tasso—the spicy, smoky Cajun pork that gave the dish its rich color.

He passed the tureen to his left. "Might I serve you, Mrs. Worth?"

She laid a hand on Mayhew's sleeve. "We've no need to be so formal," she purred. "Call me Liberty."

Mayhew cocked a brow. "Liberty, you say?"

"Liberty Belle, actually." Flickering candlelight from the overhead chandelier danced across the woman's golden hair and played over a sultry smile. "My father had a wicked sense of humor. And yes, you may serve me."

"Brilliant." He proceeded to fill her bowl, then leaned toward her and set the tureen closer to where René sat.

Felice broke off a hunk of hot, crusty bread, dipped it into the thick broth, then popped the juicy morsel into her mouth without spilling a drop. She groaned. "Heavenly."

Mayhew stared at her for a curious moment. "I do say,

my proper English manners stretch only so far. This part of your tradition is where I shall draw the line."

"As does my Virginia comportment," Liberty said, rejecting René's offer of bread.

Felice shrugged. She didn't know whether it was all the champagne, or the idea that Bastien sat to one side of her and Mayhew to her left, that caused her to relax clear to her bones. At last, she was having a good time.

René, who sat directly across from her, paid no attention to the flirting taking place between Mrs. Worth and Mayhew. Instead, he studied Felice through lowered lids, as if judging her reaction.

Well, if he thought the little tête-à-tête between her fiancé and René's companion would bother her, he could think again. Mayhew was an outrageous flirt. Hell's bells, he'd even flirted with his ninety-year-old great-grandmother when they'd visited her. And it must run in the blood, because the dowager duchess flirted right back. If René thought his lady friend had been singled out as someone special, he'd a great deal to learn.

He quit studying her and pulled off a hunk of bread for himself. Dunking it into the thick broth, he dipped his head just enough to gracefully pop the laden piece into his mouth. "Mmm. *Voilà comment savourer un plat digne des dieux.*" The only way to eat food from the gods.

A wave of raw, pagan pleasure gripped her. How many times had she heard that phrase along with the first bite of anything Creole or Cajun? But never had anyone performing that little ritual caused such a reaction in her. Lord, but the man was a curse to her fickle body.

Mayhew paused in his eating. "I say, does anyone know of a daguerreotype establishment in town where I might secure the latest equipment? I rather fancy keeping myself busy whilst Felice is toiling away, and I find these imaging devices fascinating."

Mrs. Worth touched his sleeve again. "My friend's husband owns a shop in town. He carries all the latest photographic equipment. I'd be happy to take you to meet him." She leaned around Mayhew to address Felice. "That is, if you don't mind my stealing his lordship away for a bit."

The woman was beginning to irritate Felice. Nonetheless, she merely shrugged a shoulder. "Lord Ainsworth is his own man, just as I am an independent woman. You've no need to seek my permission."

"Well," Mrs. Worth said, and turned to Ainsworth, "that's settled, then. My home is here in the Garden District, so why don't I collect you in my carriage at, say, ten of the clock?"

Once again, René's eyes were not fixed on the woman he'd brought to the table, but on Felice. Emboldened, she stared back. He lifted his wineglass to his lips and continued to watch her over the rim. She could've sworn he'd tipped it in a silent salute.

The devil.

"Jolly good," Mayhew said. "On the morrow, we shall venture forth at ten sharp."

"If we finish early enough," Mrs. Worth said, "and you aren't too fatigued, perhaps you'd enjoy another jaunt about the outskirts of town on one of Michel's fine steeds."

Felice frowned. How did the woman know Mayhew and Felice had ridden today? And on Michel's horses, no less?

"Brilliant idea," Mayhew said. "I do enjoy a rigorous gallop."

He directed his attention toward the men at the table.

"Might any of you know if there is a gentlemen's boxing club in town? I visit one regularly at home, and I quite miss the practice."

René shot Bastien a speaking glance. "*Oui*. My brother and I can help you with that."

Was that a smirk on Bastien's mouth? She jabbed him in the ribs and spoke through her teeth. "Behave yourself."

Mischief filled his countenance. "*Oui, chère*."

The conversation turned to politics, a subject that bored Felice half to death. The political arena had preoccupied her brother ever since she could remember. Retreating into her own world, she let the voices around her drone in the background like a swarm of honeybees. Her gaze settled on the low floral arrangement in the center of the table. Directly behind the flowers sat René.

She couldn't help it—her vision drifted beyond the centerpiece to where he sat. Paying no attention to his spoken words, she watched the sensual movements of his mouth—a mouth that had once set her on fire with his delicious kisses.

She dropped her gaze to her plate. Mayhew, who was intent on keeping their relationship pure until their wedding night, had never kissed her in such a soul-wrenching way. His were chaste kisses made with closed lips brushed over closed lips. His impeccable manners did not allow him to take her in his arms and envelop her with his essence while murmuring endearments and planting featherlight kisses along the curve of her neck.

Only René had done that.

Realization struck her like a lightning bolt. She'd been four years old when her mother died. The nanny assigned to her had been a mere fifteen—a young girl herself who hadn't been equipped to nurture Felice when she cried out for the mother she missed. The nanny never rocked her back to sleep, nor did she dry tearstained cheeks.

Felice had been surrounded by males: her father, her three brothers, and Cameron, a cousin close enough to be called a brother. Papa saw to it that she had most any material thing she'd desired, but the one thing he could not give at the time was himself. He'd been so wrapped up in grief over the loss of his wife that he'd buried himself in his work for most of Felice's growing years. Along the way, he'd built an empire in Mama's honor while leaving his offspring to run wild on their upriver plantation.

Papa and her brothers loved her. Of that she'd never had any doubt, but until René happened along, she'd had no idea what it felt like to be held. And in such a way as to feel as though she'd been enveloped in a loving warmth that reached clear to her soul.

No wonder she'd fallen hard for him—he'd been an oasis in the dry desert of her life. Until him, she'd had no idea what she'd been missing. She'd had no clue her soul had been nearly bankrupt.

A sense of relief washed through her. Why, it hadn't been René she'd cared for back then. It had been what he'd given her.

She turned to study Mayhew—handsome, perfunctory, well-mannered Mayhew, who was adamant they wait for their wedding night before he crossed certain boundaries. He had a lovely mouth; surely it was time he used those lips to smother her with deep kisses that would kindle the fire in her that had been banked for far too long. He had strong, well-made hands that made her skin tingle whenever he tenderly brushed her cheek with the backs of his long fingers. It was time he used those hands for other things.

They would soon be wed; surely he could lower his rigid standards a little and embrace her in the warmth of his loving arms. The devil with his trying to do the right thing. She needed to be held. She needed to be kissed. And by the heavens, before the night was through, she would walk with him in the garden and acknowledge her feelings outright. She'd tell him what she so desperately needed. She'd find a diplomatic way to convey to him that her hunger for human touch threatened to wither her soul and skew her thoughts.

All that illicit passion she'd once felt for René would then evaporate into the ether. Forevermore.

"Felice?" Mayhew nudged her. "Darling, your brother speaks to you."

She gave her head a shake. "What is it?"

"It's time I saw Brenna home," Michel said.

"Right this moment?" Hell's bells. She needed that walk in the garden.

Brenna struggled to her feet and lumbered from the room. No doubt she was headed for the necessary before the ride home. The poor woman had disappeared three times during dinner.

Michel withdrew his gold watch from his vest pocket and checked the time. "It's a wonder she lasted this long."

Felice wanted that kiss from Mayhew, and by the saints, she'd get it. She leaned into him and lowered her voice. "Will you walk with me in the gardens? I'd prefer we say good night in private."

"But you're leaving now."

"Not quite yet. I'm sharing Michel's carriage, but instead of leaving together, the driver can return for me after seeing them home. They only live a couple of blocks away, and Brenna moves so slowly, we'll have a good fifteen minutes. What say you?"

He stood and held her chair for her. "Of course, darling."

She rose, made her farewells, then turned to Michel. "Please have your driver return for me after he sees you and Brenna home. Vivienne can fetch me in the gardens."

Michel frowned and glanced about the room. "You have ten minutes to meet the driver out front."

Chapter Four

Felice clasped Mayhew's arm. Together, they descended the steps onto a cobbled path that meandered through the glorious back gardens of Le Blanc House. Cleverly hung lanterns lit the walkway, which was lined on either side with a swath of flowers. The scent of night-blooming jasmine filled the air. Above them, stars glittered like diamonds against a black-velvet sky. Here and there, fireflies danced among the flowers and flitted through the branches of stately oaks and magnolia trees.

"What a breathtaking night," she said, and gave his arm a squeeze. Muscles beneath the cotton fabric of his jacket tensed. Puzzled, she glanced his way. A beam of moonlight slanting across his face exposed a frown. "Is something amiss?"

He paused. Removing her hand from his arm, he stepped away from her and released a heavy breath. "Gads. That gathering in there. What a cocked-up attempt at civility. Their manners—as well as yours—were appalling."

She laughed softly. "Come now, don't be a curmudgeon. Cajun food is considered country fare. That manner of dining is meant to be casual and fun. I thought you'd enjoy the experience."

"Well, I did not. The entire evening was a fiasco from

start to finish. And might I mention that in addition to your questionable manners tonight, you consumed entirely too much food. If you don't start limiting your intake, you'll end up fat as a sow."

Aggravation pinched the edges of Felice's good mood. She wasn't about to let it take hold. "Oh, bother, Mayhew. I've always had a hearty appetite, and look how slender I am. My father told me that my mother enjoyed food with the same passion as I. Even after birthing several children, she never gained an extra ounce. I'd be thin as a stick and feel half-starved if I were to eat sparingly. As for my manners, you've had many an occasion to note how impeccable they are. Dunking bread into Cajun food is acceptable in this part of the world; you've missed the chance to experience a regional custom."

"Might I remind you that you are not a Cajun?"

She couldn't resist a jab at his haughtiness. "I shall never grow fat as a sow, so mind *your* manners and do not speak ill of me. If you wish to compare me with critters, then consider me healthy as a horse. Like my lovely mother before me."

He paused to study her for a brief moment. Good humor filled her once again and she responded with a triumphant grin. He rolled his eyes but failed to hide the twitch at the corners of his mouth. He worked up another frown. "Your brother's wife showed up at the table barefoot, encouraged by Thibodeaux. Is that a regional Cajun tradition as well?"

Good heavens, she didn't care to discuss the Thibodeaux penchant for going barefoot. "In case you haven't noticed, Brenna is soon to give birth. A lady's feet often swell while in such a condition, which can make footwear painful. Do take pity on her." She narrowed her eyes at him. "Are you itching to cast a pall on my good mood?"

He cocked a brow. "Do you have a problem with my being honest?"

She shoved a loose tendril behind her ear. "This gathering was assembled so I could meet Brenna. Now I wish we had waited a day or so. I would rather we had met in the privacy of her home."

"As would I. Then perhaps those dreadful brothers would not have been present."

"I take it you don't care much for them."

"Truth be told, I'm having trouble understanding how a couple of lowbred Cajuns could have come by such lofty positions in your family's business."

Felice couldn't hide the smile that flickered over her lips. "My cousin Cameron hired them when he was in town. And I do believe you hold my business-minded cousin in high regard."

Mayhew frowned. "What could have possessed him to hire those two?"

She shrugged. "Cameron figured it was better than having them steal from him. As it turned out, both men have become invaluable assets to the company. Besides, he hired them to please Josette, their sister."

Mayhew's jaw dropped. "Sink me! Do you mean to tell me that Cameron's lovely wife is their sister?"

"Indeed."

"That elegant, beautiful woman is a lowbred, bayou-born Cajun? Who would've thought?"

"She is that, if you choose to describe her in such a dreadful way. If she was raised in the same swampland shanty as her brothers, yet can hold her own over high tea with your queen, perhaps her brothers can redeem themselves as well."

"I doubt it. For one thing, their accents are peculiar. Not at all like your brother's. Their English is filled with words I've never heard of. Their French is so ragtag, I cannot begin to decipher the rubbish that comes from their mouths."

She laughed. "The Cajun language is a mix of French, English, and Indian. As for their English, it's filled with a playful kind of slang."

"Can you understand them?"

She nodded. "Even though I was taught to speak proper French, I enjoy the lazy, lyrical cadence of their speech, and I find the Cajun expressions colorful."

At the memory of the tender phrases René had once murmured to her, her cheeks heated. She glanced away, lest Mayhew take note.

He harrumphed. "What were those two up to before your brother employed them?"

She needed to get him off the subject. The sudden nervous tension roiling about in her bosom caused a thread of soft laughter to erupt. "I doubt whatever they were doing was much aboveboard. Do not underestimate those two. Just because they were thieving ragamuffins growing up doesn't mean they are not intelligent. In fact, they are clever as foxes. And as for their offering to help you locate a gentlemen's fighting club, I'd take care if I were you."

"There are rules in a gentlemen's club."

"Humph. While you learned fisticuffs according to strict rules, those two fought in streets and alleys for survival. They make their own rules."

Mayhew snorted. "I am a man of honor who defends his own, and I don't care for the way René watches you."

Her throat was suddenly parched. "Watches me?"

"Oh, come now, Felice. You are the most intelligent woman I have ever known, so don't try to tell me you haven't noticed his interest in you. He didn't take his eyes off you all evening."

She swallowed against the dryness in her throat. "He was sitting directly across from me. It's only natural for one's gaze to settle straight ahead. Mayhap he didn't care to watch the flirting going on between you and his paramour."

"And why bring a paramour to a dinner party such as this? Never mind. He's lowborn. Doesn't know any better. And perhaps he doesn't know any better than to keep his hands off you."

"Why tell me I'm the most intelligent female you've ever met only to insinuate that I wouldn't know how to take care of myself should a man make untoward advances? You aren't making a bit of sense."

"I don't care for the idea of you two being confined in one working space. Not at all."

"Oh, for heaven's sake. Michel will be on hand. You can set your watch by his habits. He will arrive before anyone else and will be the last to leave."

"And what of your brother's wife?"

"What of her?"

"In case you didn't catch her ginger hair and thick brogue, she's Irish, Felice. Couldn't he have found one of his own to wed?"

Felice bristled at this sign of Mayhew's rigid upbringing. He believed that anyone who wasn't British and didn't hold a title or carry a certain status was beneath him. Before her racing mind could form a coherent response, he continued. "Gads, what a bunch of ne'er-do-wells. Thank the gods we are only here temporarily. Please, let us dine alone tomorrow."

A rogue thought skittered through her mind. Papa, English himself by birth and of noble rank when he'd settled in America, had cast aside his title and severe upbringing—along with a cruel and heartless father, so she'd been told. Despite Mayhew's wicked sense of humor, would his staid deportment and unyielding attitude clash with her father's laissez-faire approach to life?

Her head was beginning to ache. "This walk in the garden is not going the way I had anticipated."

"What did you expect after that fiasco?"

Exasperated, she blew out a breath. "Mayhew, we need to talk about something else entirely."

He turned and studied her in the moonlight. He stepped back toward her and, curling a finger under her chin, tilted it upward. "What is it, darling?"

Suddenly, she wasn't so sure she was doing the right thing. *Oh, bother, get it over with.* "Are you truly committed to spending a lifetime with me?"

His brows knitted together "Of course. What in blazes has gotten into you? Are *you* having second thoughts?"

"Heavens no. Just the opposite."

"Good, because once I ask your father for your hand and he agrees, we can wed right away. Look, darling, if you don't care to wait until we are back in England, I'm perfectly willing to speak our vows here."

She shook her head. "I want a grand wedding in that lovely abbey you showed me. And with any luck, I'll convince my father to return with us to England. The only family members who would be missing at the wedding would be Michel and his wife. Perhaps I can talk them into coming along as well."

"His wife? In England? You must be joking."

"Why do you say that?"

"Can't you tell she's not been long in this country? I doubt she'd ever agree to set foot on English soil. And were she to do so, the upper crust wouldn't tolerate her. At least not abovestairs."

Oh, Lord in Heaven. Felice had forgotten. Come to

think of it, Brenna hadn't spoken a word to Mayhew all evening. Hadn't so much as glanced his way, in fact.

Better to bite my tongue on this prickly issue for now.

She slipped her hand into the crook of his elbow and continued their stroll. "I had something else in mind when I asked you to walk with me out here."

He paused beneath a large magnolia tree. Shadows obscured his face. "You're beginning to worry me. What is it, love? Are you having doubts about us?"

"No, Mayhew."

"Then what is it?"

"I wish there was warmer affection shown between us. I . . ."

He turned to face her. "Warmer affection? Dear heart, how can you say that?"

"We don't kiss as lovers do. You don't hold me in your arms. Why, just look at us now. Here we are, standing face-to-face, yet inches apart, like two people just getting acquainted. I would think since we are to wed, we could take a few liberties."

He leaned forward. A shaft of lantern light caught the frown creasing his brow. "Are you saying you wish to become intimate lovers before we are wed?"

"I . . . well, no . . . not exactly. But I . . . I need more. Oh, bother. I need more passion in our relationship . . . I need . . ."

"Stop, Felice." Looking toward the heavens, he heaved a breath.

Had she gone too far? "Have my words angered you?"

He bent his head as if to study his shoes. "I'm not angry, darling. I'm frustrated. Not only is it a tradition for those of noble rank to wait until the wedding night to be intimate . . ."

She reached out and touched his arm. "I'm not asking

we go that far. I simply wish for a little more affection. There are times I wonder if you truly desire me."

The breath gushed from his lungs. He turned and walked away from her a few paces, paused, then returned, as if he'd taken a brief moment to collect his thoughts. He took her by the shoulders and touched his forehead to hers. "My naïve, innocent darling. You obviously do not understand the carnal desires of men. For your sake, my intention has been to keep our relationship chaste until we are wed. If we were to go any further than we have, I'm not certain I could control myself, and I refuse to compromise you."

Tenderly, he kissed her forehead, then the corner of each eye and the tip of her nose. And then he lightly brushed his lips across hers, his mustache prickling her mouth. "Darling, you are my goddess. It might be wrong of me, but I have placed you on a pedestal, and I would like to keep you there until you are mine. Fully mine."

As he smiled down at her, he ran the back of his fingers along her cheek and down one bare arm, raising goose-flesh along her skin. "I promise you, my dear, the wait will be worth it. When I take you, it shall be in our marriage bed, and nowhere else. You are to be the mother of my children, Felice. I must keep you innocent until we wed."

Innocent? Oh, Lord in Heaven.

Flashes of that night in Paris went through her head, memories of the terrible mistake she'd made, giving herself to a man who'd only vaguely resembled René. She'd ruined herself over someone not worth a deuced fig. What was she to do now? Should she tell Mayhew the truth? How could she go into their marriage burdened with a lie?

"Under the circumstances," she said, "is being chaste so important?"

"Yes, Felice. It is to me, and certainly it should be to you."

She took in a breath to fortify herself. She must tell him the truth. But she couldn't do it. She couldn't bring herself to tell him about that night. At least not right now.

"What is it, darling?"

"Nothing. You're right. We need to wait." She glanced around the garden, gathering her wits. What she needed to do was sleep on this entire, muddled conversation and forget their little disagreement—their first. "We had best go. They'll be waiting for us."

"Of course, love. Will I see you tomorrow at all? Dinner after your long day?"

She nodded.

"Jolly good. But do let us dine alone."

Once again, things had not gone the way she'd envisioned. She lifted her chin and gave him her best smile. "We'll dine at Antoine's. It's the finest restaurant in the city. My favorite, by the way, and I hope it becomes yours."

"I pray they do not serve Cajun food."

She laughed. "Mostly French."

Chapter Five

Vivienne hurried along the corridor toward the front door with Felice and Mayhew at her heels. She glanced over her shoulder as she spoke. "Madame Andrews, she be weary. *Monsieur* would like you to hasten, *s'il vous plaît*."

Felice wasn't certain she'd heard right. "You mean to tell me they never left?"

"*Non, mademoiselle*, they have not."

"Oh, for heaven's sake. Honestly, Mayhew, there are times my brother can be exasperatingly stubborn."

Mayhew's lips curved. "I just had a brilliant flash of insight, my dear."

"Which is?"

"Stubbornness runs in your entire family."

"Pishposh. My being practical has nothing to do with being pigheaded. Did you or did you not hear me tell Michel to make his way home and then have his driver return for me?"

Mayhew gave a soft chuckle. "As I said . . ."

"Humph. And to think his poor wife has been waiting for me all this time."

Vivienne held open the front door. "*Non, mademoiselle*, the fault be not yours. Madame Andrews, she been dawdlin' all this time. Only been a moment since they took their leave."

Together, Mayhew and Felice moved onto the veranda and down the few steps to the walkway leading to the street. Vivienne closed the door behind them and disappeared into the house. Felice noted four figures gathered beneath the street-side gaslight. A low hum of indistinct conversation between René, Michel, and his driver floated through the sultry night air. Brenna, her shoes dangling from one hand, sat inside the covered carriage while a tight-lipped Mrs. Worth, arms crossed over her ample bosom, stood between Michel's vehicle and the gig Felice had noted upon her arrival.

So that fancy contraption must belong to René.

"There you are," Michel said, and nodded toward the gig. "René will see you home."

Good Lord, no!

Mayhew's hand slid from the small of her back to grip her arm. Her heart did a flip in her chest. "That makes no sense. Three cannot possibly fit into that contraption. I'll either ride with you, or your driver can return for me."

Michel shook his head. "Mrs. Worth lives nearby, so she will ride with Brenna and me. You shall ride with René."

Mrs. Worth, obviously unsettled by the turn of events, whispered in René's ear. He frowned and murmured something Felice couldn't make out over Mayhew's soft cursing.

This will never do.

"Your idea makes even less sense, Michel." Felice waved her hand toward Le Blanc House. "Monsieur Thibodeaux would have a long trip back home after dropping me off."

"*Non*," René said. "I now live in the Vieux Carré."

Thoughts scattered in ten directions. She glanced at Mayhew. A muscle ticked in his jaw.

Michel dipped his chin and gave her one of his I'm-running-out-of-patience looks. "A bit silly to send my driver when René's town house is a mere two doors from ours."

What? Oh dear. Say something clever.

She turned to René. "Surely you don't wish to end your evening with Mrs. Worth so early. I'm happy to wait for my brother's driver to return. It's well past twilight and too late for watching fireflies, but I can count the stars while I wait. I've always loved doing both."

Michel scowled. "Must you make things difficult, Felice? The *Cerise* docked just after sundown, bearing a full load of Barbados rum, which means René has a long night and day ahead of him. Not only will he be required to check on the guards surrounding the ship before he retires for the night, but he must also rise before the cock crows to see to the vessel's proper unloading."

"Well, where is Bastien at a time like this?"

René leaned a hip against the gig and casually folded his arms over his chest. "He be on the ship as we speak, don'cha know."

Oh dear.

She took in a long, slow breath while doing some quick thinking. Any further reluctance on her part and the situation was bound to become even more awkward. She mustn't let anyone, especially Michel and Mayhew, think anything was amiss between her and René.

"I see," she said on a heavy exhale. "I fear I've been a silly goose. I do apologize for any misunderstanding."

She turned to Mayhew, ignoring his stiff demeanor. "Do enjoy your outing tomorrow. I'm sure Mrs. Worth will be a delightful tour guide. I look forward to our dinner in the evening, when you can tell me all about your day."

He nodded, saying nothing. With a roar of blood in her ears, she bade the others a good evening, slipped her hand into Michel's, and allowed him to help her into the gig.

The vehicle dipped as René climbed aboard and took the reins. She swore she could feel the power that coiled within him when he moved. Was it her imagination, or could she also feel the heat emanating from him? In one cruel instant, his nearness reawakened old memories— a mixture of pleasure and pain.

With a click of his tongue, the gig gave a slight jerk, then rolled smoothly into the night. She stared straight ahead, feeling the heat of Mayhew's gaze boring into her back and excruciatingly aware of the man sitting beside her.

Breathing had never been so difficult. Silence had never been so deafening. Lord, but the ride home had to be taking ten times longer than the trip over. And to think she'd have to work in the same room with him beginning tomorrow.

René turned left when he should've driven straight. Surprise sent a shock up her spine. "What are you doing? This isn't the way home."

"*Non*," he said in a voice as rich and dark as the rum he'd been drinking throughout dinner. "There is something I want you to see."

"Well, this isn't one bit proper. Do take me home."

"Give me five minutes, *s'il vous plaît*. If you do not like what you see, I will deliver you to your home *tout de suite*." He ensnared her with a steady gaze that made her breath catch. "Do not fear, *mon amie*. You are safe with me."

"I am not your friend, so please do not call me *mon amie* again."

"As you wish. But trust that you *are* safe in my company, *chère*. I am harmless, don'cha know."

"You? Harmless?" she sputtered. "Better to make a pet of a gator. And *chère* is not acceptable either. I am Mademoiselle Andrews to you."

His low rumble of laughter shut out the world around her. Her pulse tripped. How could the sound of a man's amusement be filled with so much magnetism? Damn. How could she still harbor hurt and anger because of him?

He turned another corner with the gig and all but left civilization behind.

"Dash it all, where *are* you taking me?"

"A moment and we are there." He urged the horse along a narrow dirt path through a bottomland thicket smelling of loam and cypress. Soon, they emerged onto a grassy field fronting a bayou.

"Oh!" she cried.

At the far end of the meadow, an immense full moon hovered above the treetops on the other side of the waterway. The cool glow of moonlight rippled over the slow-moving, dark waters. Stars peppered the sky. Fireflies, as far as the eye could see, danced like so many fairies in and out of the tall grass.

Mesmerized by it all, she closed her eyes for a brief moment, trying to gather her wits about her. Trying to slow her rapid heartbeat. Trying to block out his inescapable essence.

He'd done this for her.

And she had no clue how to react.

He leaned forward, wrapped the reins around the brake lever, then leaned back. Settling his shoulder into one corner of the gig, he stretched out his long legs over the front of the frame and crossed them at the ankles. Casually, he draped one arm across the back of the seat, mere inches behind her.

The languid way he sat was deceptive. This was a man who'd grown from child to adult in the streets, a man who instinctively moved at lightning speed in the presence of an enemy—a man she'd never known to let down his guard. She'd bet it wasn't down even now.

He didn't look at her. Instead, he stared straight ahead, as if to let her lose herself in the beauty of the night.

"I . . . I thought fireflies only come out around twilight," she said.

"Not here along Bayou St. John," he said. "As a boy, I used to sneak in here when the Allards still owned the land. I knew fireflies would be thick 'most all night." A hint of a smile touched his lips.

What was she supposed to say now? She tried to breathe in the night air, only to catch his clean, musky scent. Her peripheral vision caught his magnificent profile. Those marvelous lips. He knew how to use that mouth. He'd used it to set too many fires inside her. Lord, no matter how she felt about him now, there was no denying that when it came to sensuality, here sat a gifted man. Memory after memory rolled out of her numbed brain and down into her bosom, piercing her heart.

Well, all that was in the past. *He* was in her past. What she needed to remember was their last few moments together, his cruel rejection of her. With as much inner strength as she could muster, she pushed aside her painful thoughts and concentrated on listening to the chorus of frogs along the water's edge. She studied the moon and stars, watched the fireflies. None of it managed to negate her awareness of the man sitting beside her.

"We need to talk, *chère.*"

His words, like a knife piercing the fabric of the night,

jarred her. She turned to him as her anger reached an instant boil. "You . . . you! Is this the reason you brought me here, to talk?"

"*Non*," he said quietly. "Not tonight. I heard you tell Michel you liked watching the stars and fireflies. I brought you here to enjoy nature."

She stared at him, realizing that it still took little from him to unnerve her.

"You should know that before you arrived for dinner, your fiancé asked me why you call my brother by his Christian name, but you address me in a formal manner. I saw your brother watching us and he gave a slight nod in agreement. So, he's noticed, as well. This here bad blood between us, it be no good, *chère*."

She folded her hands in her lap and managed to take in a ragged breath. "I see."

"We've been thrown together," he said. "And if we do not take care, we will end up in big trouble—each for different reasons. A truce is needed, Felice. Soon, we must talk."

She clasped her fingers together to keep them from shaking. He was right; something had to give. "What's done is done. We have nothing to say to each other. I'll be fine after a good night's sleep."

He gave a shrug of his shoulders. "I have something to say, and I am asking you to hear me out before either of us leaves town. The sooner, the better."

She nodded her acquiescence. His voice, so familiar, nearly cracked the thin veneer of her fragile comportment. She could feel herself falling apart inside. "Please, take me home. I've had enough for one night."

"*Oui*," he said softly. He leaned forward, took hold of the reins, and turned the gig around.

When they reached her town house, René tied the reins

to the brake and exited the gig. He moved to where she sat and held out his hand to assist her from her seat. Her hand heated at his touch. She ignored the sensation and, bending her head to avoid his disconcerting gaze, fished the key to the front gate from her reticule.

"Good evening . . . René," she managed to say as she opened the filigreed gateway, stepped inside, and closed it behind her.

"You as well," he responded.

She turned to face him.

He watched her with a steady gaze. And then he gave her a slight grin and spoke to her in lilting Cajun that rolled off his tongue like golden, heated honey. "I'll be seein' you tomorrow in the shipping office, Felice. Where we shall work together in a friendly and businesslike manner, *oui*? And we shall soon have this talk I spoke of, *oui*?"

She had no choice but to agree if she wished to keep their past a secret from Mayhew and her brother. With a nod, she surrendered to the truce. *"Oui."*

René drove to the docks with an image of Felice burning in his mind and an odd heaviness in his chest. At least she'd given her word she'd listen to him. He turned a corner in the gig and the *Cerise* loomed before him.

He pulled the buggy up to the dock, sprang from the seat, and secured the reins to a hitching post. Six armed guards stood sentry over a cargo worth a good-sized fortune. Lanterns lit the fore and aft decks of the ship while one window belowdeck shone bright. Bastien would be in there, overseeing a crew being paid extra to toil through the night.

As he strolled along the dock, he nodded his greeting

and addressed each guard by name. He was respected by these men—had personally hired every one of them. He was a fair and scrupulous employer, but when it came to rules, his were rigid and inflexible. The guards and crew knew not to try to bend a one of them lest they lose their positions. Nor would they dare commit even the smallest theft while he was in charge.

Who knew better than he the ins and outs of relieving a ship of its entire cargo with none the wiser? As a matter of fact, when it came to clandestinely removing anything from anyone, only his brother matched his abilities. After all, they'd had a lifetime of honing their skills on the very streets René now called home. Stealing an entire shipment of rum from the company now employing him was what had gotten him and Bastien hired in the first place.

Indeed, he was a clever thief. Always had been. But a few years ago, he'd grown weary of being the bastard son of the wealthiest man in town and a bayou-born voodoo priestess. He'd grown tired of being looked down upon, especially in the Vieux Carré, where the elite French Creoles lived. He'd yearned to better himself—if only the right opportunity would present itself.

And one day, present itself it did, when Cameron Andrews, Felice's cousin, began bedding René's sister. When one of the Andrews Company ships pulled into port riding low in the water, and he'd learned it contained expensive Gosling's rum out of Bermuda, René had seen his chance. He'd laughed when he'd hidden his booty under Michel and Cameron's very noses and then bargained with Cameron for a return of the plunder in exchange for a position in the company. It was a risk he'd taken, but one that had paid off in spades. Bastien soon followed him into the company, and his life had been changed for the better as well.

They had proven themselves worthy, both within the company and in town. At last, they were viewed with a modicum of respect. Soon, they'd moved out of the bayou and into Le Blanc House. Eight months ago, he'd seen another dream fulfilled—he'd purchased a town house on prestigious Rue Royale, right in the heart of the Vieux Carré.

His thoughts drifted back to Felice. He'd nearly spoiled it all for both himself and Bastien when he'd dared to use her to avenge himself against Cameron for having an affair with their sister. In the end, he couldn't go through with his plan to ruin Felice by bedding her and flaunting it in Cameron's face—not after he'd realized what she'd begun to mean to him.

He raked his fingers through his hair and, looking to the sky, dragged in a heavy breath. Christ, what had he been thinking, taking her behind the old Allard plantation tonight? Never again would he attempt anything so foolish. No matter that he still found her captivating. No matter that he could barely keep his hands off her.

He turned and studied the white clapboard building with the green roof and the company name etched in gold letters. At the thought of losing everything he'd worked so hard for—his position in the company, his standing in the community—a coil of fear snaked through him.

Calmly, he shifted his thoughts, pushed aside the dread striking his heart. He'd be damned if he'd risk either himself or Bastien's way of life over a woman. Firm resolve turned into cold determination. It was how he'd survived all these years.

One thing he knew for certain: He needed the Andrews Shipping Company more than he needed air to breathe.

Chapter Six

René scrubbed a hand across his tired eyes. Blinking a few times, he focused again on the bills of lading in front of him. Barely nine of the clock and he ached to call it a day. He'd ended up working alongside the crew of the *Cerise* until dawn, then returned to the office and continued on. He would remain in place long enough to see every man get his pay, then he'd take to his bed. Which should happen shortly after the noon hour—if the bookkeeper ever decided to show. Damn it.

His stomach growled.

Michel glanced up from a stack of papers on his desk. "When did you eat last?"

"Doan remember." Forget about putting food in his belly. A strong cup of café au lait mixed with molasses and chicory would relieve the fatigue plaguing him. The mere thought of his favorite brew and his stomach barked at him again. "Where be your sister?"

"Hell if I know." For the third time in less than a quarter hour, Michel withdrew his watch from his vest pocket and checked the time.

Frustration agitated René's empty gut. "She be knowin' the crew gets their wages by noon. I heard her say dat much over dinner last night."

"Do you realize your Cajun accent gets heavy when you're annoyed? Gives you away every time."

René raked a hand through his hair. "We've never been late paying our people. This close to doin' so doan sit right with me, don'cha know."

No sooner had he commented when a cloud of pale blue—hat, gown, parasol, reticule—swept into the room. A light scent of magnolia trailed behind, causing his senses to reel. Suddenly, his fatigue disappeared.

"Good morning, Michel. Good morning, René," she sang out as she plucked a long hatpin from her fancy bonnet and set the oversize piece of blue fluff on a chair. So, she'd done some pondering during the night. Must have realized her negative attitude toward him would raise questions if she didn't mend her ways.

He watched as she removed a ledger from the glass-fronted case and, with a pert bounce, seated herself behind Abbott's desk. Retrieving a pencil, a pen, and a small bottle of India ink from a drawer, she flipped open the record book.

Michel's chair squeaked as he pulled his watch from his vest pocket yet again. "Nine of the clock. Had you delayed a bit longer, dear sister, you might've managed to arrive in time for lunch."

She offered no response, merely ran a finger down a column of numbers. Her brows knitted together. She muttered something under her breath.

Michel paused in what he was doing. "Are you talking to yourself, Felice?"

The corners of her mouth twitched. "Of course. Who else in the room would I go to for expert advice?"

Despite his foul mood, René nearly laughed aloud. Merde, *but I do believe things are about to get interesting*.

She turned a page on the ledger, gave a quick perusal

of the column, then settled her gaze on the back of her brother's head. "My wages don't seem to be listed here, Michel. Kindly supply me with the correct numbers so I can include the figure with the other employees' wages."

Michel scoffed. "Your wages?"

"Indeed. I require the correct amount to insert in the ledger."

He heaved an exaggerated sigh. "You are a volunteer until Abbott returns. Stop dawdling and see to balancing the figures lest the crew fail to collect their hard-earned pay by noon."

Setting down the pen, she folded her hands atop the open ledger. "Are you saying you expect me to work for nothing?"

"Did I or did I not make myself clear?"

"Why? Because I am a woman?"

Michel cursed under his breath. "Don't start with me, Felice. You are family. Family helps out when needed, just as you have done in our other offices."

"And so are you family, Michel. So is our brother Trevor family. So is our cousin Cameron family. You *men* in the family are all well-compensated for your work, yet you expect me, the lone female, to toil away for zero compensation?"

He leaned back in his chair and spread his arms wide, palms up. "At last, you get the message."

"Well, here's my message to you. I refuse to labor here for heaven knows how long without a penny coming my way. Now give me the cursed figures, you dolt."

Michel cursed under his breath. "Get to work."

"No. Not unless I am paid."

Michel snarled at her. "You are wasting everyone's time.

I repeat—we have a payroll to get out by the noon hour, so see to it."

"Are you aware the word *no* is a complete sentence, brother?"

With the conversation fast approaching a heated argument, René sat back in his chair, folded his arms over his chest, and took in the sibling quarrel with a tight jaw. *Christ, what are you thinking, Michel?*

Felice removed herself from her chair and proceeded to pin her hat back on her head. Chin lifted in defiance, she snatched up her reticule and parasol and, gliding past her brother, sailed out the door.

A litany of curses fell from Michel's mouth. "Felice, get back here!"

Stunned, René stared at the open door and at the blue cloud disappearing around the corner. Despite the predicament she'd left them in, a humorless chuckle erupted from his throat. "Ain't she just full of sass this morning."

"Humph. My sister is always full of sass."

"You need to pay her. We're in a tight spot."

Michel glared at René. "Unlike her brothers and cousin, who've had to work for every dollar earned, she has a trust fund greater than the worth of a few small countries, which she has managed to increase on her own, thanks to her penchant for numbers and some clever investing. The last thing my sister needs is to further enrich her overflowing coffers. She's traveled to nearly every one of our offices and checked the company books without asking for so much as a dime. Now, thanks to whatever wild bee she's got buzzing around that oversize bonnet of hers, she's decided to be stubborn."

"And you are not?"

Michel turned to stare out the window at the *Cerise*

while he rubbed the back of his neck. A long moment of silence ensued while René's brain worked overtime trying to decide if he could pay the crew and have Felice balance the books after the fact.

Of a sudden, Michel laughed. "Damn if I didn't need a break from the grind of all this paperwork. I knew she was up to no good when she waltzed in here late and in a fanciful mood. Once again, that rebellious streak of hers is at play."

"*Mon Dieu.* She picked a mighty bad time to be up to no good." *And a hell of a time this is for you to quibble over money when whatever she'd get wouldn't put a dent in the company coffers, you damn fool.*

"Oh, she knows exactly what she's doing," Michel said. "Don't think for a moment she didn't time this little escapade in order to get her way."

Despite the anger boiling under the surface, René managed to keep his tone even. "Seems to me you should go after her. Give her whatever she be wantin' and sack her later, but let's get the job finished or we'll be in a mess of trouble. I could use some sleep."

"You go after her."

A jolt ran through René. "Me?"

Michel nodded. "Offer her the same wages we give Henri."

"You're tellin' me to chase her down after you refused to compensate her for her work? And now you're wantin' me to offer her an errand boy's wages? *Non, mon ami.* Leave me out of your family squabble. You need to be the one collecting her; you're the one who started this chaos."

Michel stood and, with a wide yawn, stretched his arms overhead. "I started it? She's the one who waltzed in here two hours late. Do you think if I went after her that she wouldn't hesitate to argue with me in public? I do not need that kind of negative attention drawn to me or to this business. Drag her back here if you have to."

René rose from his chair and set to pacing. "Why offer her an errand boy's wage?"

Michel stepped to Abbott's desk and flipped through the pages of the ledger. "She's temporary. And she's never demanded compensation before, so now is hardly the time to start."

I can't go after her, not with what's gone on between us. "Won't offering what Henri earns offend her?"

"Start by offering his income, then work your way up. She thrives on negotiation. Be forewarned—she can be shrewd. And she's unflappable. Don't let her play her trump card."

"What trump card?"

"That she's a woman and therefore not given the same privileges in the family business as the men. Remind her she has a more than ample trust fund."

"*Mon Dieu.* Why would I have that kind of personal information?" Anger and fatigue coalesced and punched him in the gut. He grabbed up a glass paperweight and thought about throwing it across the room. Instead, he took a deep breath and set the thing back down on his desk.

Michel, his eye on René's action, smirked. "Your sister married into the family, which practically makes you family as well, so you could easily be privy to Felice's wealth."

René pinched the bridge of his nose. "Where the hell is Bastien? He should go in my stead. I've work to do."

"He went to the bank." Michel checked his pocket watch once more.

René cursed again. "He's been gone a lot longer than it takes to get there and back. He's somewhere else lettin' off steam, if you get my meanin'."

Michel shrugged. "He'll return with the bankroll before noon. Always does."

"What if I manage to get her back here and she's too slow with the numbers to be meetin' the payroll on time?"

"Rest assured, she will make the time limit. Far be it from me to admit this to her, but she's even better at figures than Abbott. Even though he trained her for his own amusement, she can add a page of sums in her head and recite the total before he's halfway down the column."

He scowled at René. "By the way, what's going on between you and my sister?"

"What do you mean?" The hair on the back of René's neck stood on end. He knew exactly what Michel meant.

"Up until this morning, when she breezed in here and made it a point to greet you by your Christian name, I would've sworn the frigid air between you two could've frozen a bayou in midsummer. Anything I need to know?"

Merde, the last thing he needed was for Michel to demand an explanation. The fatigue that had plagued René before she'd waltzed in hit him again, as if he'd run head-on into a brick wall. He shrugged and swiped a hand across his aching brow. "*Non*. Nothing wrong between us."

Michel returned to his desk and picked up another stack of papers. "Then work your mother's voodoo magic if you have to, but get Felice back here within the hour."

René grabbed his jacket and headed for the open door, shoving his arms into the sleeves as he went. "What if she doesn't let me through the gate to the town house?"

"She won't be there. Try *Les Deux Bonbons*."

He paused, one foot over the threshold. "You cannot be serious. It's barely half past nine."

"Iced cream is my sister's opium. It's never too early in the morning to feed her addiction. You're sure to find her there. Bring me back a chicory coffee and a couple of beignets while you're at it, if you will."

Sacrebleu. How had he gotten himself into this one? He was so fatigued he could drop on the street, and now he had to chase after the one person he had every intention of avoiding. In a sweet shop no less. This whole mess was more Michel's doing than hers.

Stubborn Andrews clan.

The whole damn bunch of them.

He'd have been blind not to have spotted Felice the moment the sweet shop came into view. She made a fine advertisement for *Les Deux Bonbons* as she sat at a round, marble-topped, wrought-iron table in the bay window directly beneath the establishment's name etched in gold on the glass. Her skirts billowed around her like some heavenly blue cloud. She'd somehow managed to attach a fresh magnolia blossom the size of a dinner plate to her bonnet. Where she'd got that along the way, he could only guess.

Mon Dieu, but she was a vision.

He stood like a statue in the middle of Rue Dauphine, staring at her. Time stopped. The breeze, the street sounds around him—his anger—all ceased to exist in the thud of his heart beating against his ribs. After all this time, how had he failed to leach her out of his blood?

She held a long-handled spoon over a tulip-shaped glass filled with what had to be the iced cream she favored. Her opium, as her brother had called it. In a graceful move, she dipped into the confection, then lifted a heaping spoonful to her lips. He could've sworn her eyelids fluttered shut in ecstasy as she slid the sweetness into her mouth. How did such a willowy woman manage such a healthy appetite and still maintain her slender figure? He'd bet she wasn't even wearing a corset.

A rush of guilt washed over him. He knew damn well she wore nothing of the sort. Had no need to. He knew this because he'd once come dangerously close to divesting her of her gown and unmentionables.

He'd nearly ruined her.

Had nearly ruined his own life.

A shouted curse sent René jumping backward as a horse and rider bore down on him, barely missing him.

"Are you daft?" the man roared and sped off, hurling profanities over his shoulder.

"Pardon," René muttered and let loose a few obscenities of his own. The bothersome fool had no business using the street for a racetrack. Shoving his runaway emotions into a dark place inside himself, René strode to the shop's front door.

Her back was to him when he entered. In a quiet voice, he ordered a chicory coffee, a couple of beignets to take to Michel, and a molasses and creamed chicory coffee for himself to consume in the shop. Then he strolled to where Felice sat and slid into the chair across from her.

She paused with the spoon hovering over her glass. Her pupils flared for a brief moment. Then, with a little smirk, she collected herself and dug into the confection again. "Did my coward of a brother send you in his stead?"

René couldn't help but grin. "I do not know about the cowardly part, but *oui*, he sent me. He thought you'd be less likely to raise a fuss with me, don'cha know."

He tilted his head and studied her. "Are you enjoying your day so far, *chère*?"

"Immensely." With her gaze fixed on his, she dipped up another helping of the ice cream. This time she turned the silver spoon's full bowl over and pressed the frozen confection to her tongue. Slowly, she slid the spoon away, swallowed, and gave the inside of it a purposeful lick.

René's groin tightened.

Christ!

He drew a hitching breath and, tearing his gaze away, stared out the window while he collected his thoughts. "Your brother says he'll pay you Henri's wage because you've made no demands for compensation in the past."

Her eyes sparkled with mischief. "Are we about to negotiate upward?"

He swallowed a laugh just as a waiter set René's chicory coffee in front of him. He took a long drink and reveled in the sweet concoction. "You've not requested payment of any kind in other ports, so why now?"

"Because, silly goose, I had specific plans when I arrived here that have been upended. Because I have not seen my dear Papa in three years. Because I've a wedding to attend . . . my own."

He glanced over her shoulder at the stately clock standing in the corner. Noting the time, he fixed his gaze on her again. "Because we only have until noon to pay the crew, let us not be playin' games, *s'il vous plaît*. I'll offer you half of Abbott's wages, which is more than fair, and that's final."

"And if I refuse?"

"Then I return without you, figure out on my own what is owed, and worry about balancing the books later because I have not been to bed this past night, and I don't give much of a damn if the books are balanced today or next week. Either we return together or I leave on my own, so make up your mind, *tout de suite*."

She shrugged and dug into the last of her ice cream. "All right. You should finish your coffee. The drink's stimulation might put you in a better mood. If I have to work in the same office with you, I'd rather you not be out of sorts."

Having settled the problem, he sat back in his chair, stretched out a leg, and took a slow sip of his coffee, his gaze fixed on her over the rim of his cup.

Her cheeks flushed.

He nearly laughed. He set down the cup. "Do I bother you?"

"No." The disquiet left her eyes, replaced by a hint of amusement. She lifted a brow. "Do I bother you?"

He took his time as his gaze scraped her lovely figure from the top of her head to her slender fingers and waist. For a brief moment, he allowed the sight to heat his blood. "*Oui.* A little."

She tilted her head in query. "Interesting. How so?"

Because it is all I can do to keep from reaching out and touching you. From leaning over this table and planting my mouth on yours. From wanting to bury myself deep inside you.

He shrugged and drank the last of his café noir. "Because in about two hours we'll have seventy-five sailors lined up at the company door, each with his hand out. Meanwhile, the person meant to inform me as to what each man is to receive sits in a sweet shop stuffing herself on ice cream—a large serving of the sweet stuff—while everyone else in here is busy taking their morning coffee and beignet."

She laughed—a light, breezy sound that settled in parts of his restless body that refused to obey his commands.

He studied her as she slowly, purposefully, took in another mouthful of the ice cream, this one chocolate. "How many layers of mischief do I see in your eyes, *chère*?"

"Whatever do you mean?" In went another dollop of sweetness, followed by a bright smile.

The minx. "You've decided to stop being so formal with me, and now you play the coquette. Why is that?"

Her gaze dropped to his fingers, which were slowly running over the rim of his cup. Again, her cheeks flushed. *So, the little tease, she is not as bold as she pretends.*

Chapter Seven

Felice watched René cradle his cup with both hands while his fingers leisurely circled the rim. A keen awareness of his actions set her skin to tingling. Her cheeks heated. Lord, he might as well be caressing her directly, the way his movements affected her.

So graceful, those hands. Yet a smattering of tiny scars betrayed the life of a man who'd survived a childhood very different from her own. She knew how capable those hands were. How they could tuck a wayward curl behind an ear with the barest of touches. How they'd once lightly traced the outer edges of her lips before he'd leaned in and kissed her senseless.

Lord in Heaven, she didn't dare look up lest she catch sight of that luscious mouth—and those heavy-lidded, mesmerizing eyes. Most likely, the man could seduce a woman with a mere glance. For pity's sake, she had to get hold of herself. She was an affianced woman, while he was nothing but a scandalous rogue. And lest she ever forget, a scoundrel whose rejection had once pierced her heart like a lance.

Mayhew.

Think of Mayhew.

He would not be pleased to find her sitting here

with René. What the devil had she been doing that had caused René to refer to her as a coquette? He'd been mistaken. She had not been flirting. When she'd stepped into the office this morning and spied a scowl on her brother's face, her rebellious nature had taken hold. Michel knew very well what a defiant nature she possessed.

She hadn't been flirting with René.

Not at all.

Collecting herself, she scraped the last bit of the melted confection from the bottom of the fluted glass and offered him a perfunctory smile. "Finished."

He stood and offered his hand. "Come along, *chère*. We've work to do."

Henri, the errand boy, hustled past the window. Catching sight of them, he paused. René signaled him with a nod and the boy rushed inside.

"Take Monsieur Andrews the coffee and beignets the waiter will bring you," René said.

"Yes, sir."

There was no mistaking the hunger in the lad's eyes. "And take several for yourself," Felice added.

"*Merci, mam'selle.*" Henri grinned and hurried to where the waiter stood.

Felice donned her gloves and, slipping a hand into René's, allowed him to help her to her feet. She let go of his grasp with a flick of her wrist. Was it her imagination or had he smirked?

When they reached the door, he guided her over the threshold with a light touch to the small of her back. The electric heat of his body gave her pause. She moved away from his hand but misjudged the distance. She collided with the door frame, then lurched smack into him.

"Easy, *chère*," he murmured.

"Pardon." She caught his enticing scent as she brushed

past him and stepped onto the wooden boardwalk lining the street. He'd been up all night, yet his shirt appeared fresh and crisply starched, as though he'd just stepped from a bath. However did he manage to appear so well put together?

She clipped along at a fast pace, eager to distance herself from him. His long stride leisurely ate up the sidewalk, using half the effort she'd been putting forth. No sense exerting herself when she'd be forced to spend the day in the same workplace as he—or half the day, because he intended to leave soon after noon. Slowing down, she peered into the storefront windows as an excuse to turn her head away from him and maintain her silence. She was relieved when they finally reached the docks.

Marching into the office, she ignored Michel's smug grin. *The bugger thinks he's won, does he?* Removing her hat and gloves, she dug into her reticule and removed an envelope. "Henri, please rush this over to the next steamboat heading upriver. See it gets delivered to my father. I must alert him that I am being held prisoner here and I'll be up to see him as soon as Michel sets me free."

Michel snorted. "Won't he get a chuckle out of knowing his cheeky daughter has not changed one bit."

"I've invited him to come stay with me in the town house. Mayhew can ask him for my hand right here."

Michel leaned his head back, crossed his arms over his chest, and spoke to the ceiling. "Papa won't come."

"Why not?"

"Because he's elderly and set in his ways, Felice. He's aged tremendously these past three years, and his memory fails him from time to time. Just so you know."

Her brother's words struck dread into her heart. "Which is why I must talk him into returning with me to England."

"If he won't leave Carlton Oaks for a jaunt to New Orleans, what makes you think he'll agree to pack up and move an ocean away? Give it up, Felice. We've all tried and failed."

"Well, I have not tried. Therefore, I have not failed. I intend to give it a go." Despite the confident sound of her words, a chill settled deep in her bones. She slid her bottom lip between her teeth and worried it. Dear Papa had reached old age? His mind was failing him? Oh, she couldn't bear to hear this.

She caught René studying her with those dark and penetrating eyes that left her feeling emotionally naked. She turned her back to him and took in a fortifying breath while she collected herself.

"Well," she said as she recovered her composure and parked herself behind Abbott's desk. "I had best get to work, hadn't I? After all, everyone needs to get paid come noon. I do hope I can manage to meet our obligation."

Michel huffed. "God in Heaven, Felice, you are intent on driving me around the bloody bend, aren't you?"

She laughed. One thing she knew for certain was that she'd have those figures for René long before the clock struck twelve, so she might as well get in a few more verbal jabs at her brother. She glanced up at René. His head was bent over a stack of papers, but a muscle in his set jaw twitched and his lips were set in a straight line. Good, he could use a set down as well.

Bastien strolled in with a carpetbag in hand. He went directly to the safe, opened it, and stacked a pile of bills inside.

"Good gracious, Michel," Felice said. "You mean to tell me this dashing thief is privy to the safe's combination?"

Bastien chuckled as he walked over and kissed her on one cheek, then the other. "*Bonjour, ma petite.*"

"Did you just come from the bank?"

"*Oui.*"

She sniffed at the air around him. "Since when does the bank hand out samples of perfume? Very expensive perfume, by the way. Malmaison, to be exact."

René snorted. "What did I tell you, Michel? My brother, he be lettin' off steam of a particular kind."

"I worked the night through, right alongside you, brother, so hold your tongue, *s'il vous plaît.*"

Michel turned to Felice. "You know damn well what you are up to with your bantering. Now get the numbers for René. Time is running out."

Felice grinned. "Oh, this is so very rich. I have waited for years to pay you back, dear brother."

"For what, pray tell?"

"For all manner of things. We could start with the frogs you used to put in my bed."

"Frogs?" René and Bastien said in unison. "He put frogs in your bed?"

"Indeed. Did you not play tricks on each other growing up?"

They both shook their heads. "*Non,*" René said. "We were too busy trying to survive. What other tricks were played, and which ones were you guilty of?"

Michel grunted. "Tell him your diabolical part in the family histrionics *after* you've made payroll."

"There are far too many of my brothers' misdeeds to mention. Besides, at this particular moment, I am deep in the process of getting these figures to you. However, I will say this—Michel's worst transgression was leaving me alone right after Trevor and Cousin Cameron were sent off to England." She glanced at René. "Oh, wait, you and

Bastien know all about that. After all, you two took part in the brothel scandal that got my brother and cousin exiled—"

"Enough!" Michel turned to Felice. "Is that why you've been rude to René since your return? For something that happened years ago? You were a child, for pity's sake. You couldn't possibly remember anything."

The teasing ceased. She glanced at Bastien, who leaned a shoulder against the wall, arms folded over his chest, legs crossed at the ankles. He merely shrugged, as if he couldn't care less. But the look on René's face startled her. His dark and piercing gaze caught hers and held steady. It was as if an invisible current connected them, buzzing right through her.

Something told her there was far more to all this than she'd gleaned from overhearing conversations as an eight-year-old. Her instincts told her that whatever emotion she'd triggered in René, it had something to do with the two of them.

Whatever the case, she had to put an end to Michel's suspicion. "I heard the tale often throughout the years. What hurt most was that Trevor and Cameron left me, and within the year, you decided to run off to university, abandoning me as well. I was left with Papa still grieving *Maman*'s passing, and a baby brother who wailed away night after night. And what did he do when he reached age twelve? He sailed away with Trevor to England. Truly, I was left alone and bereft."

Michel scrubbed a hand over his eyes. "Meanwhile, Papa saw to it that you were kept busy by giving you the finest education a girl could have."

"Loading me down with a bevy of tutors was not my idea of a close-knit family, Michel."

"Do you really think now is the time or place for this discussion?" Michel asked in a softer tone.

"No indeed," she returned. "Now, if you'll excuse me, I've work to do."

An hour and a half later, and thirty minutes before the noon hour, Felice put down her pen. Silently congratulating herself on a job well done, she felt her lighthearted mood return. "You may collect my figures, René. Why don't you distribute the payroll now, because your efficient bookkeeper has completed her task early? And in case you hadn't noticed, a long queue has formed at the door."

Michel shot her a speaking glance and rose from his seat. "I shall refrain from making comment. Consider my tongue well-bit."

Bastien opened the safe while René moved to stand beside her instead of taking the ledger to his own desk. The sleeves of his shirt were rolled back, revealing arms dusted with dark hair and corded muscles that bunched as he leaned on the desk. His scent enveloped her again, leaving her light-headed. Why the blazes did her fickle body react to him when she didn't even like him? She kept her eyes on the pages in front of her lest he spy the confusion in them.

She rose from her desk and passed behind him. "You three can manage without me, so I shall retreat to the back rooms and help myself to a cool glass of lemonade." *And the necessary room, if I can remember where it's located.*

Surprise awaited her as she stepped through the door and found herself in a small, whitewashed sitting room. Two straight-back chairs flanking a barley twist table took up one side of the room, while a narrow cot lined another. A bookcase, lounging chair, and small side table were tucked in a corner. A carved armoire and mahogany sideboard holding a pitcher of lemonade stood on either side of a door across from her.

"Cozy," she murmured, and wondered whose idea it was to carve a space such as this out of the warehouse. Michel didn't seem the type to bother.

Henri emerged through the door leading to the warehouse. He carried a block of ice held between large metal tongs. He staggered to a stop. "*Mam'selle.*"

"*Bonjour*, Henri. I came for the lemonade."

"If you will allow me, I shall deposit this below the cupboard and break some off for you."

"Please," she said, and waited while he completed his task of loading the ice into a bin and using an ice pick to break off small chunks, which he deposited into a glass. Filling it with lemonade, he handed it to her.

"Thank you, Henri. You seem to be responsible for any number of chores around here. I'm impressed with your efficiency."

He blushed. "*Merci*. I work hard, but it be pleasant enough work, *mam'selle*. Much better than gigging frogs, don'cha know. I used to gig all night, then sell my catch to restaurants in the morning, then sleep all day. I never saw much of the sun."

"Are you related to the Thibodeaux family by any chance?"

"*Oui*. I be their cousin's son."

"Which cousin?"

He dropped his gaze to the floor. "Lucien, *mam'selle.*" *Good Lord, the prince of darkness himself.* "I see."

Henri looked up, wearing a forlorn look. "I know he be a bad man, but he never lived with my *maman* and me after I was born, so I doan acquaint myself with him at all. Excuse me, *s'il vous plaît*. I must see if I am needed up front."

At his departure, she sat at the table and sipped her drink. Curious as to what the ornately carved armoire might contain, she rose from the chair and made her way to it.

Opening the double doors, she found shirts. Clean, freshly laundered white shirts. There was no mistaking to whom they belonged. The interior of the cupboard carried a familiar scent that could belong to only one person. The inside of one of the doors held a small mirror and shelf containing a comb, tooth powder and brush, and shaving paraphernalia.

So this is how he manages to look so dapper at all times.

She slammed shut the doors and stepped back, appalled that she'd invaded René's private space. She might as well have broken into his bedroom and snooped. The man must work long hours to be leaving clothing in the company warehouse. Besides René's mistress, did he have any kind of life other than here?

The door opened and Henri poked his head in. "*Monsieur*, he be leaving now they be finished. Said to let you know."

She rushed into the main office in time to catch Michel slipping into his jacket and heading for the door.

"Wait!" Felice called out.

"What now?"

"Who sees to the ledgers during Abbott's absence?"

"The three of us," Michel said. "Why do you ask?"

"You've all made a mess of things, that's why. Now I'm burdened with the task of having to trace back to heaven knows where and correcting all the mistakes. Where are you going?"

"I'm off to check on my very pregnant wife. I'll return in a couple of hours."

"But Bastien is nowhere in sight and René is leaving as well, so—"

"*Non*," René said. "I cannot leave you here by yourself. I shall wait until Michel returns."

"Oh, for heaven's sake." But she knew he was right. Leaving a woman alone in a dockside building with deckhands coming and going would not do. She should thank him.

Michel disappeared and suddenly, the space seemed too confining.

"You did a fine job of meeting the payroll on time," René said, not looking up from his work.

She seated herself behind Abbott's desk once again. "I never doubted that I could."

"Oh, I do understand now. You were giving your brother the devil of a hard time."

She couldn't help grinning. "Truth be told, I had a jolly good time of it. And oh, that ice cream did taste heavenly so early in the morning."

"You can leave now."

She shook her head. "The ledgers need a thorough going-over. There's no sense my frittering the day away on nothing in particular, especially when Mayhew is out and about with your mistre . . . with your lady friend."

René went back to what he was doing, but Felice swore she saw his lips twitch. She opened a ledger, and in moments, she was lost in a sea of numbers, unaware of the passing of time until Michel stepped through the door.

"Quiet as a cemetery at midnight," he said.

She glanced at the simple school clock on the wall. "Apparently, you don't know what being gone a couple of hours means."

"Humph." He removed his jacket and seated himself at

his desk while René stood and, donning his, bade them a good day.

She paused and watched him disappear, aware suddenly that as they had tended to their tasks, the environment hadn't been uncomfortable at all. She could manage this. She could show up every day, bury herself in the ledgers. Then, once Mr. Abbott returned, she'd be free to leave. Turning a page, she sighed contentedly and lost herself once again in columns of numbers.

"It's getting late, Felice. Go home."

She jerked up her head and saw that dusk had somehow managed to descend upon the city. "Gracious. I lost track of time."

Mayhew popped through the door, concern knitting his brows together. "Have you been here all this while? Evening, Michel."

"Evening, Ainsworth."

Felice arched her back and stretched her neck from side to side. "The books are in dire need of my attention. Once I get going, I forget about all else. However, I couldn't be more pleased to see you."

"I grew concerned when Mrs. Dawes said she hadn't seen you since you left home early this morning. I thought we were to have dinner."

What a handsome man she would soon marry. Even with a scowl on his face, he was a sight to behold. "And we shall. If you think I'm presentable, then please, let's away to Antoine's. You'll love the food and ambience."

"I've dined there already. After Mrs. Worth showed me the sights, we ended up at the restaurant for our noon meal. Come, darling. Your maid, Marie, tells me she has fresh shrimp and something else whose name I didn't catch. I've had quite a day of it and you must be quite fatigued. We'll dine at the town house, if you don't mind."

"Of course." Collecting her reticule and donning her hat, she passed by her brother. "You get yourself home as well. Brenna needs you more than your work does."

He reached out and, catching her hand, gave it a squeeze. "Thank you for helping out. Truce?"

"Always, dear heart." She planted a kiss atop his head. "At least until tomorrow."

He gave a dry chuckle.

"Listen to you. You're so tired you are hoarse. Off with you."

"I'll lock up in a moment."

"Promise it will only be a moment?"

He nodded and waved her off.

It was nearing midnight and Mayhew was still rattling on about the photography equipment he'd purchased from Mrs. Worth's friend's shop, the sights he'd seen, and what he intended to do the following day.

Slipping off her shoes, she tucked her feet under her gown and rested her weary head on the back of the blue velvet Chesterfield sofa. Fatigued as she was, she listened with great contentment to the wonderful man she was about to marry. Could any woman be so fortunate? "I'm so pleased you've taken to this fine city. Perhaps you'll be able to manage the heat after all?"

"Frankly, darling, I hardly noticed. I doubt I've ever seen a town such as this. To think I've barely scratched the surface."

"Mrs. Worth turned out to be a priceless guide, so it would seem."

"Oh, her head is filled with all manner of tidbits. And what a tale she had to tell about those Thibodeaux brothers. Did you know their mother is some kind of voodoo priestess?"

"Yes, I did know that, Mayhew."

"I am absolutely fascinated. I wish to meet her."

Felice's spine stiffened. "No, you do not want to come in contact with Odalie Thibodeaux."

"You've met her?"

"I have. I once went to her home in the bayou to fetch my cousin."

"Cameron? What the devil was he doing there?"

"It's a long story. Suffice it to say, he'd taken ill while in the bayou and Bastien brought him to her home. Odalie was none too happy about our presence. Stay away from her, Mayhew. She's trouble."

"What of Bastien? Mrs. Worth told me he's a traitor. Have you any idea what he's done?"

"He happens to be a *traiteur*, which is Cajun for healer. Bastien has the gift of healing, and he's very good at it. He once saved Cameron's life."

"I say, this is quite a spectacular town. And filled with all manner of people. I had no idea I would be so taken with it."

"Told you so."

Across the street from the Andrews town house, René kept to the shadows. He'd slept a few hours before waking with an ache in his head and a fierce hunger in his gut. Having decided on shrimp remoulade to fix what ailed him, he'd been on his way to Tujague's on Rue Decatur when he'd spied Felice and Ainsworth heading his way on the opposite side of the street.

He'd watched them enter her town house, noted the lights appear in the two windows he knew to be the dining room and parlor. He'd continued on to the restaurant, where he'd doctored his ailing head and empty gut with some hearty fare. For some unfathomable reason, upon his return, he'd parked himself in front of her place, a mere two doors from his own home. Weary as he was, he waited.

A rustle coming from the side street caught his attention. Bastien slid in beside him, silent as the night. He spoke to René in their mother tongue. "You leave that woman alone. Don't you go messin' with her again if you expect to see another sunrise. She belongs to someone else now."

"I know," René said. "He's in there with her."

"Then let them be. What she does with her fiancé is none of your business."

His rational mind told him his brother was right, but his instincts told him otherwise. "There's something a bit off with his highness, don't you think?"

"He's arrogant and he thinks he owns the world, but that doesn't mean there's anything wrong with him."

The bell on the wrought-iron gate sounded. Bastien muttered a curse as both men slid farther into the shadows.

The gate opened and Ainsworth strode out. He paused long enough to say something to whoever had let him out, then strolled down the street—in the opposite direction from Le Blanc House, where he resided.

Marie, a servant both René and Bastien knew and who could easily recognize them, peered up and down the street, then locked the gate and disappeared into the darkened courtyard.

"Looks to me like his highness got his north mixed up with his south," René whispered.

"So it would seem," Bastien responded

René grunted. "Why do I have a feeling we should follow him?"

"Because why would we not?"

Together, René and Bastien stepped from the shadows. Matching the sound of Ainsworth's footfalls, they stayed well behind him. They trailed him for as long as it took to reach Madame Olympée's—the finest brothel in all of Louisiana.

"Must be that Mademoiselle Andrews, she be saving herself for the wedding," Bastien said. "But his highness, he is not."

René folded his arms across his chest and rocked back on his heels. "Didn't *Maman* once tell us that everyone has a side that no one knows?"

Bastien shoved his hands in his pockets. "*Oui*, that she did."

"Then why don't we find his?"

Chapter Eight

Wandering the city streets before dawn was akin to a living prayer for Felice. Especially here in the Garden District, where not a soul crossed her path. The seductive perfume of jasmine blossoms clung to the night air while somewhere in the branches of an oak tree lining the walkway, a lone bird's soft trill gave notice of the coming sun.

This wasn't the first time she'd been out and about at this hour, nor would it be the last. Should Michel somehow learn of her escapades, he'd likely give her the what-for, but with her lifelong independent streak, he shouldn't be surprised to discover she'd done this sort of thing for years.

Venturing out so late would not only be considered scandalous for a respectable female, it could also be dangerous. Felice, however, had a definite edge. She was tall for a woman. And slender. With her hair tucked beneath a cap pulled low over her brow, and wearing masculine riding garb, she could pass for a boy. It was doubtful anyone would question her gender.

A movement on Rue Conery caught her eye. A lone figure was headed her way. Lengthening her stride, she matched the swing of her arms to her masculine gait and passed him by. She heard him cross to her side of the street, the tap of his footsteps behind her. Her heart skipped a beat.

"You. Ho there, chap!"

Oh Lordy, that voice! Surely that can't be Mayhew.

She quickened her steps.

"Slow down, would you, boy? I merely wish to know if I am headed in the right direction."

That is Mayhew! What in Heaven's name could he possibly be up to at this late hour? Oh, blast it all, one way or the other, she was caught. She halted beneath a gas streetlight.

Whipping the cap off her head, she let her hair tumble down her back. She turned. "Mayhew, what in the world are you doing out at this late hour?"

He stumbled to a halt. "Felice? God's teeth, what are *you* doing here?"

"I'm on my way to Le Blanc House. Have you been out all night?"

"Um, no . . . I couldn't sleep, so I went for a stroll. But by jove, I got a bit turned around in the dark."

An odd feeling swept over her that he wasn't being entirely truthful. "You're wearing the same clothing as last evening. Did you not take to your bed at all?"

"I told you, I couldn't sleep." He looked her up and down, irritation replacing the hesitancy in his voice. "Enough about me. You failed to answer my question. What in Hades are you doing here dressed like that?"

Stepping forward, he reached for her arm. "I shall see you home at once."

She shrugged off his grasp and retreated a step. She gave him a once-over of her own, then continued toward her destination. "And how, pray tell, would you manage to find your way back to Le Blanc House on your own if you got lost taking a little stroll?"

He strode alongside her. "What in hell are you up to, Felice?"

"I'm off to the stables. I intend to enjoy a ride along the levee before daybreak—before reporting to work, where I shall be required to sit the day long."

They turned a corner, and magnificent, pristine Le Blanc House loomed before her.

"I'll not have you traipsing around town dressed in that ridiculous getup. Nor will I have you riding out alone. Whatever possessed you?"

"Lower your voice, Ainsworth. You'll wake the dead." They moved to the rear of the house and the stables, where a glimmer of light shone around the edges of the door. When they entered the dimly lit interior smelling of hay and horses, a stableboy shot from his chair. Wide-eyed, he grabbed a whip.

"It's all right, I'm Mademoiselle Andrews. I've come for Jingo."

The boy visibly relaxed and reached for the lone side-saddle. "I'll ready him for you, *mam'selle*."

"Not that one. Michel's English-made one will do," she said.

Mayhew grunted. "You daren't use a man's saddle."

She lifted a brow. "Why not? Because it's considered indecent for a lady to spread her legs over a horse's back?"

"Watch your tongue around that lad, Felice."

He turned to the stablehand. "Boy, saddle me that gray over there."

He stalked over to the saddles. "I do wish you wouldn't be so foolish as to use a man's saddle, darling."

"I'll have you know, I've been riding this way since I was three years old."

"Humph. Not while in England, you didn't."

"That was there. Must I remind you that I was raised around men? I wasn't about to race around the countryside with one leg thrown over my horse's withers. I've a brilliant idea, Ainsworth. Because you are intent on seeing me home, why don't *you* ride sidesaddle?"

For a long moment, she studied him. Her gaze dropped to his wrinkled cravat, then back to his eyes. A churning mixture of anger at his controlling ways and mistrust of his story that he'd merely taken a stroll hung heavy in her chest. "I doubt you'd last an hour. Especially when you must be weary after all the tossing and turning you did last night."

He glanced away, as if to gather his wits; then, lifting a brow, he gave her a cocky grin. He brushed the back of his fingers across her cheek. "You're back to calling me Ainsworth, which means you are mighty frustrated with me."

She turned to the stableboy. "I'll be taking Jingo over to our company town house for the duration of my stay, so don't fret when I fail to return him."

Mayhew placed a hand at her elbow. "I will not allow you to go off alone. Once it's daylight, I'll have no trouble finding my way back."

She huffed an exasperated breath. "If you must. But heed my words—I prefer to take my predawn rides in silence."

With a wink and a dimpled grin, he mounted his horse. "My, aren't you the cheeky one."

Four hours into digging through the ledgers, nausea rolled through Felice's stomach. Something was definitely amiss with the books. The bad mood she'd walked in with worsened. "Michel, when do you expect Mr. Abbott's friend—whoever he is—to stop by with a report on Mr. Abbott's condition?"

Michel shrugged. "Hard to say." He turned to René. "When was Farouche here last?"

"About ten days ago. Why?"

She wasn't about to report that someone might have tinkered with the books. Not until she met with Mr. Abbott. "I need to speak with this Mr. Farouche. Where might I find him?"

Michel rubbed at the back of his neck. "I don't rightly know. René?"

René shrugged. "He shares a home with Abbott, who is particular about his privacy."

Michel frowned at Felice. "Is there something amiss that you cannot handle on your own?"

No sense discussing the matter with her brother until she investigated further. He had enough to worry about. "I simply would like a little chat with the man."

"If you intend to track down Farouche for the purpose of seeing Abbott, I forbid it. I'm certain I already informed you that he doesn't wish to receive visitors during his recuperation."

"Oh bother, Michel. I find it hard to believe my dear friend would not be glad to see me. In fact, a visit from me might very well lift his spirits. Now, how do I go about finding this Mr. Farouche? Or what of the physician? Surely he would have Mr. Abbott's address. What's the physician's name?"

Michel swiped a hand over his eyes and cursed under his breath. "God in Heaven, please protect me from my stubborn sister."

Felice decided her brother's rising temper required a change of subject. "Speaking of visits, when will you invite me to your home so I may meet your children and visit with Brenna, dear brother of mine?"

"In due time, dear sister of mine." He stood. "If you do not have a pressing problem, I'll take my midday leave to check on my wife. If this babe doesn't show itself soon . . ." He grabbed his jacket and swept out the door.

René leaned back in his chair, his piercing gaze locked with hers. "What be the matter, *chère*?"

As if she'd confide in him. He was a clever man. Beyond clever in far too many ways. Was he capable of doing something so underhanded and which required such a keen understanding of accounting?

She shrugged. "Nothing. I'm just a bit fatigued. And I do miss Mr. Abbott's presence."

René stood, still studying her with that aggravatingly astute gaze of his.

He doesn't believe a word I said.

"I'll fetch you a glass of iced lemonade." He turned and strode to the rear of the office.

She watched him disappear through the door into what her brother referred to as the relief room. He'd mentioned earlier that either he or René would on occasion use the cot while awaiting a ship's late arrival. Had René slept there last night after the *Jolie* anchored before dawn? Had he been here all along while she'd been walking the streets alone and riding about the levee?

Oh, bother . . . why was she even pondering such a notion?

He returned, glass in hand, and set it on her desk.

"Thank you," she said, preferring to keep her focus on the beverage and not on his muscled forearms. His habit of rolling back his shirtsleeves was disconcerting to say the least.

He merely nodded in reply and returned to his desk.

Instead of sitting, he grabbed a stack of papers and strode to the door. "I'll be aboard the *Jolie*, but I'll keep watch on the entry. Henri is involved in a task in the relief room. Should you need anything, have him fetch me. Will that suit you, *chère*?"

"Indeed." She'd given up asking him to refrain from using personal endearments when speaking to her. After all, every Cajun male finished his sentences in like manner when addressing a female. Had he used the word on Mrs. Worth? She couldn't recall him having done so.

She took her time drinking the cool lemonade. Feeling refreshed, she returned to concentrating on the column of numbers in front of her. Perhaps she'd excuse herself from dining with Mayhew tonight and take one or two of the past year's ledgers home with her. No, she would not sacrifice her evenings with him. It was bad enough that she saw little of him during the day. However, puzzling out what exactly was amiss would take some time, and it was all she could think about.

She was lost in thought when a noise at the front door brought her out of her deep concentration. A quick glance up and then back to her books left a mental image of René slouched against the door frame, watching her—the lout.

Wait.

When had he changed into loose clothing?

She glanced back up only to discover it wasn't René, but a stranger observing her with eyes as dark and intense as René's. He appeared to be of equal height and wore his ebony hair the same length, but his was unkempt, as though he might be in the habit of combing it with his fingers and nothing else. He was a handsome man to be sure, but something about him set her on edge. "You aren't René!"

He sauntered in, a brow cocked. "And who might this fine lady be?"

The hair stood up on the nape of her neck. "Mademoiselle Andrews. Who are you and what do you want?"

"I be Henri's papa, don'cha know. Where he be?"

Lucien Thibodeaux. The houngan! She'd never met René's cousin, the voodoo priest, but she'd heard he walked a dark path. Rumor had it he could be more dangerous than the devil himself when crossed. Felice's stomach curdled, and chills ran up and down her spine. She hoped Henri remained behind the closed door.

"Henri is not here," she lied. "I believe my brother sent him on an errand some time ago, so you may leave."

"*Non.* I be waitin' here for him."

His gaze flashed dark as sin. Danger lurked in his countenance as he approached, so close she could see the telltale red in the whites of his eyes.

He's been drinking.

"You need to wait outside for Henri's return."

He gave her a half smile and continued his slow approach.

Where the devil is René?

She remembered the emergency bell atop the roof. The long rope leading to it hung a few feet from her grasp. Could she get to it if need be?

The door to the warehouse opened and Henri walked through. He nearly tripped over himself. His cheeks flamed. "Papa. What you be doing here?"

"You got some coin, yesterday, *oui*?"

Henri rubbed his hands up and down the sides of his trousers as his eyes shifted back and forth from his father to the door.

"Doan even think of runnin', boy. Now where you be

keepin' dat money? It ain't at home with your *maman*, so where be it?"

"I . . ."

René stepped through the open door, his body angled toward Henri. He paused for a brief moment, then tossed the papers in his hand onto the chair beside the door. He turned. Like a fire-breathing dragon, he faced Lucien.

"*Laisser*." Leave was all René said, but the power of that single word, little more than a growl that erupted from his throat, left Felice light-headed. Breathless, she watched the scene unfold before her as if it were taking place in slow motion.

"Henri, he be my son, not yours," Lucien replied in Cajun French. "He will do as I say."

René moved toward Lucien in a measured, threatening manner. "*Laisse-le tranquille*," he responded. Leave the boy alone.

A rapid-fire verbal encounter ensued. The next thing Felice knew, René thrust Lucien up against the wall so hard, the room shook. His hand gripped the houngan's throat. "If I ever hear of you going anywhere near Henri or his mother again, I swear on your mother's grave, I will carry this one step further."

With a quick flip, he had Lucien turned around with his arm twisted behind his back and one side of his face plastered against the wall.

Lucien grunted.

René heaved his cousin out the door. The man stumbled, then regained his footing. As he backed away, he spit out a vile curse, then disappeared.

René shoved his hair from his face and wiped his sweat-soaked forehead with his shirtsleeve. He turned to Henri, who stood like a statue, eyes wide. "You go home and tell your *maman* I will be paying her a visit."

Speechless, Henri only nodded.

René's voice had softened, yet his words were filled with authority. "Tell her you will be moving soon."

"But we . . ."

"Not to worry, *mon ami*. I have a much better place for you." René strode to the chair, grabbed the papers he'd dropped on the seat, and moved to his desk. "Now go. You be the man to your *maman*, you hear?"

Henri bobbed his head.

"Tell her she will like her new home. And tell her if that sonofabitch ever so much as looks at her or you again, she is to come to me."

Henri started for the door. One foot over the threshold, he paused. "He is the houngan. He will not let this pass."

"I am aware," René said. "Now go."

Felice sat at her desk, unable to say or do anything other than blink. René glanced her way, then, without a word, disappeared behind the door leading to the back room.

She let out a breath she'd been unaware of holding. "Good heavens," was all she could say before René returned, rolling up one sleeve of a fresh shirt.

"My word. I surely wouldn't want to agitate you," she said, unable to tear her eyes from his intimate movements.

He tilted his head, eyeing her through half-closed lids as he continued to turn back the other sleeve. "Ah, but perhaps you have, *chère*. Only in a different way."

Finished with his dress, he headed for his desk, only to pause in the middle of the room. He turned to face her, his stance wide, hands on hips. Something shifted in him as he focused on her with a feral intensity that rattled her to the quick. His indecipherable, knife-sharp gaze set her heart pounding against her rib cage.

"What?" was all she could manage.

"Come now, you must be aware of what is on my mind," he said.

Lord, it wasn't longing she saw in him but something far more dangerous to her sensibilities. "How should I know? Reading your mind would be like trying to catch dandelion fluff."

With a catlike grace, he moved to where she sat. He leaned on her desk with both hands splayed palm down. He bent over, so close there was no escaping his essence. "It is not finished between us, *chère*."

For a moment, she was afraid he was about to kiss her, and that she'd be helpless to stop him. "We were finished when I left."

"*Non*. That will happen only when we have the talk I spoke of."

He hovered over her, so close she could make out the subtle differences between his black pupils and those dark irises. A wide chasm opened low in her belly. Deep in that chasm, an indecent flame lit.

This wouldn't do.

Not at all.

She had nowhere to go but against the wall behind her, so she remained seated and racked her brain for a response that would send him back to his desk. "My, aren't we overflowing with male virility after that little spat with your cousin. Do not assume you are entitled to dominate me just because you are suddenly full of yourself."

His smile was brief. Had she blinked, she'd have missed it.

He leaned closer and spoke in a low murmur. "Make no mistake, *ma petite*. Whatever exists between us is potent and incendiary. Until we have our little chat, there is no putting out this fire."

Torn between wanting to slap him and wishing he'd

go ahead and kiss her, she struggled to catch hold of her runaway emotions. Even with the windows and door open, the air felt suddenly suffocating.

She couldn't breathe.

She had to get out of there.

Had to think.

Her mind raced in a crazy pattern that made her head spin and her stomach turn over. She was on her feet and around the desk without knowing how she got there. "I'll have no more of this ridiculous conversation. And in a business environment no less."

Marching past him, she stomped off. "I'm away to find something to eat. I'll return . . . whenever I please."

She was already out the door when he called out. "You forgot your hat and parasol. And your reticule."

"Bugger off," she muttered and headed for home.

Chapter Nine

Midnight had come and gone by the time René reached his town house on Rue Royale. He was so damn tired, it was all he could do to fit the key into the gate's lock. A twist to the right, and metal screeched against metal in the silence. He winced. This would not do now that new tenants were installed on the ground floor. Stepping into the courtyard, he locked the gate behind him and cursed under his breath at the repeated jarring noise. He'd have Henri oil the lock on the morrow.

Christ, even his bones ached. What he craved was a full night of uninterrupted sleep. He'd risen before dawn these past four days. In a couple of hours, he'd do the same. Three clippers with full cargoes had sailed into port all at once, which meant a hell of a workload lay ahead of him. Unless Bastien returned a day early from upriver, René would be on his own.

Little good Michel was of late. Granted, he could be depended upon to see that the crew from all three ships got their pay by noon—after Felice provided the proper figures, that was. But clearly, the man was not his usual steadfast self. He'd made errors of late. Had René not caught the mistakes, they'd have proven either costly or dangerous. For someone known to be the epitome of calm,

Michel's work discipline had gone adrift under the stress of his wife's confinement.

Then there was the problem of the missing *Endeavor*. Had the long-overdue clipper failed to make her way around treacherous Cape Horn? Christ, he hoped not. He'd hired every crew member on board—including the captain. The thought of them lost at sea, along with the few passengers the merchant ship carried, wrenched his gut.

If all that weren't enough, he had Felice to deal with. She'd barely spoken to him since their encounter three days before. He damn well wasn't sorry for having confronted her. He'd been right about the banked flames threatening to ignite between them. When he'd leaned over her desk, close enough to catch her scent, her breath hitched, her pupils dilated, and color rose to her cheeks. He knew raw emotion when he saw it. When she slid that lush bottom lip of hers between her teeth, she looked at him as if he was about to devour her, and there was little she could do about it—or wanted to.

Thank God she'd bolted.

He hated to think what might have happened had he followed the command of his randy cock and climbed right over the top of the desk. The last thing he needed was to repeat the mistake he'd made three years ago. Now, more than ever, it was time she agreed to a private conversation. If things continued like this much longer, Michel was sure to take notice. As would everyone else.

A thought niggled at him. Something more than the fire between them was disturbing her. She'd shown up the next day with barely a greeting, then buried her head in those damn ledgers, where she remained until taking her leave. He would consider that later. What he desperately needed now was his bed.

He passed by what had once been the old servants' quarters and took note of the shuttered windows.

Bien.

Henri and his *maman* must be settled in for the night. Not only were they safe from Lucien behind the locked front gate, but their new home was a far sight better than the sparse room they'd been living in. And Monique's days of having to take in laundry were at an end. She worked for René now.

He hadn't seen her for a few years. She couldn't be more than thirty, yet she appeared older, with her pinched features, gaunt frame, and lackluster dark hair. She'd been attractive once—pretty even. Given time, perhaps her new situation would revitalize her. Until he'd shown up to move them to his home, he'd had no idea of their plight. Henri had said nothing of their situation when he'd hired on with the company.

Providence could move in remarkable ways, René decided. Because he previously had not employed live-in help, he'd had no use for the old servants' quarters. Rather than let them sit empty, he'd had the space refurbished, used it to store excess furniture. As luck would have it, his once-a-week cleaning lady had recently returned to Metairie to care for her elderly folks. Thus, René needed to hire someone new when Monique happened along. It only took a day of rearranging furniture and putting a little shine on the roomy, two-bedroom space to make it ready for her and her son.

When they stepped inside their new home for the first time, Henri beamed. Monique wept. And René bit his tongue to keep from cursing Lucien out loud. How the hell could the man abandon his family, leave them to fend for themselves? But then, Lucien never did think of anyone but himself.

René moved silently through the courtyard. His sweet-smelling garden, filled with local flowers and exotic plants he'd managed to collect on his travels, edged the entire perimeter of the courtyard. By this time next year, everything should be well-established. He was proud of all he'd accomplished—had every right to be. He'd come a long way from the bayou shanty he'd been born and raised in. Everything he'd ever dreamed of had come to pass—he had a lofty position with a highly respected company, a home in the coveted Vieux Carré, and ever-expanding wealth, thanks to decent wages and wise investments. Yet, as he climbed the stairs to the main living quarters, his footsteps echoed with the odd emptiness hounding him of late.

Spying a light shining through the edges of the curtains on either side of the door, he paused. Had Monique forgotten to turn off a lamp? Gaslighting wasn't something to be left unattended. He reached for the handle, but the door swung wide and Monique stood before him.

"*Bonsoir, monsieur.*"

He stepped inside. "What the devil are you doing up so late?"

"I thought it best to remain here for your return," she said in her Cajun tongue.

"*Merci,*" he responded in kind. "But I come and go at odd hours. In the future, do not wait up for me unless I send Henri to inform you otherwise. He will also let you know if I intend to return for dinner, which will be a rarity because I take my meals in restaurants. All I require of you is to keep my living quarters in order; otherwise, you may do as you please."

He noted her hands were clasped in front of her so tightly, her knuckles were white. "What is it?"

"You have a guest waiting for you, *monsieur*." She nodded toward the staircase leading to his bedroom.

"A woman?"

"*Oui*. A pretty woman."

Liberty.

"Did she give her name?"

"*Oui, monsieur*. Mrs. Worth."

Oh, hell.

"She said she was your lady, and that I was to allow her entry, under your orders. Was I wrong in letting her in?"

"*Non*. You could not have known, but from now on, no one enters without my permission. Is this the reason you waited up for me?"

"*Oui, monsieur*. I—"

Christ, she was nervous. "When only you and Henri are present, call me René." Tired and out of sorts as he was, he managed to offer her a smile. "Remember, we are practically cousins."

She blinked, as if to hold back tears, then dropped her head and settled her gaze on the floor. "I . . . I am so grateful to have a lovely home for my son and me. I do not wish to do anything to cause you disappointment."

He moved to the Louis XIV side table and reached for a cut-crystal glass on a tray next to a decanter of Armagnac. He poured himself two fingers and turned back to her. Good God, the hemline of her old gown was quivering. "Have no fear, Monique. Your home is here for however long you wish. What we need is a little patience while we get used to each other, *non*? Forgive me for not taking the time to get to know you in the past, but you were with Lucien, so I had reason to keep my distance."

"*Oui*," she whispered. "I am aware of your dislike for each other. He can be quite charming with the ladies, and I was young when we met. Too young. It wasn't until we married and Henri came along that my husband showed his true face to me."

René's jaw clenched. She was a good woman wed to a good-for-nothing man. "You can relax now. You are safe."

"I hope so, *monsie . . .* René."

Frustrated, he raked his fingers through his hair. Tomorrow, he would have a dressmaker come in with orders to get rid of Monique's goddamn rags. "Go. Get some sleep."

"*Bonsoir,*" she murmured and scurried out the door.

He watched her disappear, then moved back to the Armagnac and poured another two fingers. The last damn thing he needed was Liberty Belle in his bed. He climbed the stairs and strode to the door, opened it, and stepped inside. Liberty lay in the middle of his bed, wearing nothing but a rose in her hair.

"Darling," she purred. "I thought you'd never get home. I nearly fell asleep waiting for you."

He drained the glass with a hard swallow and set it atop the rosewood chiffonier beside the door. "I didn't see your carriage out front."

"I sent my driver away."

He noted her clothing scattered about the room. Gathering it up, he laid the pile at her feet. "Get dressed. I'll see you home."

A flare of anger lit her eyes. With an upward tilt of her chin, she recovered and gave him a seductive half smile. "It's much too late to leave now, so I may as well spend the night. And why is it you've never invited me into this lovely room before? Why do you never spend an entire night with me?"

Because I have never cared enough to allow any woman

into my private space. He raked a hand through his hair. Damn it, he wasn't about to give her an answer.

She bent her head and gave him a faux pout. "Don't you miss me, darling? It seems all you do is work, which leaves me quite bored."

He turned his back on her and moved to the window. Shoving his hands in his pockets, he stared down at the empty street below. "How can you be bored when you've been busy showing Ainsworth the town?"

She laughed, a soft, velvet sound deep in her throat. "Why, I do believe you might be jealous. And here I didn't think you were the sort."

Christ, that was the last thing he was. He never questioned the amount of time Ainsworth spent with her, but if what he suspected was taking place, why the man's nightly visits to a whorehouse? "Liberty—"

"I am not sleeping with Ainsworth, if that's what you think."

He could always tell when she fibbed. Which occurred whenever she wished to hide her flamboyant ways. Tonight, she spoke the truth. He wasn't about to question what took place between her and Ainsworth. What he needed to do was figure out the kindest way to ease himself out of a relationship that had gone flat before Ainsworth arrived on the scene. The woman had a temper.

"He takes photographs of me. That is all," she said. "He's absolutely obsessed with this newfangled equipment and tinkers with it for hours."

Her words got René's attention. He kept his back to her. "What kind of photographs?"

She laughed again—soft and throaty. "Why don't you ask him to show them to you?"

Like hell he would. As soon as he found the time, he'd

call on Madame Olympée, try to find out what her regular customer was up to during his nightly visits. After the first time René and Bastien had spied the man entering the brothel, René sent a telegraph to their Boston office. He figured it was the fastest way to get a message aboard the next ship to England. At the moment, Ainsworth was being investigated both here and on the other side of the Atlantic. Sooner or later, René would have answers to a few of his questions.

He drew in a slow breath, carefully choosing his words. "You are a lovely woman with many fine attributes. Why you would choose to be with a man like me—"

"Darling, don't tell me you think you've fallen out of love with me. I won't have it."

He closed his eyes against the frustration about to burst inside him. He didn't love her, had never led her to believe he might one day. "There's that word again."

"Come to bed. Let me show you a new meaning to it."

Whatever reserves he had left drained out of him. He could no longer put up with her manipulations. "*Madame*, things are over between us."

A hush fell over the room. He didn't know which was worse, the silence or one of her fits of temper.

"You are weary, darling. Come to bed. You'll feel differently in the morning," she said, but the sultriness in her voice had given way to a familiar edge that appeared whenever things didn't go her way.

"*Mon Dieu*, Liberty. Leave things be."

"It's her, isn't it?"

He knew of whom she spoke, but he damn well wasn't about to acknowledge it. "Get dressed. I'll see you home."

"I saw how you couldn't keep your eyes off her that evening at Le Blanc House."

"You don't know what you're talking about."

"Oh, but I do. We women are like finely tuned instruments. Our instincts tell us when an odd chord has been struck, when something is out of tune, or when just the right note has sounded to draw two people together."

He kept his focus on the darkened street below, knew to hold his tongue despite her goading.

"You can't have her, you know. Even if she weren't engaged to a man of noble blood and will spend her life in faraway England, she'd never have you. Oh, she'll toy with you. But you're a Thibodeaux from the bayou—a bastard son of a voodoo witch and an arrogant French aristocrat who thinks nothing of openly keeping mistresses."

A rustle of silk and petticoats told him she'd climbed off the bed and was donning her clothing. "He's approached me, you know. Your father, I mean. Seems he is in the market for yet another mistress. This time, one to share with his illegitimate son. Might you help me on with my corset?"

Hearing the subtle changes in her voice, he wasn't about to touch her. She was a woman growing angrier by the moment. "Hooks are in the front. Always have been. I'll tend to the fastening of your gown if need be, but you got out of your clothing on your own, so I suspect you were clever enough to think of what to wear before you ever stepped out your door."

"You are being a cad, René."

"*Non.* I am being honest."

He felt her anger explode. Like a vibration running through the room and right up his spine. He heard her telltale scramble toward the fireplace.

Merde!

He ducked sideways.

The vase shattered against the wooden window casing. Barely missed the glass. He would like to throttle her. Instead, he kept his voice low, his words precise in their delivery. "Well done, Liberty. You just destroyed an irreplaceable Chinese urn. An ancient one at that."

"You coldhearted Cajun bastard. I'll not have you toss me away like yesterday's newspaper."

He glanced at his bed. Ah, hell, he'd see her home, then return to the office and catch a nap on the cot. "Unless you wish to assist me in preparing the carriage, finish dressing. You can meet me in the courtyard. But do so quietly, I've people asleep downstairs."

"Oh, yes, that woman who let me in. She's far too pretty to be a maid. Where'd you find her?"

When he failed to respond, she eyed the matching vase atop the fireplace mantel.

"Do not touch it, Liberty. I'm warning you." The one she'd destroyed had been his first legitimately acquired work of art, which was why the pair sat on the mantel in his bedroom—a reminder from whence he'd come, and where he might go in life. *That vase can never be duplicated, goddamn it.*

She reached out and ran a finger down its delicate side. "It amazes me how a Cajun bastard growing up in a bayou hovel could know how to choose anything of value, let alone pull everything together in a room befitting an aristocrat."

An angry response leaped to his throat. He swallowed the words, kept them to himself. *That's because I was raised to steal anything I could get my hands on. I soon learned to spot the difference between cheap goods and quality. I grew to respect an object—not for its monetary value but for what it represented in the heart of its creator. But I'll be damned if I will give you the satisfaction of*

*knowing my thieving ways made me want a better life,
and that it would take years to figure out how to go about
changing my circumstances in a town that always rejected me.*

"On second thought," he said in a casual monotone, "I
won't leave you alone in my home, lest I return to a pile of
rubbish." He moved to the linen-covered Bergère chair
beside the fireplace. He sat, propped his elbows on the
armrests, and steepled his fingers beneath his chin. As relaxed as he hoped he appeared, he was poised to react. A
few slow intakes of breath and he was in control of his
faculties. No longer would her words have the power to
rile him.

She continued dressing without looking his way. "A
self-taught aficionado of the finer things in life—is that
what you are? Or perhaps your taste comes from your
aristocratic French father. I doubt your Cajun voodoo
mother would know the difference between a porcelain
vase and a chamber pot."

He laughed. "Aren't you just chock full of sophisti-
cation?"

Chapter Ten

Shock gave way to denial. Denial gave way to hurt. And some time during the night, hurt gave way to anger—an anger so fierce, Felice could barely see straight. "Curse your black heart, Mr. Abbott," she muttered as she tramped through town in the predawn darkness. "Curse any good thing I ever thought you stood for."

"Beg your pardon, *mam'selle*?" Henri said, as he scurried alongside her.

"Pay me no heed, Henri. I awoke in a foul mood."

Except for the occasional vendor getting an early start, and a lamplighter making his rounds to extinguish the gaslights, the streets were empty. She and Henri reached the front door of the office, only to find a pitch-black interior. To their right, three majestic clippers, their cargo yet to be unloaded, floated low in the water. Lanterns lighting the fore and aft decks cast eerie patterns across the surface of the water. An amber glow shone from the portholes of all three ships.

"Monsieur René must be belowdeck on one of them, *mam'selle*. Ain't no one inside the office."

Good, let him stay there. They hadn't spoken since he'd

nearly climbed over her desk the other day. She had enough on her mind without running into him.

Several armed sentinels patrolling the dock paused and turned their way. One called out, "Who goes there?"

"I'll speak to them." Henri ran to the first guard, who nodded and waved a greeting at Felice. The boy hurried back to her. "They'll keep an eye on the entrance while I get your coffee and beignets, but he said to lock the door behind you anyway."

"Can you bring something for each of the guards as well?" Felice asked. "Perhaps one of them would be willing to help you carry everything back."

"*Oui*," Henri responded, and returned to the first sentry, who joined him.

Using the key Michel had supplied her, she slipped into the office and locked the door behind her. Removing her gloves, she used the faint light coming through the windows from the ships to locate the tinderbox on the wall next to the door. She lit the sconce and turned up the gas flame.

Working her way around the room, she set each wall lamp alight. As she mumbled another curse meant for Abbott, she headed for the relief room to ready it for Henri's return, and flung open the door.

"You're not Henri," René said in a voice thick with sleep.

She bit back a squeal at the shadowed figure lying on the cot. "My word! You frightened me half to death."

The bed gave a squeak as he rose from his prone position. Swinging his legs over the edge, he rested his elbows on his knees and raked his hands through his disheveled hair. "Light the sconce, *s'il vous plaît*."

Trying her best to keep her hands from shaking, she lit the wall lamp and turned it full up.

He blinked and shielded his eyes. "*Merde*. Not so bright."

Feigning nonchalance at finding him asleep, she lowered the flame until a soft glow infused the room. "Better?"

"*C'est bon*. What be the time?"

He wasn't his usual immaculate self. His shirt was wrinkled, his hair mussed, and dark stubble shadowed the lower half of his face. A quiver ran through her belly. She couldn't have felt more intrusive had she stepped into his bedroom. "Nearly five o'clock."

He stood and made his way to the wardrobe, where he retrieved a fresh shirt. He set the folded garment on the chair beside him.

Mercy! Did he intend to disrobe in front of her? Now more than her hands trembled. When he said nothing, she struggled to find words. "Why are you not working?"

"I decided that if I was to make it to the noon payroll without falling asleep on my feet, I needed to close my eyes for a bit." He scrubbed a hand over his face and picked up his shaving brush. "I've already labored for several hours."

"I'm sorry if I sounded rude. You surprised me when I thought I was alone." Good Lord, he did intend to shave right in front of her. Would he do so shirtless, as her father had? She backed toward the door.

He glanced her way. "Why are you here so early? A woman shouldn't be on the streets alone at this hour, *chère*. It is far too dangerous."

She would've laughed had she not been caught up in a whirl of emotions assaulting her senses. If only he knew how often she wandered around New Orleans at odd hours.

He paused with the brush in midair, his gaze piercing. He lifted a brow. "Well?"

"You are correct, petticoats do not belong on the streets after dark. Alone, that is." Well, she wore men's clothing whenever she was out and about in the wee hours, so she spoke the truth, didn't she? "Henri accompanied me. I sent him for coffee and beignets."

"You did not answer my question. Why come here so early?"

I couldn't sleep. That damn Abbott and his swindling kept me awake.

Instead, she said, "In case you hadn't noticed, we have three ships presently docked with crews keen to fill their pockets by the noon hour, and just as eager to empty them in town thereafter. I need to make certain I get all three payrolls ready on time. Michel will be in a little late, by the way. Honestly, he needs to hire more help around this place. At least two or three more would do."

"It has been decided that my brother will remain in town from now on. He has already taken on more duties. We usually have two other regular employees, but presently they . . ."

He picked up his shaving cup, swirled the brush around in the soap, and went about slathering the creamy white mixture over his jaw.

"But what?" My word, she might as well have been watching him bathe for the sensual reaction his act aroused in her. She should turn and leave. It was the right thing to do. Instead, she stood transfixed, watching the slow swirl of the soft brush as he swept it over the lower half of his face, and damning herself for the heady rush the sight gave her.

"Our two other employees are—or were—aboard the *Endeavor*," he said as he continued lathering.

"Oh my, René. You think the ship's gone down, don't you?"

"At the moment, I choose not to consider such a disaster. It will cast a pall on a day that has barely begun. What's been the matter with you these past few days?"

She stiffened. "What makes you think anything is wrong?"

"Has Lord Mayhem done something to upset you?"

"Lord Mayhem? *Lord Mayhem?* Oh, for pity's sake, René. His name is Mayhew. Lord Ainsworth to you."

Humor danced in René's dark-as-sin eyes. He picked up his razor, gave it a few swipes along the leather strop and, setting the blade to the side of his face, gave it an expert stroke. "Then why have you been so out of sorts? Did you not enjoy your evening with your fiancé? Does Lord Mayhem's behavior need correcting?"

"By whom?" she sputtered, her gaze fixed on the slow slide of the razor. "He has done nothing wrong. *Mayhew* and I are fine. Perfectly fine. As a matter of fact, we greatly enjoy our evenings together."

He paused and lifted a brow at her through the mirror. A shadow clouded his expression, but in one blink it was gone. He wiped his blade clean with the towel, then returned to shaving. "Something has you in a dither, *mon amie*. And I do not think it has to do with our private conversation a few days ago. You are made of sterner stuff than that."

Fury over Abbott's criminal deeds flooded her veins again, leaving a bitter taste in her mouth. She wasn't about to tell René what she'd discovered. Her nerves in a jangle, she turned to make her exit. "Leave it be. I have duties to attend to."

"Ah, but something has you acting peculiarly, *ma petite*. After you left here last evening, Michel asked me what I thought was the matter with you. He's asking questions, Felice. If I know your brother, he will soon be openly demanding answers, and I prefer he not link the two of us to whatever has you on edge."

Oh, she wanted to strangle Abbott. "Leave my brother out of this. He's beside himself with worry over Brenna. He is scared out of his wits she might not make it through the delivery of their child."

René finished using the razor, picked up a towel, and wiped his jaw clean of any soap residue. "She's had six children. Surely—"

"Brenna is not doing well of late." Felice tried shifting her gaze away from his clean-shaven face but failed miserably. "The doctor has ordered her to bed for the duration. Michel is sorely aware that far too many women lose their lives giving birth. Frankly, I'm worried as well."

"What else is bothering you? One way or another, I will get it out of you, so you may as well tell me now."

"I . . . I cannot . . ." She whirled around and headed for the office.

He reached her before she made her exit, took her by the shoulders, and turned her around. The heat of his hands made her heart lurch. She wished he wouldn't touch her. A shrug of her shoulders and he dropped his hold on her. The scent of his shaving soap wafted over her, leaving her oddly light-headed. "I cannot risk telling you because you will run right to Michel, and he has enough to worry about. I will speak to him when the time is right. Not before."

His eyes narrowed. "I am a man of my word. I will leave it up to you to tell Michel. Now, what is it?"

Their gazes locked. He wasn't going to back down. She sighed. "All right. M . . . Mr. Abbott has been embezzling company funds."

René's dark eyes snapped with fire. "Are you certain?"

"Numbers don't lie. He's worked for this company for thirty years. And he's been embezzling for twenty. Now do you understand? I cannot tell Michel the company's most trusted employee is a thief, at least not while his wife's condition has him so concerned."

Anger flowed through her again like a fever. "Before I take my leave of New Orleans, I will find and expose Abbott if it's the last thing I do."

René took a step back and assessed her through half-shuttered lids. "He was special to you, was he not?"

She turned her head so he couldn't see angry tears spring to her eyes. "I am certain I now hate the man."

"*Chère*," he said, "you cannot hate someone unless they have meant something to you. It is only natural to feel pain."

Funny how anger and sadness could both cause tears to form in one's eyes. "I . . . I once thought of him as family, as my adopted uncle, actually."

René reached out and laid a hand on her shoulder again. She fought a terrible urge to lean into him, to seek his comfort. A sob rose in her throat, but she let it die there, unborn. Scrubbing at the corners of her eyes, she jerked her shoulder from his touch. "I need to tend to my duties."

A knocking on the door caught their attention.

"That must be Henri. I have the door locked," she said, and hurried to the entrance. To her surprise, Bastien peered through the window alongside Henri.

"*Bonjour!*" He stepped inside, carrying a tray of coffee and beignets. Henri, weighed down with the same, hurried over to the guards.

Felice grabbed a beignet and a mug of café noir. "Where did you disappear to all this time?"

Bastien cocked a brow. "No one informed you of my whereabouts?"

"I'm the slave here, remember? No one ever tells me anything."

He chuckled. "I was upriver at the Houma plantation. John Burnside is a force to be reckoned with, but when it comes to dickering over a contract, there is none better than *moi*."

She laughed at his arrogant remark. "I take it you did well."

"*Oui.* With all the land Burnside owns devoted to sugar crops, he is now called the sugar prince. Landing his shipping contract means huge profits for us. By the way, I stopped to visit your father on my way home."

She nearly choked on the beignet in her mouth. "Oh my! Do tell me, is he well?"

"*Oui.* And looking forward to seeing you soon. He's amused by your letters, don'cha know. Would like you to send more *tout de suite*."

She laughed. If only she could feel this at ease around René. "Thank heaven you've returned. Michel won't arrive until time for payroll, but your brother is in need of your assistance. Not only is he exhausted from the heavy workload, he's quite concerned about the *Endeavor* having yet to make an appearance."

"*Bonjour, mon frère.*" René strolled in, clean-shaven and wearing a fresh shirt. He grabbed a mug of coffee, stuck a beignet in his mouth, and strode out the door toward the clippers. "We shall talk while we work. *Au travail.*"

Bastien watched him walk away, then grabbed a mug for himself and headed for the ships. "As my brother said, do let us get busy."

Dawn broke with pink tinting a part of the sky, while a ribbon of ominous thunderclouds stretched along the horizon, warning that a slow-moving storm was headed their way. Felice retrieved the ledgers from the locked case and seated herself behind the desk. She took a moment to watch the dock come alive with men emptying the ships like ants stealing crumbs from a picnic. Finding the scene before her strangely comforting, she settled into figuring the payroll.

She had no time to contemplate Abbott's misdeeds, nor did she pay attention to who came or went. As the hours ticked by, ever-efficient Henri supplied her with either coffee or lemonade.

At ten minutes to ten, her brother walked into the room. She put down her pen. "Dear heavens, Michel, are you planning on taking a trip somewhere?"

"No, why do you ask?"

"Because you could pack a week's worth of clothing in those bags under your eyes."

He managed a tired chuckle. "What would I do without you to brighten my day?"

She would've liked to have hugged him. Instead, she handed him the stack of payroll slips for the first two ships. "I'll have the final count for the other within the hour. How's Brenna?"

"Still pregnant." He sat at his desk and leafed through the pages. He paused to sweep a hand over his eyes. "God, Felice, what if she doesn't survive this?"

"She's given birth six times, Michel. She'll be all right."

Neither of them said anything further. They worked in silence until Felice handed him the last of the numbers.

Bastien entered the office. "Ready for my trip to the bank?"

"I'll handle it this time," Michel said. "Finish what you were doing."

Bastien nodded and returned to his duties while Michel retrieved the carpetbag from the safe. "I'll return within the hour."

She was left alone again. Reaching behind her, she rubbed at the ache in the small of her back. René walked inside. She straightened her spine and asked, "Finished?"

"Not quite," he said. "But close enough that I can sit down for a moment."

"*Mischie! Mischie!* Help me!" A young boy ran into the room carrying a flour sack dripping water, and tears tracked down his dirt-smudged cheeks.

"Whoa, Tad," René called out. He grabbed hold of the bag and carried it back outside.

"Please, Mischie," the boy pleaded through sobs. "They might still be alive."

"What in the world?" Felice scrambled after the two of them. Whoever the boy was, he couldn't be more than six, and he'd used the shortened, familiar term of *mischie* for *monsieur*. His clothes appeared to be of good quality, but they were dirt-stained, and the edges of the cap he wore was ringed with sweat.

René set the sack on the ground and turned it upside down. Two small, limp puppies tumbled out. "Where'd you get these?"

"Saw someone toss them in the water, so's I fished 'em out," the boy said, hiccupping through his tears. "Please, *Mischie*, can you save them?"

"Take hold of one and do exactly as I say," René ordered. He held one of the pups upside down and gently shook it. The boy did the same. "We need to empty the water out of their lungs. Felice, fetch some towels. They're in—"

"I know where they are." She hurried to the wardrobe where René stored his things. Retrieving a stack of towels, she rushed back to find him kneeling on the ground and softly blowing into the mouth of one of the pups.

"Do the same, Tad," he ordered between breaths. "Go easy."

She sat next to them, her heart beating a hard tattoo against her chest as she watched the scene unfold before her. René was down on his knees, handling the pups and the boy as if they were made of spun glass. What a difference from when he'd heaved Lucien out the door with such powerful force the walls shook.

One by one, the little legs of the bedraggled animals twitched. "They're alive," she whispered.

René held out a hand for a towel. "*Merci*," he said, and wrapped his pup in the towel, then handed another to the boy, instructing him to do the same. Holding the little beast in his arms, he rubbed at its soaked fur.

He glanced at Felice with a tired smile. "So much for sitting down for a bit." He looked at Tad. "Good boy. Keep drying its fur."

"Aye, sir," said the boy, his dirt-and-tear-stained face red from the effort.

Poor thing, she thought and, lifting the hem of her skirt, she used the corner of her petticoat to tenderly wipe clean the boy's face. He watched her with solemn eyes the color of summer leaves. She removed his sweat-soaked cap. One look at the crown of red hair plastered to his head and she knew to whom he belonged. "You're one of Brenna's boys, aren't you?"

"Yes, ma'am." He hiccupped and swallowed.

"I'm Felice, Tad. I'm your papa's sister, which means we are family." At hearing her own words, a strange sensation bloomed in her chest. "You can call me Auntie."

She glanced at René, who sat with one leg crossed and a hand dangling over his knee in a casual kind of grace. The pup, still wrapped in the towel, lay beside him. René watched her with those unreadable onyx eyes. She looked away from his riveting gaze. Only then did she notice a small crowd of sailors had gathered.

"Can I keep the pups?" Tad asked her.

"I . . . I don't know. You'll have to ask your father."

Just then, Michel rounded the corner at a trot, carpet-bag in hand. He slid to an abrupt halt. "What the devil's going on here?"

Tad scrambled to his feet, clutching the wrapped puppy in his arms. "Papa, I have me an auntie!"

Then he held the bundle out for Michel's inspection. "And doggies. See? Someone tried to drown 'em, but I fished 'em out of the drink, and Mischie, he saved them. Can I have 'em, Pa?"

Michel scrubbed a hand through his hair. "Tad—"

"I'll take one if your boy is allowed to have the other," René said. "He worked hard saving these little fellows."

Michel bent back his head and stared at the sky. Then he heaved a sigh and looked down at the wet bundle in Tad's arms and at the shiny, expectant look in his round, little-boy eyes. "What the hell is one more animal in that madcap home of mine?"

Felice's mouth dropped open at Michel's words. "Madcap? Now I do need to get over to your place and meet your family. If only you'd give me a moment's break from work."

A husky chuckle left René's throat.

She glanced at him and noted that, once again, those eyes of his radiated amusement. Was he so pleased to take one of the pups that the fatigue she'd previously noted in him had vanished?

Tad buried his cheek against his father's waist, the soaked towel and dog between them. "I'll make you proud, Pa. I promise."

Michel ruffled Tad's hair. "Son, you always make me proud."

Good heavens! Felice blinked back a rush of tears. Never would she have believed this had she not seen it for herself—her brother, the once confirmed bachelor, taking to Brenna's brood as if they were his own. She looked up with new respect in her eyes.

He held out a hand to help her to her feet. "Don't say it," he said.

"Don't say what?" She grinned. "That you are easily persuaded when it comes to boys and dogs?"

"Humph," he grunted. "Let's get to the payroll. René, go home. Get some sleep. We'll take it from here."

René rose to his feet, the shirt he'd donned a few hours earlier now wet, transparent, and clinging to his hard belly and muscled arms like a second skin. He shoved a hand through his hair. "*Non.* I'll see every man gets his pay. Then, I will gladly find my bed."

He turned to Henri, who stood among the small crowd. "It looks like these pups have been weaned. Can you find a few edible scraps aboard one of the ships?"

"There's some leftover stew in the galley of the *Golden Swan*," one sailor called out. "Ain't fit for anything but dogs."

The crew guffawed. A sailor wearing a stained apron punched him in the arm and cursed.

"Lady present," René called out.

Felice returned to her position at her desk. The others followed, and soon the room was a beehive of activity. Tad sat cross-legged in the far corner of the room, hovering over the two pups while Bastien, Michel, and René made ready to hand out the payroll to the long line of sailors just beyond the open door. Here she was, the only female among all these men. The situation left her with the same feeling as when she'd grown up surrounded by males—comfortably at home.

Michel summoned Henri. "While we're doling out wages, hurry on over to Tujague's. You need to buy lunch for all of us before these hungry sailors descend on the place like a cloud of locusts and leave nothing but crumbs in their wake. Will everyone be happy with the beef brisket?"

Felice glanced up from her ledgers. "If they still serve cold shrimp with that lovely piquant remoulade, I'll have that. Bring some warm rolls as well. And butter."

Michel rolled his eyes. "Fresh bread comes with the brisket and vegetables, Felice. Dash it all," he muttered. "Henri, include enough brisket for my sister. She has a hollow leg and will only steal mine."

"Oh hush, Michel. I'd only be tasting yours, not stealing the entire meal."

She ignored the chuckles around the room and went back to her ledgers while the men took charge of handing out the wages. By five minutes before noon, they were finished.

No sooner had the last sailor walked away, stuffing his wad of cash into his pocket than Mrs. Liberty Belle Worth hurried in alongside Henri. Both carried wicker baskets that filled the air with savory aromas. Felice's stomach grumbled.

"I ran into Henri trying to cart all these vittles by himself," Mrs. Worth said, "so I decided to help out."

Gads, in all this melee, Felice hadn't given a single thought to Mayhew. She wondered where he was and why he wasn't with Mrs. Worth, but she wasn't about to ask.

Henri and Mrs. Worth began dispensing the food. When she reached René's desk, Liberty murmured something and bent to kiss his cheek. He leaned away slightly.

Well, would you look at that. He wasn't one bit glad to see his mistress. Not one bit.

In a smooth-as-silk move, Liberty turned to Bastien. "I understand you are having a *bal de maison* next week to celebrate your birthday. But I have yet to receive an invitation, my friend."

Bastien cocked a brow. "I thought it was understood you would be on my brother's arm."

"Well," Mrs. Worth said as she donned her gloves, "if that is settled, I shall take my leave. Henri, do see to returning all the crockery and cutlery to the restaurant."

As soon as she was out of earshot, Bastien turned to his brother. "You finally gave her the boot, didn't you? You should have warned me."

"I hadn't expected her to waltz in here like nothing was amiss." René rose and donned his jacket. "I'm going home."

"I'll walk with you." Bastien turned to Felice. "You will be coming to my house party, *oui*?"

"Of course," was all she could manage after overhearing the stunning news.

"You may bring Lord Mayhem, of course."

She threw a pencil at him. "His name is Mayhew, you dolt! Lord Ainsworth to you."

The brothers left, laughing.

Michel chuckled. "You should go home as well."

"I need to finish this one column in the ledger before I take my leave. What of you?"

"I'm locking up as soon as you are gone, so make haste." He glanced at René's desk and the brown leather satchel atop it. "Damn, he forgot the papers I gave him."

He picked up a stack of papers from his desk, moved to the bag, and slipped them inside. "I also tossed in some documents needing his signature. Drop these off to him on your way home, will you?"

Hell's bells. The last thing she needed was to find herself alone in the same room with that man. "Can't Henri do it?"

"I gave the boy the rest of the day off. He's gone crawdad fishing."

"I'll hand the packet through the gate to Henri's mother, then. She can pass it along to René."

"I prefer you give it to him directly. And make certain to tell him that I added documents requiring his signature. They need to go to the bank on the morrow."

She cursed silently.

Michel paused and gave her the once-over. "Damn it, Felice, don't give me that sour look. He only lives two doors from you. How hard a task can this possibly be?"

Harder than you might imagine.

Chapter Eleven

Felice stood outside the wrought-iron gate leading into the courtyard of René's town house. Eight o'clock and it was still as hot as blazes. It didn't help that a storm was brewing and the air had grown heavy enough to bathe in.

"Where are you, Monique?" Impatient as she was, Felice could hardly fault the woman for being cautious about allowing anyone in, not after having met Lucien. But dash it all, what was taking her so long?

Curiosity had her inspecting the exterior of René's red brick town home. It certainly was tidy, she thought. Cascades of green ivy in waist-high twin pots flanked either side of the gateway. She took a few steps back to scrutinize the second floor, with its fancy ironwork and deep veranda. Black shutters edged tall windows set inside gleaming white casings. Flowerpots overflowing with bright blooms hung from the veranda's ceiling. A third-floor balcony mirrored the second.

His place had to be half again as large as her family residence two doors down. "My oh my, Monsieur Thibodeaux," she murmured. "Don't you have a statement to make to the world, though?"

Stepping forward, she peered through the gate. A

two-tiered, marble fountain stood in the middle of a pristine brick courtyard. Water spilled from the upper tier to the lower in a merry water dance. A colorful display of flowers and plants graced the courtyard's perimeter. More black shutters flanked interior windows. To the rear and down the long carriageway leading to the stables, a chestnut bay stuck out his head from the upper half of a stall.

"Hey, boy," she called out. His ears perked up. "Do you remember me? You transported me home one evening." A flash of summer lightning cracked overhead, and in the distance, thunder rumbled. The humidity nearly sucked the breath out of her lungs.

Monique appeared, unlocked the gate, and escorted Felice to the stairs leading to the main living quarters. "A dressmaker is awaiting me, so *monsieur* said you may let yourself in. No need to knock."

"Well, that's hardly proper . . . letting myself in, that is."

Monique glanced at the darkening sky; then her head dipped as she pursed her lips against a smile. "He's in his favorite chair in the front parlor, *mam'selle*. Says he won't be leavin' it any time soon, not unless the house be on fire. He's fair exhausted, don'cha know."

"Well, then. Good afternoon to you, Monique. And *merci*." Felice gripped the polished wooden handrail and climbed the stairs. A wave of apprehension washed over her. The courtyard itself felt intimate, as if she were once again invading René's personal space, but now she was required to enter his home on her own? She really didn't care to know how he lived. Blast it all, why was she feeling so at odds with herself? She'd curtsied to the queen in London, for pity's sake. The sooner she got away from New Orleans, the better—away from all the burdens wearing her down of late. Away from *him*.

Clutching the satchel of documents to her chest, she

reached the top step. She paused, welcoming the distraction of the grand courtyard below. So, this was what René encountered every morning when he set out for the day. A far cry from his meager upbringing in a bayou shanty.

She turned to enter his home. Her throat constricted. Little good it did, trying to picture him as he once might've been. The man's formidable presence had a way of turning her insides into porridge. Especially when he settled those piercing midnight eyes on her.

She swept a gloved hand over her damp forehead and tucked a strand of limp hair behind her ear. He'd better not take this opportunity to begin the private conversation he'd threatened or she'd turn on her heel and leave. Yes, that's what she'd do, she'd walk out on him.

"Oh, do get this over with," she muttered, and stepped into a sumptuous interior bathed in a soft, gaslit glow. She didn't know what she had expected, but it certainly wasn't this . . . this understated display of . . . hell's bells . . . of studied refinement.

Slowly, she moved through the first room. No heavy floral wallpaper to be found here, only the subtle sheen of pale Venetian plaster such as one might find on the Continent. Aubusson rugs were scattered atop gleaming polished wood. Billowy, translucent silk curtains instead of dark and weighty velvet graced the tall windows. She glanced up at the ceiling and sucked in her breath at the sight of an elaborate fresco, reminiscent of palaces in Europe.

"Mercy me," she whispered as she worked her way toward the front of the house. An elaborate, curved staircase to her left led to the upper rooms. *And to his bedroom*, the devilish sprite on her shoulder whispered.

Her stomach lurched.

Instead of a wall and doorway separating this room from the front parlor, she faced a grand, open archway. Heavens. Referring to the next chamber as a parlor was downright laughable. It rivaled any grand salon in Paris.

She stepped through the archway. At the sight of René lounging in an oversize upholstered chair, his bare feet propped on a matching ottoman and the rescued dog curled up in his lap, everything else around her—walls, furniture, windows—dimmed into one big blur. He wore the same dark trousers as when he'd left the office, but he'd since changed shirts. He now wore a garment of soft muslin. Whatever the fabric, the way it draped his upper body left no doubt as to how well-formed the man was.

He sat near the open French doors leading to the veranda, a glass of amber liquid in one hand, the fingers of his other leisurely sweeping through the sleeping pup's fur.

Oh, to be that little dog, the sprite on her shoulder whispered. The flesh on her arms broke into goose bumps. The thrum of her own blood pounded in her ears. "Have you named him?"

"Her. It's a her," he said in that honey-soft drawl that seeped right through her skin. His gaze dropped to his lap, and he gave the little beast a tender caress. "She hasn't yet shown me what she wants to be called."

The sprite on her shoulder nudged her. *Those supple fingers . . . you remember, don't you?* Felice swallowed the lump in her throat. She wasn't about to turn and run, but sure as the sun would rise in the morning, she wouldn't be staying long. "I have the papers you neglected to take with you. Also, Michel sent a few documents requiring your signature. They need to be dropped off at the bank by midmorning latest. I'll just separate them for you and be gone. Do you mind if I use this table over here?"

With a bare movement of his head, he indicated the commode beside his chair. "Set them here, *s'il vous plaît*. I'll take care of everything before I retire."

"You haven't slept yet?" She didn't know what else to say. It was all she could do to get the words past her dry throat. She placed the satchel next to him and stepped back.

"For a couple of hours." He glanced through the open veranda doors. "The rain, she has arrived. You should remain until it is over. Won't be long. This kind of torrent will be short-lived."

He lifted the glass to his lips, openly studying her over its rim. "But you know that because you are from these parts."

Don't look at me like that. "I live two doors down. Do you think I would melt?"

"Sweet as you are, *chère*, you just might."

She opened her mouth for a sharp retort but closed it when she saw humor dancing in his eyes. "You've papers to sign."

He set down his drink and gave a little shrug of one shoulder while his fingers continued to slowly stroke the pup's fur. "In time. First we shall have our little chat."

A buzzing shot through her brain. She heaved a sigh meant to send him a hostile message. "I was afraid you'd say that."

When he said nothing in response, she turned and stepped onto the veranda. Hadn't she promised herself she'd make a prompt exit were he to bring up the subject? Then why was she standing here? With no wind to speak of, the rain poured down in a noisy, straight curtain, mesmerizing her and holding her hostage. It had stormed like this that awful night three years ago when he'd uttered those horrid words to her.

Anger straightened her spine. "Get it over with, then."

Silence.

Despite the nerves buzzing in her ears, she made up her mind to remain and hear what he had to say. She stood stiff and unmoving, listening to the rain pound the roof as it turned the street into a sea of mud. Just as she was about to give up and walk off, he spoke.

"I'm sorry I bruised your heart," he said.

What? Those were the last words she'd expected to hear. Shock sent her hand flying to her mouth. She closed her eyes against the tears blooming beneath her lids. But then the old hurt rose up in her chest and set her blood boiling. She had nothing to lose by responding with the truth because she would soon leave here. "Bruised it? You damn well tore it to shreds."

"No more than my own," he mumbled.

Startled, she turned an ear his way, as if doing so might catch a repeating echo of his words. "What did you say?"

"Nothing that matters," he murmured.

"What do you want from me, René?"

A movement behind her told her he'd risen from his chair. "I am trying to apologize for the way I treated you."

He'd drawn closer. She could hear it in the volume of his words, could feel it in the air shifting around her. A strange and sudden awareness of his nearness scorched her skin. What if he reached out and touched her? What would she do? "No need. What's done is done."

"I got involved with you for the wrong reasons," he said. "That was wrong."

She wrapped her trembling arms around herself to steady them and turned around. He stood not three feet from her. He leaned a shoulder against the door frame, his feet crossed at the ankles, his shirttails hanging loose. The light from the wall sconce behind him shone like a nimbus around his body, making him a dark angel of the night.

Emotion tightened her throat until she could barely find her voice to reply. "What wrong reasons?"

He lifted his chin, just enough to watch her through veiled lids. "When your cousin Cameron returned to New Orleans and bedded my sister, I was furious. I wanted revenge."

"He married her."

"*Oui*. But you are well aware that years earlier, he'd seduced my other sister, who died bearing his child."

"By her own admission, Solange was the one who did the seducing. That youngest sister of yours was looking for a way out of the bayou and tricked my wealthy cousin, a seventeen-year-old . . . oh, please, René. Everything's been settled. What difference does all this make now?"

"At the time, nothing was settled for me. I was determined to ruin whatever I could of Cameron's life. The two of you are close enough to consider each other siblings, and when he took up with Josette, I figured the best retaliation would be to seduce you. I had every intention of coaxing you into falling in love with me, then abandoning you. I planned to leave you with your reputation in shreds. In the end, I could not go through with my plans."

"But why did you find it necessary to say such hateful things to me when walking away would've been enough?"

His gaze broke with hers, shifted over her shoulder. He stared into the darkness. When had the rain stopped? She was close enough to spot a faint wash of color darkening his cheekbones. So, he truly was upset.

"Because a man like me has no business even speaking to a woman like you, let alone doing what I did."

She sucked in a breath.

At the sound, he went back to watching her with those

black-as-midnight eyes. "When things had gone too far between us, when I realized I was taking you to my bed because I wanted you in a way I didn't think I could ever want a woman, I realized I did not have the strength to simply walk away."

His startling words, the way he studied her, were doing strange things to her heart. "But—"

He lifted a hand to silence her. "I knew I had to permanently destroy what was happening between us or I wouldn't be able to stay away from you. I had to make you hate me—hate me enough to leave town and never return. I needed you to despise me so heartily you would forget you ever knew me. I can see you've done a good job of it, agreeing to marry a high-ranking Englishman. Going off to live the rest of your life across the ocean."

Mercy, what was he telling her? "But I did return."

A muscle twitched in his set jaw. "I thought I knew what betrayal was, thought my emotions were immune to duplicity, but it wasn't until that very moment that I learned how sharply betrayal can sting," he said.

They stared at each other for a long while, the air between them electric. With each moment ticking by, the hammering of her heart increased until she thought it would burst from her chest. "How do you feel about everything, now that you've apologized?"

He raked his fingers through his hair, shifted his shoulder against the door frame. "Ever since you left, the burden of what I did to you has weighed heavy on me. I need to make things as right as I can. I need to hear that you forgive me before I'll have any peace."

She didn't know what to say. She had to get out of there. And fast. The last thing she wanted was for him to see her weep. "It's a little late for that, isn't it? What now,

René? We are stuck working in the same building day after day; how do we go on as if nothing ever happened?"

"We simply do, *chère*."

"I . . . I should leave." She stepped forward.

He reached out, blocking her way. "You haven't said the words I need to hear. Will you forgive me?"

She nodded. "Of course."

He stood with his hand at her waist, so close she could see the pain in his eyes. "I need to hear the words, Felice."

His nostrils flared, as if he'd caught her scent. His lips parted, then closed. He wanted to kiss her. She could see it in his entire countenance. What was worse, she wanted him to. They stood together, the heat of his fingers penetrating fabric and flesh.

She placed her hand on his arm, intending to nudge him away from her. Heat radiated from the muscles flexing under her touch. Instead of distancing herself from him, her body relaxed of its own accord. She leaned closer, until she was enveloped in his very essence. Every part of her being seemed to melt into him. Her fingers splayed across his solid chest as if to stop him when she was the one edging closer. His heart beat hard against her palm. She reached up and touched his mouth, outlined those familiar, sensuous lips with a slide of her fingers.

"I . . . I'll forgive you," she said, her words barely a whisper. "But I want something from you first."

"What is it?" His voice came as little more than a husky rasp.

"I want you to kiss me one last time, René."

She felt the subtle jerk of his body. His gaze dropped to her lips as his parted once again, and his warm breath fell against her mouth. "But why?"

"I want to try to erase the last time we were together. Just the two of us. Like this. I want to blot out my horrid memory of that night. I want one final kiss to replace those last terrible words you spoke so I can truly forgive you. Then we will forget this ever happened. And when tomorrow comes, we will carry on as colleagues, as acquaintances who happen to work together. You will be relieved of guilt. I will be cleansed of painful memories. And we can both get on with our lives, free from the pain that has obviously plagued both of us."

The intense energy they created just by standing next to each other slid beneath her skin and dripped into her blood. She was at a loss to explain the baffling emotions building inside her. She stepped closer, put her face to his throat and breathed him in.

A soft, guttural sound left his throat. Vibrated through her. He slid a hand into her hair and tilted her head back, and for a long while, looked deep into her eyes. Then he wrapped an arm around her and pulled her against the length of him. He was all hard muscle. And fully aroused.

He dipped his head and pressed his lips to hers. Softly at first. A bare brush. Then his tongue worked her lips apart and touched hers. She moaned and wrapped her arms around his broad shoulders. For a long moment, she was lost in the wonder of a kiss that made the world disappear around her.

Slowly, he pulled back, pressed his forehead against hers. "Yours is the sweet taste I could never get out of my mouth."

Oh, God, what have I done?

"I . . . I need to go," she said.

"*Oui.* It is for the best." Slowly, ever so slowly, he dropped his hold on her, eased her from him. He leaned back, his eyelids and thick lashes veiling his thoughts. "I'll see you out."

"No, don't," she whispered, and forced herself to step away. "I need to see myself out."

He nodded. "Go, then. Monique will open the gate. She will watch until you are safe inside yours. *Bonsoir.*"

She walked away, then paused and looked over her shoulder. "I forgive you."

A corner of his mouth tipped up. "*Oui.* I could feel it."

She turned to leave.

"Felice," he called in that smooth, sultry voice.

She halted and stared ahead. "What?"

"You're one hell of a woman. One of a kind."

She smiled to herself and, without replying, moved through his home and down the stairs in a daze. "Heaven help me."

She hurried to the gate. Instead of Monique letting her out, it was Henri. Good Lord, she'd forgotten all about the satchel and separating the papers. "I . . . I delivered some documents to Monsieur Thibodeaux. Please remind him there are some requiring his signature. They need to be delivered to the bank before noon tomorrow."

"*Oui, mam'selle.* Would you like me to see you to your door? The fog—"

"Heavens, no. It's only two doors down. If you'll watch until I'm inside my gate, that will be enough." As she stepped into the mist, she spied the outline of a man standing at her gate, and a horse tied to the hitching ring attached to the side of the town house. She halted.

The man turned. "Felice? Is that you?"

Good God, Mayhew! "Yes, I'll be right there."

She turned to Henri. "It's Lord Ainsworth. You may go back in now. Good evening."

Sweeping loose tendrils from her face, she moved forward. Guilt weighed upon her so heavily, she could barely make her way along the sidewalk. She hadn't given him a single thought today. How could that be?

"Mayhew. Forgive me. I didn't realize the time."

"Who the devil was that, and what were you doing with him?"

"It's only the company's man . . . well, boy," she stammered. She knew full well René stood on his veranda overlooking the street—it was where she'd left him. "You must remember Henri. He's the one who brought us lemonade when we arrived in town. I . . . I had to deliver a packet of important documents on Michel's behalf."

"Surely not to a boy. Who in blazes resides there, anyway?"

Struck dumb, she stared at Mayhew while she tried to push out the guilt long enough to respond, but all she could think of was René's teeth biting softly down on her bottom lip, the heat of his fingers spread at the small of her back, the hardness of his body.

"Answer me, Felice. What's got into you?"

"It's René Thibodeaux's residence."

"Bloody hell! That cur lives there?"

"Indeed." She made a fast recovery. "Now, let's get ourselves inside. This humidity is sucking the life right out of me and ruining my dress."

Shaky fingers had her fumbling for the pocket hidden in the seam of her skirt. Were her lips swollen from René's kiss? Did his scent linger on her clothing? Would Mayhew guess she had done more than deliver papers? "Blast it all, I neglected to take my key today. Mrs. Dawes will have to let us in."

She pulled on the bell chord and kept at it until she heard her companion call out that she was on her way. At the sound of a braying donkey, they both turned. The beast careened around the corner, pulling a cart down the street helter-skelter. The wagon weaved back and forth and seemed near to tipping over. "Auntie!" Someone called out. "It's time!"

"What in blazes?" Mayhew shouted.

A young man she'd never set eyes on before pulled the small cart to a halt in front of her, its wheels sinking halfway into the mud. "It's Mum; she's about to have the babe. Pa wants you and your lady to come along."

"Who are you?"

"Donal," he said through heaving breaths. "Pa's oldest. He's in a terrible fix. The midwife ain't arrived, and the doctor ain't home. He sent me to fetch you. Please hurry."

Mayhew untied his horse. "I'll follow behind."

"No," she snapped. "A woman about to give birth has no need of a bachelor. Go back to Le Blanc House. I'll see you on the morrow."

Felice hiked her skirts, stepped into the muddy street, and took hold of Donal's hand. "Why the donkey?"

"Dunno. It was dark in the stable. Grabbed what I could." He heaved her aboard.

Mrs. Dawes reached the gate and unlocked it. Felice called to her. "Have you ever delivered a babe?"

"Oh, dear. Only one, but it's been years."

"Then climb in, Mrs. Dawes, because I have never done so. Nor has my brother."

Chapter Twelve

René stood on the veranda with the pup nestled in his arms and watched as the wagon careened around the corner with Felice and her lady's companion bouncing about in the back. He'd nearly laughed aloud when she'd hiked her skirts, scrambled through the mud into the wagon, then hauled Mrs. Dawes up behind her. So now, plucky Felice was about to have a go at being a midwife.

He turned his sights on Ainsworth. No sooner did Felice disappear than the man climbed on his horse and headed, not in the direction of Le Blanc House, but exactly where René expected—Madame Olympée's parlor house, as she liked to call it.

When the hell would Felice realize the man was not for her? *Merde.* René was hell bent on learning more of what Ainsworth might be up to. Was it possible the lord's nightly visits to Madame's were meant to save Felice's virtue for their wedding night? If so, he sure as hell was a randy son of a bitch.

And an ornery one as well, if tonight's exchange between them had been any indication. René had only meant to linger on the veranda long enough to make certain Felice got home safely. That was, until he'd spied Ainsworth waiting at her gate. When the ill-tempered man began grilling Felice, it was all René could do to keep from making his way outside to defend the woman who'd just left his home.

Christ, his lips still pulsed from their kiss. His tongue still tasted her sweetness. It was a good thing she'd stepped away from him when she had. He'd gotten so lost in her essence that before he knew it, a perilous hunger had him at the edge of no return. If their incendiary kiss had given her some peace and put an end to their rift, so be it. But for him, the physical contact had done nothing but fan old embers into flames. His groin tightened as raw need rushed through him again.

At least she'd forgiven him. Which was something in itself. It was as if a weight had been lifted off his very soul. Tomorrow, he'd force himself to walk into the office with the pitiful knowledge that all he'd ever have of her was friendship.

Wandering back inside the house, he poured himself another two fingers of Armagnac and settled into his chair once again. Her delicate scent. The sweet taste of her. It still clung to him. He doubted the feel of her mouth on his would fade anytime soon.

He pressed the glass to his forehead, as if doing so might soothe the dull ache beginning to tug at his temples. The pup grunted and squirmed in his arms. "Time to go out, little one?"

With a groan, René rose from the chair and took her outside, to the rear of the house, near the stables. He placed the pup on a small plot of ground he'd set aside for her. "Three days, little one. Three days and I'll have you trained to handle this private matter on your own. I'm the master with animals, don'cha know."

Commander stuck his head out of the stall and gave a quiet nicker. René moved to the stall and stroked the horse's velvet nose. "Oh hell, there's no way I'm going to get any sleep, so I may as well take a jaunt over to Madame Olympée's and try to get her to see me. If she'll let me through the door."

Then he'd hunt down Bastien. He'd let his brother know Michel would not be in on the morrow, and he'd be required to take his place. He doubted Felice would show up either. Perhaps by morning he'd drop by the house to see if the babe had been born. Who knew how long this sort of thing took?

The pup whined, and with a yip, it waddled down the corridor toward René. He plucked her up and held her in a shaft of moonlight. "What the hell have I done, taking on a snippet like you?"

He drew the little animal to him. She gave a soft grunt and snuggled into the crook of his arm. A sharp pang ran through his chest. "Guess you're a keeper, *oui*? But I've got someplace I need to go, so I'll leave you here in the stall next to Commander. He'll look after you until I get back. There's water to drink and hay to lie in."

He grabbed a saddle blanket, folded it, and placed her atop it. "I need your name soon. Can't keep calling you 'little one.'"

Making his way back inside, he changed his shirt, donned a tie, jacket, and shoes, then headed for the brothel, where Ainsworth's horse was among those tied to a hitching post. Just as he'd figured, the burly guard at the door refused him entry. "Tell Madame Olympée I wish to speak with her in her office. It'll only take a few minutes."

He waited on the street while several of the city's upstanding gentlemen entered and exited the club. He recognized one man, an official from the bank. No one batted an eye at being observed coming or going.

"Madame will see you," the guard said.

He trailed behind the sentry and entered Madame Olympée's inner sanctum. Beneath the soft glow of a gas wall sconce, he seated himself on a red velvet chair opposite her. Madame sat at an ornate Louis XV desk, its corners, legs, and front panel decorated with gilded brass. She studied him for a long moment while taking sips of her bubbly. A clock ticked somewhere behind him, growing louder by the second. Madame tapped a matching rhythm on the desk with her scarlet-lacquered nails.

"Don't tell me you intend to turn my establishment into rubble again," she said.

"That was seventeen years ago and best forgotten."

She took another sip of champagne. "One never forgets such an eventful night."

"Had you not hired my sister, the fight would never have occurred. She was only fifteen."

"Only fifteen, but clever as they come. She begged me to let her work here, insisted she be assigned to only one man, Cameron Andrews—her ticket out of the bayou. She knew what she was up to from the beginning. I taught her all the ways to keep from getting with child, yet she had his, which was exactly what she'd intended."

Old pain nicked his insides. "And then she died giving birth."

The Madame took her time setting down her champagne flute. She leaned over her desk and, clasping her hands together, speared him with her gaze. "I suspect her death had something to do with your mother, so unless you want to travel down that ugly road, I suggest we drop the subject. Since Bastien is not with you, my security detail will find it rather boring to throw you out. So tell me why you are here, and then kindly leave."

He took in a slow, deep breath and exhaled just as

slowly. "You have acquired a new client who has become a nightly visitor. A British fellow. Lord Ainsworth."

"What about him?"

"He is Miss Felicité Andrews's fiancé. Her brother, a married man who does not wish to be seen entering your establishment, asked me to come in his stead," he lied.

"Monsieur Thibodeaux. I take great pride in assuring my patrons that they can enjoy my establishment with the utmost privacy and confidentiality." She shoved back her chair and made to rise. "You should leave."

He lifted a hand and, catching her gaze with his, held it steady. "Hear me out, *s'il vous plaît*. Miss Andrews's brother simply wishes to learn if her fiancé is of sound character. Lord Ainsworth may be frequenting your establishment as a way of saving Miss Andrews's purity for their wedding night, but *madame*, if he has any peculiarities that might prove dangerous or hurtful to Mr. Andrews's sister, he would like to be advised. Despite the business you are in, you are respected in this town. Mr. Andrews is well aware of your reputation for honesty. He is merely concerned about his sister's well-being."

Something flared in Madame's eyes. She lifted her chin and stared over his shoulder. "There are many men who enjoy long and successful marriages by keeping their activities in the marriage bed rather boring. They choose to confine their peculiarities to establishments such as mine. Lord Ainsworth may be no different."

René's heart kicked up a notch. She damn well knew something. His jaw tensed. He forced it to relax. He needed to keep his temper under control and keep her talking. "There's probably not much you haven't seen throughout the years. I should think you'd be an expert at weeding out the dangerous ones to keep your own girls safe. Tell me this much at least—could he become a menace to a young wife?"

Madame turned her head to the side and focused on a landscape painting. She heaved a heavy sigh. "The man in question is no longer allowed physical contact with any of my girls."

The hair stood up on the back of René's neck. He leaned forward in his chair. "Quite the statement coming from you. If he is no longer allowed to touch anyone, why continue to come here?"

"He got a little rough with one of them, something I do not allow. It seems he is obsessed with some kind of newfangled photography, so he pays quite handsomely to photograph those who agree. That is why he returns."

A little rough? At this establishment, where almost anything goes? "The women are positioned without clothing, I would assume?"

She nodded. "He prefers having two girls pose together in . . . shall we say rather risqué attitudes. Apparently, he's rented a back room at Monsieur Fournier's Photogravure, where he develops his work. He has offered to pay my ladies a good deal extra to accompany him there for additional work, but because I am skeptical of his intentions, I forbid their accommodating him under threat of being permanently banned from working here."

Christ! "I see. Is there anything else I can pass on to Mr. Andrews that might be of concern? I assure you, we will keep what you have told me to ourselves."

"It's no secret that some of my rooms have viewing panels behind the walls where voyeurs may enjoy watching others in the act. He also pays handsomely for time spent there. And oddly, from time to time he requests that drink and food be sent in."

René was beginning to feel sick.

Madame rose from her chair. "Monsieur Thibodeaux, I suggest you return to Mr. Andrews and inform him not only of what I have said, but that perhaps it would be wise of him to make further inquiries of this Lord Ainsworth in the man's home country. Now, if you'll excuse me—"

René thanked her for her time and, finding the same guard who'd escorted him waiting just outside the door, he followed the man to the front exit. The sentry couldn't walk fast enough to satisfy René.

Once outside, he leaned his back against the wall and sucked in fresh air. He hoped to hell the wire he'd sent to Boston had made it onto the next ship to England. He wouldn't know anything until he received word back, but after what he'd learned tonight, from now on he'd do more than simply follow Ainsworth.

"What the hell are you doing here?" Bastien called out in his native tongue.

René replied in the same language. "Don't tell me you are headed inside?"

Bastien shook his head. "I was entertaining a young lady at Antoine's. I saw her to her door and am now headed home. What are you doing here?"

René nodded toward Ainsworth's horse. "Third one down. Recognize one of Michel's fine steeds? I just had a most interesting chat with the owner of this *splendid* establishment."

Bastien cocked a brow "And you have much to tell me?"

"*Mais oui.* Come along home with me. I could use a drink, and you might as well join me; you have a long day ahead of you on the morrow. Brenna is about to become a mother for the seventh time."

"At last. *Mon Dieu*, but she was riper than a summer watermelon. I take it Michel will not make it to the docks in the morning and I am needed in his place."

"Exactly." Remembering how easily he'd overheard Ainsworth and Felice talking, René kept their chatter along the way about nothing in particular.

They reached the gate to René's home and slipped inside, only to hear a howling coming from the rear of the property.

"What's making all the racket?" Bastien asked.

"That, *mon frère*, is the rascally pup I rescued. I've got her locked up, and by the sound of things, she is not happy about it." They made their way to where Commander was pacing in his stall, tossing his head about and nickering nervously while the pup in the stall next to him howled and cried.

René opened the stall door and out waddled the pup, yipping up a storm. "Can you believe something this small can make such a racket? Hush, you'll wake the dead."

Bastien laughed. "I do believe she's scolding you for leaving her. Good thing she isn't any taller or your bollocks could be in jeopardy about now."

René chuckled and picked up the little dog. "Well, aren't you the sassy one." *You remind me of a certain plucky lady I work alongside. She's full of sass too. That's it—I've got your name!*

The idea of secretly naming the pup after Felice filled him with devilish humor. He turned to Bastien. "Say hello to Miz Sassy. Now come along. I've got some good Armagnac on hand, and there's much to discuss, so you may as well spend the night."

Chapter Thirteen

Felice stepped away from the ornate mahogany bed while Mrs. Dawes eased newborn Emma from Brenna's breast and placed the babe in the bedside cradle.

"Would ye mind cracking the windows a wee bit?" Brenna asked. "I could use some fresh air, so I could."

"Of course." Felice drew the emerald-green velvet curtains aside, opened all the windows, and then the balcony doors overlooking the back yard. A pleasant cross breeze flooded the room. Somewhere outside, a rooster crowed. "Sounds like the sun will soon rise."

Brenna smiled. "As will the children, blessed be their energetic little hearts."

Her melodic Irish accent was music to Felice's ears. She returned to the bed where Brenna—who'd been given a sponge bath and helped into a crisp, white cotton nightgown—rested atop fresh linens and against a stack of downy pillows. A floral counterpane matching the roses on the wallpaper lay neatly folded across the end of the bed. Overstuffed chairs in the same emerald velvet as the curtains flanked the fireplace.

After slipping a white lace bed jacket over Brenna's shoulders, Felice braided the new mother's still-damp hair into a single plait, then drew it over one shoulder. "There you go; toilette is complete."

Brenna gave Felice's hand a squeeze. "Ye've gone and spoiled me, ye have. As for helpin' my beautiful baby girl into the world, to say thank you a thousand times would be pitifully lacking."

Felice's eyes stung with fresh tears. "Good heavens, I am still in awe of it all."

Brenna glanced at Mrs. Dawes. "I am truly beholdin' to you as well."

Mrs. Dawes blushed. "I would not have traded taking part in this joyous occasion for all the tea in China."

Michel strolled into the room, a duck waddling behind him. "Have I returned too soon?"

"Perfect timing," Felice said. "Did you know there's a duck at your heels?"

He shrugged. "That's Goose. Follows me everywhere."

"No, it's a duck," Felice responded.

He approached the bed, his gaze locked with his wife's. "The boys found an egg in an abandoned nest. Hid it in their room and named it before it hatched. Therefore, the blasted thing's name is Goose."

His hair was unkempt, bristle shadowed his jaw, and his red-rimmed eyes bore the telltale signs of fatigue, yet an air of elation still clung to him. He took his wife's hand in his, kissed the back, then tenderly touched his lips to her forehead. "How are you, my dear?"

She gazed up at him, a soft glow in her eyes. "A mite better than when ye last set eyes on me."

He smiled down at her. "My dear, you were beautiful then. You are even lovelier now."

Felice had no words to describe the tender exchange taking place between her brother and his wife. She'd never been privy to such intense love. Oh dear, she should give them their privacy.

Mrs. Dawes stood. "If you please, I'll take a bit of a respite downstairs. The children will soon awaken; should I coordinate meals with Cook? I could also bring you both a tray."

"Thank you," Michel said. "While Mrs. Andrews could use a meal brought in, it would be best for me to break the fast with the children. Left on their own, the little devils would likely run amok. Right, darling?"

Brenna, her hand still in Michel's and her gaze still locked with his, nodded. "Aye."

"As you wish," Mrs. Dawes said and headed for the door. She paused. "Miss Andrews is at the shipping office these days, so I've little to do as her companion. Would it be acceptable to everyone if I remained here to care for wee Emma and the missus?"

Brenna sighed. "What welcome words. Are you agreeable, Felice?"

"Certainly."

"Then so 'tis," Brenna said. She glanced at the duck hunkered down beside Michel. "Fair warning, Mrs. Dawes— our six children will seem more like a dozen, and they play host to an odd menagerie, they do."

A smile split Mrs. Dawes's face. "I was raised in just such a home." She scurried from the room.

"I should take my leave as well," Felice said. "You two . . . make that three . . . need your privacy."

"I can wake Donal to escort you home," Michel said. "But I'd rather you remain in the guest quarters for some well-deserved rest. Once the tribe is up, however, you'll likely find a few climbing into your bed, books in hand. They know no shame."

She laughed. How very good it felt to be among a jolly family.

Michel studied her through eyes gone soft. "You've

been a godsend, Felice. I didn't know you had it in you to deliver a child into the world."

"Do stop. You're about to get me all weepy again." She wiped at a corner of her eye. "Lord, what an incredible miracle life is."

Growing quiet, she observed the touching scene before her. "I rarely envy anything or anyone, but tonight, I must admit, I am envious of the precious life you two share."

She swept her hand to the babe in the cradle. "Brenna was incredibly stoic tonight, Michel. You married an amazing woman." She sniffed. "Oh bother, now that the excitement is over, I can't seem to stop the tears. Joyous though they are."

The duck quacked.

Felice laughed again. "Even the duck is contented. By the way, there was a small goat wandering the stairwell a few hours ago. I don't know where it got off to, but with the children asleep, should I go look for it and get it outside?"

"That would be Blackie the pygmy goat," Brenna said. "Tommy's had it since its birth. The little beast makes the worst bleatin' noise if it doesn't settle in with the boys every night. Now there's Tad who won't let the rescued pup out of his arms. Colleen wants to hunt René down and talk him out of the other one."

Michel folded his tall frame into the chair beside the cradle and ran his fingers lightly over his daughter's cap of thick auburn hair. "Isn't our Emma beautiful?"

"Aye, so she is," Brenna said before Felice could speak again.

"Really, I should leave you two alone," she said. "I'm intruding."

Michel rose from the chair. "Stay with Brenna until Mrs. Dawes returns, if you will. I'll be down the hall in Donal's room, grabbing a quick nap, should you need me."

He departed with the duck quacking along behind. Felice turned to Brenna. "Shouldn't you try to get some sleep?"

Brenna shook her head. "Nay, I'm wide awake."

Emma squeaked.

Felice rushed to the cradle.

A beatific smile graced Brenna's lips. "She's only dreamin' of her next meal, she is. Do take a seat."

Felice took the chair beside the bed and next to the cradle. Needlessly, she tucked an edge of the blanket around Emma. "I suppose with six others, you're quite used to these little noises, but I find them rather terrifying. Did you in the beginning as well?"

"Aye," Brenna said. "But after the first one, ye get used to their signals. Do you want a large family?"

The question startled Felice. "Why . . . I hadn't given it much thought. I mean, Mayhew and I have certainly discussed . . ."

No, we have not.

"What I mean is, we naturally assume there will be offspring. At least an heir and a spare, as is expected of the nobility. Heavens. It sounds like I'm not keen on having children, which isn't true. It's just that I'd been traveling around the world for some time when Mayhew happened along. After a whirlwind courtship, I found myself back here, so not a lot of planning has gone into our future yet. But of course, I would very much like a family."

She took in a ragged breath and begged her suddenly curdling stomach to settle. What was wrong with her? But she knew darn well what was amiss. Not nine hours ago she'd been kissed by another man—a slow, deep, passionate kiss such as her fiancé had never given her.

And she'd liked it.

Too much.

Heaven help her.

Brenna's gaze held steady. "Do you love your Lord Ainsworth?"

The blunt question jolted Felice. "What's love anyway?" she blurted out.

She pressed her fingers to her lips, as if doing so would take back her words. *What's love? I've just witnessed it, for God's sake!* "I don't know where that came from. I suppose I do . . . I . . . but of course I am in love with him."

"Has he confessed his love for you?"

"Indeed, he has." She placed her hands in her lap and fiddled with her fingers.

Brenna studied her for a long while, then said, "Ye've never had a blood sister, but I have. We were never apart until the day I sailed away. We could talk about anythin', knowing our secrets were safe. I could use such a sister here in America."

"As could I," Felice breathed.

"Ye're a strong and independent woman," Brenna said. "So tell me, what drew ye to someone like Lord Ainsworth to begin with?"

"We met at a fabulous dinner party soon after I landed in London . . . from Paris. As it turned out, the hostess had arranged the seating in hopes of making a match. I was quite taken with him straightaway. Not only was he handsome and debonair, he possessed a keen wit, high intelligence, and enough charm to dazzle me. The next morning, my hotel room was filled with flowers. Always the gentleman, he went about courting me in the most wondrous ways. I grew exceedingly fond of him and quite comfortable in his rather proper English world, so when he proposed, of course I said yes. He insisted on formally asking Papa for my hand, which is why we are here."

"Gracious, I would think most any woman would be

thrilled to become his fiancée," Brenna said. "But then, ye are no ordinary woman, are you? Why are you looking so ill at ease of a sudden? What's amiss?"

Absolutely nothing, other than I need to dismiss that encounter with René, shake off the guilt from my Paris liaison, track down the blackguard Mr. Abbott, and get some sleep.

"At the moment, I'm feeling somewhat perplexed about . . . well . . . about most everything in my life. I'm certain it's all the excitement of the past few hours. With fatigue setting in, I doubt I'm thinking straight."

"Tell me what ye think might have you at sixes and sevens."

If it's honesty she wants, honesty she will get—without mention of a certain Cajun rogue who's had my head spinning.

"Several things, I suppose. It's obvious Mayhew is a fish out of water here. He doesn't fit in at all, which I believe rather distorts my perspective. Another thing is that my work has me buried in numbers all day, which is something he has little interest in and gives us virtually nothing to discuss. To make matters worse, we only see each other in the evenings, when I am quite fatigued and he is eager to make a night of it."

"And once ye're back in England, ye figure things won't be so muddled?"

She didn't dare discuss the effect René's kiss had had on her. Had it somehow shifted her outlook even further?

Dear God, let my confusion be temporary.

"Once back on English soil, I feel certain things will straighten out."

"Now ye're fair chewin' on your bottom lip. What else is givin' ye conniptions?"

Felice tucked a stray curl behind her ear. "Since we

agreed to share confidences, I . . . I would like to bring up a rather . . . ah . . . indelicate subject."

Brenna nodded. "Isn't that what close-knit sisters discuss?"

Felice dragged her bottom lip between her teeth again, then realizing what she'd done, set her mouth to rights. "I . . . I need to be quite frank."

"I am a-listenin'."

Felice closed her eyes and breathed in a lungful of courage, then spat out the words. "Mayhew is intent on saving my virtue until the marriage bed. Therefore, the physical aspect of our relationship has been . . . ah . . . rather chaste." She gulped. "The trouble is, he assumes I am an innocent, which I am not."

At her disclosure, her stomach lurched and her chest tightened until she could barely manage a decent breath. "I feel so guilty."

She set a steady gaze on Brenna. "I have reached the conclusion that it is only right to confess to him. Still, I fear the consequences, so I delay."

Brenna scoffed. "Is he himself an innocent? Of course not, yet he expects ye to meet him at the altar as a chaste woman for him to deflower? Bah! I would say nothing."

"You don't care much for him, do you?"

"I cannot say as I do or do not like the man after spendin' only one evening with him. Truth be told, I cannot imagine ye livin' the rest of yer days in England. I cannot see a spitfire like yerself takin' much joy in the restricted life of a duchess. Which you will be once his elderly father knocks on the pearly gates. Ye've family here, Felice. And a familiar life that gives ye comfort."

"Indeed, I do feel at home here, but remember, I have kin in England as well. Trevor and Cameron's families are greater in number than my relatives here."

"But they're livin' in Liverpool, while ye'll be expected to live on yer husband's country estates, with visits to London few and far between. Do ye fancy such a life?"

Felice was back to chewing on her lip. "I felt comfortable with the notion at the time."

"It's one thing to be courtin', another to be wed. Not only will yer life not be yer own, ye won't even be allowed to tend to your own children. Won't get to know them, so t'speak."

The feeling of hollowness in Felice's stomach spread throughout her body. "Of course I will know my own children."

Brenna shook her head. "We raise our own in this household, Felice. We do not cast them off to nannies on some third-floor nursery to be nae seen nor heard, as happens to those born to nobility. Yer wee ones won't even be allowed to break bread with ye 'til they're grown. Any sons ye might have will be trotted off to boarding schools, where ye shan't see them except fer a few holidays a year. Little more than strangers they'll be when they come to visit."

Felice's heart dropped to her toes. She didn't want to hear this, but a part of her knew Brenna had the right of it. "You have just given birth to a beautiful child. We should be speaking of this joyous event instead of discussing my plight. Also, I am curious as to how you and my brother came to meet. All I know is that you emigrated from Ireland with your husband, who then passed away."

"Aye," Brenna said. "Colleen was barely a year old when her pa went and stepped on a nest of hornets, he did. Dead in an hour, so they said. His demise left me to run our restaurant on me own. Donal watched the other kids, swept floors and waited tables. 'Twas a hard life, to be sure. Jack and Tommy had to stand on stools to wash dishes.

With no pa and a mum too busy to tend to their needs properlike, they were growing wilder by the day.

"Yer brother started coming in more regular. He'd take the same table and sit for a long while. Did so for well over a year. One day, Colleen crawled onto his lap. When I rushed over to fetch her, he looked deep in my eyes, and something passed between us that left me weak in the knees. Next day, he showed up with an entire staff, includin' a woman to watch my little ones. Then he marched me down the street to another restaurant. By the end of the meal, it was plain as day we couldn't get enough of each other. I don't guess I need to say anything further, only that he's made my children his own. He fathers them with a steady hand, but doesn't drive the spirit out of them."

"What a wonderful story, Brenna. I'm touched. My brother can be very private about his personal life."

"Now that you know my story," Brenna said, "I've just one more thought to burden ye with. Then I'll leave ye be. You seem to be too much of a free thinker to be content with what will be expected of you as a duchess, and too loving to leave your children to be raised by others. Can ye truly live such a rigid life?"

Felice picked at imaginary lint on her skirt rather than look Brenna in the eye. "I fear I shall never be a well-behaved woman. Having been raised around men, I emulated and competed with them. My nanny was the fifteen-year-old daughter of our cook, for heaven's sake. By the time I was old enough to talk, I had taken to slipping one over on the poor thing at every turn. And as for my teachers, I used to read naughty books to one of them—wicked stories my father didn't know I'd gotten hold of. Not to mention, I was smashingly good with numbers, while none of them were, which intimidated them."

They both laughed.

Brenna lifted a brow. "Anything else?"

Could this woman possibly have guessed about René? Guilt flooded her anew. "Only to confess that I had a brief affair in Paris. It turned out to be a disastrous assignation I very much regret. Not only because I lost my virtue."

"I do hope ye'll give yerself a wee think when it comes to deciding the right time to walk down the aisle," Brenna said. "Do not let the journey be one filled with regret, because there will be no turnin' back. Not in England, at least. And especially not wed to nobility."

A knock sounded on the door. Mrs. Dawes entered with a tray. "I brought tea, along with buttered toast and scrambled eggs, Mrs. Andrews. The children are awake, and Cook has breakfast near ready to serve, Miss Andrews. Your brother requests you join them."

"Splendid." Eager to end the conversation now, Felice rose from her chair. "Not only am I looking forward to dining with the children, I am suddenly quite famished."

Chapter Fourteen

No sooner had Felice breezed out of Brenna's room than a wave of fatigue washed over her. Slowing her pace, she descended the stairs, taking her time to observe her surroundings—something she hadn't done when she'd raced to the master suite last night.

Despite the elegant interior, subtle signs indicated a well-lived-in home, complete with scuff marks on the stairs and a banister bearing a few nicks and scratches. A wide corridor ran from front to back with large rooms on either side. The less formal rooms were easy to spot. Especially the library, which was filled with over-stuffed chairs, well-worn leather sofas, and sturdy tables topped with open books, toys, and sundry periodicals scattered about.

A mélange of robust aromas wafted from the rear of the house. Her empty stomach rumbled. Laughter came from the same direction, drawing her in. Heavens, they must all be talking at once.

She stepped into a large and sunny morning room filled with six noisy children who let out a *whoops* of delight at her entry. Michel, sitting at the head of a sturdy oak table, rose to greet her.

As did his children.

And good Lord, so did Bastien and René!

Her heart did a quick flip. What in blazes were they doing here? Coming face-to-face with René outside of work so soon after their intimate encounter was not what she'd expected.

Michel grinned. "Look who stopped by to congratulate the family on our new addition. It didn't take much to convince them to join us once they caught sight of the feast Cook had prepared. Come along, Felice, before hungry mouths leave you with nothing but scraps."

Felice collected herself and called out, "Good morning, everyone." She took the only empty chair, opposite the Thibodeaux brothers, and sat. Except for Bastien's blue eyes and sculpted, close-cropped beard, the two ridiculously handsome men could pass for twins. Even their deportment was much the same.

At the sight of a salver of sliced tomatoes and a platter of fluffy scrambled eggs surrounded by thick, aromatic boudin sausages, her stomach rumbled. A bowl of creamy grits swimming in butter and brown sugar set her mouth to watering.

"Obviously, you employ an excellent Cajun cook," she said and poured herself a cup of aromatic chicory coffee, added a dollop of cream, then collected a basket filled with hot buttermilk biscuits. Dropping one onto her plate, she hesitated, then took two more for good measure.

René, eying her with a half grin, handed her a crock of strawberry jam and a bowl of sliced peaches. "You won't get feasts like this in foggy old England."

Bastien took a swallow of the rich coffee and nodded in agreement. "I was once a guest in a fine home in Mayfair. To my surprise, I was expected to start the day with a boiled egg, kippers, watery porridge, and cold toast. And no conversation. Do those stiff British really savor greeting the day with smelly salted fish and complete silence so the patriarch can read his *Times*?"

He placed a hand over his heart. "Forgive me, Mam'selle Andrews. Lord *Mayhem* would surely enjoy such a morning. *Oui*?"

"Lord Mayhem," four-year-old Colleen parroted, and handed her plate to her father to fill.

Felice shot Bastien a scowl. He merely smirked and took another swallow of coffee.

As the children broke into a noisy round of chatter, trays were passed, biscuits grabbed, milk poured—often sloppily—and the clamor of several forks hitting the platters of juicy tomatoes rang like bells throughout the room.

"Sheer bedlam," her brother said to Felice with a wink.

"Rather like our growing years, wouldn't you say, dear brother?"

"Dear brother," Colleen repeated.

Something odd brushed against Felice's ankle. She gave a squeak of surprise and jerked her leg aside.

Michel peered beneath the table. "Finn, take your tortoise outside or I'll have Cook make soup out of it. Your pardon, Felice."

Colleen giggled. "Mischie Bastien, can you tell Mischie René I need him to leave the pup here?"

Bastien, busy spooning sausage and eggs onto his plate, cocked a brow. "Why don't you tell him? He's sitting right next to me."

"Becauthe, he won't lithen to me. You're hith brother. He will lithen to you."

"Pass the biscuits," Tad said through a mouth full of grits. When no one responded, he repeated himself.

"Chrissakes," eight-year old Tommy muttered. "Will someone at that end of the table pass Tad the damn biscuits?"

Michel dropped his fork onto his plate with a loud clatter. "Hush your mouth, son. Would you like to skip breakfast and stand in the corner?"

"No, sir. Sorry, sir."

He passed the biscuits to Tad while addressing Tommy. "Where did you learn such language?"

Tommy shrugged. "Dunno, sir."

"Well, if you know what's good for you, you won't be repeating yourself."

"You were very, very bad," Colleen whispered to Tommy, loudly enough for everyone to hear.

"And you hush your mouth, Colleen." Michel glanced at Felice. "Remind you of anyone?"

Bastien and René exchanged a knowing glance and kept on eating.

Felice set her serviette against her mouth to cover her grin. "You didn't mention breaking the fast meant every man for himself."

"As you said, reminiscent of our growing years—only with more bodies," Michel responded.

"Papa," Colleen called out while grabbing a handful of biscuits and popping them onto her plate.

"What?" Michel responded.

She licked her fingers. "Do ants have toes?"

Michel glanced at Felice. "Ask your auntie. She'll know."

Bastien chuckled, shoved his empty plate aside, and stood. "Thank you for your hospitality, but I must get home for a change of clothing before making my way to the office. My regards to Mrs. Andrews, *s'il vous plaît*."

Felice noted Bastien's neat attire and frowned. He intended to change? Could he be worse than his brother, who changed his shirts at the drop of a hat?

René caught her eye. "He spent the night at my house."

He turned to Bastien. "Do you want to take my buggy?"

"*Non*. I'll walk the two blocks. I also need to fetch my horse."

Mrs. Dawes entered the room. "Sir, Mrs. Andrews is eager for the children to meet little Emma. Might they have your permission to go to her?"

Chaos broke out as chairs scraped and chatter reached a new, raucous level. "Halt, all of you!" Michel called out as he stood. "Do you wish to frighten your new sister to death before her eyes are even open? We will go to your mother and the babe in a dignified manner."

Silence fell over the room. "Good, then follow me. Mrs. Dawes, please take up the rear and see they keep to a single file. Felice, we'll be having a family celebration this evening at eight o'clock. You are welcome to bring Lord May . . . Lord Ainsworth."

"Lord Mayhem," Colleen singsonged as she slipped her small hand into Donal's and followed along.

In a single moment, the room emptied, leaving only René and Felice at the table. *Lord a'mercy.*

He settled his gaze on her. Mischief sparked in those dark eyes of his. "Tell me, *mam'selle*, do ants have toes?"

She laughed. "Never in my wildest dreams could I have imagined my brother as a family man with a house full of rambunctious children."

René lifted a brow. "Is that a bad thing?"

"On the contrary. I am rather enjoying the circus. They are spirited children but good-hearted."

"*Oui*," René said softly. "Michel's doing a fine job of raising them up right." His gaze dropped to her mouth.

She felt a shift in him. Her pulse tripped. Was he remembering their kiss? She certainly was. The feel of his mouth on hers, the taste of his tongue touching hers.

In one easy, languid move, he leaned back in his chair. His lids lowered until he watched her in a way she found too seductive for her own good. No man should have lashes so thick, nor eyes so gorgeous. Or a mouth so . . . drat! She placed her serviette beside her plate and rose. "I shall take my leave before I am too weary to find my way home."

He kept a steady gaze on her. "Will you spend your day resting at home rather than going to the office?"

She nodded. "Michel offered me a bed here, but I've not seen my own since the night before last. Familiar comfort beckons me. I could also use a good, long soak in a hot bath."

Something flared in René's eyes.

Her cheeks heated. *Hell's bells, what in the world made me mention something so intimate as my bed and a tub with me naked in it? I definitely need to distance myself from this man.*

He pushed back his chair and stood. "Come along, *chère*. My buggy is out front. I'll take you home on my way to work."

René's rapid, fluid movements left Felice's mind scrambling for a decent response. She tried stuffing strands of loose hair into the disheveled chignon at the nape of her neck and failed. "What would people think if they saw you driving me through the streets in the early hours of the day? I couldn't possibly look worse for wear."

A slow and sultry grin lifted a corner of his lush mouth.

An odd buzz shot through her body. *Oh dear, did his imagination just travel along the lines of something other than a night spent as impromptu midwife? I need to watch my tongue, blast it all.*

His gaze still fixed on her mouth, he took his time responding. "Do you really give a damn what anyone in this town might think?"

His words came from somewhere deep in his throat—a raspy, velvet sound. Unwelcome heat rolled through her belly. They were to be friends now, were they not? She'd forgiven him, and they had agreed to carry on as if nothing in their past mattered. Nonetheless, her body was fast betraying her commitment to view him as a mere acquaintance.

Swallowing hard, she cursed her wayward emotions and lifted her chin to meet his sultry gaze straight on. "No, I suppose I do not. But you certainly care what people think of *you*. Look how hard you've worked to lift yourself up by your bootstraps."

He gave no response, either in words or by so much as a flicker of change in his expression. Did he know what he was doing, watching her as if he harbored salacious thoughts? Time slipped into slow motion while her heart hammered in her ears. Every second he stared at her seemed like an hour. Defiance finally overtook her runaway emotions. Unexpected words spilled from her tongue. "But then, I suppose caring what others think of you does not include your questionable reputation regarding women."

Now why did I say that?

"Or so I've heard." She swore she heard him chuckle under his breath.

Blast it all!

Instead of moving toward the front of the house, René strolled to the back door, disappeared into the gardens and returned with a puppy in his arms.

"That's the dog you rescued, isn't it?"

"*Oui*," he said.

"You don't intend taking it to work, do you?"

He grinned. "*Mais oui.* Come along. I'll let you hold Miz Sassy while I drive the buggy."

Felice put the final touches to her hair, removed her dressing gown, and donned a midnight blue frock trimmed in white. This one had a front closing, something she could manage on her own.

She was irritated that Mayhew had declined to accompany her this evening. You'd think the missive she'd sent him this morning, inviting him to join her for afternoon tea followed by dinner at Michel's at eight, would have him at her door moments before the appointed hour.

The last thing she'd expected was the delivery of a bouquet of flowers, along with a note telling her he was indisposed but would meet her at Michel's. The nerve of the man. What the devil had him otherwise engaged?

How many times did he complain of not seeing enough of her? Now, when he could've spent the better part of the day with her, he'd begged off. For what? Or was it *for whom*? Could it have anything to do with a certain widow René had given the boot?

She stomped around the room, looking for her shoes and chastising herself for allowing Mrs. Dawes to remain with Brenna. Oh bother, what an inconsiderate thought.

She slid her feet into soft slippers and headed to the courtyard and the waiting carriage.

Once inside the vehicle, winding her way through the streets, she mulled over her predicament. She'd been so certain of her decision to wed Mayhew. At the moment, however, her enthusiasm for marrying anyone at all had dwindled to nothing. Had her conversation with Brenna put her mind in a muddle? Had it been the incendiary kiss she'd shared with René that had her vacillating? Would everything return to normal once she was back in England?

By the time she arrived at Michel's, she'd grown even more flustered. Entering his home through the unlocked door, she made her way to the large, informal sitting room. The family gathering included not only the children and Mrs. Dawes, who hovered near Brenna, but also Bastien and René. They stood with Michel near the fireplace, drinks in hand and discussing business with the boys hovering nearby.

But no Mayhew.

Blast it all, what was she to do? She straightened her spine, lifted her chin, and, after waving a greeting to the men, made a beeline for Brenna. Should anyone inquire as to Mayhew's absence, she'd act as if she was well aware of his whereabouts, then inform her hosts he'd be along shortly.

Brenna, ensconced in an oversize, cobalt-blue velvet chair appeared regal in her impressive brocaded robe, with pearls woven through her hair. Had she worn a tiara, she could have passed for royalty. "Brenna, you are beyond lovely, but I am surprised to find you sitting up and looking so rested."

"Well, my time visiting everyone down here may prove

to be short-lived," Brenna responded. Her hand rested on the cradle beside her and gently rocked it, even though Mrs. Dawes held little Emma in her arms. "Would ye look at my family? Aren't they something to behold?"

"Indeed." Felice noted Brenna's offspring dressed in their Sunday finery and behaving as if they were cherubs in church.

"Don't tell me," Felice said. "Mrs. Dawes did your hair and Madame Charmontès fashioned your exquisite gown."

Brenna nodded.

Mrs. Dawes smiled.

"While I'd recognize the couturier's work anywhere," Felice said, "the woman never ceases to amaze me with her innovations. I must remember to have something like this made when my time for motherhood arrives."

If it ever comes to pass. The somber thought did little to lift her mood.

Brenna traced her fingers over the golden threads woven into the silk that flowed about her like a cream-colored cloud. "Madame presented this lovely creation as a gift, so she did. And 'twas Mrs. Dawes who insisted on stringin' pearls through my hair to complement the robe. Where's yer man, Felice?"

Ever the blunt one, isn't she? "He's been delayed. He'll be here shortly." She hoped.

Colleen, her hair done up like her mother's and wearing a matching miniature robe, held a doll wrapped in a blanket like Emma's. "I got to hold Emma. Wanna hold Mary?"

"I'd love to, darling," Felice bent low enough for Colleen to slip the doll into her arms. Thinking she might have heard someone at the door, she excused herself.

"I'll come along," Colleen announced.

"You may," Felice said. Carrying the doll and with Colleen at her side, Felice opened the door to a scowling Mayhew.

"It's about time. I've been pounding until my fist is bruised."

Felice bristled. "And a pleasant good evening to you as well, Lord Ainsworth."

Mayhew tossed his hat onto an entry table and glanced around. "What, no servants?"

"Everyone is helping with the festivities. Where have you been all the day long?"

"I told you, I procured some photographic equipment," he said. "I've been busy fiddling with it. Took me longer than I expected."

"No, Mayhew, you mentioned no such thing. You merely mentioned looking into a purchase the night we had dinner at Le Blanc House."

He glanced down at Colleen as though he'd only now noticed her presence. "Don't tell me these . . . these imps are allowed to join the adults?"

Brenna's words regarding the nobility's views on children echoed through Felice's mind. Her spine stiffened. "This is a special occasion, so yes, they are allowed to mingle with the adults. Come now, Mayhew, don't be persnickety."

They stepped into the sitting room. At the sight of Bastien and René, Mayhew cursed under his breath. "Since when does one drag the hired help to a family gathering?"

Felice was fast losing her patience. "Come now. You are well aware their sister is married to my cousin, which makes their offspring not only my nieces and nephews, but those of the Thibodeaux brothers as well. Under those circumstances, Michel has reason to include them."

Colleen lifted up a turtle to Mayhew. "Wanna pet Finn's turtle before Pa finds it in here?"

Mayhew took a step back. "No, I do not care to touch the filthy thing."

He turned to Felice and whispered in her ear. "How long will this ragtag bunch of heathens be allowed to remain in the room? Surely they won't be sitting at table with us."

Felice fought to keep her temper from exploding. "Don't," she said through clenched teeth. "Just don't."

Colleen looked quizzically at Mayhew, then shrugged and, handing the turtle off to Finn, gathered her doll from Felice's arms and set it in Emma's cradle. She ran over to René and stretched out her arms to him.

René lifted her up, settling her on his hip. She began to chatter away. Whatever the girl had to say, it prompted a laugh from deep within his belly. Stunned, Felice thought she had never heard such a wonderful sound.

Colleen slapped a hand on each side of his face and squeezed until his mouth looked like a fish. "Lithen to me," Colleen said.

He leaned his head back, and his hearty laughter erupted again.

Felice couldn't help it; she giggled.

René shot her a quick glance. His penetrating gaze locked with hers for mere seconds, but the sheer intensity of it pierced the distance between them like a bullet aimed straight for the heart.

He turned his focus back to Colleen as if nothing had occurred. Nonetheless, Felice had lost her breath and now struggled to regain it.

Mayhew bent to her ear. "What the hell was that about?"

"What was what about?" she responded.

"The look he gave you."

"I have no idea what you're talking about."

"Like hell. The bastard is like a rutting bull around you. Has he forgotten where he came from? Which gutter he crawled out of?"

Felice had had enough. "Mayhew, please accompany me to the library."

"What the devil for?"

"We need to talk."

"Any place is better than here," he mumbled.

Once in the library, she shut the door behind them. "I don't know what's put you in such a foul mood. I do hope it has nothing to do with lively children and a contented family celebrating a babe's birth. Under the circumstances, it would be best if you took your leave."

His jaw slackened. "You don't actually think to order me around, do you?"

She lifted her chin. "You don't belong at this function, so whatever you were up to today, I suggest you carry on and leave us be."

He leaned toward her, fury burning in his eyes. "You've a tongue like an adder tonight."

Instinct nearly had her taking a step backward. Instead, she held her ground. "If you disapprove of how the Andrews family chooses to conduct itself, then I doubt you'd be content if you were to wed the likes of me."

His eyes widened. Turning on his heel, he gave her his back and moved to the other side of the room. He shoved a hand through his hair and stood before a bookcase for a long while. Finally, he returned to where she stood. Oddly, he was once again the Mayhew she knew. "You're right, darling, I am out of sorts. It does happen to everyone now and then, right?"

She could only nod, fearing she would say something further she might regret.

He reached out and, lifting her chin with a curled finger, planted a light kiss on her forehead. "I'll see you on the morrow, darling." He winked. "Perhaps I'll have a little surprise for you."

Which was the last thing she needed. Today's spectacle had been revelation enough. "I'll see you out," she said.

"No, darling. I shall see myself out. Enjoy the evening with your family. Heaven knows you've been laboring much too long and hard. No one deserves a night of frivolity more than you."

He brushed his lips across her forehead again and made his exit.

She shut the door to the library behind him and heaved a sigh. What she needed was time to collect herself before returning to the fold. Tomorrow, she'd quietly begin the task of searching for Abbott's replacement. Once she located Abbott, she'd inform Michel of the crime the man had committed; then she'd make haste to leave New Orleans.

In the meantime, she'd have to work alongside René, but that was all the contact she intended to have with the scoundrel who, with little effort, set every nerve in her body tingling. She could no longer deny the mutual attraction. She wasn't about to make the same mistake with René that she'd made in Paris. From now on, she would no longer so much as meet his eyes.

She wandered about the room, feeling as though she'd like to disappear for a while. A quick exit out of New Orleans held more appeal by the hour. But where would she go if she actually did choose to vanish? What if, instead of sailing to the shipping offices to inspect the company books, as she'd done in the past, she were to simply step aboard one of the family ships, bid adieu to everyone, and start over?

Spying a globe sitting on a shiny brass stand, she walked

over and gave it a spin. She closed her eyes and waited for it to stop, then set her finger on the globe and opened her eyes. "Colombia? What in heaven's name would I do down there?"

She took in a long, slow breath, and on the exhale decided she was not one to run and hide. She'd rejoin the festivities, refusing to make excuses for Mayhew's behavior. It was no one's business what went on between them.

And she darn well wasn't about to let his nasty disposition affect hers.

Chapter Fifteen

René and Henri reached the docks just as dawn peeked over the edge of the earth, painting a swath of glorious pink along the horizon.

"*C'est magnifique*," René murmured.

He loved mornings like this—calm waters, the scent of night-blooming jasmine still lingering in the air, and a heavenly promise of cloudless blue skies all day long. He set down the pup long enough to unlock the office door.

Michel strode around the corner of the building. He paused and fisted his hands on his hips. "Do not tell me you expect to keep your mutt inside."

"*Mais oui*." René fought a grin, one he couldn't account for.

"Leave the beast at home. Let Monique watch it."

"*Non*. Miz Sassy, she be my responsibility, don'cha know." He summoned Henri, who followed him inside and laid a small makeshift bed on the floor beside René's desk. Sassy climbed right in, turned a couple of circles, then plopped down into a furry ball and closed her eyes. "One more day and she will be trained to see herself out whenever the need arises."

Michel raised his hands in a sign of surrender. "I could've stayed home for this kind of tomfoolery."

"Why the glum mood this fine day?" René asked. "Family life not agreeing with you?"

Michel grunted. "A full night's sleep would do wonders to sweeten my sour disposition." He slid a document from under a paperweight on his desk, his frown deepening before he tossed it aside. "Worry only adds to my foul temperament."

"What did you just read that you didn't like?"

"Bastien's report on the *Endeavor*. I doubt she made it around the Horn, it's been so long. Damn, I hate losing a ship."

René's gut wrenched at the morose thought of a crew drowning at sea. "You can't give up just yet. *Maman* made Captain Thomas a gris-gris."

Michel glowered at René. "What in the Sam Hill does one of your mother's voodoo charms have to do with any of this?"

"The captain, he wears the amulet under his shirt to protect against a bad journey. *Maman* swears the *Endeavor* will return. She says giving up hope curses both ship and crew. This is one time I shall not go against her word."

"Oh God no. Let us never defy the powerful voodoo priestess." Michel yanked open the drawer to his desk and set out his pencils, inkwell, and pen, then slammed it shut. "What do you suppose went on between Mayhem and my sister last evening?"

Remembering the argument he'd overheard between the two of them, René frowned. "It is not for me to suppose anything where those two are concerned."

"Humph. What's your opinion of the man?"

He's a rake of the worst kind. Close to losing his temper, René managed an indifferent shrug. "It is not my place to judge him."

Michel gestured toward the top of his head. "Do you see anything up here besides hair?"

What the hell kind of mood is this man in? "What be your meaning?"

"It means, I am not wearing a dunce cap. I have not been ignorant of certain goings-on around here. I don't much care for Ainsworth, but I cannot put my finger on just what bothers me about him, which is why I ask. Suffice it to say, I wasn't disappointed when he made a hasty exit from my home last evening. And seeing as how you had your eye on Felice for the entire gathering, to say you harbor no opinion is laughable."

Christ. René picked up a sheaf of papers from his desk and leaned back in his chair, feigning indifference. "Henri went for coffee and beignets. I told him to get enough for all of us, including Bastien and your sister. Both should arrive shortly."

Michel grunted. "I am still not wearing a dunce cap, *mon ami.* You insist on being evasive, so I figure now is as good a time as any for a much-needed conversation."

"Oh?"

"You've proven yourself to be an invaluable asset to the company. I hope you look forward to many successful years to come."

René ignored the chill snaking down his spine. Whatever Michel was up to, he had a feeling he wasn't going to like it. "Go on."

"That said, I can think of only two reasons why I would sack you."

No longer bothering to disguise his irritation, René mumbled a curse and tossed the papers back on his desk. "Is this the part where I am supposed to inquire as to what those two reasons might be?"

Michel snorted. "One reason would be if you ever stole

from the company—which is highly unlikely because theft was precisely what persuaded Cameron to hire you. I must admit, stealing a shipload of the company's rum and holding it for ransom in exchange for gainful employment was an act of sheer genius. I couldn't see it at the time, but thankfully, Cameron did."

"And your second reason?"

"Ah, that would be if you seduced my sister."

"Christ." Alarm shot through René like a bolt of lightning. The old sense of not belonging anywhere in the world swamped him. He worked to keep a neutral tone in his voice. "Look to Bastien if you want to warn anyone. Those two are thick as thieves."

"They are merely friends, something you well know. Do you think I failed to take note of how she barely spoke to you when she arrived, but remained her spunky self with everyone else? The tension was so thick, I could've cut it with a knife. There's an undeniable connection between you two. Knowing your reputation with women, I find your attraction to my sister a rather worrisome prospect."

Merde. Michel's dark suspicion could ruin René's life in a heartbeat. To say he wasn't attracted to Felice would be a damnable lie. But to swear he had no intention of seducing her would be God's truth. The last thing he'd want would be to ruin her, for in the process, he would destroy everything he'd worked so hard for.

He'd learned long ago it was best to keep a lie as close to the truth as possible. "A man would be blind not to notice your sister's beauty and zest for life," he said. "But that doesn't mean every man who notices her is out to take her to his bed."

Michel shot René a searing gaze. "If she decides to give Ainsworth the boot, she could end up vulnerable to your advances. I warn you, my sister is out-of-bounds. You will share the same office, and you are free to socialize with her as it relates to this company or our family gatherings. Cross those boundaries and you will never work in this city again. Or in any other shipping company in the world, for that matter."

René forced the muscles in his set jaw to slacken as he fought the anger roiling up from deep in his gut. Pausing to tamp down his frustration, he took in a few breaths, but lost the battle as the old cynicism returned. He'd be damned if he'd sit here like a dumb goose and let Michel tear him apart. "I haven't forgotten I am a Cajun bastard, born and bred on the banks of Bayou Laurent. Nor have I forgotten that I do not carry the respected name of my *illustrious*"—he snorted—"father, Émile Vennard. Believe me, I know my place, and it is not with the likes of your sister. Or anyone of her ilk, for that matter."

Michel tossed his pencil across his desk and cursed. Jumping to his feet, he paced back and forth, raking his fingers through his hair. He made his way to the window facing the docks and, thrusting his hands in his pockets, stared out at the busy scene before him.

René leaned back in his chair and tossed his own pen down. "What the hell's gotten into you?"

Michel scrubbed his hand over his face and heaved a breath. "I am well aware of what went on between you and Cameron when he started seeing your sister three years ago."

"You mean when your cousin bedded Josette."

Michel turned on his heel and faced René, fire in his eyes. "He married her, goddamn it! You know bloody well what I'm talking about. You sought revenge by ruining Felice."

The blood in René's veins turned to ice. *How long had*

Michel known? "But I didn't follow through. What the devil kind of story were you told?"

"When I visited England three months ago, Cameron told me he'd learned what had gone on between you and Felice after she landed at his doorstep in Liverpool. When he heard she was heading here with Ainsworth, he figured there was likely unfinished business between you and her."

Michel's scowl deepened. "I knew something dire had happened when my carefree sister suddenly left New Orleans as if the devil was at her heels. You may not have ended up bedding her, but you used your wiles to tear her life to shreds."

René's insides roiled at the memory. "What I did was wrong. When she returned, I asked for her forgiveness, and she gave it to me. Rest assured, there is nothing further going on between us, nor will there be. The past has nothing to do with the here and now."

"Oh, but it does."

"How so?"

Michel paced again, the heels of his shoes hitting the floor so hard the wood vibrated. "I have always had a penchant for politics. Although I am no longer interested in a career in Washington, there is much for me to accomplish right here, and I wish to toss my hat in the race for mayor. Also, my family needs me, and I owe it to them to be the father I promised Brenna I would be when we wed. I cannot continue working from sunrise to sundown and leave our six offspring to Brenna. My newborn is asleep when I leave and also when I return."

"What does this have to do with Felice and me?"

"I am desperate to retire from here, René. Truth be told, you are better at what I do than I am. I want you to take my place."

"What?" René's heart stuttered in his chest. "How long have you been pondering this?"

"Nigh on three months. Since traveling to England for my annual meeting with Cameron and Trevor. When I expressed my desire to spend more time with my family and enter the local political arena, Trevor brought up the idea of making you a partner."

Partner? The breath froze in René's lungs. Christ, this was more than he'd ever expected or hoped for. A partnership meant he'd have all the security he'd ever need. A lifetime of it. He would have one of the most coveted positions around—not only in town but in the entire Andrews Shipping Company the world over.

Michel returned to his desk and plopped down with a heavy exhale. "We've decided to make Bastien a partner as well—move him into your position."

Merde. For the first time in his life, René's glib tongue fell silent.

"Bottom line is, if you value a partnership in this company for both you *and* your brother, then stay the hell away from Felice. Keep your cock in your trousers when you are around her. I need your word that you will not touch her."

René's head reeled. He could barely think straight. Hell, he'd avoid her like the plague if doing so would garner such security for Bastien and himself.

"You have my word," he managed to say. Suddenly desperate to get the hell out of there and breathe some fresh air, he picked up the sheaf of papers and started for the door. "Let me assure you, I have no thought for your sister other than that she does a fine job with the ledgers."

"Oh, for Christ's sake, René. Do you really expect me to believe that? You even named your goddamn dog after her."

"Miz Sassy is not—"

"Stop." Michel raised a hand, palm out. "How many times have either one of us commented on how full of sass Felice is? Then you waltz in here with a pup you've named Miz Sassy?"

"Christ Almighty! I'll change the dog's name to whatever suits you."

"Oh, hell no." Michel picked up his pencil and, twirling it in his fingers, smirked at René. "I look forward to Felice's reaction when she learns you named a hound after her."

Even though he'd been shaken to the core, René could feel amusement spilling, twitching his lips. "You would inform her?"

Michel chuckled. "I won't have to. You'd better hope to hell there's not a loaded pistol around when she figures things out."

Henri walked in carrying a basket of warm beignets and a tray of mugs filled with steaming coffee. "Bastien took his vittles dockside. Said he spied two ships on their way in and will wait for them to make port."

Felice waltzed in behind Henri. She snatched a beignet on the way to her desk. "You speak of the *Meridian* and *Alexia*. It'll take two days to unload their cargo, so we'll have an easy go of things today." She glanced at the pile of fluff wagging its tail, and paused. "You brought your hound?"

"*Oui.*"

Michel snorted.

She ruffled his hair in passing, then slid into the chair behind her desk. "I can see by your wicked smile that the dog's presence pleases you to no end, brother dear. How's our wee Emma? Did she sleep through the night?"

He grunted. "I shall wait to respond once you've brought your first child into the world, sister dear."

For a brief moment, something unreadable passed over Felice's countenance, an expression akin to sadness. René shot a speaking glance at Michel, who lifted a brow in response.

She turned to the locked case, extracted the ledgers, and set about deciphering figures.

They weren't five minutes into the day when Ainsworth crossed the threshold and headed straight for Felice, barely giving René and Michel a nod. He pressed a kiss on her forehead. "A good day to you, my love."

René's appetite for beignets evaporated.

"What are you doing here?" she asked. "It's not even eight o'clock."

Ainsworth gave an exaggerated huff. "Well, sink me. Cannot a fiancé decide to surprise the love of his life?" Reaching into his jacket pocket, he pulled out a narrow, black velvet case and set it atop her desk. "Go ahead, love, open it."

I'll be damned. When Felice's expression could've frozen icicles in Hades, René no longer pretended to work. He leaned back in his chair and watched the goings-on.

"Mayhew," she said. "While I would otherwise appreciate your unexpected visit, we have two ships about to make port, and because I missed work yesterday, I have fallen behind in my duties. I'm afraid I'll have to ask you to excuse yourself."

So much for her announcement that today would be a slow and lazy day.

She gave the box a push toward her fiancé and went back to the ledgers. "Perhaps you could give me this over dinner."

Ainsworth paused, then turned to Michel as if he'd not

been dismissed, a broad smile on his face. "I say, old chap. Might you excuse your sister from her duties long enough for the two of us to make our way upriver for a spell? It's past time I asked her father's permission for her hand in marriage."

Felice's head shot up from where she'd been bent over entering figures in the books.

René swore she turned pale.

Michel turned to her. "Your fiancé's request certainly seems reasonable. Once we've finished with these two ships, why don't you take a couple of days off?"

"Capital!" Ainsworth fairly shouted.

She openly glowered at Michel, then stood. "Mayhew, a word." She marched outside, far enough away to be out of earshot, but clearly visible through the window. While she stood with her back to them, Ainsworth faced her, his expression clearly visible.

René turned to Michel. "You baited her, didn't you?"

Michel's mouth twitched. "It worked, didn't it? What do you suppose she's saying to him?"

"After the conversation you and I had before she arrived, do you think I would bother with whatever is going on between those two?"

Michel pointed to his head. "Dunce cap. Bring me my dunce cap, *mon ami*."

"Bugger off. You—" René's retort trailed off as the harbormaster stepped through the door.

"I beg your pardon, Mr. Andrews," the man said. "You've got two ships coming in to port, and I can't seem to locate the proper registrations on the ships."

"Let me have a look." Michel took the documents to inspect just as a tall, slender man with a gray beard entered the premises.

Farouche!

René shot a glance out the window, where Felice stood with Ainsworth.

Farouche removed his top hat and gave Michel a quick bow of his head. "*Bonjour*, Monsieur Andrews."

Michel glanced up from his paperwork. "Farouche. I'll be with you in a moment."

"I can see you are busy, *monsieur*. I shall return on the morrow, *s'il vous plaît*."

"Stay. I want to hear all about Abbott, and I also want you to meet my sister." He nodded toward the couple, standing outside, engaged in what now appeared to be a heated argument. "She's taken Abbott's position until his return. He taught her all she knows, so he's certain to be pleased."

René caught a flash of movement out of the corner of his eye. He looked out the window in time to see Ainsworth stomp off. Felice headed for the door, head down, brows knitted together.

"There you are," Michel said when she entered. "Monsieur Farouche, meet my sister, Mademoiselle Felicité Andrews."

Felice's spine stiffened. Her cheeks flushed. "Monsieur Farouche," she said, her words clipped. "Please step over to my desk for a chat."

She wasn't the only one in the room with color rising. Farouche turned so red, even his hawklike nose pinkened.

"I . . . I must hurry along," he stammered. "Much to do. I simply wanted to inform your brother that Monsieur Abbott is not yet ready to return to his duties. I shall inform him that you are keeping up with the ledgers in his stead."

He turned on his heel and made a rapid exit.

Felice scooted from behind her desk and chased after him. "Stop, Mr. Farouche. We need to talk. Monsieur Farouche!"

Michel turned to René. "Go after the little fool."

"Me? I thought I wasn't to go near her."

"Damn it, René, you can see I am otherwise engaged. Not only is she a woman running helter-skelter through the streets alone, but she is off to who knows where. Get her back here before she does something stupid."

Chapter Sixteen

René dashed out the door and down the street, the heat of the day hitting him full in the face. A flash of blue skirt disappeared around the corner. "Felice," he called.

Little good that did.

He'd not run two blocks and already perspiration drenched his shirt. He swiped at his wet brow and kept on running. *How the devil can she move so fast? And in this heat no less?* He drew up behind her, but she disappeared around another corner and into an alley.

He cursed aloud. Did she know she was headed straight into a disreputable part of town? He slid around the corner, nearly losing his footing. She was nowhere to be seen. He sped up and continued racing down the back-street. Reaching the end of the alley, he didn't know which way to turn, left or right.

He paused.

In the quiet, he heard a faint, "Mr. Farouche! Stop, I tell you!"

He ran toward the sound only to find Felice frantically pushing open the heavy entry door of a run-down, rattrap of a building.

"Felice!" He caught up with her just as she stepped

inside a squalid courtyard. Stumbling to a halt, she covered her mouth and nose against the stench.

He grabbed her by the arm. "Do not take another step."

She coughed and pointed to a door on the second-floor landing. "Farouche disappeared up there. Could Mr. Abbott possibly reside in this horrid place?"

The tumbledown building contained a multitude of cramped apartments surrounding a dirt courtyard scattered with debris. In the sudden silence, several women tending to steaming cauldrons over open fires paused to stare at Felice and René. Children of every size and age collected into a group. Clad in tattered clothing, their heads bald, their faces filthy, they began to slowly close in on the intruders.

René tightened his hold on her arm and murmured in her ear, "If you value your life, let me take you out of here."

Speechless, she backed out with him, her eyes wide. He pulled her from the building and slammed the entry door shut. With a shout, he promised a grim death to any who tried to follow them.

"What was that . . . that . . ." she sputtered as he escorted her away at a fast clip. "Why did those poor children have no hair on their heads? What could've caused such a dreadful condition?"

"Their heads are shorn on purpose."

"Whatever for?"

"To keep down the vermin infestation. I reckon the women wearing scarves on their heads are bald as well."

A small groan left her lips. "I think I'm going to be sick."

"Keep walking," he said, knowing full well where he was headed. "Let me get you to a safe place."

She stumbled along in a breathless daze, allowing him to lead her by the arm. "My brother said Farouche and

Mr. Abbott live together. Mr. Abbott was well paid. He would have no reason to reside in such terrible conditions. I do not understand why he would choose—"

"I think I do," René said, and kept walking, guiding her with a hand at the small of her back. Finally, he halted in front of a two-story building. "Let's take a moment to catch our breath before we venture inside."

"Where are we?"

"At the tax office. We're about to discover who pays taxes on the building Farouche disappeared into."

"The records should tell us who owns that miserable place, right?" At his nod, the confused look in her eyes cleared. She took in a deep breath and stepped forward. "Then let's not waste another moment."

It took half the coin in René's pocket to convince the clerk to allow him access to the archives. "Just as I thought. Your friend Abbott owns the decrepit building."

Felice stepped back from the open pages, not bothering to discreetly lower her voice. "You suspected this when we escaped, didn't you?"

"*Oui.*" He ran a finger under one line. "See here. This is Abbott's address. He lives in the Garden District, not four blocks from Michel."

She pressed her palm flat to her forehead as if to aid her thinking. "Yet he allows those poor people to live under such wretched conditions."

"Farouche's intention was to lead you away from Abbott and into harm's way."

She stepped forward again and studied the paper as if she meant to brand the words into her brain. Moments later, she gripped the table's edge, her face draining of color. "Please, take me out of here before I publicly sicken."

He rushed her from the building and into a garden park

across the street. Settling her onto a bench that offered privacy, he eased himself down beside her.

With a low moan, she gripped her midsection and rocked back and forth, swallowing hard and gulping air.

René slipped an arm around her for comfort. "Shh. Take in your next breath and hold it for as long as you can, then slowly let it out."

She nodded and did as she was told.

"That's it, *chère*. Breathe slow and easy and the dizziness will subside." For want of anything else to do, he began soothing her with small talk in his native tongue until he felt her relax.

As color returned to her cheeks, she let go a deep sigh and leaned her head against the inside curve of his arm. At her innocent movement, his heart thudded. He fought an urge to pull her even closer, comfort her with a gentle kiss atop her head, but Michel's words gave him pause.

"What was Monsieur Farouche doing in that awful place?" she asked. "I thought he was employed as Abbott's gentleman companion."

"He purposely led you away from Abbott for a reason, Felice. It was no accident he disappeared and left you to fend for yourself in that courtyard. Had I not happened along, you might never have made it out of there."

A shudder ran through her. Suddenly, she stiffened and sat up straight. Determination filled her countenance. "We know his address. Let's go after the rat right now."

"*Non*, *chère*. Things have taken a dangerous turn. It is time you informed Michel of what has transpired."

She shook her head. "Abbott was my mentor, not Michel's. He seemed like an uncle to me. Papa was more than generous with Abbott, treated him like family. I want to . . . no, I *need* to confront the pigeon-livered man on my own. Afterward, I will inform Michel; then, together, we will have him arrested."

"Felice, I am no tenderfoot when it comes to confronting danger. I've learned that the more clearheaded I am, the better my decisions. You might want to pause before you choose your next course of action. Especially now that you've decided to keep Michel in the dark."

What the hell kind of position will this put me in if her brother learns of it? Christ.

"Good advice, but I doubt I will feel any different where Abbott and his lackey are concerned."

"Lackey? My dear, Farouche is no hired hand. He is Abbott's lover."

Her eyes widened. "What? How do you know this?"

René shrugged. "It became obvious when Abbott was hospitalized. Farouche hovered over him as only a close partner would. The man who placed you in grave danger did so to protect his companion of many years. He's likely informing Abbott at this very moment that you are aware of the embezzlement. They both have a great deal to lose now, so you must take care."

She locked her gaze with his, held it far too long to leave René unaffected. A beat passed as he tore his gaze from hers and took to counting flowers on a bush until his blood settled. For the love of God, why was he so attracted to this untouchable woman?

"I never gave any thought to Abbott's private life," she said. "I grew up thinking him a saint, most likely living alone in a small house with his cat. Oh, Midnight. His cat. I wonder—"

"Farouche collected the little beast from the office once Abbott was released from the hospital. Felice, I do not think it wise for you to continue riding around town at all hours of the night. And once again, I urge you to inform your brother of Abbott's crime."

Her lips parted in surprise. "How did you know I go out riding at night? Have you been spying on me?"

Despite what had just occurred, and despite Michel's warning to leave Felice alone, he fought another inappropriate urge to lean in and kiss her lush, sweet-tasting mouth. His words left his throat in a husky rasp. "I suspect you take Jingo out at the most unholy of hours when you have trouble sleeping. Whenever I feel restless, I leave my bed and sit on the veranda. We often keep the same nocturnal hours."

Her gaze dropped to his mouth. Her pupils dilated and her exhale left parted lips. "What do we do now?"

He knew that look, knew she felt what he was feeling. He leaned closer. Her breath fell on his lips. So close. So very close.

Mon Dieu. This would not do. She was forbidden fruit.

Catching himself once again, he eased his arm from her shoulders and rested it along the back of the bench. *Merde.* He shouldn't have embraced her. But what was the harm? His action was meant to comfort.

Wasn't it?

The fire in her steady gaze burned through him, clear to his toes. Fire was a dangerous thing when not properly tended. He knew better than to play with it.

He stood and, offering his hand, helped her to her feet. "What we shall do now, Mam'selle Felice, is set out for a scoop or two of ice cream. Isn't that your inclination whenever you've a need to soothe your soul?"

She stared at him for a long moment, as if puzzled by his suggestion. And then her lips twitched. "What a marvelous suggestion, Monsieur Thibodeaux."

* * *

Felice sat across from René, trying to decide which was more delectable, the iced confection sliding off her spoon and onto her tongue or the luscious man sitting across from her. No other word for him would do—handsome was too vague, attractive inadequate.

Those dark eyes scrutinizing her deepened in color— if that were possible—before a hint of amusement flickered through them. He eased back in his chair, his chin tilted upward, his lids lowered. Something all too familiar rolled through her belly. Could the man be ignorant of the provocative effect such a movement had on a woman? She noted several young ladies surreptitiously eyeing him.

What was it about him that drew her to him like a magnetic force when she knew firsthand he was nothing but trouble? One thing she had to admit—he certainly had the ability to smooth troubled waters using few words. With the worst of her anger having subsided, she could actually admit to enjoying herself. He'd been right—she'd do nothing at the moment regarding Mr. Abbott. Stepping away from the predicament could offer insight as to what next to do.

"Thank you for talking me down from a cliff I nearly jumped off," she said. Dipping her long-handled spoon into the tall, fluted glass, she came up with a dollop of sweetness that nearly made her moan with pleasure.

René merely gave her a nod of acknowledgment. A wave of heat curled through her belly again. It wasn't enough that he lazily observed her through a veil of thick lashes; his fingers were now caressing his coffee cup as if stroking the flesh of a woman. Another spark shot through her. Lord have mercy, her thoughts were turning indecent.

She swallowed hard. Her next words tumbled out of her mouth without practicing the pause he'd taught her. "Back there when we sat on the bench, you wanted to kiss me, didn't you?"

The brief hesitation of his fingers circling the rim of his cup told her she'd caught him off guard.

He lifted a brow in question. "Or was it you who wished to kiss me?"

She mirrored his action by lifting one of her own. "Are we playing games now, Monsieur Thibodeaux?"

What are you doing flirting with him, you goose? Get hold of yourself.

He extended a leg, hooked the tip of his shoe beneath the bottom rung of a chair next to him, and drew it closer. Shifting in his seat like a man who had the entire day with nothing to do, he stretched his arm across its back and settled further in his seat.

Another wave of heat passed through her belly. Heaven help her, this man could even manage to make a simple movement intoxicatingly sensuous. She doubted there was a female in the place who wasn't fixated on his every move by now.

Raising his coffee cup to his lips, he took a swallow, watching her over the rim. He took his time setting down the drink. "I like you, *chère*. And I'm fairly certain you like me, but the kiss we shared the other night was meant to be a peace offering and nothing else, *non*?"

Like? Lust was more like it. She took another scoop of ice cream, turned over the spoon, and slid the cool silkiness slowly over her tongue. "You would be a liar if you denied wanting to kiss me back there. I merely inquire."

His eyes were fixed on the action. "What is your purpose in asking when anything other than a mere friendship is out-of-bounds to me? Always will be."

Lord, but this toying conversation was pleasurable. Not to mention exceedingly stimulating. And dangerous. Especially for a woman with a fiancé. She shoved thoughts of Mayhew aside. "Just feeling a bit cheeky, I suppose. Trying to distract myself from the horrible discovery of Mr. Abbott's secret life."

Her attention remained fixed on his cup as he set it down, and his slow-moving fingers went to work caressing the porcelain once again. She wondered what it would be like to have him caressing her the way he stroked the cup. *Come with me and I will show you the most wicked delights*, his movements seemed to say. She swallowed, and went back to spooning ice cream into her mouth.

His gaze dropped to her mouth, then lifted back to her eyes, where they locked. "Your brother scoured my innards with a few choice words this morning."

She failed to hold back a little laugh. "What an odd way of putting things." Her spoon hovered over the goblet. "Because our immediate discussion centers around us and a certain kiss, am I to suppose my name was brought up in this dissecting of your entrails?"

"Michel drew a line in the sand where you and I are concerned."

"My brother set boundaries for us?"

"*Oui.*"

Anger rose up in her like a sudden summer storm. "Well, isn't that rather revealing? He is determined to control me and my every move."

"Take a deep breath, *chère.*"

She shoveled another spoonful of ice cream into her mouth. Then another. "I am practicing the pause, René. But oh, that brother of mine could drive me to Bedlam with the way he's determined to govern me. I took note of your metaphor, by the way. Didn't Jesus draw a line in the sand when he addressed those eager to stone women for adultery? Does my brother think something is going on between us?"

"More that he is aware of something having *once* gone on between us. He wants whatever occurred to remain in the past. I gave him my word that I would not seduce you. I also assured him that I was not inclined to do so."

His words stung. "Ah, but you once were. We've established that much with your apology."

"Your brother swore he'd see to it I never worked in this town again. So, Mam'selle Felice, did I want to kiss you back there? *Oui*. Did I? *Non*. Will I do so in the future? Most certainly not."

"I don't know whether to be hurt by your announcement or so furious with my brother I could breathe fire."

"And fire is not something I am going to play with where either one of us is concerned. Besides, have you forgotten you are soon to wed? That is, unless you are reconsidering your commitment."

A shaft of guilt speared her heart. She wasn't about to tell him she was indeed having second thoughts. "Let's not bring Mayhem into this discussion."

René chuckled. "Do you realize you just called your fiancé Mayhem?"

"I did not."

"Did too."

"We shouldn't be having this discussion," she sputtered. "We should . . . oh my. Don't look now, but the most intriguing couple just stepped through the door. Would you care to place a wager as to who they might be?"

Instead of glancing over his shoulder at the shop's entrance, René turned his attention to the street-side window.

Felice followed the direction of his gaze and caught the reflections of Liberty Belle Worth and Émile Vennard,

René's wealthy, aristocratic French father. "You cheated. You caught their images reflected in the glass."

She leaned over the table and lowered her voice. "What are your father and the widow up to?"

René shrugged. "What they do is not my concern."

"If there is no betting on who the couple might be, how about a wager on whether or not she makes her way over to our table?"

"She will."

"You are certain?"

He gave a slow nod, his deportment unchanged.

"You don't give a fig about them, do you?"

"Does it look as if I do?"

"Let us take our leave. My soul has indeed been soothed, thank you very much. I've no desire to engage in a tête-a-tête with your paramour."

Amusement curled a corner of his mouth. "Former paramour. As you are well aware. You are trying to egg me on, aren't you? Finish your ice cream."

She dug into the bottom of the flute, filled her spoon, flipped it over, and slid the ice cream along her tongue.

Something dark flickered in his eyes, then quickly vanished. "Why turn your spoon over with every bite?"

"Why do otherwise when taste is on the tongue, not the roof of one's mouth? Besides, the confection is cold. When it touches the roof of my mouth, my brain hurts."

"What?"

"You heard me." She took the last mouthful, and with her eyes locked with his, slowly and deliberately slid the overturned spoon along her tongue; then, with a satisfied noise in her throat, she dropped the silver implement into the glass with a clink.

A deep laugh rolled out of his belly. Heads turned their way. Young girls, and those not so young fluttered fans over the lower part of their faces and leaned in to whisper to one another. If looks were candy, they were consuming luscious René with fleeting glances.

"Now you've done it," she said. "Here comes Mrs. Worth. Drat, I do wish we'd wagered on the time it would take her."

"Darlings." Mrs. Worth swept to their table. "How lovely to see you, Miss Andrews." She glanced at Felice's throat. "I see Ainsworth hasn't given you his little surprise or you'd surely be wearing it."

She pressed a forest-green glove to her lips. "Dear me. I spilled the beans, didn't I? Do act surprised when he hands you that little black box. Men like to think themselves rather heroic when bestowing gifts."

Lord in Heaven, what has Mayhew been up to with this woman? Not a spoon or fork jingled throughout the room as all eyes settled on their table. Determined to act as if the shocking news meant nothing to her, Felice nonchalantly touched the corners of her mouth with her serviette. "Have no fear, Mrs. Worth, I shall act supremely surprised and impressed."

The woman turned to René. "I'm thoroughly enjoying spending time with your father. Do consider the offer we recently discussed. He asked me to remind you."

René took a steady bead on her, his countenance suddenly cold and hard. "Being rude to a woman goes against my grain, Madame Worth, but sometimes it's unavoidable. Especially when the person in question stands at the brink of making a fool of herself in public. I suggest you take your leave."

Gasps and hushed whispers ran rampant throughout the room. No doubt sizzling gossip would reach countless wagging tongues by nightfall.

Liberty's cheeks flushed. "Good day to you, then. I'll be certain to mention seeing you out and about to your fiancé, Miss Andrews."

"You do that, Mrs. Worth." She watched Liberty Belle's retreat, her brown taffeta gown making a swishing sound as she went. "That went well."

"Humph," René snorted. "It's time we returned to the docks. The ships are likely in by now."

"Might we first take a short detour to—"

"No, *chère*. I will take you by Abbott's place after dark."

"Tonight?"

He shook his head. "I have plans. Another night."

He's off to spend time with a woman. Disappointment that had nothing to do with Abbott swept through Felice. Had René taken another mistress so soon? Or was he merely in the first stages of seduction? A mental image of him trysting with a faceless female nearly ended her pleasant mood. Why should his private life be of any concern to her? Really, it shouldn't matter one bit. But for some odd reason, the idea of him with another woman bothered her more than figuring out that Mrs. Worth had been present when Mayhew purchased what had to be a necklace of some kind.

Chapter Seventeen

Felice stared at the black velvet box Mayhew slid across the table. A wayward thought gripped her—she'd like to toss it across the room along with a few choice words. However, sitting center stage at Antoine's Restaurant was hardly the place to make a scene.

"Open it, darling," he urged.

Practice the pause. Curious as to whether or not Ainsworth would admit he'd had help in choosing the gift, she lifted a glass of port to her lips while she waited for her boiling anger to reduce to a slow simmer.

He reached across the table and nudged the unwanted gift closer to her, his eyes fairly glittering with anticipation, his smile as benevolent as ever. "You are intent on teasing me mercilessly, aren't you, love? Now, open the blasted thing before I end up grinding my teeth together."

"I cannot wait," she managed to murmur as she lifted the lid.

Lord help me to remain calm.

Felice did not wear complicated jewelry. She preferred clean lines and simple designs. He should know this from what he'd seen her wear. Here was a necklace that belonged around Liberty Belle's neck, not hers. Four strands of pearls made up the upper part of the necklace, meant to fit snugly around her neck. Three long strands hung below the choker in loops with large drop pearls suspended from the middle of each strand. For heaven's sake, what was he thinking?

"Do you like it, darling?" The glint in his eyes brightened.

Practice the pause.

Another slow breath in and out.

"Isn't this something?" she managed to say. "I know most of the jewelers in town—I'm wondering where you found this . . . this gem."

He took a long swallow of his wine. "Oh, darling, you know men pay no heed to such trivial things. I spotted this in the window, so I walked in, purchased it, and walked right out. I doubt I even noticed the name on the establishment's sign."

Dear God, she'd bet her entire fortune Mrs. Worth had purchased this on her own. He'd had nothing to do with it. *Damn you, Mayhew.*

Practice the pause.

When she failed to respond, a look of puzzlement replaced his smile. "Darling?"

When her anger subsided, the sounds of her heart spoke to her. Right then and there, she decided to forge another path for her future. Where or what it was to be, she had no clue. She only knew this was not the man meant for her.

Mayhew's brows knitted together. "Say something, love. You're beginning to worry me. If you don't care for it, I can always—"

She snapped the lid closed and slid it back toward him. "I don't think this is for me. Not at all."

"All right," he said, his words coming slowly, his changing deportment telling her he realized something other than the necklace was at stake. "We'll take it back tomorrow. You may choose whatever your heart desires."

"I don't mean the necklace, Mayhew. I mean us. I don't think we are right for each other after all."

He paled. "You cannot possibly mean that."

"I do." She reached out and covered his hand with hers, but he withdrew it and gripped the stem of his wineglass.

Oh dear, he's not taking this well. What to say next? Best to try another tactic.

"You deserve someone who will better serve you as your eventual duchess. I'm afraid it is not in my disposition to follow strict societal rules. Nor do I wish to spend my life running a household in the countryside while required to do or say whatever is expected of me. You can do far better than someone like me, Mayhew."

His focus shifted from her to the pecan cake sitting in front of him. He swallowed hard, his Adam's apple bobbing up and down. Then he seemed to brace himself. He looked back up at her and smiled, his entire countenance changing. "Nonsense, darling. The problem is, we've been gone from England far too long. Once we return, I am certain you will settle back into the life you were obviously enthralled with before our departure."

This time it was he who reached out and covered her hand with his. "This is not the time to be making such a drastic decision. I know without a doubt that you will make the perfect wife for me. There is no one but you to stand by me through life. No one. Sleep on things, and tomorrow let's discuss our wedding plans. With or without your father's consent, I intend to get you down the aisle posthaste. I simply cannot wait to make you my wife, and show you what a wonderful husband I will be."

He wasn't going to let her go easily, was he? Her throat

went dry at what she was about to say. Guilt over her sordid affair in France had plagued her long enough. It was time to confess—a surefire way of breaking off the engagement.

"Another reason I am not fit to be your wife is that you've put me on a pedestal with regard to my chastity. It is time I told you the truth."

He cocked a brow. "Go on."

A sudden calm swept through her. She took in a slow breath and released it, sure now she was doing the right thing. "When you and I met at that party in London, I had just come from Paris. On the heels of an affair."

Streaks of red snaked up Mayhew's neck and onto his cheeks. A thick vein throbbed at his temple and his jaw clenched.

"Should I continue?"

He emptied his glass of port and poured another. "Why not? I cannot help but be curious as to the why and what of it all."

"I met the man through an acquaintance. He reminded me of someone who had recently broken my heart." She shrugged. "I offer no excuse for what I did, and I've grown weary living with the burden of guilt. I don't want to try to fool you into believing I am virginal on our wedding night. Doing so is not in my character."

Fury etched lines in his face and spilled over into his eyes. Or was that hatred, pure and volatile? "Seeing as you were in Paris, I am assuming this fellow was French, was he not?"

She managed a nod.

Mayhew's face looked as though it might be fashioned out of porcelain and could crack into a thousand pieces were it to be touched. A muscle along his jaw twitched.

"Per chance, did your midnight lover sport black hair and resemble anyone with whom you are currently acquainted?"

Though Mayhew looked as if he wanted to reach across the table and throttle her, she felt not only relieved by her confession, but oddly at peace. But she wasn't about to admit he'd guessed the truth regarding René's part in her irrational decision to lose her virginity to a near stranger. "I believe enough has been said."

"Never mind. The answer is obvious." With a hatred-filled gaze fixed on her, he removed his serviette from his lap, placed it alongside his untouched dessert, and slipped the velvet box back inside his jacket pocket. He stood and without another word turned on his heel and strode through the room as if he were doing nothing more than making a trip to the necessary.

René crouched down in front of the door to Monsieur Fournier's establishment. Extracting a thin piece of steel and a wire from inside his jacket pocket, he inserted both into the lock. "*Merde.* I'm rustier at this than I thought."

"It doesn't help that there's no moon," Bastien responded.

"Black as pitch." René slid the slender tools into the lock and gave them a few twists back and forth until he heard a soft snick. "Got it."

They entered the store with Bastien in the lead, easing their way around counters by touch toward a door Bastien figured had to be Ainsworth's rented space.

"I hope to hell your map of the place is accurate," René said.

"*Mais oui.* The floor plan, she is permanently fixed in my mind, much like *monsieur*'s photographs are fixed on paper."

René snorted. "Your ego astounds me."

Bastien chuckled. He'd visited the shop a few days before, feigning interest in a new hobby so as to memorize the store's layout.

Reaching a door they hoped would lead to their targeted area, René ran a hand down the side of the panel, searching for the handle and lock beneath it. "Christ, I may as well be blindfolded."

Bastien grunted. "Could you have guessed when Michel offered us the respectability of full partnerships that in little more than twenty-four hours we'd be breaking and entering?"

"Hush," René said. "I hear someone outside."

A night watchman strolled by, swinging a lantern in one hand and twirling a police baton in the other. Crouching behind a counter, René and Bastien waited until the swaying light flickered off down the street. "I hope you closed one eye while he passed," Bastien said.

"I believe I'm the one who taught you that little trick, *mon frère*." Having caught a view of the lock when the light shone through the shop's window, René inserted the narrow picks into the opening. A couple of clicks later and the door swung open.

With no windows to reveal their presence, and with the door shut behind them, Bastien lit the whale oil lamp. Shallow wooden boxes filled with photographs lined a long wooden table. René stood at one end, Bastien at the other, as they riffled through the photographic engravings.

"They seem to be sorted by subject," Bastien said. "In this box, the women are all naked. In that one over there, they are scantily clad but touching themselves intimately."

"*Mon Dieu*." René's gut wrenched at the sickening sight. "Would you look at the ones in this box?"

Bastien stood beside René as he flipped through images

of unclothed women. Each of them had something tied around her neck—ropes, scarves, a man's necktie.

The sight made René's skin crawl. "What do you suppose Mayhem is up to? Does he fantasize about strangling these women? Does he intend to eventually do someone harm?"

"Hold on," Bastien said. "I just remembered an erotic Marquis de Sade novel that was passed around to us when we were boys. In it, the heroine suffered erotic asphyxiation by one of her captors and survived."

"*Ou Les Malheurs de la vertu*," René muttered. "You don't suppose Ainsworth seeks sexual gratification through strangulation?"

Bastien shrugged. "I've heard of men who can only get their cocks up through this method. The rush is said to be no less powerful than cocaine. Maybe one or both peculiarities are Ainsworth's problem. In any case, the man is a bit twisted."

"What if he had Madame's ladies partially strangle him, which is why she forbids him to visit her house as other men do? But why all these photos? And why has he separated them into categories?"

René tossed the stack back in the box. "Christ, this is disgusting." Fisting his hands on his hips, he tipped his head to the ceiling and sucked in a deep breath. "Would you have wanted our sister to marry a man who is aroused by this sort of thing? One who also visits a brothel nightly?"

"If you are thinking of informing Michel, I would say he's likely to cut off the man's cock and use it for bait. Do we tell him?"

"Or do we inform her father? Ainsworth is eager to ask for his daughter's hand."

"Which reminds me," Bastien said. "A piece of mail arrived on the London ship for Felice's father. I thought it strange because the return address indicated it was from Scotland Yard. It was labeled private and confidential, for his eyes only, so I sent it upriver on the next paddleboat. I wonder if it has anything to do with Ainsworth."

"What other business would Andrews have with the law than to have his daughter's suitor investigated? Didn't I send off to do the same?"

"*Oui*," Bastien replied. "What do we do now?"

"We sleep on this bit of news. But I'm thinking it's about time we offered to accompany Lord Mayhem to the gentlemen's boxing club he inquired about."

Still looking through the photographs, Bastien said, "Let me guess. You want me to fight the sonofabitch first, and the winner of the bout—which would be Mayhew because I would be taking a fall—fights the next opponent. Which would be you, and you'd proceed to pound him bloody?"

René tossed the last of the photographic images back into a box, the acid in his stomach now up in his throat. "Something like that."

"When we're finished with him, you must remember something, *mon frère*."

"Which is?"

"Felice will still be forbidden to you."

René's chest tightened to the point of pain. "She always was, *mon frère*. Always will be. How could I forget?"

Chapter Eighteen

René headed for home, deep in thought as he tried to figure out how he and Bastien might best go about exposing Ainsworth. What he needed was a response to the inquiry he'd sent off to England. Or should he cook up an excuse to travel upriver, seek out Felice's father, and confide in him? Could the packet from England contain anything of significance?

The clip-clop of horses' hooves against stone caught René's attention. He didn't have to guess the sound's origin. Damn stubborn woman. Quickening his pace, he reached Felice's town house just as she was leading her horse from the cobbled courtyard onto the dirt street.

The light from the streetlamp shone against her white cotton blouse and danced off the toes of her polished riding boots. His gaze shifted to the fawn-colored riding breeches hugging her every curve. Lust hit him like a punch to the gut.

Great.

She paused, watching him watching her. She lifted a brow. "Well?"

He released his breath, then took another more controlled one so he could think straight. Desire faded, replaced by irritation. "Damn it, Felice, I told you not to venture out alone at night."

She locked the gate, then mirrored his perusal of her with a bold one of her own, scrutinizing him from head to toe and back again. "You *told* me not to go out alone. And here I thought that was a mere suggestion—one I chose to ignore."

"Let me guess. We located Abbott's address in the tax records, so you are headed for his residence."

Grabbing a hank of mane, she pulled herself onto Jingo's bare back and gripped the reins with both hands. "Move aside if you don't wish to be stepped on. Better yet, go home."

René crossed his arms over his chest and stood his ground.

"Get out of my way, Thibodeaux."

"You are so damn stubborn, Felice."

Her chin lifted. "I've a mind of my own, and I do not cotton to anyone else trying to make it up for me. Now move, before I run you down."

God knew what danger might await her once she reached Abbott's. He couldn't live with himself if she was harmed. So much for getting any sleep tonight. Cursing under his breath, he set about removing his jacket and waistcoat.

"Why on earth are you disrobing in the street?"

"I'm of a mind to go with you, so I'm dispensing with a bit of cumbersome clothing." He wasn't about to mention the set of burglary tools and various weapons tucked inside his jacket. The last thing he needed was for the metal to jingle about while he was astride the horse.

"Oh, no, you don't." She urged Jingo forward.

René took hold of the bridle, stopping her. "I wouldn't

try that if I were you. I've been exercising him in your absence these past three years. He obeys my commands."

He shot her a wicked grin. "Did I forget to mention he responds to my voice? You'd be flying off him ass over teakettle the minute I whistled for him to halt."

The horse danced a step to the side.

"You wouldn't dare."

"Try me." As if he had all the time in the world, René folded the clothing he'd shed, gave it a toss through the gate's wrought-iron rails and onto a bench. He turned back to Felice. "Going bareback is one thing, but no bit in his mouth is a little foolish, isn't it?"

She stuck her nose up in the air. "You may have him trained to your voice, but I have him trained to bridle only. So there."

With an effortless vault, René mounted Jingo. Landing directly behind Felice, he knocked her cap off her head and sent the hair tucked inside spilling out in a tumble. The sweep of her sweet-smelling locks across his face and chest was like being stroked, right in his privates. His stupid cock reacted with an erection so hard it hurt. Damn good thing straddling Jingo's back kept his trousers stretched away from his crotch.

"Pardon," he muttered, and brushed the cloud of waist-length curls over her right shoulder. "Your hair tickles my nose."

"Then you might want to slide right off the back end of *my* horse and head for home."

"Not a chance." He pressed his heels into the beast's sides, nudging the gelding forward. "We'd better take it slow. No sense inflicting undue pressure on Jingo's back."

The horse's rolling gait set the two of them rocking together in a rhythm as ancient as life itself. He kept his hands positioned atop his thighs, but good Christ, nothing separated them but the thin fabric of shirts, breeches, and trousers. Now here was a form of torture he didn't want repeated any time soon.

He'd expected lively banter along the way, but she grew quiet as they ambled through the Vieux Carré and onto the street heading toward the Garden District. Her scent surrounded him, arousing him in ways he hadn't anticipated—or even thought about when he'd made the irrational decision to join her. But what was he to do? He couldn't let her wander about on her own at this hour. Not after what they'd discovered about Abbott and his good-for-nothing partner.

They turned onto the street where Abbott lived. René felt a jolt run through Felice. The horse halted in response, a quiver running through its muscles, its ears laid back.

"Oh, my word," Felice muttered. Before them stood the grandest three-story mansion on the block. Lights blazed in every window. "So much for the cozy cottage I once envisioned Abbott residing in."

"I've always been curious as to who lived here," René said. "Never bothered to inquire."

She tilted her head one way, then the other, as if attempting to peer through the many beveled and stained-glass windows.

"You're sitting here figuring out how to sneak inside and get a look around, aren't you, *chère*?"

"With every window lit, I doubt we'd disturb anyone's sleep. What say we pay those two worms a visit?"

"You stubborn, stubborn woman. Have you any idea the danger you could be facing?"

"Surely you carry a weapon or two on your person. Come along with me, René."

"*Non.*"

She huffed a deep sigh. "If you'll help me, I promise to inform Michel of everything first thing in the morning."

"And if I don't?"

"I shall carry on alone."

"Oh, hell." Dismounting, he tied the reins to a hitching post, then held out a hand to Felice. "No wonder you exasperate your brothers."

She laughed as she slid off Jingo. "Don't forget my father. I managed to perturb him the most."

"No surprise in that." Together, they strode up the steps to the front door. René lifted the brass lion's head knocker and let it fall with a resounding bang. The double-wide, carved panels opened, answered by a dark-skinned, gray-haired man dressed in full uniform.

"Mr. Abbott, please," René announced. "Tell him Monsieur Thibodeaux is calling."

"He ain't here no more," the butler responded in a calm voice, yet his deportment altered, if only briefly.

An alarm sounded in René's head. "Then get Farouche."

"He ain't here neither, sir. They done left for the Continent this afternoon."

"What?" Felice cried. "The Continent? On one of the Andrews's ships?"

"No, *mam'selle*. They done gone upriver, where they's expectin' to take a train to the coast."

"May I help you?" A golden-haired Adonis strode down the hallway dressed in attire similar to what René wore to the office. The man was in his early twenties, his features an odd mixture of both masculine and feminine. Were his cheeks rouged?

René guided Felice inside. "Who are you, and where have Abbott and Farouche gone off to?"

"I am Hudgins, sir, the estate manager. As the butler said, they've retired to the Continent. I have been left in charge of seeing the furnishings stored and putting the slaves up for auction. I also hold the power of attorney for the sale of the residence."

Felice gasped. "Slaves? Abbott owns slaves?"

"Indeed, *madame*."

Felice turned to René, eyes wide and cheeks blotching. "What kind of monster is he? All these years he's worked for the family, he knew how we felt about owning slaves. I thought he agreed with us."

She gave a wide sweep of her arm. "And would you look at all the wealth he's reaped by stealing from us."

The elderly butler slowly backed away, fear replacing decorum. Heads peeked out of doorways only to disappear in a flash. A maid, looking like a startled owl in her crisp, gray-and-white uniform, halted in the center of the staircase.

This was about to become a helluva lot more complicated than merely exposing Abbott's twenty years of embezzlement. "Fetch your brother, Felice."

"Now?"

"Now."

She held René's gaze, as if begging him to help her find some semblance of order in her confused mind. "Oh, Lord. Michel is going to kill me."

Her face was filled with so much anguish, looking at her was like a thorn thrust in his heart. "Have him send for the constable."

As she raced down the steps, he turned and addressed the butler in a voice loud enough for others to hear. "Do not fear us. Abbott is a criminal. Therefore, he will not be allowed to benefit from a slave auction. The woman who left to collect her brother and the constable is Mademoiselle Andrews of the Andrews shipping empire. If you've heard of them, then you know the family does not abide slave ownership. Neither do I. Let me assure you, something will be done to aid every person here."

He turned to Hudgins. "Except, perhaps, for you. Are you a free man who receives wages?"

Hudgins, pale as his snowy cravat, gulped. "I am"—he cleared his throat—"indentured, sir. I merely follow orders." He stared past René's shoulder, his voice trailing off. "As always."

"How long have you been employed by Abbott—or whatever you wish to call your time here?"

"Four years, sir."

"How old are you?"

"Twenty, sir."

Damn. He's likely been abused by both Farouche and Abbott. "And the others. How have they been treated?"

Hudgins looked to his shoes. "Not always well, sir. I expect the Andrews family will want to inspect the premises. I'm sorry to say, they'll find a room set aside for the delivery of punishment."

René's skin crawled. Nonetheless, he softened toward the man. Who knew what his role in all this might turn out to be? "I'll take a look around now. You will accompany me." He turned again to the butler. "I'd like you to assure the others they are safe. There will be no auction. Nor will families be separated." His words snagged in his throat. "Tell them . . . tell them their lives are about to take a turn for the better."

He and Hudgins went from room to room, with Hudgins describing the high-end furnishings, statuary, paintings, and collectibles of varying sizes. René figured there had to be a small fortune in those acquisitions alone.

"Abbott couldn't have attained all this simply through embezzlement. What more do you know?"

"He is a genius at numbers, sir. He invested well." Hudgins gave a nod to a door at the end of the corridor. "The punishment room, sir. I'll have to fetch the key."

René had seen about all he could stomach at the moment. "I'll skip it. At least for tonight."

A commotion at the front of the house told him Felice and Michel had returned. She stood beside her brother, looking as if she were close to falling apart. For a fleeting moment, this strong-willed, independent woman reminded him of a frightened dove. Had she been anyone other than Michel's sister, he'd have reached out and offered her comfort. Blast it all.

"Felice has had enough of a shock for one night," Michel said. "Either see her home or take her to Brenna, whichever she chooses."

She took a step forward. "I'd rather go home."

After informing them of all he'd learned, René turned to Felice. "Come along."

With barely a nod, she allowed him to lead her down the steps and back to Jingo, passing both Donal and the constable as they arrived. They rode home in silence, surrounded by the quietude of the night.

Reaching Felice's gate, René slid off the horse and offered his hand to her. "If you'll give me your key, I'll unlock the gate. I may as well take Jingo to his stall while I'm at it. Why don't you go to bed?"

"But how will you get out without leaving the gate unlocked?"

"I can lock it behind me and toss the key into the courtyard." He closed one eye, as if he were taking aim, and pointed to a spot near a fern. "In the morning, you'll find it right there."

"So accurate?"

He managed a smile, "*Oui*. The best." He glanced at her, his emotions a wreck. "*Bonne nuit, chère*. Sleep well."

He led Jingo through the courtyard, down the back alley and into a stall, murmuring to the horse along the way. He took time to give the beast's coat a few strokes with a bristle brush. Wearily, he headed for the exit.

"Don't go," came her words from somewhere in the darkness.

He glanced to his right, to a bench where Felice sat, her white shirt a beacon in the moonlight. He halted. "I thought you'd gone inside."

"Stay with me, René. I cannot bear to be alone."

He'd already been struggling to resist offering her solace, but to stay would mean too great a risk. They were both vulnerable for different reasons. "Let me take you back to Michel's."

"That would be worse. All the noise and questions. Not to mention Michel's forthcoming wrath. I cannot face it all. For the first time in my life, I . . . I feel as though I need help making it through the night."

Good God, was she asking for the very thing Michel had forbade? The very thing that would ruin René's life?

"Never mind," she said when he failed to respond. "I'm being foolish. Go."

Didn't he feel the complete prick now? "Would you like me to sit with you awhile?"

She stood. "No. I'm perfectly capable of climbing the stairs to my quarters. If we remain here much longer, we're likely to wake Marie. She can be such a curmudgeon when she's not had enough sleep."

He watched her walk away and slowly climb the stairs to the main living quarters. "Good night, then."

Without looking back, she lifted a hand and waved goodbye.

Collecting the jacket and waistcoat he'd left folded on another bench, he exited the gate and, after pausing to toss the key to the spot he'd earlier pointed out, he made his way inside his own courtyard. He took his time going to his living quarters. He paused long enough to remove his shoes and stockings. Then, as he'd done all his life, he planted his bare feet on Mother Earth's replenishing soil and waited for the faint buzz to ground him. Climbing the stairs, he met Miz Sassy on the upper landing. The dog wiggled her behind in a glad-to-see-you greeting. His heart gave a little lurch. "Aren't you already the loyal one, though. Come along."

Once inside, he set down his shoes. "Don't go chewing on them, Miz Sassy." He headed for the stairs leading to his bedroom, only to pause. He scrubbed a hand over his eyes, wondering if he could use a shot of Armagnac.

"Damn," he muttered, and moved to the veranda with the pup at his heels. She went directly to the bed he kept out there for her and curled up with a little plop and a grunt.

A movement to his right caught his eye. Glancing over at Felice's balcony, he saw that she stood in the shadows, her telltale white shirt like a beacon. She leaned against the wall, watching him.

He stood there in the dark, listening, waiting for her to say something—anything. He heard his own harsh breathing, felt it rasping in his throat. Knowing her gaze held his as surely as if it were high noon, he drew in a deep breath, forced his heart to slow down.

Oh, hell. He might have been unwilling to go so far as to enter her home, but he could damn well sit on the veranda with her until she decided to find her bed. Seduction was the farthest thing from his mind. What kind of heartless prick would attempt to seduce a woman under these circumstances? And then he decided, to hell with Michel's warning. Damn it, she was in dire need of comfort, and who the hell's shoulder did she have to lean on?

And if her brother thought otherwise, he had the problem, not René.

Apprehension falling by the wayside, he climbed over the wrought-iron railing, using the fretwork as toeholds. He had to grin when he heard her gasp. His bare feet hit the boardwalk without a sound. He strode past the door separating their town houses and using the ironwork similar to his own, scrambled up to her balcony and hopped over the railing.

"Aren't you a regular monkey?" she said in a velvet-lined voice.

"*Non.* You've merely been witness to the by-product of my years of thievery."

"Regrets?"

"About what, my past or hauling myself up here?"

Their eyes met and lingered for a long moment. "I'm glad you came," she said.

"Me too."

"I could use a hug," she said in a soft, wavering voice. "That is, if you don't mind."

"I figured you might." He stepped forward and opened his arms. She slipped into them like a rose petal on a summer wind, all soft and sweet-smelling. She rested her cheek against his chest, her body aligning with his, radiating warmth. He put his face in her hair, moved a hand along her back in a slow, soothing gesture. Her breath, as she relaxed against him, penetrated his shirt and heated his skin. At that moment, he wasn't quite sure if the deep need he was feeling belonged to him, to her, or to the merging of two desperate people seeking a safe harbor in an uncertain world.

He paused his movements along her back and, with his eyes closed, simply held her, embracing her with both touch and mind until he felt her shift a foot. "Better?"

She nodded against his chest and pulled her head back. "Would you care to sit with me awhile?"

He released her, managed a half smile, and moved in the shadows to the piece of furniture against the wall. He nudged it with his knee. The darn thing moved. "Is this some kind of rocker?"

"It was my father's design. Had it constructed years ago. He made sure it was large enough for someone to sleep out here should any of us have the notion to do so—which we did quite often back then. It's been reupholstered many times over, but the framework is still in fine condition. Try it."

They sat, he at one end, she at the other. He used his bare foot to keep a gentle, steady rhythm going, one he found comforting. He hoped she did as well.

"Have you ever had one of those moments that sort of redefines things for you?" she asked.

Like right now? "I suppose. What about you?"

"I've had two of them today . . . perhaps three. Time will tell about the third. I've decided I need to get away from all this mess. Travel upriver and spend some time with my father. The last thing I need right now is my brother haranguing me."

Her words, barely above a murmur, sounded as if she was talking to herself rather than to him. He ventured a response. "You've had a long day of it, *chère.*"

A soft sigh escaped her lips. "It seems like a lifetime ago that I went chasing after Farouche."

By the sound of her voice, she was beginning to relax. He kept up the slow rhythm of the rocker, moving it with the ball of his foot. After all she'd been through today, he wondered how she'd respond to learning about Ainsworth's secret life. Perhaps her father had information on the man that would cause him to forbid the marriage.

If so, she wouldn't need to know what kind of man she'd nearly wed.

"Why have you not married, René? You are certainly good with Michel's children, and they obviously think the world of you."

Startled by her question, he responded without thinking first. "I have no intention of wedding, *chère*."

"Whyever not?"

"Because I don't want to continue the Thibodeaux name. And I do not wish to raise children, only to have them learn what a bastard their father is—not just because I am illegitimate, but because of my past and background."

"What of Bastien, does he feel the same?"

"*Oui.*"

"You make no sense, René. You obviously love the company of women. Surely you've considered the risk of begetting your own illegitimate offspring?"

"I thought you wanted me here to avoid being alone, *chère*, not to discuss my personal life."

A long moment of silence ensued before she spoke again. "You and I, Monsieur Thibodeaux, are more alike than you care to admit."

If only it were true. I'd never let you go. "Us? We couldn't be less alike. You come from privilege, while I come from the lowest of the low."

A soft noise left her throat. "You've no idea where I'm coming from at the moment."

With that, she closed her eyes, slid down on the bench, and curled up with her head next to his thigh. "Don't mind me. I fear I can no longer keep my eyes open."

"Then you should go to bed."

"Mmm, no," she murmured. "I cannot yet bring myself to crawl into bed alone. I shouldn't presume to be so bold, but would you mind staying with me until I fall asleep?"

He liked this soft side of her. With her guard down. Her sassiness cast aside. A familiar warmth heated his chest. "Rest your head in my lap or you'll end up with a crick in your neck."

She slid up, swept her hair over her shoulder, and rested her head on his thigh. "Better?"

Without thinking, he brushed a stray lock from her cheek, then caught himself and stretched both arms across the back of the settee.

"Please," she murmured. "Don't stop. I cannot tell you how soothing that felt."

He gave up the fight and gently stroked his fingers through her hair in tender comfort. He leaned his head back against the soft padding of the rocker and closed his eyes. In moments, her breathing grew rhythmic. Though he knew she slept, he sat there for a long while, comforted by the intimacy of the moment.

Like Felice, he'd also had a moment of realization this night. Sadly, he'd reached the conclusion that she was likely the one woman in the world who possessed the unwelcome capacity to commandeer his soul.

Chapter Nineteen

Felice closed the cover of the last ledger, signifying the end of her days working alongside her brother. At the thought of what she was about to announce, melancholy slipped in sideways and settled under her skin. Folding her hands atop her desk, she pushed aside the gloom threatening to grip her and took one last look around the shipping office.

Michel sat at his desk, head bent over the day's bank deposits. Even in profile, he appeared weary. Guilt tugged at her heartstrings. How she regretted their heated exchange when she'd first arrived this morning. Bastien, sitting at the opposite side of the room, glanced up as if he'd heard her thoughts. A brief nod, and he went back to working his way through a stack of documents.

At the map table in the middle of the room stood René, the very reason for her imminent departure. His tender care of her last night had only deepened her unwanted attraction to him. Lord, she couldn't even look at him now without her entire being wanting him to spirit her off somewhere to have his way with her. If she didn't leave New Orleans soon, something was bound to happen between them. Something they'd both regret.

He leaned over the map just then, his palms flat atop the

table. The fine fabric of his shirt and waistcoat stretched taut across his firm, broad shoulders, while his rolled sleeves exposed the muscles cording his forearms.

Her breasts tightened and her stomach did a wicked little flip. No man had a right to be so well-formed. So sinfully gorgeous. She looked away only to catch Michel quietly observing her. Heat crawled up her neck. Embarrassment flushed her cheeks. "What?"

He merely shrugged. Then he shifted in his chair and his eyes took on a mischievous glint, telling her he was about to lighten the mood by teasing her. "Are we through quarreling, dear sister?"

Good, he'd abandoned his anger. "I wasn't arguing, dear brother," she teased back. "I was merely giving you all the reasons I was right."

A throaty noise escaped Bastien's lips.

"Oh, hush," she said.

"I didn't say a word."

"No, but you were thinking with prejudice. And so loud, I could hear your brain rattling from over here."

Michel rolled his eyes. "See what I put up with?"

Bastien chuckled.

"Don't tell me you've never had an argument with your brother," she said.

"*Oui*," Bastien responded. "But we use fists, not words."

Michel snorted. "Even bone-crushing blows would be a good deal quieter than the volume of my sister's voice once she's riled."

"Poppycock," she said. "I had to shout above your demeaning insults in order to get you to hear me."

"Oh, the whole town heard you, dear sister."

"I had good reason to be angry. Any woman with starch in her would shout down being called feather-brained."

Michel pursed his lips against a grin.

"Admit it," she said. "Had I not happened along, Abbott's well-hidden crime would have gone undetected. No man you hired would've discovered what I did."

"So you say."

"Blast it all, Michel. The least you might do is swallow your foolish pride and give me credit for what I exposed. But no, you have to focus on the fact that I made an error in judgment by not informing you right away."

He raised his hands in the air, an affectation of surrender. "All right. You win. Accolades to you for discovering the missing funds. But had you told me right off, we could've had Abbott arrested and at least got back some of what he stole."

"Silly goose. It's not as if this blasted company is going to be left in the poorhouse because of his disappearance. And we *will* get back what's left after the sale of Abbott's house and furnishings."

"It's the principle."

"Humph." Shoving pencils, ink, and pens into the drawer, she sat back. "For your information, this feather-brained sister of yours now has the company books in perfect order. My work here is finished. Pray do not mess them up whilst recruiting my replacement."

Michel flipped his chair around and straddled it, surprise etched on his face. "You don't mean to leave us?"

She reached for her hat and reticule. "This moment, in fact."

Bastien paused in his work.

René turned around, his eyes veiled, his face an unreadable mask. His favorite pencil in hand, he slowly flipped it through his fingers, the ruby tip reflecting the sunlight arcing through the window.

Michel stood and raked his hand through his hair. "My apologies if I've been too sharp-tongued with you."

"I'll say," she said. "Any sharper and you could've shaved with it."

Instead of laughing at her attempt to tease, he gave her a sorry look. "I've been out of sorts—for many reasons of late. I should never have taken out my bad mood on you. Before you run off in anger, why don't you take the next few days off? Come back on Monday and we'll talk."

She shook her head. "I intend to be on the next paddleboat upriver. I very much need to visit with Papa before I leave here for good."

"For good?" A frown burrowed lines across Michel's brow. "Surely you aren't serious."

"I am." She took in a deep breath and slowly exhaled in a feeble attempt to loosen the tight muscles restricting her chest. Why did she suddenly feel close to tears? This leaving was turning out to be more troublesome than she'd anticipated. "Truth be told, my life has been so turned upside down since my arrival, I need time to myself to think things through."

"What about my *bal de maison* this evening?" Bastien asked.

Oh, for heaven's sake, how could I have forgotten? "I wouldn't think of missing your fête. I'll leave here first thing in the morning, then."

Silence permeated the room. Lord, but she was weary from all the upheaval in her life. That and too little sleep last night had left her exhausted, and here it was barely two of the clock.

Michel stood and began to pace. "After spending time with Father, what then? Where will you be off to?"

"I don't rightly know just yet. Perhaps visit family in Liverpool for a short while. I very much enjoy working with numbers, so I'd like to continue doing so. Perhaps

I'll travel around the world again. This time, I'll be on the lookout for a port that suits me. Settle in."

"What of Ainsworth?"

What about him? Lifting her chin, she glanced out the window at nothing in particular. "My relationship with Mayhew is not open for discussion. That said, I shall take my leave. First, I'll visit Brenna and the children. After which I—"

"Will stop by the sweet shop for ice cream," Michel teased.

She couldn't help but laugh. "Oh my, what a fabulous idea. Thank you ever so much."

Michel walked over to where she stood and chucked her under the chin. "Good to see Miss Ferocious Felice has taken a back seat to Miz Sassy."

At the sound of the nickname, René's dog gave a little yip and waddled to where Michel and Felice stood.

Michel shot René a guilt-ridden grin. "Oops."

Felice stilled. She glanced from Michel to René and back to the hound. "What's this pup's name?"

Michel headed for the door. "Seems I heard someone on the dock shout my name."

She turned to René. "Well?"

Bastien bounded for the exit as well. "Your brother has called for me."

Leaning a hip against the map table, René folded his arms over his chest and crossed his feet at the ankles, a smile at the edges of his mouth. "Her name's Miz Sassy."

Lord, she couldn't look at him, especially at what crossing his legs had done to the juncture where his hips met his thighs. *Good heavens!* She focused on his upper torso. Still, it took a moment before she managed to speak, the words binding in her throat. "You named this dog after me?"

"More like she chose her own name." His voice had deepened. His lilting Cajun cadence was now thick and smooth as honey.

At a loss for words, and her body abuzz with a current as strong as an electrical storm, she leaned down to pick up the pup. "Come, Miss Sassy."

"It's Miz Sassy, not miss."

Again, the little beast yipped at the sound of her name. Felice gathered the ball of fur in her arms. Miz Sassy collapsed, as if her bones had gone to jelly, and nuzzled Felice's neck. She gave a little sniff at Felice's hair, then licked her cheek, melting Felice's heart into a puddle. "Why, she's nothing but a bundle of fluff. Weighs hardly anything."

René lifted his hip off the table and slowly approached her. A muted shift took place in his eyes as his gaze turned direct and personal. Felice, with the dog in her arms, retreated until her back met the wall. Her ears roared and her heart thundered. Confused thoughts wrapped her like a net, holding her in place. What in heavens was he up to?

He stood in front of her now, so close, heat emanated from him in waves, his scent surrounding her. Flattening his hands against the wall on either side of her head, he caged her in. Only the pup separated them. His eyes held fire, like the night he'd nearly bedded her. "You really intend to leave for good?"

She could barely nod. When had the air grown so heavy? She wanted it to rain. Perhaps if it rained, the storm would wash away the electricity in the air around them.

He leaned in, touched his forehead to hers. Then he pulled away, just enough to connect his gaze with hers once again. This time, his eyes were filled with anticipation and . . . and need?

What is going on inside this man?

His lips parted and his nostrils flared, as if he were breathing in her entire essence. And then he stole the rhythm of her breath, matched it with his, seeming to capture her very soul.

Suddenly, she wanted to weep for what was never to be.

"It's for the best," he murmured. "We're both nearly past the point of no return, which would ruin us."

She nodded again, her attention fixed on his lush mouth. Her heart thrummed at the notion of what she was about to request. "Would a goodbye kiss be so terribly inappropriate?"

He studied her for a long moment, so close she saw the golden striation in his eyes—eyes that were not pure onyx after all. He leaned in and gently, ever so gently, touched his lips to hers in a kiss so soft, it whispered against her lips, yet left her without the capability of thought. She locked her knees to keep from sliding to the floor.

Lifting his mouth, he raised his gaze to hers. It was filled with the promise of dark, delicious sin. Such a simple kiss this was. A tender kiss, but one that very clearly said he wanted her. He was so very good at making her want him back.

"Will you dance with me tonight, *chère*?"

She held on to the moment for as long as she dared. And then she tore her gaze from his and pressed her cheek to his. "Yes," she whispered. "I will dance with you."

Shouts erupted from outside, pulling them apart. Henri stuck his head inside. "It's the *Endeavor*. She's listing something terrible, but she's here!"

"Thank the heavens," René muttered and was out the door in a flash. Felice followed.

With tattered sails and a crew looking just as ragged, the *Endeavor* limped into port. "Get the crew off, and rescue as much of the cargo as you can," Michel shouted.

"Then get the ship back to deeper waters. If she's going to sink, it cannot be here."

Everything was happening at once, with both Bastien and René flipping off shoes and shirts and helping crew onto the dock. The captain called down to Michel. "Not much left aboard, Mr. Andrews. We had to jettison everything that wasn't nailed down to keep from sinking."

In minutes, the crew was off the ship. René and Bastien climbed aboard. "What are they doing?" Felice asked Michel. "I thought you said the ship was about to sink?"

"They're helping the captain collect his logs and whatever else is needed. Then I'll take it to deeper waters and set it afire."

"Have you done this before?"

"Don't worry. I know what I'm doing."

"Please take care, Michel." She gripped his arm. "I am sorry we had words."

He gave her hand a squeeze. "Me too." He let go her hand and shouted to Henri. "Run over to the company boardinghouse and alert the McGanns we've hungry sailors coming their way. Tell them to heat water for baths, then hop over to the city bathhouse and alert them as well."

Felice stood at the edge of the dock, watching as the two brothers readied the ship to be scuttled in deeper waters. Her gaze landed on René's bare and muscled torso, stunned at the sight of so many scars. She'd heard that his father had hired thugs to kill him, but she'd never imagined the damage done.

"Watch out, Felice!" someone called.

Too late, she tripped over a mooring line. In she went, straight into the water like a bullet, her skirts billowing over her head.

Someone help me—I cannot swim!

She thrashed about, desperate to reach the surface, her skirts twisting about her head and upper torso, trapping her.

Hands grasped her, pulling her up and out of the water. Gasping for breath, her skirts still wound about her head, she fought for breath through wet fabric clinging to her mouth, choking her. White light flashed in her mind as she struggled to keep from drowning. Her mindless flailing landed a kick to someone's body.

"Hold still, let me do the work," someone commanded. More hands grasped her, lifting her out of the water.

"I've got her." *Was that René's voice?*

Coughing and sputtering, she gagged as someone slapped her on her back. "Are you all right?"

Her brother's voice echoed in her ears. She could barely manage a nod.

"I'll see to her, get her dried off," René said and, lifting her in his arms, carried her inside the office and into the back room. "Henri, get some towels."

René set her on the cot and knelt down in front of her, sweeping her hair from her eyes with his fingers, then used a towel to wipe her face. "We need a few more, Henri."

"*Oui*, m'sieur." Henri scurried into the storage room, returning with the towels.

"Leave us," René ordered. "See to the boardinghouse and the bathhouse."

He began rubbing her arms with the towels Henri had given him. "I'll dry you off a bit, then take you home."

"No, you've too much to do here. I'll wait for Henri to return. He can escort me."

He stood, the water beading off his golden, scarred torso. "You're certain?"

"I am. Please leave me. You've waited so long for the *Endeavor* to make it home, and you are needed here. I'll see you this evening."

He slicked back his wet hair with the flats of his hands and nodded. "I'll hold you to the dance you promised."

She nodded. "Indeed. You'll be quite busy; shall I take Miz Sassy to Monique?"

"*Oui, Merci*." He paused for a brief moment, then rushed from the room.

As soon as Henri returned, they made their way along the streets to her town house. Handing over Miz Sassy to him, she sent them on their way. Once inside her home, she bathed, and then Marie washed and tended to her hair. She really had no need of Mrs. Dawes, not with Marie to help her. She had been with Felice since she was a child, knew her needs better than anyone.

Not twenty minutes out of the tub and into a thin dressing gown, the bell rang, announcing someone at the gate. "I'll get it," Marie said.

She returned with a scowl on her face. "That Lord Ainsworth, he be at the gate, but I wouldn't let him in, seein' as how you are indisposed. He said he'd wait. Said it was mighty important he speak with you."

"How did he know I was at home? Oh, never mind. Help me into a day gown, and then show him in."

"If'n you say so, but somethin' about dat man doan sit square with me. Not that it's none of my business, mind you."

Moments later, Mayhew followed a scowling Marie into the room, his hat in hand.

Marie stood between them, her hands on her hips. "Should I be stayin', *mam'selle*?"

"You may be excused." Felice turned to Mayhew. "That is, unless you would like coffee or some other refreshment?"

He shook his head. "No, I'm fine. What I am in need of is a private conversation with you."

Marie humphed and stomped off to the rear of the house.

"How did you know I was home?"

Mayhew, looking like a sad puppy dog, set his hat on a side table and turned to her. "I stopped by the shipping office. Michel told me where you'd gone off to."

She folded her arms around her waist and tapped a foot. "What do you want, Mayhew?"

"I came to apologize for my reprehensible behavior last evening."

When she said nothing, he continued. "Darling, I do not want to lose you. I don't give a fig that you've had an affair. Who's to know if you are not a virgin when you meet me at the altar?" He raked his hand through his hair. "Say something, Felice. Anything."

"All right," she said. "How about this—I don't care much for liars."

He paled. "What do you mean?"

"I do not for one moment believe you purchased that necklace on your own. In fact, I do not believe you so much as stepped through the door of a jewelry store. You engaged your *friend*, Mrs. Worth, to do the purchasing, didn't you?"

He muttered something, heaved a breath, and swiped a palm across his brow. "You are correct on all counts. Darling, please believe me when I tell you that I am entirely lost in this city without you. You're swallowed up by that blasted shipping office the day long, and it seems we are becoming near strangers, which I cannot bear."

"How does our being apart justify having Mrs. Worth do the purchasing? And what in the world have you been up to every day?"

"I've buried myself in my new hobby of photogravure. I have been trying to become skilled enough to surprise you, so I can take a fine portrait of you. I lost track of time the other day when I wanted to do something special for you, so I asked her to do me a favor."

"Are you bedding her as well, Mayhew?"

His mouth dropped open. "What? No, Felice. I would never . . ." He shook his head. "No, not possible. Please, we've gotten off on the wrong foot. Neither one of us is thinking straight. We need time."

She closed her eyes against his words, too tired to even string rational thoughts together. "You're right, Mayhew. I need time to think things through. I'm off to visit my father on the morrow and—"

"Brilliant. Allow me to accompany you. We'll speak with your father—"

"No." She raised a hand, stopping him. "I shall see Papa alone."

He began to pace. "Will you promise to return to me?"

Oh, her thoughts were getting more and more jumbled. "I cannot promise anything at the moment."

"Can you at least give me your word you will return, and we will meet. I want to prove to you that I am the man you want to spend your life with."

What could she say? To dismiss him entirely right now would surely create a ruckus—one she couldn't cope with. Better if she waited to remove all hope of a reconciliation until after she visited Papa. She nodded. "I'll return, but I cannot say precisely when."

"Jolly good, then." He tilted his head to one side and winked. "Can we at least attend Bastien's gathering together before you take your leave?"

"How can I say no when the ball takes place at Le Blanc House and you reside there? However, Michel will be collecting me, and you will already be on the premises, so I shall meet you there. Now, if you will excuse me, I am in dire need of some rest. I've had a long day, and if I don't lie down soon, I will be in no condition to attend anything."

"Brilliant!" His face lit up as though nothing about their relationship was out of place. Reaching inside his jacket, he retrieved the black velvet case containing the necklace, set it on the table next to her, then stepped forward and kissed her on the forehead.

With a noisy, exaggerated shuffle, Marie stepped from the shadows and escorted him out the door.

Felice found the nearest chair and, with a loud exhale, plopped down in it and scowled at the velvet box he'd left behind. "Heaven help me."

Chapter Twenty

René leaned a shoulder against the wall near the ballroom's exit. Once again, his gaze swept the crowd, then settled on Felice seated in the far corner next to Michel. A muscle pinched in the middle of his chest. Ignoring the odd sensation, he lifted the glass of mint-laced rum to his lips.

He'd take his time, wait until the band played the last tune; then he'd claim the dance she'd promised him. Until that time, he'd be damned if he'd approach her while her watchdog of a brother hovered.

Her English prick of a fiancé sat to her left, deep in conversation with René's mother. Why would an arrogant nobleman bother to chat up a voodoo witch? Odds were, he was up to no good. René would worm the gist of their conversation out of her, even if it meant priming the gossip pump by telling her about Ainsworth's deplorable photographs. Tight-lipped as *Maman* could be, she surely did relish someone else's chin-wagging.

"A good evening to you, Monsieur Thibodeaux." Andre Marchand, a wealthy cloth merchant, paused in front of René. He extended his hand in greeting.

René liked the widower, a French émigré from Bourgogne. Found him to be an agreable businessman with impeccable standards. He returned the handshake. "Marchand. I was surprised to see you here tonight."

The man grinned, his plump cheeks rosy, his eyes twinkling. "I'll wager your brother sent invitations to his neighbors in order to make it difficult for us to complain of the noise. He didn't expect a one of us to accept, did he?"

René chuckled at the man's accurate insight.

Marchand twirled the points of his waxed mustache. "A Cajun *bal de maison* is something new to me, so— voilà!—here I stand. Enjoying myself heartily, I might add."

René took another swig of his rum. "What do you think of our kind of music?"

"First off, it would be remiss of me not to mention the sumptuous food." He patted his rotund midsection. "And as for the music, I'll request a favor, if I may."

"Which would be?"

"A discreet glance over my right shoulder will show you a circle of five giggling young ladies, all with fans aflutter."

"*Oui.*"

"That midge of a girl dressed in pink froth with an abundance of sparkling pink feathers in her hair—her choice, not mine—is my daughter."

René nodded. *Pretty little thing, but what's the connection between her and a favor?*

"Cosette is eager to experience her first turn around a dance floor. However, the lads eager to accommodate would rather walk through fire than dare to approach that closed circle and risk a cut direct in front of their peers. Do me the favor of dancing with her."

Disbelief shot through René. "Me?"

Marchand hiked a brow. "Indeed. Is there a problem?"

I'm a bayou bastard with a past that follows me everywhere, and your daughter is an innocent—that's the dilemma. Trying to appear undaunted, he shrugged. "Among other things, I'm a bit old for her, not to mention my less-than-golden reputation in this town."

"It's merely a dance. Who else might I trust to know the steps to this fast-paced music? Besides, with my good standing in the community, who would dare cast aspersions on you?"

René spotted Henri eyeing the cluster of girls and wearing a hound-dog look. So, even he feared to approach the formidable closed circle. "I'll give it a go."

"Splendid," Marchand said. "I'll wander off so as not to be accused of meddling." He turned to leave, then paused and gave René a long look. "You've been good to me, Thibodeaux. Four different times you've caught errors in my shipments. You could've said nothing, lined your pockets with a good deal of coin, and neither I, nor your company, would've suspected a thing. I owe you one."

He owes me? Whatever the hell that meant. He waited until the band was about to strike up the next tune, then moved to where the cluster of girls stood. "Would you care to dance, Mademoiselle Marchand?"

Cosette gasped. The circle parted, and her fan went into high motion, her doe eyes wide and blinking as fast as her fan fluttered. "*Monsieur?*"

"I'll wager you've not danced to Cajun music. And because I was born to these kinds of tunes, I thought you might like to give it a try." He held out his hand in invitation.

Heads in the room turned.

One of her slack-jawed friends gave her a quick jab to the ribs. She wheezed, then lowered her fan, revealing the heightened color of her cheeks. "I . . . I would be pleased to dance, *monsieur*, but being ignorant of the steps, I should make a fool of myself."

"Do you know the waltz?"

"This music in no way resembles that dance, *monsieur*."

"Ah, but in its own way, it does." He stepped forward and lifted her trembling hand to his shoulder. Taking the other in his, he eased her into the throng of dancers. "Relax. Let me lead and you'll do fine."

Three fiddlers drew down hard on their bows, and with a high-shrilled "*Ayeee*," the distinctive Cajun music sprang forth. Mandolin and banjo players, spoons and washboard players joined in, tapping in time to the lively rhythm.

René whirled Cosette about the room, surprised to find her so light on her feet. In no time, she caught on to the steps. With pink skirts swirling, and her feather headdress twinkling under the lit chandeliers, she shouted above the din, "*Laissez les bon temps rouler, monsieur*. Let the good times roll!"

He chuckled and circled the room with her, dancing past her father, who beamed with pleasure. Marchand gave him a small nod of approval. Others standing around the perimeter paused to stare openly.

Realization struck René like a bolt of lightning.

By urging him to dance with Cosette, Marchand had publicly declared a bayou bastard and son of a voodoo witch as his peer. Was it possible a curtain could be drawn over René's wretched past? With the merchant's elevated status extending well beyond New Orleans, would others follow suit? Had Marchand made one of the most important moves in René's sorry life? Had the man just accomplished in a single gesture what René had spent years trying to achieve?

Elation shot through him.

He glanced down at his rosy-cheeked partner. And to think he'd almost refused to dance with her. Christ, he felt good.

By the time the song ended, both he and Cosette were laughing and out of breath, albeit each for different reasons. She looked to her father and then to her awestruck friends. As her father approached, she practically bobbed up and down on the balls of her feet.

"Well, doesn't that just take the cake," came a throaty female voice thick with what René recognized as an overindulgence of spirits.

Anger shot through him. A muscle twitched in his clenched jaw. "Madame Worth. I didn't expect to see you here."

The band started up again and Liberty Belle had to raise her voice to be heard. "If you recall, Bastien gave me a verbal invitation directly in front of you. Tell me, what the blazes are you doing, flirting with this young thing barely out of the nursery? I thought you'd be all over that Andrews chit tonight."

The heightened color in her cheeks, the glassy look in her eyes fueled by lust and too much liquor—he'd seen her this way before, one of the many reasons he'd distanced himself from her. "Watch your tongue, Madame Worth."

She slid her hand through the crook of his arm and looked down her nose at Cosette. "You shouldn't flirt with Monsieur Thibodeaux. Men like him are known to devour young misses like you in a single bite. Go on, be off with you, little one."

Cosette's eyes grew wide. Marchand stepped forward, his brows knitting. He looked from Liberty Belle to his daughter. "It seems your dance lessons have paid off, Cosette."

She gave her father a brief hug, then hurried to her circle of friends.

"*Merci beaucoup*," Marchand said to René. "I figured if anyone would be willing to indulge my request, it would be you."

"Cosette was surprisingly quick to learn." René purposely avoided introductions between Marchand and his former mistress. *Now, to discreetly rid myself of a drunken Liberty Belle.*

Marchand ignored her as well. "My Cosette is now the envy of every young girl in attendance. She and her friends will be chatting about this night for weeks to come."

Liberty ignored Marchand and tugged at René's arm. "Darling, we need to talk."

It was all René could do to remain civil. "Would you excuse me, *s'il vous plaît*?" With a raised brow, Marchand nodded and, turning on his heel, disappeared into the crowd.

"You are making a scene, Liberty." He held the hand tucked in the crook of his arm and led her toward the exit. "You need to leave before things get any worse."

"Unhand me," she cried, trying to extract herself from the hold he had on her. "I am not ready to call it a night."

"You are foxed," he growled between his teeth. "I'll see you home."

"Oh no, you won't." She wriggled free, and with every eye in the room on them, she weaved through the crowd to where Ainsworth sat between Felice and René's mother.

René shoved a hand through his hair. "Christ."

Bastien sidled up to him. "Do you want me to take her home? Perhaps I can reason with her."

"*Non*. She is my burden. Why the hell I ever got mixed up with her in the first place, I'll never know." He started toward the widow.

By the time he'd managed to remove her from the

ballroom and get her down the stairs to the front of the house, she'd turned the air blue with her curses.

Bastien followed behind and assisted René in getting her into the carriage. "I strongly suggest I should be the one to take her home."

"*Non.* It's your fête, brother. Return to your guests. I am sorry to have caused you embarrassment."

"It was I who invited her, so it is I who should apologize. You'll return?"

René shook his head, his dignity snuffed like a flame gone to black coal. "I'd rather swim in a cesspool than venture back into that crowd."

He glanced around at the onlookers who'd stepped outside for fresh air. "Not only did she make a complete fool of herself, she also destroyed Marchand's effort to elevate our standing in town. And she managed to do so in about the same number of minutes."

"I am aware," Bastien said. "I saw everything."

Liberty made to exit the carriage, mumbling something incoherent. René stepped in front of her. "Damn it, Liberty, stop your foolishness."

"Take me back to the ball and dance with me as you did with that child."

He took her by the shoulders and set her firmly on the seat. She cursed him. He turned to Bastien and lowered his voice. "I'd like to wring her neck. Go on, see to your guests and leave her to me."

"Do you think I cannot hear you?" She laughed and peered over his shoulder at the stunned onlookers. "He says he wants to wring my neck, but his temper will mellow once he's in my bed. It always does."

René cursed under his breath again. The sultry air closed in around him. He slipped out of his jacket and cravat, laid them behind the seat, then climbed into the gig beside her. With a crack of the whip in the air above the horse's rump, they took off, while Liberty chattered at full volume. Fortunately, she lived a mere two blocks away.

Nonetheless, he had an argument on his hands when he tried to remove her from the carriage. Her raucous outbursts brought not only her maid onto the porch, but servants from adjacent homes, who stepped outside and craned their necks as well.

"You'll pay a price for tossing me aside," she called out, and waved his cravat in the air like a white flag of surrender. He'd sooner find that cesspool to swim in than return for the blasted necktie she'd grabbed from behind the seat. At least it wasn't his new jacket.

Instead of going home to an empty house, he drove out to the old Allard place and parked the gig in the grassy meadow fronting Bayou St. John. Unlike the night he'd driven Felice out here, there were no fireflies to speak of, only the sound of cicadas in the cypress trees, and a chorus of frogs along the water's edge. A damnable lonely sound tonight.

Propping a foot on the dashboard, he leaned back in the seat and studied the vast sky overhead, fatigue gripping him. He was tired. Tired of trying so hard to be accepted in a town that would never forget his past indiscretions. Tired of fighting an internal war he'd never win. Tonight's ruckus had broken something inside him. One moment he'd shot to the heights of euphoria at Marchand's grand gesture, while the next, he'd escorted a drunken ex-lover past the town's finest and plummeted into a black hole he never wanted to visit again.

I give up.

As despair leached into his bones, he heaved a breath and swiped a hand over his eyes. He'd leave New Orleans. Find somewhere else to settle down. On Monday, he'd turn down Michel's offer. The manager in the Jamaica office was retiring. Why not ask for a transfer there? The island was close enough to return home on occasion, and no one there cared about his past. If Michel refused his request for relocation, he'd find employment at a shipping outfit elsewhere, because damn it, he was good at his job. Better than good.

Felice.

At the thought of her, a pain shot through his chest. She'd be gone on the morrow. What the hell, he'd be gone soon enough as well. He reckoned the ache he felt was because she lived in his heart, but there was no place for her in his arms. He didn't weep at the thought of leaving everything behind, at never knowing a life with someone like her, but he sure as hell felt like it.

The trees behind him and along the bayou filled with wind, tossing about shadows that seemed to battle with one another. In the distance, lightning pulsed in clouds that had begun to gather over the gulf, signaling an incoming storm. Picking up the reins, he urged Commander homeward. Filled with dread at the thought of returning to the house that represented the life he'd worked so damn hard to achieve, he took the long route back home.

A new kind of hollowness opened up inside him. He'd sell the place, leave everything behind.

Turning the corner onto Rue Royale, he spied his town house, the exterior lit only by lamplight. He squinted through the darkness. Who the devil was sitting at his front gate?

He drew closer until he was able to make out his visitor. Gut wrenching, he tightened his grip on the reins. Commander tossed his head. "Felice? What the devil are you doing sitting on the ground out here?"

"Petting Miz Sassy through the bars." As if on cue, the pup gave a pitiful whine and then barked.

"Hush, you'll wake the neighbors." He set his jaw against the pounding of his heart and climbed down from the gig. "This is darn foolish of you, sitting out here alone. What if some no-account happened along and snatched you up?"

She stood and dusted off her backside. "Nothing happened, did it? Monique and Henri are still at the soiree, so I've no way in. Thought you'd never return."

He opened the gate, one hand on the reins. "You should go home, *chère.*"

She stepped closer, her light, sweet scent surrounding him. A flood of want and need surged through him. His heart hammered hard in his ears. The last thing he needed was Felice at his door, because the one thing he needed most right now was her. God help him, he wanted to be deep inside her. Wanted her with a force so powerful he was near to carrying her up the stairs to his bed. For one blinding moment, he couldn't find his voice. "Don't," he managed in a husky murmur. "I cannot—"

"Cannot what?"

"Touch you." He drew a hitching breath. "I'm in no frame of mind to—"

"To what?" Something shifted in her countenance. She took another step closer.

He studied her upturned face. She was so close now, if he were to lean forward another few inches, his mouth would be on hers. Her breath against his skin whispered to his hunger and need.

Realization hit him like a punch to the gut, and the pieces finally fit. She was the missing piece in the puzzle of a pitiful life that was little more than veneer. All he ever really needed was her to complete him. But there was no forgetting he was the no-good, illegitimate offspring of Émile Vennard. No forgetting he was a bayou bastard, son of a voodoo priestess, someone who could never give her what she required in life. They were never meant to be.

He heard the heavy intake of his own breath, felt the tightening of every muscle as he struggled to govern his emotions. "Felice, I am only so strong and disciplined a man. Whatever you came here for, *go home*. If you know what's good for you, you'll stay away from me."

She retreated a step, and their gazes locked for a long moment. Sadness filled her eyes. "You are a strong man, René. Stronger than I am. I will not beg you, so I shall say goodbye and leave it at that."

She turned and walked away.

He froze.

The simple act of Felice turning her back on him was enough to tear out his insides. For the second time this night, something broke in him.

He leaned his forehead against the gate's iron bars as if they'd afford him a cool respite. "Don't go."

She paused with her back to him. "I am leaving on the morrow, René. We will not see each other again. But we have unfinished business, you and I."

Jesus. He'd be leaving as well, so what did her brother matter? No, he'd given his word, and a man was only as good as his word. "I cannot take you to my bed. I gave your brother my word."

She turned to face him, but kept her distance. "It is not you doing the seducing, is it?"

He didn't know what else to say except, "What of Ainsworth?"

"I cannot marry him. I am free to do as I please." She tilted her head, waiting for his response.

Her voice, a silken caress, shifted his resolve. Nonetheless, he couldn't ruin her only to walk away. "But I would know, wouldn't I?" His voice cracked. "And that makes me unworthy of you."

She stood unmoving, as if studying his very soul. Then, bold as you please, she marched back to him and set her open palm against his taut chest, her eyes never wavering from his. The heat of her touch seared his skin. Then she crushed the fabric of his shirt in her fist and tugged him to her.

His heart stilled, then gave a painful thump as he lost his resolve. This time, he couldn't make himself push her away. "You had better damn well be certain of what you're after, *chère*. Because if you want what I'm pretty sure you do, then know this—I will take you to my bed, and by morning I will have known every inch of you."

She sucked in a quick breath, then lifted her chin. "I want you. If for no other reason than to end these feelings for you that are driving me to Bedlam."

"Then God help us, because there will be a price to pay for what we are about to do." He sought her mouth and mumbled something incoherent as he tasted her sweetness.

When he lifted his lips, a ghost of a smile touched hers, one filled with consent.

Chapter Twenty-One

How they got from the gate to René's bedroom was a blur to Felice, but here they now stood, beside his large bed, the linens pulled back, and with him clad in nothing but a pair of trousers. Slowly, ever so slowly, he divested her of her clothing, his dark lashes veiling his thoughts. His featherlight touch roused a trail of shivers dancing along her skin and over her breasts, leaving them taut and wanting.

Her chemise, the last of her clothing, fell to the floor. His gaze drifted over the length of her, and a soft noise left his throat. "You drive me wild," he whispered, his husky words sending tremors through her.

His mouth settled on the curve of her neck, just below her ear, and his hand covered one breast. Did she moan or was that him? "You unhinge me, *chère*. You send me some place where I cannot manage to think straight."

You can't think straight? Lordy, I am brainless.

Setting her trembling fingertips to his bare chest, she ran them through the dark curls there, then along the line of hair circling his navel, and down a thin trail disappearing beneath his trousers. A buzz slid across her skin.

She traced several scars on his torso. Later. She'd ask about the wounds later. All she wanted right now was to take things moment by moment, drink in the beauty of his near nakedness, experience every exquisite act he'd promised to show her when he'd led her to this room. Her senses reeled as a vivid image swept through her mind of what was about to come—of the two of them naked, on the bed directly behind her.

He curled a finger under her chin and lifted it, his brow furrowed. "Your hand trembles," he said. "We can stop if you wish."

The deep resonance of his voice seemed to vibrate in her bones. Surrounded by his heat, by the fierce power emanating from him, she shook her head. "I know what I want. I desire you. Desire *this*."

His lips parted, and his hot breath fell on her mouth. His nostrils flared as his voice rasped, "Then unbutton me."

As she worked at the opening of his trousers, a riveting need tightened her breasts. Her blood, heated by the musky, clean scent of him, pounded in her ears. A hunger beyond words erupted in her, lighting a sweet flame in the tender curve of her upper thighs.

"Now drop them to the floor," he murmured. "As I did with your clothing."

She did as he directed. In one fluid movement, he stepped out of the trousers and kicked them aside.

Oh my!

She tore her gaze from his endowments and looked up into his eyes, momentarily taken aback by his glorious nakedness. Then, in a bold and wanton act, she curled her hand around the satinlike skin covering his steel-hard maleness. Tightening her hold, she moved her hand from tip to root and back again.

He sucked in a breath.

His pupils flared.

And then his lips parted as some unintelligible whisper

left his mouth. A curse as he yielded his soul to her? For the first time, she understood the eternal power a woman held over a man. It was a power she would never abuse, lest she find her own downfall riding the aftermath of his roiling torment.

His lashes swept down, veiled his eyes for a brief moment, as if he needed the time to recover the power her action had stolen from him. Then he chuckled, low and deep in his throat. He licked her temple, blew on it, and nipped at her earlobe. "We'll fit together quite nicely, you and I." Outlining her mouth with tender kisses, he eased her onto the bed.

"God, you know how to work magic," she whispered, and gave herself over to him as he settled the length of his body alongside hers.

He set his hands to her face, tilted it, and studied her while she swam in the depths of his sultry gaze. His mouth brushed against hers, a whisper of a kiss that left her boneless. "It's time we let our hearts go wherever they take us," he murmured.

"Exactly what I was thinking." She leaned into him, wanting to feel every inch of him touching her. His arms swept around her and she was enveloped—by his taste, his scent, the warmth of his skin. She wanted more of him. "Your kisses are wicked. So very, very wicked."

"And you are lovely, *chère*. So very, very lovely."

His voice, a silken caress, shifted the rhythm of her heart. Her hand scraped across his hard, flat stomach. She gripped his hip to steady herself and rolled onto her back, sought his mouth and mumbled into it as she slid one leg over his sinewy hip.

His breath against her skin as he explored every inch of her body whispered of his hunger and need, and her body responded with wild abandon. His fingers moving so lightly over her skin felt as if the air itself had come alive to caress her. He cupped her breast in a sweeping move upward, held it and suckled. She cried out, a feverish need escalating in her.

"Please," she whimpered, and rocked her hips in an attempt to ease him inside her.

In one swift move, he rolled over her and nestled his length against her heat. Involuntarily, her body arched against his. He claimed her lips once again, and then astonished her as his hand found the nest of curls at the top of her thighs. He slid a long finger deep inside her.

"Oh, God," she cried out as the slow, rhythmic movement of his hand demanded total surrender.

Pressing his thumb against a tiny ridge of flesh nestled in her mound of curls, he kept the pace of his hand going as he bent his head to her breast and again filled his mouth, while flicking his thumb against the tiny nub. A dazzling current shot through her body, and she cried out as her hips canted against his hand, her body and mind helplessly demanding more of this wondrous ecstasy that until now, she never knew existed.

In a slow and sensuous slide, he eased himself partway into her. She moaned as the heat of him entered her. He buried his face in her neck. Near to pulling out, he nipped at her shoulder and then sank halfway into her once more.

"Nearly there," came his hoarse whisper. "Tell me how it feels, Felice, my body inside yours." He sank farther into her, relaxing the length of his body against hers at last. "Tell me there were times you awoke in the middle of the night because of me."

"Yes," she cried. "Yes. It's been you . . ." Unable to finish her sentence, she wrapped her legs around his hips and tried to fit him deeper inside her.

With a groan, he drove all the way into her, clear to the

root of him. He rocked up tight against her pelvis and against the small nub nestled in her womanly cleft. He rotated his hips in small, tight movements. "Is that why you're so desperate to have me inside you, because you've wanted me since we first met?"

"Yes," came her soft cry.

"Tell me you'd lie awake at night wanting me. Just like you want me now."

His harsh whispers released a molten flow of lava through her veins. "Yes," she cried. "Oh, God, yes. Try as I might, I never forgot you, René."

He pumped inside her now—his sultry whispers sounding lush and erotic between thrusts. "But those nights were nothing like this, were they? Those were mere fever dreams. You are here now, in the flesh, and Christ, it is all so good."

Tears flooded her eyes, and she cried out as she rocked against him. On a shattering moan, an orgasm rolled through her.

He stilled, capturing the moment. And then she canted her hips once again. Closer. She was still desperate to be closer. He began to move again, but this time, each supple thrust of his muscled hips held an intense purpose far beyond the act of making love, as if the two of them had entered some sacred dimension.

He whispered to her, his words leaving his throat in a ragged rasp, filled with both pain and desire. "Thoughts of you kept my life worth living for years, Felice. I just didn't know it then."

He clutched her tighter, and a shudder went through him. "All these years you were somewhere deep in my heart and mind—you kept me from giving up."

He pushed onto his elbows so he could look deep into her eyes. Before his final thrusts sent them both into erotic oblivion, his hoarse, barely audible words found her heart. "You have no idea how much I needed this—needed you, tonight. You've kept me from dying inside."

Rolling thunder drew Felice from a deep sleep. The scent of strong coffee brought her fully awake. She opened her eyes—and found herself trapped in René's warm gaze.

"*Bonjour, mon amour.*" He lay on his side atop the covers, his head propped in his hand, his bare feet crossed at the ankles. He was clean-shaven, dressed only in a pair of charcoal-gray trousers. She reached out and ran her fingers through his thick, slightly damp hair. The right side of his mouth lifted, and his dark, glorious eyes sparkled with humor—and something else she'd not seen in those depths. Playfulness?

Shoving her hand through her own wild mass of curls, she pulled the sheet over her breasts and propped herself up against a stack of pillows. "You are already fresh and clean while I . . . I . . . What time is it?"

Something prurient crept into his playfulness. Sensing the restrained power of a man contemplating sinful mischief, she watched his sooty lashes fall against his cheeks as he lowered his lids and openly studied her mouth. "Time to be kissed again, don'cha know."

His mouth, so darkly sweet, came down on hers, sending her senses flying once again. His tongue traced her mouth, and then swept up to her ear, where his heated breath against her skin coursed through her body like hot lava. "It doesn't matter what be the time, *chère*, because it's Sunday, and the rain, she will be coming down in buckets the day long, so I have decided to hold you captive until the morrow."

"But I was to go to the shipping office today. Michel

hired a new bookkeeper, and I promised to show him the protocols. Then I shall board a steamer and go upriver to spend time with my father."

"You think to travel in this weather?" He leaped from the bed, took up a carafe on the bedside table, and poured a rich chicory and coffee blend into two cups. "Besides, Michel has likely hauled his small army to church."

"He's in a holy place while you and I—"

"Lounge in our own temple." He shot her a mischievous grin. "At least it must be holy, considering the number of times you called out, 'Oh my God,' during the night."

"René!"

He laughed. Then he seated himself on the edge of the bed, plunged a fork into a bowl of peaches and lifted a slice to her mouth. "Here, I crushed some mint on them."

"Mmm," she crooned, grateful for the fruit and mint to freshen her mouth.

He lifted another slice to her lips, set down the bowl, and picked up a cup of coffee.

"I think I am perfectly capable of holding the cup on my own."

He chuckled. "Ah, you don't like being pampered? But I like to feed you."

She'd never seen him like this, so relaxed, so . . . so unrestrained. His soft laughter ran through her, melted all her resolve to dress and return home. Pressing her lips to the edge of the cup, she waited for him to tip it.

A drop of coffee pooled in the middle of her lower lip, about to spill over. Before she could react, René leaned over and lapped up the sweetened liquid with his tongue.

"Oh!" Thought evaporated. His breath fell hot against her mouth, and she knew she wouldn't stop what was about to happen. His hand at the back of her head gently

drew her closer into him. His tongue slid upward to the
wet underside of her lip with only the barest of touches.

A soft whimper escaped her lips. "Should we be doing
this again?"

"Only if you've a mind to." His tongue touched one
corner of her mouth, sending an exquisite rush of heat
straight to her womb. His kisses traced a tender line to her
earlobe and then to her neck.

He eased back the covers, raised her knee, and kissed
the soft inside, his mouth sending a passionate message.
"We've had a night of it, haven't we, *chère*? Perhaps you
are feeling too tender to try again."

She started to say no, but he eased her from the bed, a
sultry look overcoming him. She clung to the bedsheet,
dragging it along with her. "What are you doing?"

"You owe me a dance." Snatching his shirt from where
he'd tossed it on the chair, he gently pulled it over her
head. Taking her hand, he led her to the middle of the
room.

"But there's no music."

Lightning split the sky and thunder shook the walls.
"There be our music, *chère*. Rolling around in the heavens."

He was so handsome, so devastatingly beautiful a man.
And powerful. Did he even know how very magnetic he
could be? Again, she noted the scars on his bare torso, but
something told her not to break the magic of the moment.
Instead, she smiled at him and slipped her hand into his in
a show of acquiescence.

"You are even lovelier when you smile," he said.

"And you as well, sir. You should do it more often."

Taking her in his arms, he moved them about the room,
all the while trailing kisses over her face and atop her
head. "Kissing is so underrated, don'cha know. It happens

to be one of my favorite things to do. Therefore, we should spend hours at it today. What do you think?"

She could only nod, reveling in the moment. Reveling in a side of this man she never knew existed. Yes, she would give him—no, she would give both of them—a day and another night together. She would savor every rich moment, experience him in any way he offered himself to her. She'd grapple with her emotions later.

He danced her about the room, through lightning blazing across the sky and thunder shaking the timbers. Then he paused. "Now it is time you had the pleasure of being bathed by my hand—in water scented with herbs that will relieve any tenderness, and then your body will be mine and mine will be yours."

Monday's noon hour had come and gone by the time René strolled into the bustling shipping office, the corner of one eye scraped and beginning to bloom with color. Bastien followed in his wake, looking the worse for wear.

Michel glanced at both of them. "What the devil happened to the two of you?"

Ignoring the question, René and Bastien greeted Meirs and Beauchamp, the two men off the *Endeavor* who'd been hired to lighten the heavy workload. From there, they moved to where Felice stood beside the new bookkeeper, who was seated at her old desk.

When René's gaze met hers, she quickly looked to the books, her cheeks flushing. A flash of memory coursed through him, of their time together and how he'd managed to taste every inch of her. He reckoned by the color rising to her face, she shared his visions.

Christ, he found her even more beautiful today. How the devil was he going to let her walk away and never see her again? At least her memory was etched in his soul and would likely remain there evermore.

She turned to her brother. "Why do you ask what happened to their faces when it's plain they got into it with each other? I doubt it's anything new where those two are concerned." She shot René a knowing look. "I am curious as to the why of it, though."

Fighting his intense physical reaction to her sheer presence, he merely shrugged and made his way over to his desk. Bastien, on the other hand, leaned a hip on the bookkeeper's desk and chuckled. "Suffice it to say, we paid a visit to the gentlemen's boxing club by invitation of Lord-High-and-Mighty. He got the worst of it."

Felice's jaw dropped. "You didn't."

"Has anyone seen my good pencil?" René was already at his desk, riffling through the drawer.

"When did you see it last?" Michel asked.

"When I left on Friday." He glanced at Felice. "Lord Mayhem didn't happen by, did he?"

Michel spoke up. "As a matter of fact, he did. He was in here looking for Felice, but she'd already gone home."

"Had I known my pencil was missing, I would've pounded him a bit harder." René sat back in his chair and tried to keep his attention off Felice. "That was my favorite writing instrument, and I intend to retrieve it."

He'd meet in private with Michel this evening, resign his position after she'd gone upriver. The thought left him feeling raw inside. He glanced about the room, his sense of hurt at leaving all this behind growing. Damn it, he'd broken his word to Michel; he couldn't stay. And there was no pretending that the debacle with Liberty Belle had never happened. By now, every ear in town had heard of the degrading fiasco. His gaze drifted to Felice again.

Her head snapped up and her face drained of color.

"Papa," she cried as she rushed toward the entry. "What are you doing here?"

René turned to see the elder Andrews walk into the room with Jean Robicheaux, one of the company attorneys, at his heels. Christ, he hadn't seen Justin Andrews since he'd gone upriver to have him sign some legal documents. The man looked as if he'd aged years, not months. Why, his hair was now completely white. Must have something to do with Abbott's betrayal.

Michel rose and made his way to where his father stood, but Felice was already in her father's arms. "I've come to petition the court on behalf of those slaves Abbott kept," Justin said. "According to Robicheaux here, it seems I have to purchase the slaves before I can set them free. But set them free I shall."

"What puzzles me," Michel said, "is how Abbott hid everything from us for so long."

"Indeed," Justin responded. "We learned today that Monsieur Farouche had been the cover for all of Abbott's affairs for years. If you recall, Farouche had a demeanor that suggested a certain class. Apparently, he'd been a merchant in France who'd run into financial difficulties, so while Abbott had the funds, Farouche had the profile to keep Abbott's extravagant lifestyle hidden. I intend to see to that run-down tenement he owns as well. Once Robicheaux apprised me of the situation, I couldn't get here fast enough."

"Good heavens," Felice said. "I was about an hour away from taking a steamer upriver. We would've missed each other. Now there's no need for me to go at all. You *will* be staying with me at the town house, won't you?"

"Unless you prefer that I board at Le Blanc House." He lifted the packet he held in his hand. "At some point, I would like to discuss this with you."

René shot Bastien a speaking glance. With everyone talking at once, his brother made his way to René's desk. "That packet Andrews has, is that the one from London you sent to him?"

"*Oui*," Bastien said. "Looks like whatever is in it has something to do with his daughter, don'cha know."

"Well, I wish to hell the information I sent for would arrive." Not that it mattered, he supposed, now that Felice had broken off with her fiancé. Nonetheless, with Ainsworth's penchant for taking sordid photogravures, René still wanted to look into the man's past.

Suddenly, the room grew silent, and everyone turned to the entry. "What the hell," Bastien muttered.

René turned to see four police officers walk through the door, led by their district captain.

"We're looking for René Thibodeaux," the lead officer announced.

René stood. "That would be me. What is this about?"

All four officers surrounded him, cudgels in hand. "Monsieur René Thibodeaux," the captain called out. "You are under arrest for the murder of Mrs. Liberty Belle Worth."

Chapter Twenty-Two

René eased himself onto the narrow cot shoved into one corner of the jail cell. He took a deep breath. Pain froze the air midway into his lungs. Stifling a groan, he fingered the raw area on his right side. Damn thugs probably cracked a rib. Maybe two.

Forced to stick with shallow breathing, he stared at the bare ceiling with the one eye not swollen shut and tried to make sense of this chilling turn of events. Christ, would someone—anyone—fill him in on the particulars? What the hell had happened to Liberty Belle? Who could've murdered her? All he knew was that he'd seen her home and then spent the next two nights and a day locked inside his town house with Felice.

Felice.

My one alibi.

A muscle ticked along his jawline. She was the last person he'd bring into this living nightmare. If vigilantes didn't end up lynching him tonight, and if he managed to get out of this mess unscathed, he'd ask Michel for an immediate transfer to Jamaica. No matter which way things went, his life in New Orleans was over. What a ludicrous joke—just when he'd decided to make a quiet exit from the decent life he'd built here, Providence stepped in to make certain there'd be no turning back.

His mind in a muddle, he glanced around the small cell with its clean brick walls and stone floor. At least there was something to be said for being locked up in a newly built jail here in the wealthy Garden District. Incarceration in the Fourth District would've meant a flea-infested blanket and piss-stained mattress. If that. He swiped a film of sweat off his brow with his dirty sleeve. Too bad whoever designed the place lacked the intelligence to position the windows properly. With no cross breeze, the holding area was muggy. Not to mention hot as hell.

The sound of conversation caught his attention. He stilled and listened to the rise of angry voices. Eyeing the doorway separating the three cells from the outer room, he could only catch sight of the lanky jailer with his booted feet atop his desk, a rifle across his lap, and a holstered revolver hanging off one hip.

A litany of Cajun curses erupted from a familiar voice. *Bastien.*

Thank the saints, you've come.

By the sound of things, his brother was undergoing a thorough search for weapons. And none too pleased about it. Despite René's miserable condition, a corner of his mouth curled as the volume and string of blasphemes increased. Bastien did not take kindly to being touched by anyone. Unless the fondling involved a lovely female— and by invitation only.

René swung his legs over the bed, pressed his palm against his side to support his injured ribs, then eased himself into a standing position. Making his way over to the cell's iron bars, he gripped them for support and waited.

Bastien stalked through the open doorway, muttering and tugging at the shirt cuffs beneath his tailored jacket.

One look at René's face and at the blood staining his once-white shirt, and Bastien halted. Color drained from his face. He cursed and broke into their native tongue. "What the devil happened to you?"

"Seems I ran into a few fists along the way to this fine establishment."

Bastien said nothing for a long moment, his formidable gaze raking René's disheveled appearance. "I know what a scrapper you are, so how many sonsofbitches did it take to hold you down and beat the hell out of you?"

René swiped the back of his hand over his sweaty brow again. "I doubt not a one from this precinct missed his golden opportunity to get some licks in on a Cajun."

Fury blazed in Bastien's eyes. "Well, it damn well won't happen again. I'll need to collect Vivienne, have her help me tend to you."

René shook his head and, trying for a breath, bit off another groan. "This is no fit place for her."

Bastien's eagle eyes watched René struggle for air. "Cracked ribs?"

"Most likely."

"You're going to need a couple of stitches alongside your eye, don'cha know. Vivienne, she be better at stitching up faces than I am, but I can take care of the rest. I'll collect some healing herbs from the back garden at Le Blanc House to take the swelling and soreness down."

René touched the side of his eye. The pain was so damn bad elsewhere, he hadn't realized the seriousness of the injury. "I doubt they'd let either one of you into my cell to tend to me. Besides, healing my injuries might not matter; they've got a hanging planned sometime around midnight. Or so I heard."

"Like hell, they will!"

René leaned his forehead against the bars. "I'm guilty

as charged, so they say. After the hanging, they intend to dump me in a bayou for the gators to feed on, then tell everyone I managed to escape. How about that for a tidy solution to a dastardly crime I didn't commit?"

Fresh blood seeped through a cut on his lip. He touched two fingers to the wound and came away with a smear of crimson. "Right now, what I could use is some water and a cloth to clean my face."

Bastien turned on his heel, ate up the floor with long strides, and bellowed at the jailer. "Get my brother a clean cloth and a bucket of water, damn your hide."

"Did you find out what happened to Liberty Belle?" René asked.

Bastien nodded. "I was at the meeting with our company attorneys, along with Justin, Michel, and the police commissioner. Liberty Belle was strangled. With your cravat."

René's jaw dropped. "*My* cravat?"

"*Oui*. No mistaking it was yours because your initials were found in one corner, and her maid swears to have seen you with her mistress."

"*Mon Dieu*. My necktie, of all things." René gripped the bars of the cell and lowered his voice. "Do you recall that I removed my jacket and cravat before I escorted her from Le Blanc House Saturday evening?"

"*Oui*."

"When I reached her residence and helped her off the buggy, she swiped my tie. Then she waved it about in the air like a white flag of surrender, daring me to go after it. Which would've meant following her as she scampered indoors. I wasn't about to go looking for more trouble, so I ignored her little game and drove off."

He shoved his hand through his hair and paced. "This

had to be Ainsworth's doing. We need those photographs he's got stored at the photogravure."

Bastien nodded. "I doubt her death was deliberate. Most likely, they were dallying in their erotic strangulation game and got carried away."

"What if he runs? I'll be certain to hang. Did you mention any of this at the meeting?"

"*Non*. I figured I'd make a midnight call on Fournier's shop first, help myself to a couple of those telltale images before we let the attorneys in on what we already know. We don't want them filing a search warrant and Ainsworth getting wind of it. He could destroy the evidence before the ink is even dry on the document."

"Do they have any idea as to when she was killed?"

"Her lady's maid found Liberty's body already cold in her bed on Sunday morning. She said it was around seven o'clock, after Liberty failed to come down to breakfast. I recall it being around ten when you two left the soiree Saturday evening, so the crime would've taken place sometime between when you dropped her off and when the maid found her. Did you go straight home?"

"*Non*. I drove out to the old Allard place." At the look on Bastien's face, René explained, "I didn't feel like returning to an empty house straightaway. Wanted to think."

"Did you happen to see anyone after you left her?"

René shook his head.

A chill ran down his spine. He'd be damned if he'd involve Felice. But he wasn't about to admit to anyone that he'd been with her from midnight Saturday until Monday morning. Once authorities got hold of Ainsworth's photographs and took him to trial, René would be in the clear. Then he'd get the hell out of town as planned. A wave of sorrow washed through him like a swollen river of mud.

Bastien studied René through narrowed eyes for a

long moment. "You're certain no one saw you after you left her?"

"Not a soul. Her maid and a few of the neighbors' servants saw me deliver Liberty to her door. She was so loud, I'm certain they easily overheard the conversation."

Bastien leaned a shoulder up against the bars and crossed his legs at the ankles. "You know gossip spreads like wildfire around here. People love a juicy scandal. Especially if it be a Thibodeaux in the thick of things, don'cha know. Some of the guests at Le Blanc House Saturday were outdoors when you left with Liberty. They heard you saying you'd like to strangle her."

"*Mon Dieu!*" René paced again. "How could this not be Ainsworth's doing? What if he's already left town?"

"Why should he? The weasel has no idea we're on to him. And since you're in custody, with everyone certain you're the criminal, I'll wager Lord Mayhem feels no pressure to leave the city. He's probably enjoying the whole fiasco, and already making plans to attend your trial."

"Humph. He'll likely bring a picnic lunch to the hanging as well."

A cacophony of chatter in the outer room brought their conversation to a halt. Bastien moved to the doorway, peered into the outer room, and returned to stand in front of René, a flash of humor in his eyes. "It appears the jailer, he be giving Justin and Michel a dutiful search for weapons. They not be liking it much."

"What the devil are they doing here?"

Bastien cocked a brow. "Perhaps they showed up to offer their support."

Despite the muggy air, another chill slithered down René's spine. Whatever had possessed him to risk taking

Felice to his bed? God Almighty, what had he gotten himself in to?

Justin marched in ahead of Michel and nearly stumbled to a halt. One look at René and fury mottled his skin. "Who did this to you?"

The jailer walked into the holding area, water slopping over the top of one of the two buckets he carried. His eyes darted around the room. His Adam's apple bouncing up and down, he set the buckets on the floor beside the cell's bars and turned to leave. "You'll have to be usin' yer pocket handkerchief, cuz we don't got no extry rags."

René spread his arms wide, palms up. "The square of fabric you refer to happens to be in the pocket of my jacket—the one your colleague stole off my person, don'cha know."

The jailer shot René a sneer. "No, I don't 'don'cha know,' you dirty Cajun."

"Indeed, my brother is rather dirty." Bastien removed his clean, folded handkerchief, handed it to René, and peered into the buckets. "Don't tell me the empty one is intended for a piss pot?"

"Ye got that right."

Curses fell from Bastien's mouth. "You expect your prisoner to not only reach through the bars to clean the blood off himself, but he has to aim through the bars to take a piss?"

"I ain't opening the door to this here cell, so that's jess what he's a gonna have to do. Yes siree."

Michel, having been silent throughout the discourse, eyed the jailer's scraped knuckles. "If I were you, I'd turn around and hie out of here before you get some of what you did to this man who is under your care."

The jailer glanced from one man to the other, then

shoved his hands in his pockets. "You ain't got no right to be telling me what to do. I—"

"Do you know who we are?" Justin growled. "We refrain from asserting our authority over anyone unless they've done something so foul as to require it, but you and your cohorts have done exactly that. You'll have the devil to pay now. When I leave here, I shall go directly to the mayor and the police commissioner. By day's end, you and every single man who laid a hand on Mr. Thibodeaux will find himself removed from his position and gone from the city for good. If you know what's good for you, leave."

The jailer backed out the door, his pock-marked face flushed. "Well, I cain't very well leave this here place empty, so I'll be sitting square in the other room 'til my replacement shows up at the next shift."

"Then you do just that," Michel said.

With the jailer gone from the holding area, Justin turned to René. "Did you murder that woman?"

René locked gazes with Felice's father. The hair on the back of his neck stood on end. "*Non, monsieur.* I did not."

A long moment stretched out while Justin stared at René as though he were searching his very soul for the truth of René's words. Then the elderly man gave a slight nod and stepped back in line with Michel. "Our company attorneys are the finest around. They're working on setting you free now."

He reached in his pocket, extracted a clean hand-kerchief, and handed it to René. "Use mine as well."

Michel followed suit with his snowy white hand-kerchief. "There'll be a trial, of course, but our attorneys are good. They'll find a way to set you free."

Bastien lifted his shoulder off the cell's bars. "Seeing

as how my brother overheard some locals who plan to take
the law into their own hands by way of a hanging, might
we borrow a few guards off the docks and position them
around this building tonight?"

Michel made his way to the doorway, where he checked
on the jailer's position, then returned to address Bastien.
"See to it your brother is kept safe by whatever means you
find necessary."

He turned to René. "Your counsel has arrived, so we
shall take our leave. Rest assured we're with you all the
way on this. Just tell them everything you know and let
them take it from there."

Bastien waited until the two men made their exit and
said, "I'll collect Vivienne and have Henri bring in some
ice for the swelling, a few clean towels, and a fresh shirt.
Anything else?"

"*Non*." René watched Bastien disappear through the
doorway, then made his way back to the cot, suddenly so
fatigued he could barely stand, let alone bother to clean
himself up. Easing onto the thin mattress, he grimaced as
he stretched out onto his left side, facing the wall. He
shut his eyes, his head swimming, his body aching.

A dull sense of self-disgust passed through him. In the
past, he'd always stuck with one woman at a time, had
always been careful to make clear his intention of remaining a bachelor, had always managed to end a relationship
on good terms. But Liberty Belle? Whatever had possessed him to get mixed up with her was beyond him
now. His gut had told him she was one to avoid, but he'd
ignored his instincts. Had he thought he could overlook
her demanding ways and the sharp edge that lay beneath
her appealing veneer so long as there was no depth to the

relationship? When had she begun playing the kind of games that had ended in her death?

As he waited for the attorney, he drifted off, a vision of Felice swirling in his head. Whatever took place hereafter, he'd not so much as mention her name. He'd be damned if he'd involve her in this mess, which would likely become the scandal of the decade.

Chapter Twenty-Three

"Well, look at you, living in the lap of luxury. Why, they even provided you a pillow on which to rest your head."

A lilting voice, so familiar, so bloody sweet-sounding to his ears, pulled René from the drugged sleep he'd fallen into. He lay still for a long moment, his face to the wall, his pulse tripping. This wasn't good. Not at all. "Mockery is not courteous, Felice. What are you doing here?"

"I've come bearing gifts in Henri's stead," she said. "A clean shirt, towels, and, as per Bastien's instructions, some ice for your swollen eye. As for my greeting, do forgive my attempt at a lighthearted approach to your terrible situation. How are you feeling?"

Gingerly, René rolled over, forced his aching body into a sitting position, and fixed her with a steady gaze. "Go home."

Eyes flaring and jaw slackening, she gasped at his appearance. "Good Lord, René. What have those monsters done to you?"

With a grunt, he rose and made his way to where she stood just outside the iron bars. He took note of the water bucket and piss pot, now sitting inside the holding cell. The hair stood up on the back of his neck. Had he slept so soundly he'd failed to hear the turn of the jailer's key?

Failed to hear the wooden pails being repositioned? *Mon Dieu*. Anyone could've knifed him in the back and sent him swimming with the gators.

He'd also failed to hear the ruckus Felice had no doubt made getting past the jailer. What the hell kind of personal search had she been forced to submit to? he wondered. "Where is your lady's companion?"

She shot him a pointed look. "You know full well she is at my brother's home, caring for his wife and newborn."

"You should not have come at all, let alone with no chaperone to accompany you, *chère*. It is not safe for you here. Any number of wicked things could happen, and here I'd be, locked up with no way to protect you. Go home."

With an indifferent shrug, she dismissed his concern. "Actually, I came along with the company watchmen Papa sent to oversee your safety, so I was in fine company. A pity when it becomes necessary for guards to guard the guards. In any case, your time here is about to end."

"What makes you say that?"

"Once I sign a sworn statement admitting I was with you in your own home during the very hours when Mrs. Worth was murdered, you shall be set free."

"*Non!*" Gripping the bars, he lowered his voice, and his words left his throat in a feral growl. "You must not breathe a word of our time together. To do so would mean your ruin."

"Foolish man. When it comes to choosing between my reputation or you hanging by the neck until dead, I have no hesitation in selecting the former."

Merde! He couldn't have her involved in this disaster. For both their sakes, he needed to cut her out of his life.

For good.

But how was he to get rid of her without causing her

undue pain? He couldn't tell her about Ainsworth. Not yet anyway. Nor could he reveal Bastien's midnight raid on Monsieur Fournier's Photogravure lest word somehow got out.

The truth.

He could at least divulge a bit of what had happened. "As you well know, I am innocent, but I did not go straight home after I delivered Liberty Belle to her residence."

Her brows furrowed. "Where did you go?"

"To the old Allard place."

"Where you took me after dinner the first night I arrived?"

He nodded. "So, you see, until I returned home and found you at my gate, I saw no one and can provide no alibi."

"Oh, dear."

"I have the best attorneys, and your father intends to hire a detective to find whoever murdered her. Once this person is discovered, I'll be set free. When such time arrives, I shall leave New Orleans."

She stilled. "For good?"

At the thought of leaving his home, at the thought of never seeing her again, a wild shaft of pain tore through him. He could feel himself beginning to fall apart. He tried to draw air deep into his lungs, but it barely seeped in. He managed a nod despite the pain. "I'm through trying to build a life here, *chère.* And after this debacle, which the tongue-waggers will never forget, I have no desire to remain."

"Since I do not intend to remain in New Orleans either, what does it matter if my reputation is torn to shreds? I care little about what others think of me, and you'd be set free."

His heart stammered and his mouth filled with cotton.

"Damn it, Felice. Your brother warned me that if I were ever to lay a hand on you, not only would I never work for the company again, he'd have me blackballed from the shipping industry worldwide. I have worked my tail off to get where I am. If I have any hope of a decent life, I'll need a transfer to another post, but if you reveal our time together, I will be left with nothing. I can take up thieving again, which I am damn good at, or I can hang on to life by my fingernails. I do not intend to do either."

She stood in silence, staring at him for a long moment, as if disoriented. And then, with a lift of her chin, bold resolve appeared in her eyes. "Well, then, let's get on with things, shall we? I retrieved a clean shirt for you from those you've stored at the office. They were nicely folded until that ill-tempered jailer in the other room insisted on inspecting everything I had in hand. And with no regard whatsoever for your personal items, the ornery dolt."

Anger shot through him like a hot arrow. "Exactly what manner of search were you forced to submit to?"

She shrugged a shoulder. "The matter is done with, and of no consequence."

His jaw clenched. "What happened?"

Amusement did a ghost dance across her mouth. "When it came to laying hands upon a female member of the Andrews clan, the oaf was wise enough not to risk the consequences. And in my silent but menacing manner, I *dared* the coward to try touching me."

"Oh, Christ," René muttered. "*Vous êtes une fille naïve.*"

"Really, René? Do not underestimate my ability to look out for my own well-being. And your remark does not signify, because I am far from naïve. As you well know."

Frustrated, he scraped a hand through his hair, only to realize the motion was too painful. "I only meant you were naïve to have risked coming here."

"Humph." She set down a shiny tin pail lined with straw. "Here's the ice. I also brought along a bar of Pears soap."

"I do not use Pears soap," he growled. "Go home."

"In due time." She passed the shirt and towels through the bars. "Set these on the cot, then come back here and let me help you clean your face."

"I can damn well wash myself."

"Seeing as how you have no mirror, I think it will be helpful for me to reach through the bars and at least assist your endeavors. Are you even aware of all the damage done to that gorgeous face of yours? Thankfully, your nose seems to have escaped the pounding."

He mumbled another curse, deposited the shirt and towels on the cot, then carried over the stool at the foot of the bed to where she stood. It took all the strength he had in him to lift the water bucket atop it. Taking up the three handkerchiefs he'd been previously given—figuring they'd be softer than the towels—he dipped them into the water and gave them a squeeze. Moving to the bars, he handed them to her.

She stepped closer and gently set her fingertips beneath his chin to steady him. Her head tilted back and forth as she studied him, then carefully set about dabbing the damp cloth along one side of his face.

It was either close his eyes or focus on her—on her creamy, flawless skin, on those intelligent eyes holding emotion that could not be expressed in words. His gaze dropped to her lovely, lush mouth—a mouth he'd so recently spent hours exploring with his own. Despite the pain in every muscle, his body reacted to her.

She paused. A question formed in her eyes. "Did I hurt you?"

Embarrassed, he stepped back, snatched the blood-stained cloth from her hand and rinsed it in the bucket. "I can manage this myself," he growled. "Better yet, I'll wait for Bastien, so go home and don't come back."

His voice sounded all wrong, as if it had come from someplace outside himself. Damn it, she was trying to help while what he wanted to do was reach through the metal bars separating them and hold her close. He wanted her. Wanted her to fill the hollowness inside him—just as being with her over the weekend had worked to fill a lifetime of emptiness. He couldn't do this to her, couldn't place her in harm's way because of his own selfish, unfulfilled needs—couldn't involve her in this catastrophe for more reasons than he could count.

"Stop being so stubborn," she ordered. "Bastien has gone along with my father and brother to meet with the mayor, so he'll be a while. And why are you suddenly acting so strange? One would think you'd suffered brain damage, the way you are behaving. Frankly, I find the notion somewhat dismaying."

He held his side as he tried in vain to gulp in air. "Pardon, *chère*. I am not myself. Rest assured, my mind has not suffered in the manner you suggest."

Something in her demeanor softened. She stretched out her hand, palm up. "Please," came her soft reply. "Do me the favor of giving me the cloth. Allow me to finish cleaning your face."

The velvet resonance of her voice soaked right through his skin and vibrated in his bones. He returned to stand close to her, his heart beating a hard tattoo against his chest. This time he closed his eyes against their intimate proximity, but doing so only served to heighten his awareness of her soft touch, of her clean, magnolia-scented skin, of her sweet breath falling softly against his mouth.

Mon Dieu. He must send her away before Bastien arrived. If not, his brother would take one look at the two of them and know something besides mere friendship existed between them. When it came to women and intimacy, Bastien was an astute observer of the human condition.

She touched the corner of his mouth with the damp cloth.

He winced and opened his eyes.

"Sorry," she murmured. She stood so close that the heat emanating from her body mingled with his. "There, this is the last of it. Now off with your shirt and don the clean one."

Once again, he fought a clawing hunger to reach through the bars and drag her to him as some caged beast would. "While you watch, I suppose?"

She lowered her chin and set a hard gaze on him. "It's not as though I hadn't seen every inch of you during our oh-so-intense love affair."

He paused with his shirt half off. His chest tightened, and a dull ache settled in the vicinity of his heart. Casting off the garment and tossing it onto the cot, he shoved aside all thought of their time together. Here was his opening— an opportunity not only to remove her from harm's way, but to dismiss her from his life for good.

Ainsworth would be held accountable for Liberty Belle's murder, and things would soon be set to rights. No one need know of his affair with Felice. Her reputation would be left unscathed, and then he'd ask Michel for another assignment and leave this town forever.

Every nerve in his body rebelled at what he was about to do, at the hurt his act was bound to inflict. Forcing a sneer, he turned to face her.

"Our *love* affair, Felice? We spent thirty-six hours fornicating, and you have the nerve to call what we engaged in a *love* affair? It seems you are very naïve after all, *chère*."

She took a step back, her face growing pale. For a long

moment, she did not speak. Then she took in a long, slow breath and on the exhale said, "Are you saying the time I spent curled up in your arms while you read to me for hours was merely a prelude to another round of fornication?"

"You're catching on," he lied, as another little part of him died.

Her chin quivered. "What about when you insisted on bathing me, on playing chess while you had on nothing but your trousers whilst I wore your shirt? Was that just another round of seduction? Of making sure this naïve woman would continue fornicating?"

He forced his gaze to hold steady. He was reminded of the many other places he'd touched her during their glorious time together. Of how he'd taught her all manner of delicious, intimate things she hadn't known existed.

Pain slammed into his chest, yet he went on. "That's about the way of things, Mademoiselle Andrews."

"I see," she said softly, her gaze dropping to her feet. "Perhaps it would be best if I were to take my leave."

Christ! While he'd been sticking a knife in her heart and twisting, he'd managed to carve out his own with a spoon. His next words caught in his throat. He swallowed hard, then forced them out. "*Oui.* You should go."

She turned and started to exit the room. Then she paused. "You think I'm an imbecile, don't you?"

"*Non.* You were simply ripe for seduction." He managed a nonchalant shrug. "I merely took advantage of the moment."

"So, you preyed on a young woman who was attracted to you?"

"Indeed. And for that I must apologize."

"No need to apologize. I quite enjoyed being your prey. What say you now, Monsieur Thibodeaux?"

A part of him froze, then separated from what was taking place, as if to observe the scene from a far corner of the room. "Go," was all he could manage.

That stubborn chin of hers lifted again, and a storm flashed in her eyes. "You really must consider me a stupid cow if you think I actually believe the pile of rubbish you just tried to feed me."

She turned and disappeared from his sight.

Stunned, he gripped the cell bars, leaned his forehead against the hard metal, and closed his eyes against the sight of the empty doorway. For whatever was left of his worthless life, it was going to hurt like hell, knowing that while she'd live on in his heart, he'd never again hold her in his arms.

Chapter Twenty-Four

Mind and emotions in a whirl, Felice rushed past the jailer only to backtrack and stare at his bruised knuckles. "Why, you lout. You were one of those mistreating your prisoner, weren't you?"

He opened his mouth to reply, but a chair scraped behind her. "It won't happen again, Mademoiselle Andrews," came a deep voice.

She spun around. Picou, the shipping company's lead guard, sat in one corner, his brawny arms crossed over an expansive chest. Good heavens, had he heard the conversation in the other room? Had the jailer?

"Monsieur Picou. I did not see you there. Hadn't realized you'd come inside. Thank you for your time."

He nodded. "The other guards, they be outside. Nothin' bad will come to our boss man, now we be standin' watch."

"Good." As intimidating as the Cajun appeared, she doubted a kinder, gentler man existed. With his wiry black beard, strapping size, and fierce appearance, any man who didn't know him would pause before attempting to cross him. He had great respect for René, as did all the men he employed. The realization that René was in safe hands sent a wave of relief over her.

She spoke loudly enough for the jailer to hear. "I

imagine by the time my father and brother finish meeting with the mayor and police commissioner, these bullies will think twice about taking the law into their own hands."

Picou shot a hard glance at the jailer. "We got our instructions, don'cha know. Should they make any trouble, we're to hang 'em high."

She gasped.

A corner of his mouth tipped up. "By their ankles, *mam'selle*. Not their necks. We're to leave them for the commissioner to take down. Or not, as he sees fit."

"Oh my." She felt rather than heard the jailer's reaction. "You are efficient. As usual, Monsieur Picou. Good day."

"*Bonne journée, mademoiselle.*"

Exiting the jailhouse, she assured the other sentries she was quite capable of making her way home on her own. She hurried along Rue St. Charles in the oppressive heat. As rivulets of perspiration trickled down her spine, she decided to take a deserted short cut between Rue Iberville and Rue Bienville.

An elegantly dressed man strolled toward her. The late afternoon sun formed a nimbus behind him, obscuring his features and making it impossible to discern who it was, yet there was something familiar in the way he carried himself.

He paused directly in front of her, effectively blocking her way.

Émile Vennard! The wealthy Frenchman who'd fathered René and Bastien. Here stood the last person she'd expected—or wanted—to run in to. No wonder his movements seemed familiar—both his sons carried themselves in a similar manner.

"Mademoiselle Andrews." He greeted her with a touch of his fingertips to the brim of his stovepipe hat, his accent that of a well-born Frenchman. "We've not met. I am Monsieur Émile Vennard."

"I know who you are. You were Mrs. Worth's escort the day your son and I were in the sweet shop on Rue Dauphine."

At the mention of René, the man's lips curved into a half smile, one that traveled nowhere near his eyes.

Those eyes.

They were the bluest of blues—the very color Bastien had inherited. Vennard wore his graying hair and beard trimmed short, in a manner similar to Bastien's. However old Vennard might be, his olive skin remained remarkably free of any visible signs of age. He had to be in his midfifties, seeing as how René was thirty-four. The two brothers had inherited their father's height and splendid physical appearance. But could personal style be passed from father to sons as well? Despite having been raised shoeless and in near poverty in the bayou, and even though they'd never spent time with a father who refused to acknowledge them, René and Bastien's impeccable manner of dress was comparable to Vennard's.

His gaze swept over her from head to toe. "How unfortunate for me that we have never formally met. *Quel dommage.*"

What a pity, he said? Oh, the man's arrogance virtually clung to him like a cloud, seeming to mingle with his too-sweet cologne. Had no one informed him that the air in this part of the world was far too heavy for such a cloying scent?

Despite the heat, the manner in which he continued to study her sent a chill sweeping across her skin. "I am most eager to reach my home, Monsieur Vennard, so if you will kindly step aside, I shall be on my way."

Vennard gave a slight bow of his head, but did not step aside. A flick of his wrist and the elaborately gilded handle of his walking stick flashed in the ebbing sunlight. His gaze traveled the length of her body once more.

Her skin crawled anew.

"How are you faring, now that your lover is soon to be executed?" he asked. "Won't his hanging leave you with no one to warm your bed?"

How could he possibly know of my tryst with René?

"How is it you know me by name when we've never been introduced?"

He cocked a brow. "I would imagine anyone who knows the people of consequence in this town is aware of who you are. And everyone is aware that you are affianced to a proper English lord. What they might not know as yet is that you've recently taken up with an improper man. One of ill repute, and soon to hang no less. Sooner or later, gossip manages to leak out, no matter how discreet one has been—especially when it is such a delicious scandal."

Was that a veiled threat? How dare he goad her. "What are you insinuating?"

He said nothing, but something in his demeanor told her he meant her no good.

"Furthermore," she said, "you have the nerve to stand here in front of me while your son faces such a terrible fate? Shouldn't you be doing something to help set him free?"

"Humph." His right hand gripped the handle of his walking stick so hard, his knuckles turned pale. "I figured sooner or later one of those two mongrels was bound to cross the line and end up swinging from a rope."

Had she heard him right? "Mongrels, you say?"

"I ordered his mother to drown both boys at birth, but

would she listen? Instead, she hid them from me, creating years of trouble for everyone in this town."

She stared into his eyes disbelievingly. "You cannot be serious."

He took a step closer. "The two of them are a stain on society."

Refusing to retreat from his menacing stance, she held her ground. "You also cast off their mother once you tired of her. Wasn't disposing of a woman as powerful as Odalie Thibodeaux taking a rather dangerous risk? I'm surprised she hasn't leveled a wicked voodoo curse upon your dark soul."

"Oh, but she did. She cursed me with those boys, then purposely trained them up as street thieves to humiliate me."

For a long moment she stood frozen in place as she realized this was a blackhearted man who cared only for himself. Suddenly, she had a new understanding of the cruel life René and his brother must have endured during their growing years. This deep awareness grew into a tangible, sickening reality. Lord, what they must have had to do to survive in a town where everyone reviled them.

For a scant moment, her heart even held a thin thread of pity for their cold-as-ice mother. Like his sons, Vennard must have been an exceedingly attractive man in his younger years. No doubt women found him beguiling. It likely hadn't taken much coaxing for him to draw Odalie in and take his pleasure with her while giving nothing in return but empty promises. She must have cared deeply to allow him to return again and again until she'd borne three misbegotten children, only to be cruelly cast aside. But could a mother actually resort to using her children as a means of punishing their father?

Good Lord!

"You, Monsieur Vennard, are the most despicable creature I have ever encountered. I have asked you nicely to step aside. Now I am telling you, get out of my way."

He lowered his chin and glowered at her through narrowed eyes. "It would behoove you to treat me with respect, Mademoiselle Andrews."

She glanced at his walking stick, at the way he'd shifted the grip in his hand as if to extract something hidden within. How odd. What did he want of her? Well, she'd have none of whatever it might be. And she'd be damned if she'd allow him to intimidate her.

Mustering a look of defiance, she forced calm into her voice. "I am well aware it is common practice to carry a sword sheathed within a cane, Monsieur Vennard. You would do well not to attempt to intimidate me, for I have quite a temper when provoked."

He gave a soft snort and took another step closer.

Anger heated her blood. "Not only was I raised by scrappy brothers, but I learned a certain martial art during my travels in Asia. Had I a need to defend myself, I could easily take command of your weapon. Are you aware that the tendons behind the heels and knees are an ideal place to target an opponent?"

"Silly girl. Your blustering only serves to amuse me." Nonetheless, a widening of his irises darkened his eyes to cobalt.

"Oh dear, I nearly forgot about the wicked hatpin holding my bonnet in place." She tapped the jeweled end. "The sting of the hornet, so say men who've been struck by one of these vicious little things. I could have this one embedded in your eye before you knew what hit you."

The brow over his right eye twitched in response.

She nearly laughed.

He sucked in a haughty breath, his nostrils flaring. "It

would seem you are not much of a lady after all. It's no wonder you have taken carnal pleasure in the bed of a corrupt bastard."

Oh, things had gone too far. "Words are a luxury I reserve for persons I choose to converse with, Monsieur Vennard. I no longer wish to speak to you." She stepped around him and hurried off, feeling an urgent need to bathe away more than just the perspiration trickling down her spine.

Reaching the town house, she extracted a key from a pocket hidden within her skirts and let herself into the courtyard, slamming and locking the gate none too quietly.

A rush of emotion left her suddenly weak. She sank into one of the garden's wrought-iron chairs and contemplated her encounter while she caught her breath.

"Are you all right, *mam'selle?*"

She looked up to see Marie, who'd become a trusted ally over the years. "Not quite, but I'll manage."

Marie's brows knitted together. "You is in a sweat, *mam'selle*. How can I help you? Would you like a cool bath?"

"Not just yet. I need a bit of a rest. I've much to think through, and then we shall have a chat." Felice stood and managed a weary smile. "I could use a glass of your wonderful iced lemonade, though. That is, if you've a mind to make it."

"I'll bring it right up."

Making her way up the stairs to the main quarters, Felice stepped inside, and there stood her father. "Papa. I didn't expect you back so soon. Tell me what has transpired since last I saw you."

His eyes narrowed. "First off, what has happened to you? You look a fright."

Tears filled her eyes. She blinked hard. She wasn't a woman prone to weeping when sad. Angry tears were something else, however, and they threatened to cascade down her cheeks now.

A black cat with a white-tipped tail strutted out from around a table and curled about her father's legs.

"Is that Midnight, Abbott's cat?"

"Indeed." Her father leaned down and picked up the feline. It curled up in his arms and began purring. "Found it in the garden at his home—well, soon to be my home, once the legalities are taken care of. I'll return him to the office, where he belongs."

She brushed a hand over Midnight's thick black coat. "I wondered what had happened to the little mouser."

"Answer my question, Felice. What the devil's gone on? You look as if you've seen a ghost."

Crushed with sudden fatigue, she removed her hat, tossed it onto a side table, then moved to the blue velvet divan and sat, her breath leaving her lungs in a great rush. "I might indeed have seen a ghost, Papa. A ghost of a man."

She brushed her fingertips over the corners of her eyes, and as he sat beside her, he clasped her hands in his. "You're trembling, child. What's happened?"

"I've just come from seeing René. I fear he has quite given up on living." Her voice caught. "I . . . I'm afraid for him, Papa. It's as though the very life force has gone out of him."

Chapter Twenty-Five

"I would not wish to alarm you, Papa, but since René's arrest, he is no longer the vibrant man we knew. He said even if he escapes hanging, he is finished with this town. He intends to ask Michel for a transfer to another port."

"Oh no. We cannot allow him to leave, not when Michel is poised to offer René his own position in the company."

Stunned, Felice turned to face her father. "When was this decided? And why?"

"Recently. Ever since I can recall, Michel has had a yearning to toss his hat into the political arena. He also has a new addition to a large family, and several of his children need reining in or they'll run wild—or wilder than they already are. And he's just learned that our current mayor has no intention of seeking reelection. He strongly suggested Michel would make an excellent candidate and said he would back him should he decide to accept the endorsement."

She leaned her head on her father's shoulder and released a sigh. "René feels his reputation is beyond repair, no matter the outcome of the trial. I think this is the ultimate humiliation for a man who has worked hard to overcome his parentage and difficult childhood. He says no one will forget what has happened, and he seems determined to move on. I'll admit, his announcement shook me to the core, but I don't blame him one bit."

"We're working on establishing his innocence, Felice. Rest assured it's not over for him in this town. Once this crisis passes and he has the opportunity to take Michel's place, a highly respected position, he may change his mind. Bastien tells us that come tomorrow, he'll possess proof enough to have the charges against his brother dropped."

She reached over and stroked Midnight's head. "Really? I wonder what Bastien plans to produce?" Could it have anything to do with the intimate hours she'd spent with René? Surely not, if René forbade her to come forward in his defense. No, there had to be something else, but what?

Her father studied her through wise and perceptive eyes. "You care very much for René, don't you?"

Guilt flamed her cheeks. He couldn't possibly know what had gone on between René and her. Papa had only arrived from upriver this morning. She swallowed the lump in her throat. "Of course I care. He is one of our most important employees. I've worked alongside him for nearly a month, and I'd be the first to say he's about as indispensable as Michel."

They sat quietly for a long while. She was unable to get her thoughts to coalesce into any semblance of order, could practically hear her heart breaking in two. "René lied through his teeth to get rid of me when I went to visit him in jail. I fear he is at such a low point in his life that he'd as soon go to the gallows as walk this earth another day."

Her father's penetrating gaze seemed to look into the very depths of her soul. Had he guessed? Did he know that she had fallen for René?

He sat back and ran his hand over the cat sleeping in his

lap. "When are you and Lord Ainsworth planning to wed? Assuming I grant permission, of course."

Her insides jerked at the question. It was hardly a coincidence that he'd make mention of Mayhew right now. She rubbed circles at her temples. "There's to be no wedding. I've broken off with him."

"Pray tell why."

She gave her head a shake. "Things weren't right. We weren't a good fit. I made a mistake in thinking I was in love with him. Besides, I am not suitable for the life of a duchess. I am too independent and rebellious. Not only would I be bored to death, I would feel shackled by all the restrictions placed upon me."

"I see," he said softly.

Marie brought in the iced lemonades and set them on a small table in front of them. Felice reached for hers, then clasped her unsteady fingers together and slipped them back in her lap.

Her father set his hands over hers and squeezed. "You still tremble."

She took a deep breath. "I bumped into René's father on my way home. Or should I say, he ran into me."

"What the devil did he do to you?"

"Nothing. Oh, he tried to intimidate me, but honestly, I think he did me a great favor."

"Favor or not, you stay away from Émile Vennard. He is not a decent man in any sense of the word."

Something about her father's strong reaction to the mention of Vennard gave her pause. But with everything else going on, she decided not to question him. "Worry not, Father. I saw through his thin veneer of civility."

"Then what was the favor he did you?"

She grew quiet as the shadows in the room lengthened in the waning light. Sipping her lemonade, she stared across the room at a large painting of her mother, sitting on a blanket under a banyan tree, her bonnet and an open book cast to one side, a King Charles spaniel in her lap.

"Vennard told me he'd ordered Odalie to drown the boys at birth. Can you imagine a parent thinking so little of a babe?"

"And how was his saying such a terrible thing doing you a favor?"

She gave a nod to the canvas. "Look at that composition of *Maman*. It is still my very favorite depiction of her."

He huffed a breath of frustration. "What in the world does an oil painting of your mother have to do with Vennard's accosting you and wanting his bastard sons drowned?"

"Years ago, when you'd bring me to town and go off to the shipping office, I would sit in this very place for hours while I stared at the painting. In time, it seemed as if I could step right inside and sit next to *Maman*. Visit with her."

She squeezed her father's hand. He squeezed back. "I know this sounds strange, but I feel as if I got to know her."

She glanced at her father. His eyes had grown moist. "Hear me out, Papa. Something similar occurred when Vennard said the boys should've been drowned at birth. At first it was such a shock that all I could do was lock gazes with him. Suddenly, it was similar to when I used to stare at this painting—the world seemed to fall away, and it was as if I became privy to René's life. I realized that even though his mother taught him to steal, and the townspeople shooed both boys away, they desperately wanted to belong."

She blinked back tears. "Oh, Papa. He and Bastien may have stolen a ship full of rum and bartered it back to get hired by Michel and Cameron, but look what they've done for the company. Look how they've bettered themselves. And look how the townspeople have accepted them . . . until now, that is."

"Drink your lemonade" was all her father said, but he leaned his head back on the divan and studied the painting of his wife. The only sound in the room was the ticking of the ormolu clock on the mantel.

She sipped her drink, set it back on the table, and sighed. "I always thought René a handsome man. I suspect most women think so. Today, after meeting his despicable father, I realize what made René truly attractive was that dazzling fire burning inside him. I just hope the flame hasn't gone permanently cold. I doubt I've ever seen a man so miserable as he was this afternoon."

"You are so like your mother," her father finally said, his words little more than a whisper. "It amazes me that even though you never knew her, not only do you greatly resemble her, your disposition and mannerisms are so much like hers that you continually catch me off guard. And now you have shown me yet another side of her that lives on in you; she, too, had deep insight and caring for her fellow man."

Her father gave her a half smile. "All these years, I had no idea this painting came alive that way for you. It was my favorite as well. I wonder what would happen if, in your mind's eye, you were to take your mother out of this scene and place René there in her stead. I wonder what manner of conversation the two of you would share."

The shock of his words drew Felice to attention. Oh, Lord, he couldn't possibly know how painful it would be for her to imagine herself sitting beside René in such a bucolic setting.

"Go ahead," he urged. "Try it and see what happens."

Her brain tossed about, searching for what to say next, but it was the dog in the painting that caught her attention.

She knew what to do.

Scrambling off the sofa, she hurried toward the stairs leading to her bedroom. "Miz Sassy. She's what René needs."

She glanced over her shoulder at her father's puzzled look. "René's dog. He's quite fond of her. She'll give him comfort. I'll need to change my clothes, then take her to him."

"You dare not go out now, Felice. It's near dark."

In moments she was back down the stairs, dressed in her masculine riding gear, her hair tucked under a cap. "I'll be back in an hour or so. Don't worry—I've been out like this before."

She scooted out the door before her father could make another attempt to dissuade her, and rushed over to René's home. She rang the bell for Monique to let her in. Then, snatching up the pup and its leash, she hurried to the stables at the rear of her own town house. She saddled Jingo and, with Miz Sassy in her arms, guided the gelding through the courtyard.

Her father stepped from the shadows. "I'm going with you."

"But—"

"No buts about it, daughter. You are not traipsing through this town alone after dark."

She paused long enough to catch the stubborn glint in his eye. She knew that look, and it meant trouble if she fought him. She handed the pup to him. "Here. Hold her while I mount up, then close the gate behind me and hop on."

A sense of joy bubbled up at what they were about to

do. She nestled Miz Sassy in front of her and held out her hand to her father. "Use my foot for leverage."

"I know what to do," he grumbled. "I still take my daily ride around the plantation."

Despite his age, he was nimble, and easily seated himself behind her.

"Aren't we the pair?" she said, and urged Jingo forward.

"You mean threesome," Papa replied. "Again, you are so much like your mother. I find it somewhat disconcerting at times."

Felice chuckled. "She rode her horse through town at night?"

"No, but she did whatever she damn well pleased. And was never without her dog."

They rode to the jailhouse in silence under the cool glow of moonlight. Miz Sassy held still in Felice's lap, but her ears were perked up, and she stared straight ahead, as if she intuitively knew where they were headed.

"You'll wait outside, won't you?" Felice said when they reached their destination. One of the guards took the reins and held the dog while both dismounted.

"But of course." Her father turned to speak with the sentry while Felice hurried inside.

"You cain't bring a hound in here," the jailer growled when she entered the facility.

"Of course she can," her father announced as he trailed in behind her. "Didn't the mayor and police commissioner pay you a visit and give you a good talking to? You have your orders to make sure that your only prisoner is adequately cared for until his trial. We are here to see to his comfort as well. If you have a problem with that, we can send for the commissioner."

The jailer's jaw twitched and his face colored. "Won't be necessary."

"Consider yourself fortunate to still be sitting here. The mayor wanted to run the bunch of you out of town after what you and your cohorts did to Monsieur Thibodeaux. Not to mention what you had *planned* to do."

She shot her father a frown over her shoulder. "I thought you agreed to wait outside." To the jailer she said, "I won't be long."

Her father looked at Picou. "If we leave the dog for the night, will you see she goes outside to relieve herself from time to time?"

"*Oui.*"

The jailer sputtered.

Her father shot the man a dark look.

The jailer dropped his chin to his chest and muttered under his breath.

"Now, Papa," Felice said. "This time, I insist you remain out here while I deliver the pup to René. I'll be but a moment."

He nodded. "You are indeed as stubborn as your mother."

Miz Sassy began to whine and wiggle in Felice's arms, her nose and ears pointing toward the doorway to the other room. "Everything's going to be just fine," Felice murmured. "Your master is eager to see you too."

She stepped into the room where René was being held and paused, her heart tripping over itself. He stood gripping the bars with both hands, his jaw clenched and the look in his eye severe. Or was his expression harsh because he was barely holding himself together?

She'd done the right thing, bringing his dog here. She was sure of it now. She approached him and held the pup up close to where he stood.

René reached through the bars and stroked Miz Sassy's head. "What are you doing here, girl?" The dog began wiggling and whining, trying to squeeze through the bars to get closer to René.

The jailer shuffled into the room. "Mr. Andrews done give me orders to put that mutt into the cell with you, but you gotta leave the leash with the guard in the other room."

While she set Miz Sassy down long enough to remove the leash, the jailer attached one end of a manacle to René's wrist, the other to the iron bar.

"Oh, for heaven's sake," she said. "Must you?"

"The only way I open the door and go in there," he grumbled, "is if the prisoner is shackled and cain't escape."

René shot her a speaking glance, indicating she should say nothing further.

The jailer swung open the gate just enough to allow Miz Sassy to squeeze through and run to René, her behind wiggling so hard she nearly fell over. René's grin as he lifted her to him and waited for the jailer to release the manacle nearly brought tears of relief to Felice. Yes, she'd done the right thing.

René waited until the jailer left the room, then moved back to where she stood. "*Merci*," he said, and kissed the top of Miz Sassy's furry brown head.

"No need to thank me." The perfection of his mouth mesmerized her. Only recently, he'd used that mouth to drive her to sheer madness. Her cheeks grew hot and her stomach clenched. If only she were the one receiving his affections.

Her mind grasped for something—anything—to change the subject. Glancing over his shoulder, she spied a large, gray envelope atop his cot. "Is that the package my father brought with him when he arrived?"

"*Non*. This one belongs to me."

"It looks exactly like the one my father had in hand

when he walked into the office this morning. He said it was something he wished to discuss with me."

René continued cuddling a contented Miz Sassy and stroking her fur. "My packet arrived on this afternoon's ship out of London."

He watched her with a veiled, sultry gaze. Her unruly heart did a flip in her chest.

Did he know the power of that provocative look?

For a long moment, her mind went blank. Then his half grin brought her back to herself. She had never before been rattled by a man's smile. She noted the fine line of stitches Vivienne had left near his left eye. She wanted to reach out and soothe what would eventually turn into a thin scar, wanted to touch his split lip as if her actions would cause his wounds to disappear.

She searched her mind for something to say. "Have you eaten anything?"

"*Oui*. Vivienne and Bastien brought me some good Creole cooking."

Despite his wounds, René was entirely in command of himself now. He was clothed in dark trousers and a fresh shirt. The raven hair curling near his collar was swept dashingly back from his brow as though freshly washed. When he moved about, he did so with renewed power, his onyx eyes aware of everything around him.

Felice marveled at his capacity to recover from something so harsh as the beating he'd endured only hours before. She tilted her head back and studied him through shuttered eyes meant to hide her own tangled emotions. "You are like a weed springing out of a crack in a street's cobblestones. No matter how many times you are stepped on, you spring right back up and keep on growing."

"Is that a compliment?" he asked in a voice that had gone low and husky. His gaze slid to her mouth.

"I think so." Something shifted inside her. Though she and René might have shared a lust-filled tryst, one they both had agreed would be a one-time thing, that understanding didn't mean she couldn't offer him her support during this trying time.

She reached through the bars and drew a finger along his cheek. "I'm so sorry this happened to you. I wanted to do something to give you some comfort. I hope bringing Miz Sassy to you has helped."

René closed his eyes and leaned into her hand as if it was her comfort he sought. Then he opened his eyes and stepped away from her touch.

"You should go," he said in a raspy voice.

She saw pain reflected in his gaze, and she fought the urge to slip her hands through the bars and reach out to him. Oh, how she wished she could lie with him in his bed and hold him. Just hold him. She nodded her acquiescence, but the words she hadn't meant to say slipped off her tongue of their own volition. "Your face and mouth could use my healing kisses."

"Leave me, *chère*," he groaned. "I cannot take much more of being trapped in here while you are so close, yet so unreachable."

Chapter Twenty-Six

René stepped into the jail's private meeting room, a stark space except for five wooden chairs set around a plain oak table. Barred windows on either side of the room stood open to catch a miserable, sultry breeze. He paused long enough for the removal of his wrist shackles, then took his place at the table opposite Michel, Justin, and Jean Robicheaux, the company attorney. All three sat in shirtsleeves and waistcoats, their jackets hanging off the backs of their chairs. René, too, remained in shirtsleeves.

Before he could inquire of his brother's whereabouts, Bastien stalked into the room. After a brief greeting, he tossed three of Ainsworth's photographs onto the table.

Gasps and cursing met his action. Michel slid one of the images his way, the color in his face turning a deep red. "God Almighty."

Bastien draped his jacket over the back of his chair, but remained standing. "These women, they not be dead, only making like *Les Malheurs de la vertu*."

Justin's scowl deepened. "Whatever the hell that means."

"Erotic asphyxiation," René added. "Strangulation during the intimate act brings them to the edge of death. The one being choked is able to reach . . . uh . . . a greater—"

"We get the idea," Robicheaux cut in. "And you think this is what might have happened to Mrs. Worth? That she was taking part in this heinous ritual when things went too far and she ended up dead?"

"*Oui*," René responded. "It happens."

Justin's shocked gaze shifted from René to Bastien and back again. "How do you know this? Are these images yours? Do you actually participate in this . . . this depravity?"

René raised a hand, halting Justin's ramblings. "*Non*. Hear us out, *s'il vous plaît*."

Robicheaux spread all three images in front of him and proceeded to take notes. "If they are not yours, whose are they and how did you come by them?"

"Bastien . . . ah . . . acquired them last night." René nodded at Bastien for further explanation.

"How I managed to get them be of no concern to you." Nonetheless, Bastien fisted his hands on his hips. "What you need to know is that after the person in question bought photographic equipment from Monsieur Fournier's Photogravure, he leased a room in the rear of the shop. Kept it locked from prying eyes. The room and equipment were put to use after the store's closing hours, and *voilà* . . . these images were produced."

Robicheaux sat back and flipped his pen in his fingers. "I take it you have a pretty good idea who took these."

"*Oui*," René said. "Mayhew Rutherford, Marquess of Ainsworth."

"Ainsworth?" Justin sucked in a loud breath. "You're certain?"

"*Oui*," Bastien and René responded in unison. "We followed him."

Michel shot to his feet and began to pace. "I knew there

was something I didn't like about that man. Why, he's little more than a beast masquerading as a human!"

Justin reached around and retrieved a handkerchief from his coat's inner pocket and wiped his damp brow. "To think this depraved creature planned to marry my daughter."

The mere idea of what Felice might have suffered had she married Ainsworth made René's gut wrench. "There are plenty more where these images came from."

Robicheaux scribbled a few more notes. "Do you have any idea how Mrs. Worth got involved in this kind of thing?"

René shook his head. "*Non.*"

Michel, wearing a scowl so deep it nearly hooded his eyes, had a white-knuckled grip on the back of his chair. "Was she carrying on with him while involved with you at the same time?"

"*Non.* I ended things between us a couple of days after his arrival. I do not know when exactly their affair began, but I figure it took place *tout de suite.*"

Robicheaux continued taking notes. "Was her association with Ainsworth the reason you ended your relationship with her?"

"*Non.* I'd grown weary of our situation several weeks earlier, but I did not wish to cause her undue pain, so I took my time ending things. But once I became aware of her interest in him, I used it as an excuse to end our affair."

Justin, appearing a bit green, turned the images face-down on the table. "How in the world did these women agree to pose for this man? Were they eager to participate in this ungodly practice, do you suppose?"

"According to Madame Olympée, Ainsworth hired the women she employs against her bidding," René said. "He'd been a nightly guest in her establishment until something he did went beyond Madame's rules and she banned him from even touching the girls. It be my guess he paid them a good amount of coin to join him in his studio."

Michel paced again. "A nightly guest in a whorehouse, you say. I could strangle him myself. And it wouldn't be with the same motive as what was done to Mrs. Worth."

Justin shot Michel a stern look. "You cannot mean that."

"I can damn well think it."

René opened the packet he'd received from London and, despite his disgust, managed to maintain a neutral expression as he shoved the contents to the center of the table. "He has a dark past he's managed to keep hidden from the public."

Justin's eyes widened. He pulled out a stack of papers from a similar-looking envelope, slid them over to Robicheaux, then reached for René's report. "Scotland Yard?"

"*Non.* A private detective. Seems this is not Ainsworth's first time meeting this kind of trouble. His father secretly paid a princely sum to authorities to keep things quiet on three different occasions."

Justin gave a nod toward the documents he'd given to Robicheaux. "To make matters worse, Lord Ainsworth is in dire need of a wealthy bride to replenish his family's empty coffers. Who better to prey upon than the heiress of a vast shipping empire?"

Robicheaux shoved the papers René's way. "Here, take a look."

René rummaged through the documents, the hair on the back of his neck standing on end. "That Ainsworth, he be one desperate and twisted man, to be sure."

Michel, Justin, and Robicheaux began talking all at once as they decided on a course of action. René and Bastien listened, shooting each other speaking glances.

Robicheaux turned to René. "For your safety, the judge has agreed to move the trial to the end of the week."

René felt the blood drain from his face. "That's only four days away, don'cha know."

"I know," Robicheaux said. "With this new information, we've plenty of evidence pointing to the guilty party. I doubt the trial will last more than a couple of hours."

"I'm concerned he could run before then," Justin said.

René nodded.

"We'll put you on the stand first. I am certain Ainsworth will be among the court's spectators, and I'll have one of my men present a proper warrant to Fournier so we can collect the remaining evidence."

"How can you be sure Ainsworth will attend?" René asked.

A humorless laugh escaped Robicheaux's lips. "The whole town will likely turn out for the trial of the decade. Mark my words, because he thinks we have no idea what he's been up to, he'll be eager to watch the jury find you guilty of the crime he committed. Once I've finished questioning you, I'll call your housekeeper to the stand. After her, I'll bring up Mrs. Worth's maid, who witnessed your delivery of Mrs. Worth to her home. She must have observed not only your immediate departure while the woman was still alive, but the hour as well. This should give us plenty of time to collect the evidence at Fournier's. Once we have Ainsworth on the stand, presumably as a witness to the events at Le Blanc House, we'll surprise him with the acquired images."

A hundred thoughts shot through René's head. He had to think fast. Had to prevent Monique from taking the stand. She'd be forced to reveal the truth—that not only had Felice been in his home with him during the hours when

Liberty Belle had been murdered, but she'd remained for nearly two days. "Why bother with my housekeeper?"

Robicheaux lifted his pen. "Because she can verify the hours you were at home. I'll make a routine inquiry of her—was anyone with you that night, was she aware of your coming or going, etcetera, etcetera."

René swallowed hard. "Why would we need her if you're gonna call on Mrs. Worth's maid, and then Ainsworth?"

Bastien scowled. "What difference does it make? She's providing a solid alibi that will drive another stake in Mayhem's heart."

"I do not want Monique taking the stand, Robicheaux. I do not even want her in the courtroom. I forbid you to call on her in my defense."

Robicheaux scowled. "Why the devil not?"

René kept his focus on the center of the table. "I have my reasons for not wanting her there."

"*Merde!*" Bastien jumped to his feet. "We're working to set you free, yet you refuse to allow Monique to speak up for you? What's your goddamn problem, brother?"

"Christ!" René dragged a hand down his face and heaved a breath. "I don't want her there in case Cousin Lucien attends. Which he will—he'd take great pleasure in seeing me hang."

He looked to the others at the table. "Monique, she be my cousin's wife. I rescued her and her son from his brutal treatment and housed them in the ground-floor apartment of my residence. I do not know if he is aware they live on my property, but I do not think it wise to advertise her whereabouts by putting her on the stand and announcing she is my housekeeper. Why place her in danger when we have Ainsworth?"

Bastien stalked around the table, facing the backs of

Michel, Justin, and Robicheaux. He leaned one shoulder against the wall, his arms crossed over his chest, his intense blue eyes darkening as he locked gazes with René.

Merde. He's guessed who else I'm protecting. René turned away from his brother's hard stare. Well, damn it, he *was* protecting Monique as well as Felice. "Does anyone have a problem with wanting to shield her if at all possible?"

Bastien gave a soft snort. "*Non,* brother. You need to protect *her.*"

René shot him a warning glance. "Sit down, Bastien."

"Makes sense to me," Robicheaux said.

Relief washed through René. "*Merci.*"

"Save your thanks for after the trial," Robicheaux responded. "We'll call on her if worse comes to worst, but as I said, I doubt the trial will last more than a few hours. If need be, there are others we can call on for testimony while we wait for the evidence to be brought in."

"Should we inform Felice as to what we've discovered about Ainsworth?" Michel asked.

"No," came Justin's sharp retort. "The only people with a need to know are those of us sitting right here. The more people we advise, the more likely word could leak out. If Ainsworth were to catch wind of any of this and flee, we'd lose him, and by God in Heaven, there is no one more bent on seeing this man behind bars than I."

"I do not want Felice in the courtroom either." René focused on Robicheaux's note, taking it as an excuse to avoid his brother's scrutiny.

Justin shoved aside the documents he was perusing and studied René in a way that had him wanting to squirm in his seat.

After a long moment of silence, Justin said, "I agree. There's no need for my daughter to learn publicly what a horrid man she nearly married. Especially in a crowded room with everyone staring at her."

"Humph. Try keeping your stubborn daughter away." Michel returned to his seat.

"I'll see to it," Justin replied.

Robicheaux set down his pen and folded his hands on the table. "Are you aware that word has already gotten out about the trial date, and people are lined up at the courthouse to purchase gallery tickets?"

René swiped a hand across his eyes. "Christ. I'm to be the town's entertainment."

"Is this a normal practice?" Justin asked. "I know spectators are allowed in court, but I don't recall actual tickets having been sold in the past."

Robicheaux nodded. "When it's something this newsworthy, they routinely sell vouchers at the courthouse rather than end up with a stampede for seats. The practice is meant to keep chaos from breaking out."

He stood, collected the photographs, and placed them in his leather satchel along with his notes and documents, then stepped around the table and shook hands with René. "Try to relax these next few days, sir. After all the information I gathered here today, I'm feeling damned optimistic. I don't care to know how you and Bastien got wind of Ainsworth's dealings, or how these images ended up on the table today because you have done yourself a huge favor. Gentlemen, I'll see you in court."

He opened the door to make his exit, only to have the jailer scoot past him, shackles in hand.

At the sight of the ironwork in the jailer's hands, a muscle twitched in René's tight jaw. It was all he could do not to bolt.

Michel glanced from the jailer's hands to René and

back, then took a bead on the jailer. "Are those really necessary? We're a mere fifteen feet from his cell."

"I got my orders." The jailer snapped the shackles in place and led René to his cell, locked him in, then reached through the bars and removed the irons.

Bastien hung back, waited for the others to be out of earshot, then turned to his brother. He spoke in his native tongue, his words low in his throat. "Christ, René. You had to go and pluck that forbidden fruit, didn't you?"

Shame found a familiar place in René's gut. He raised the palm of his hand to Bastien. "Stop. I have crucified myself enough over something I cannot undo, so if it's torment you have in mind, I'm already full of it."

Anger drained from Bastien's countenance. He paced a few steps, then returned to stand in front of the bars separating them. "At least give me some clue as to when this all started. Was it recent?"

"*Oui*. She was sitting in front of my gate when I returned from the old Allard place Saturday night."

"How long did she remain with you?"

"Until Monday morning."

Bastien heaved a slow breath. "And you're certain Monique is aware of this?"

"*Oui*." René gripped the bars of his cell and leaned closer to where Bastien stood. "I want no more to do with this town or the people in it. If I am set free, I will ask Michel for a position in another port. He already warned me against having anything to do with his sister. Should he learn of our time together, he would ban me from working in the shipping business anywhere in the world, and I will be left with nothing."

"So not only are you trying to save Felice's reputation and protect Monique, but you also wish to salvage what you can of your livelihood."

"Precisely."

Something old and familiar flashed through Bastien's eyes, but it was gone before René could decipher the meaning. What had he seen? Helplessness? Melancholy? Despair? Whatever it was, it sure as hell twisted René's guts into knots.

Bastien stood before him for a long moment, his eyes full of conflicting emotion. Then something shifted in him, and his countenance filled with a powerful determination. "Then know this, *mon frère*—we've been through too damn much together for me to let you walk away alone. Whatever happens, or wherever you choose to go, I'll be going with you."

René stared long and hard at his brother as the full impact of his words sank in. For one fleeting moment, René was transported back in time, to the day when his seven-year-old self had decided he needed schooling. Barefoot and dressed in the only clothes he owned, he'd pushed the pirogue away from the dock, leaving his four-year-old brother behind. His brother's chin had quivered, and there was the same sadness reflected in his eyes that had flashed through them moments ago. *I'll be back*, he'd told Bastien. *I need to learn to read and write.*

He'd returned late that afternoon to find Bastien sitting cross-legged on the rickety old dock, his tearstained face lighting up as René floated around the bend in their old flat-bottomed boat. And so it went, day after endless day of reassuring his brother that he'd return, only to find him standing on the dock, waiting. The time finally came when Bastien was old enough to tag along with René to school. They went everywhere together after that, leaving their mother at home, too involved in her own world to bother with their whereabouts or how they were fed or clothed. Thick as thieves the brothers became—in the truest sense of the word.

René wasn't a man to weep, but *merde*, he was getting damn close. He had to clear his throat to speak. "We're grown men now, Bastien. We've gone our separate ways whenever we had to sail somewhere on company business."

Bastien lifted his chin and observed his brother through shielded eyes. "*Oui*, but for all our lives, whenever there was trouble, we were always in it together. No matter where we've traveled for work, *mon frère*, haven't we always returned to this one spot?" A humorless grin touched his lips. "I cannot be letting you leave here for good without tagging along."

Christ. René pinched the bridge of his nose, closed his eyes against another onslaught of pain, and turned his back to his brother, waving him off. "Go, Bastien. Go before the last nerve in my body deserts me and I end up tearing the pitiful contents of this goddamn cell to shreds."

Chapter Twenty-Seven

Despite her family's infuriating attempts to warn her away, Felice had no intention of skipping René's trial. Angry, worried, and dreading the outcome, she moved past the crowd lined up in front of the justice building, stepped around to the side and signaled the fresh-faced young guard who'd agreed to let her in through the private entrance. His fee had been a bit steep—her favorite garnet earrings, which matched the ruby-red sash fastened around the waist of her white, dotted swiss day gown.

"Felice!"

She whirled to spy Mayhew fast approaching.

Drat and blast! "Ainsworth. What are you doing here?"

"Sink me, you called me Ainsworth." He stepped up to her, his countenance filled with sunny exhilaration. "I've been summoned to appear as a witness. What are you doing at this door?"

She flipped open her parasol against the hot morning sun and ignoring his question, appraised his fine attire. "A witness? Whatever for?"

His mustache twitched above an easy grin. "Seeing as how I was a guest at the Le Blanc House ball Saturday evening, and witness to the dispute between Thibodeaux and Mrs. Worth wherein he practically dragged her from the room, his attorney requested my presence."

"*His* attorney, you say?"

"Indeed. You look ever so fresh and lovely, by the by. But dash it all, your earlobes are bare. Quite unlike you not to coordinate your jewelry with your fashions. Leaves you looking as though you've trotted off half-dressed."

At the mention of earbobs, the guilty-looking guard lowered his chin and focused on the toes of his boots, his cheeks the color of ripe tomatoes.

Felice took a deep breath and forced her frustration away. "Leave it to you to find something to criticize about my person, Mayhew."

"I meant no harm, darling. Do forgive me if I've over-stepped my bounds. My only intention was to offer a harmless suggestion that perhaps you'd forgotten to complete your toilette. But no matter; you wouldn't have time to trot home and correct the situation."

Her thoughts running in another direction, she ignored his remark. Something wasn't quite right. "I fail to understand why Monsieur Robicheaux would issue you an invitation to appear on behalf of his client. I would think it should be the prosecuting attorney wanting to expose any dissent between Monsieur Thibodeaux and Mrs. Worth."

Mayhew shoved his hands in his pockets and leaned back on his heels, glaring down his nose at her. "Monsieur Thibodeaux, is it? Whatever the case, I should not miss this occasion for anything in the world. At least I'll get to see one of those Cajun rotters get his just rewards."

Fire blazed in her belly, burning away the caution holding her emotions in check. "Step away from me, sir. After your last disparaging remark, I shall insist on making my way inside on my own."

Ainsworth took her by the elbow. "Felice, we need to

talk. This temper tantrum, or whatever it is you've been having, has gone on long enough. We are to be wed, and that is final, whether your father gives his approval or not."

Felice shook off Ainsworth's grip. "Understand this, Lord Ainsworth—I made a grave error when I accepted your proposal. Furthermore, I have come to the conclusion that I am disinclined ever to marry. I am truly sorry I dragged you halfway across the world on what has turned out to be a fruitless journey. It is high time you took yourself back to England. On the morrow, I should like to arrange first class passage for you on one of our family's vessels. In the meantime, if you will excuse me, I wish to seat myself in the courtroom before the main doors open and that insufferable crowd rushes in."

"Felice—"

She raised a hand. "Stop. Nothing you say will change my mind."

"I know you've been spreading your legs for a man who is about to hang. That's what has changed your mind about wedding me, isn't it?"

She gasped.

The guard stepped forward. "That will be enough, sir. Step away from the lady and go directly to courtroom number three, or I shall be forced to call for another guard to escort you there. Miss Andrews, kindly wait here until this gentleman has reached his destination."

"Thank you." She straightened her spine and watched as the door closed behind a muttering Mayhew.

The guard reached into his pocket and retrieved the garnet earrings. "These bobs belong on your ears, Miss Andrews, not in my pocket. Even though I disagree with the man's treatment of you, I'll admit he's right that your dress is lacking without them. It wasn't right of me to negotiate for your entry. I feel downright ashamed."

She shook her head. "A bargain is a bargain. You've helped me avoid the crowd out front, and my peace of mind was well worth the trade. I've an idea. How about I wear them now, and then, at the end of the day, I'll return them to you."

"Oh, no, miss. I couldn't."

"Please. I'd love for your wife to have something nice in return for your kindness to a lady in need."

He paused, considering her offer, then broke into a wide grin and dropped the earbobs into her hand. "Well, all right, then."

She tilted her head his way. "Here, help me on with them, will you?"

Once he'd attached the garnet jewels to her ears, Felice walked smartly down the long, vaulted corridor to courtroom number three. Showing her voucher to the attendant, she took in a deep breath for courage and stepped inside. Just as she began her march down the aisle to the front row, the main doors to the building opened to a flood of noisy ticket holders. She slid in beside Michel.

His mouth fell open. "What the devil are you doing here?"

"Having a picnic. What do you think?" Leaning past him, she took note of her father's stern demeanor. Beside him sat Bastien, appearing none too pleased either. Bastien's mother sat on the other side of him, surprising Felice. On second thought, even though the voodoo priestess ventured into town only on rare occasions, it would be fitting for her to show her support for her son. To Odalie's left sat René's cousins, Vivienne and Régine, the two women who worked at Le Blanc House.

Michel leaned to Felice's ear. "Weren't you told to remain at home?"

"Blast it all, there are three other women sitting here in support of René. Why shouldn't I too?"

"He specifically did not want you here."

And she knew why—he wanted to protect her. "He's a friend, and someone I've worked alongside for weeks on end."

"Damn it, Felice. Go home."

She raised her voice against the clamoring crowd stampeding into the courtroom. "If you don't like it, you can all go to Hades, because I do not intend to vacate my seat until the trial ends, so hush!"

Michel frowned. "You've got a tongue so sharp today, I could shave with it."

"Better than slitting your throat with it for yet another pitiful attempt to control my life."

Bastien leaned forward. "Now that's actually funny."

"That's enough." Justin motioned for Michel to slide over, and seated himself between them with a soft clicking of his tongue.

"Oh, yes," Michel muttered. "You were certain you could keep her away from here."

Justin heaved a sigh and placed a gloved hand over his daughter's. "Because you insist on remaining throughout the trial, my dear, whatever occurs, do refrain from further comment, lest you give your poor father apoplexy."

She managed a small, humorless smile and gave his hand a squeeze. "I was surprised to see Odalie here. No matter the years of rancor between mother and son, I do applaud her presence."

Taking in her surroundings, she noted the full rows of spectators and spied Mayhew seated on the opposite side of the aisle. Three rows behind him sat Émile Vennard and, of all people, René's cousin Lucien, who'd taken a seat one row behind Vennard. She'd only met Lucien the one time he'd invaded the shipping office, the day René had tossed him out on his ear. He'd been disheveled and bleary-eyed back then. Today, however, he was smartly dressed in a finely tailored suit, his hair swept from his face and falling almost to his shoulders, not unlike the manner in which René wore his. Too bad the man had such a wicked reputation.

Behind Lucien sat a line of young ladies, their fans fluttering in front of the bottom half of their faces. Heavens, hadn't she seen them at Saturday's ball? And wasn't one of them the girl René had twirled around the dance floor? Surely they were here to support him. A glance upward told her the balcony was packed as well. What a curious mixture of spectators.

"All rise!"

The black-robed, gray-haired judge walked into the courtroom to the sound of a roomful of rustling skirts and shuffling feet. Stepping up to the elaborately carved bench, he seated himself. On the wall behind him hung the great seal of Louisiana, with its white pelican resting against a blue background. Three chicks were nestled in her lap.

His Honor tapped his gavel three times. "Be seated."

He waited for the cacophony to cease and then spoke. "Before we bring forth the defendant, I wish to make it exceedingly clear that there is to be quiet in my courtroom at all times. So much as a whisper by so many spectators will sound like the buzzing of hornets. I find the noise quite displeasing, so if you find you cannot keep your thoughts to yourselves, fair warning—you will be removed from these premises with no hope of a return."

He turned to the bailiff. "Now that I've made myself

clear, kindly escort the defendant, his attorney, and the prosecuting attorney into the room."

When had the twelve members of the jury filled their box? Felice had been so intent on making note of the onlookers that she'd failed to notice. Despite the judge's orders, as René walked in beside his attorney, Jean Robicheaux, a round of whispers flared up.

Felice's heart stopped, and for a moment she felt light-headed. She'd expected him to be in chains and looking haggard. He was anything but. Impeccably dressed in a dark suit, gold-embroidered vest, snow-white shirt, and cravat, and with his raven hair swept neatly back from his face, he appeared every bit as confident and handsome as she'd always considered him to be. Except for the stitched area around his eye, which had turned a purplish yellow, his clean-shaven face appeared devoid of any markings. Even the corner of his lip seemed smooth. Bastien was indeed a gifted healer. He'd done a fine job attending to his brother.

René's dark eyes swept the length of the first row. He gave a slight nod to his cousins, mother, and brother. As he moved closer to the long table where he was to sit, his gaze settled on Felice. He stood beside his chair, with the low barrier separating them not five feet in front of her, his eyes ablaze.

She raised her chin in defiance and sent him a silent message. *I know you do not want me here because you wish to protect me, but here I am, and here I shall remain because . . . because . . . oh dear saints in Heaven . . . because I am so in love with you, I cannot bear not to be here.*

At the sudden realization that she loved him, a shudder ran through her. Dipping her head to avoid his fiery eyes, she covered her mouth with her gloved hand to keep from crying out. She closed her eyes to stop any telltale tears that might escape down her cheek.

A squeeze of her father's hand brought her back to her senses. Raising her head and opening her eyes, she studied René's wide shoulders as he turned and seated himself beside his attorney. The room grew so quiet she could hear the collective breathing as the crowd waited for the proceedings to begin.

With the judge's preliminary instructions delivered, René took the stand beside the judge's bench and was sworn in.

"Would you describe your relationship with the deceased," his attorney asked.

René stared straight ahead, though Felice could tell he was not seeing the spectators, but looking inward. Her heart jumped to her throat, making it difficult to find her breath. She swallowed hard, then sent a silent prayer Heavenward, asking that René be exonerated.

"At the time of her death, Mrs. Worth and I were no longer associated," René said.

"How long were you together?" Robicheaux asked.

"About three months."

"Who ended the relationship?"

"I did."

"Was it what she wanted as well?"

"*Non.*"

The questioning continued until Robicheaux finally asked, "Monsieur Thibodeaux, did you murder Mrs. Liberty Belle Worth?"

A flurry of whispers swept through the crowd.

"I did not."

"No further questions."

The prosecuting attorney, a round-bellied man named Monroe, took over the questioning. Approaching René, he held up what Felice recognized as René's missing ruby-tipped pencil. Her heart did another jump into her throat.

Monroe walked the length of the jury box, openly displaying the implement to the jury. "Do you recognize this unusual pencil, Monsieur Thibodeaux?"

"*Oui.* It belongs to me."

"Do you know how it came to be on Mrs. Worth's bedroom floor beside her deceased body?"

"*Non.* It went missing the day before she was murdered."

"And it ended up next to her. How do you explain that, Monsieur Thibodeaux?"

René, showing no emotion, responded, "I do not know how it ended up in her room. I only know it disappeared the day I left the office early."

Monroe went on to ask essentially the same questions as had Robicheaux, but with a sharp and accusatory tone. Interesting how the same questions, asked in a different way, threw the shadow of doubt over René's responses.

Once Monroe ended his questioning, Robicheaux called Mayhew to the stand. Felice turned to her brother and father. She swore both had stiffened at the sound of his name being called out. She leaned forward and spied a muscle twitch along Bastien's jaw. Why in the world was Robicheaux calling Mayhew to the stand on René's behalf? She turned to her father in question. He continued to watch the proceedings, but gave her hand a squeeze, warning her to remain quiet.

The bailiff swore Mayhew in and Robicheaux moved to stand in front of him. "You are acquainted with the accused, Lord Ainsworth?"

"Somewhat," Mayhew responded. "He is employed—or was employed—by the Andrews shipping firm, where my fiancée was assisting her family with the bookkeeping. She was there only on a temporary basis, I wish to add."

How dare you call me your fiancée! Felice opened her mouth to whisper to her father, but he squeezed her hand again, this time so tightly, her fingers pinched together.

"And were you acquainted with Mrs. Worth?" Robicheaux asked.

"Indeed. I met her at Le Blanc House the first evening my fiancée and I landed here from England."

There you go again, bearing false witness, you prig!

"Mrs. Worth offered to give me a tour of the city the following day, while my fiancée was otherwise engaged," Mayhew continued. "And since Miss Andrews was needed alongside her brother, Mrs. Worth was kind enough to continue keeping me company on several occasions."

It was all Felice could do to hold her tongue. Things were going much worse than she'd imagined.

Robicheaux began pacing back and forth in front of the witness box. "Tell me, Lord Ainsworth, when did you begin seeing Mrs. Worth in the privacy of her home on, shall we say, more intimate terms?"

Mayhew's eyes widened. His fingers smoothed his mustache in a manner Felice knew to be a nervous habit. "Well, that would have nothing to do with my being a witness to Thibodeaux arguing with Mrs. Worth at a ball last Saturday, when he practically dragged her from the place in front of the guests."

Robicheaux raised a hand, stilling Ainsworth. "Bear with me, Lord Ainsworth. I am attempting to get a clear picture for the jury of what went on between the time Monsieur Thibodeaux left the festivities with Mrs. Worth and the moment when her maid found her dead."

Attorney Monroe rose and objected to his opponent's line of questioning.

"Continue with your questioning, Monsieur Robicheaux," the judge ordered. "Answer the question, Lord Ainsworth."

Mayhew openly squirmed in his seat, and Felice was beginning to feel sick to her stomach. So the two had been intimate after all. But what did she care, now that she'd ended their engagement? Nonetheless, he'd openly called her his fiancée in front of the whole town and was now admitting to a tryst. It was humiliating.

"We were . . ." He shot a glance at Felice, then looked away. "I simply do not see how this has any relevance to the fact that Thibodeaux killed her."

The judge banged his gavel. "You will answer the question, Lord Ainsworth. Henceforth refrain from passing judgment on the accused."

Robicheaux turned to the table where René sat, looking questioningly at a man who'd slipped into the seat beside René. He set a packet in front of René and gave a slight nod to Robicheaux.

"Never mind responding." Robicheaux walked over to the table and took the packet in hand. "Let's move on to my next question. After your arrival in the city, did you take up a particular photographic hobby, Lord Ainsworth?"

Mayhew visibly paled. "What the devil is going on here? Thibodeaux is the one on trial, not me. What I do in my spare time is my business and has nothing to do with him murdering Mrs. Worth."

"Oh, but it does." Robicheaux spread out the contents of the packet. Picking up several photographs, he tossed one onto the prosecutor's table, placed a few onto the judge's bench, then displayed the remainder before Mayhew and the jury. "Mrs. Worth was found strangled to death by a cravat belonging to Monsieur Thibodeaux, one he has sworn under oath that she had taken from him before she entered her premises that fateful night."

Robicheaux turned to the jury. "If you will, please consider the results of Lord Ainsworth's hobby. The women you see in these photographs are not dead. Rather, they were hired by Lord Ainsworth to pose in a manner similar to the way Mrs. Worth was found—naked, and with either a scarf, rope, or cravat tied around their necks."

The bottom fell out of Felice's stomach, and the room began to whirl around her. "Dear God in Heaven," she murmured to her father. René's head turned a bit, as if he might have caught her words.

A roar went up in the crowd.

Mayhew jumped to his feet. "You cannot prove I took those pictures!"

The judge banged on his gavel. "One more outburst from you spectators and I will have the courtroom cleared. Lord Ainsworth, sit down!"

A hush fell over the room.

Mayhew took his seat, his face flushed.

Robicheaux submitted the remaining photographs to the judge, who sifted through them. The scowling magistrate then ordered the bailiff to hand out the incriminating evidence to each of the jurors, who were all sitting in stunned silence.

"You were the only person with a key to Monsieur Fournier's back room, one he'd rented to you," Robicheaux said. "Furthermore, each of these women is willing to testify that it was you who paid her to pose in such a manner."

Feeling suddenly faint, Felice splayed a hand over her

chest in a futile attempt to aid her breathing. Her father slipped his arm around her and, pulling her close, whispered in her ear, "Now you know why we did not want you here, my dear."

Robicheaux pointed a finger at Ainsworth. "Mayhew Rutherford, Marquess of Ainsworth, on the night of May 21, did you and Mrs. Worth engage in a sexual practice whereby you tied Mr. Thibodeaux's cravat around her throat for the purpose of increasing her ecstasy, only to end in accidentally killing her?"

Chapter Twenty-Eight

"Now, see here." Mayhew sprang to his feet. "How dare you try to bait me into—"

The judge pounded his gavel. "Sit down, Lord Ainsworth, or I shall hold you in contempt of court."

Mayhew's cold, hard eyes settled on Felice. Despite the magistrate's raised voice, despite the muffled whispers in the rows behind her, Mayhew's icy regard set off a high-pitched ringing in her ears. The man she'd once thought so handsome and full of charm now appeared cold and ugly.

What did I ever see in you? The entire time we were together, you barely managed to brush your lips over mine, claiming you wanted to keep our relationship pure until we wed, yet you carried on an affair right under my nose, practicing vile acts that led to her death? What kind of monster did I nearly marry?

Mayhew's gaze drifted to her left, past her brother, father, and Bastien. Then his eyes settled for a brief moment on René's mother before returning to Robicheaux.

Something shifted in Mayhew's expression.

He visibly relaxed, his shoulders squaring, his chin lifting. "While I can certainly understand your assumption, Mr. Robicheaux, fact is, I was nowhere near Mrs. Worth's residence the night in question. I have a perfectly sound alibi, if you will permit me."

Was that a twitch of a smile touching the corners of his mouth? Like a cat cornering a mouse right before the pounce? Felice had seen that expression on many an occasion. This time, though, it made her skin crawl.

Robicheaux gingerly placed the photograph he'd been holding alongside Mayhew. "And what would be your firm alibi, Lord Ainsworth?"

Mayhew adjusted himself in his seat with a renewed air of confidence. "As you know, Le Blanc House is owned by the Andrews family. It is primarily used to house their ships' captains between voyages. The mansion also plays host to other guests on occasion. Such guests include family visitors, such as myself. The accused's brother also resides there, as do his two female cousins, who manage the property. While I had been invited to the *bal de maison* that was held there this past Saturday evening, so was the accused's mother, who remained overnight. Because I had never met a woman like her, I was most curious. After introductions were made, I chatted with Odalie Thibodeaux from around nine of the evening until a buffet breakfast was served to us stragglers the next morning. She and I then parted ways and took to our respective suites, which was well beyond the hour at which Mrs. Worth was found deceased."

He pointed to Odalie. "The accused's mother is sitting just over there. Certainly she would be obliged to confirm my whereabouts under oath."

"Holy hell," Michel muttered to Justin, who'd crossed his arms over his chest as his countenance turned stern. "What do you make of this turnabout?"

"I haven't a clue," Justin responded.

"Bailiff," the magistrate called out. He pointed his

gavel toward the table where the defense attorney sat.
"Place Lord Ainsworth in the chair to the left of Monroe,
and bring another guard to stand beside him. Robicheaux,
bring forth the accused's mother."

Odalie stood and made her way past Bastien, Michel,
and Felice's father. When she was forced to turn sideways
in order to ease her full skirts past Felice's equally ample
ones, a clean, lightly perfumed scent surrounded her.
Odalie had to be in her fifties, yet her hands gripping the
railing were smooth as a young girl's, as was her face.
Her raven hair, caught up in a bun at her nape, held a
silken sheen. She was still a beauty, one who knew how to
present herself to full advantage. Even her fashionable
green day gown could've come from the same dressmaker
as Felice's.

Stoic and moving with grace through the room to the
witness box, Odalie raised her hand to be sworn in. Like
René, she stared straight ahead, her gaze fixed on no one.

"Madame Thibodeaux—"

"It be *mademoiselle*. I never married," she responded
in a smooth, lyrical Cajun accent. She was all femininity,
yet beneath her genteel deportment, beneath her honeyed
words, lay unmistakable power.

Felice glanced over her shoulder at the female spectators, the lower half of their faces obscured by fans. She
noted the men sitting rigid, their mouths grim lines of
frozen silence. No doubt most were hearing the voice of a
legend for the first time. How silent the room had suddenly become—more church than court. Not a rustle of a
skirt, nor a shuffle of feet, only the whoosh, whoosh,
whoosh of the ladies' colorful fans beating in rapid motion
against the heat, while the acrid scent of sour perspiration
and sweet perfume grew ever stronger.

Robicheaux cleared his throat "Pardon, *mademoiselle*.

Thank you for coming forward. I've only a couple of questions. My intention is to validate Lord Ainsworth's claim that the two of you kept company the entire evening of May 21, during which time Mrs. Worth met her demise."

"*Oui*," she responded. "It is as Lord Ainsworth said. We were introduced around nine of the clock on Saturday evening. We remained in each other's company until after breakfast the following morning." She narrowed her eyes at Robicheaux. "Perhaps you be questioning the wrong man, *non*?"

He lifted a brow. "What do you mean?"

"There is someone in this courtroom who is fond of picking up where his sons leave off with their women." She settled her gaze upon Émile Vennard. "It is an odd habit, to be sure, but one he has routinely indulged in these past few years. This unusual practice also included Mrs. Worth."

"Lordy be," Felice whispered. "I did see him out and about with Liberty Belle. How many men was the woman bedding?"

Whispers flooded the room.

The magistrate pounded his gavel once. "Mr. Monroe, if you have no questions, Mademoiselle Thibodeaux may step down so Monsieur Émile Vennard can take the stand."

It took all the self-discipline Felice possessed to keep from commenting. Had Vennard been attempting to seduce her the day he'd stopped her in the street? Was that why he'd made mention of an affair between her and his illegitimate son? Despite the heat in the room, a chill ran over her, prickling her skin.

"I see no reason I should be questioned," Vennard announced after being sworn in. "I was in Baton Rouge on business from Thursday until Monday afternoon. My daughter's husband, my business partner, accompanied me."

Robicheaux turned to where the man married to Vennard's daughter sat. He gave a small nod. Robicheaux turned back to Vennard. "You were acquainted with Mrs. Worth?"

"I was."

"Intimately?"

Monroe stood. "Objection. Irrelevant."

"Sustained." The magistrate frowned at Robicheaux. "Unless you have a point to make, Counselor, if Monsieur Vennard was out of the city at the time of Mrs. Worth's death, I suggest you allow him to take his seat so we can get on with this trial. It is getting mighty hot in here, and I am of a mind to call a recess."

"One question, your honor, and then I think we are all due a short break in the proceedings."

"Go on," the judge responded.

"Monsieur Vennard, did you ever practice this method of providing ecstasy to Mrs. Worth by the use of an instrument of one kind or another around her neck?"

Vennard sat without responding, his color heightened, his regard of Robicheaux forbidding.

"Answer the question." The judge slipped a white handkerchief from his sleeve and mopped his brow. "I am running out of patience here, and I intend to call a recess."

"We dabbled in it a couple of times," Vennard responded through thinned lips, "It would seem that Lord Ainsworth helped Mrs. Worth to develop peculiar tastes."

Felice bit her bottom lip and clasped her hands tightly in her lap. She couldn't let her mind wander to what might have gone on between René and Liberty Belle. Oh, what a dark and nasty business this all was.

Robicheaux walked back to the table where René was seated. "No further questions, your honor."

Attorney Monroe rose. "Your honor, before we take a recess, I would like to call our last witness."

"Good God, can it not wait?"

"Your honor, sir. I believe this witness will be on the stand for only a few minutes. I also believe she will be the witness to wrap up this entire trial."

The judge released a deliberate and heavy sigh. "Call your witness, Mr. Monroe. But this had better be good, because my patience ran out about ten minutes ago, and I'm of no mind to allow further deviation from court procedure."

"The prosecution would like to call Miss Jewel to the stand."

A gray-haired woman of plump proportions took the stand, her mahogany skin shimmering in the hot room. While she was being sworn in, Robicheaux and René put their heads together in a quick exchange of whispers, followed by a shrug of René's shoulders.

Monroe approached the witness. "Miss Jewel. You have worked for Mrs. Worth in the capacity of lady's maid for several years. Is that correct?"

"Yes, sir."

"And are you familiar with the accused, Monsieur René Thibodeaux?"

"Indeed I am."

"Did you witness Monsieur Thibodeaux visiting Mrs. Worth in her home?"

"Yes, sir. On many an occasion."

"And did Monsieur Thibodeaux spend the night with Mrs. Worth on any of these occasions?"

"No, sir, he did not. It was a right sore spot with Mrs. Worth that she could never talk him into spending the night. Furthermore, she had a burr up her behind that he refused to share his own bed with her. He just came an'

went, if'n you know what I mean. She was deep hurt
when he stopped seein' her. That's the only reason she
took up with other men—thought it would make him jealous and he'd want her back."

"Did you see him at Mrs. Worth's residence on the
night of May 21?"

"Yes, sir. He brought Mrs. Worth home from that fancy
bal de maison and left. But then he done returned."

"He returned?"

"Yes, sir, he came back all right."

"Do you know what time this might have been?"

"Yes, sir. I saw him come back into the house at near
two in the mornin'. But I didn't see when he left 'cuz I
went back to bed."

"What?" Felice's hand flew to her mouth. Her breathing grew labored. She leaned toward her father, barely
able to get her words out. "She's lying."

René turned his head Felice's way and gave it a small
shake.

"You're sure it was he?" Monroe asked.

"Yes, sir. The one gaslight in the corridor was turned
way down low when he come through the front door, but
I recognized him aw'right. It burdens my heart that he
would do such a thing to her because up 'til then, he'd
always treated her kindly."

Felice jumped to her feet. "She's lying!"

A muffled roar went up in the courtroom.

The judge pounded his gavel. "Enough! Bailiff, remove
this woman from my courtroom."

Her father grabbed her by the arm to pull her back to
her seat. Felice shook it off. "If you saw someone come
through that door, it was not René."

She looked around the room, panic nipping at her heels
as the bailiff reached for her. Whatever happened next,

she didn't care. But she damn well wasn't about to see René hang for someone else's crime.

She tried to shrug off the bailiff's grip, but he held tight. "René Thibodeaux did not murder Mrs. Worth. I know this because he was with me . . . we . . . we were together during the very hours someone else murdered her."

Her father stood.

Michel stood.

The judge pounded his gavel with one hand and mopped his brow with the other. "Bring her forward, bailiff. Miss Jewel, take a seat on the other side of Attorney Monroe. Lord Ainsworth, you sit tight where you are. Guards, no one leaves this room. And for you spectators, any noise from you and you will pay fines."

Her head and heart in a mad whirl, Felice made her way to the witness box, where she stood to be sworn in. When the judge ordered her to sit and she took in the crowded courtroom, a sudden calm washed over her and the fog in her head cleared. In what felt like slow motion, she surveyed the room. Mayhew sat with his hands clasped together on the table in front of him, his features rigid. René, his expression unreadable, stared straight ahead at some blank place on the judge's bench, his jaw tight. Directly behind him sat her father, alert and stoic. Then there was Michel. If anyone could skewer a person with a glower, it was he.

"Miss Andrews," Robicheaux began. "You claim to have been in Monsieur Thibodeaux's company during the time Mrs. Worth lost her life. However, the accused swore under oath that he was alone that night. Please remember that you are under oath. Which one of you is telling the truth?"

She took in a slow, deep breath as thoughts clicked into place, one by one. René being charged with perjury was nothing compared to receiving a death sentence. She regarded the spectators and the attorneys awaiting her next words in a courtroom that had grown so quiet even the ladies' fans had stilled. Well, if scandal was what they were feeding on at the moment, they were about to get a bellyful.

"I joined Monsieur Thibodeaux in his home just before midnight on May 21. We remained together without leaving the premises until just before noon on Monday, May 23."

A collective gasp rolled through the room.

Robicheaux shot a quick glance at René, who gave a slight nod of agreement. "You never left each other's company during that entire time? Nearly two days?"

So, René had not even told his attorney the truth. "That's right. Except to use the necessary, which did not take long."

Another collective gasp swept through the room.

"Could Monsieur Thibodeaux have slipped away to Mrs. Worth's home while you slept?"

Oh, wasn't this about to become a scorcher of a scandal. Then again, did she ever do anything in small measure? A slight smile touched the corners of her mouth. "No, Monsieur Robicheaux, René could not have left his residence while I slept because we were fully engaged with each other. We did not fall into an exhausted sleep until well after eight in the morning and, according to reports, Mrs. Worth was found dead before then."

Even Robicheaux's face turned pink. "I see."

He turned to the judge, who motioned for him to continue. Was that a glint in the magistrate's eyes? "You say you met up right before midnight at his residence?" Robicheaux was obviously groping for words. "Was this a prearranged meeting?"

"No. He wasn't expecting me. In fact, he was surprised

to see me waiting at his gate—and not pleasantly so. It took a bit of coaxing on my part to persuade him to invite me in, but once there, his attitude changed. From then on, he wasn't keen on letting me go until Monday morning."

She shot a bold glance at René, who appeared as if he wanted to shake some sense into her. There. She'd done it with those last words. She'd told the world he could not have murdered anyone while he was in bed with her.

A movement in the gallery caught her attention. She looked up to spy a well-dressed man moving with stealth toward the exit. Something familiar in his build, in the way he moved, caused her to remain focused on him. He paused and glanced over his shoulder at her, his dark hair brushing the top of his collar.

Lucien!

"My God!" she blurted out without thinking. "They could be twins standing in the shadows."

Miss Jewel shot to her feet. She looked from René to Lucien, her mouth agape. "Why, they could be brothers. He must be the man I saw. *Monsieur* would never have hurt Mrs. Worth!"

Lucien took off at a run.

"Stop that man!" the judge shouted.

Odalie stood and called out, "Lucien Thibodeaux, you will not run away and leave my son to hang for your sins."

Chaos broke out as the spectators jumped to their feet, guards wrestled Lucien to the floor, and several men nearby joined in to help hold a writhing, cursing man.

"Order in the court!" the judge shouted, pounding his gavel and wiping his brow. "Order in the court! Bailiff, bring the man here. Miss Andrews, remain where you are."

Lucien was dragged before the judge. "It was an accident. It wasn't murder," he said. "She kept wanting me to tie the necktie tighter, don'cha know. She'd done it before, and it was good. It be her fault. Pull tighter next time, she'd say."

The judge waved a hand at the bailiff. "Take him away."

He turned to where René sat. "Monsieur Thibodeaux, while the court apologizes, you did commit perjury by swearing under oath that you were alone the night of Mrs. Worth's murder. Thus, a fine will be levied. You are free to go, but you must return by ten in the morning tomorrow to hear the amount I will set. I suggest you make your immediate exit using the same rear entry as when you arrived."

With no expression on his face, and without uttering a word, René stood and turned to Michel, who leaned on the railing separating the two of them. Anger rolled off him like a fast-moving thundercloud coming in from the ocean.

"I warned you to stay away from my sister," Michel growled. "As of this moment, you are no longer employed by Andrews Shipping. Nor will you ever work for any shipping concern anywhere in the world."

Giving Michel no response, René merely walked over to the table where Monroe was stuffing papers into his satchel. He said something to Monroe, who responded by digging into the pouch. With a shrug, the attorney came up empty-handed.

René turned to Mayhew. With a scowl, he reached into an inside pocket, retrieved René's ruby-tipped pencil, and handed it to him.

René turned and strode past the jury box, past Felice. Without so much as a glance her way, he disappeared from the courtroom.

Chapter Twenty-Nine

Tears welled in Felice's eyes. Blinking them back, she lingered on the witness stand, waiting for the courtroom to clear so she could take her leave with some semblance of dignity. She clasped her trembling fingers together in her lap and, focusing on them, lost herself in thoughts of what had just transpired.

"Felice?"

She glanced up and caught the concerned look on her father's face. He stood across the room alongside her brother and Jean Robicheaux. Except for the three men, the courtroom was empty. How long had she been sitting there, trying to fit together all the jagged pieces of today's waking nightmare?

"Come along," her father said. "I'll take you home."

As she approached him, Michel intervened. "Was it necessary to go into such blasted detail about your wanton affair with René? Or was it your intention to embarrass the entire family?"

Her brother's words sent shards of pain slicing through her. Robicheaux looked from one to the other, then grabbed his satchel and, muttering a hasty goodbye, hurried off.

Had she gone too far in her determination to clear

René? Well, it was too late to change things now. And she'd be darned if she'd quarrel with Michel while at her weakest. What she desperately needed was to make her way home. Fall apart in private. Then pull herself together and figure out what to do with her life.

Her father cleared his throat but said nothing, although his scowl indicated his certain displeasure at her brother's actions.

Chin up, she stepped forward, mirroring Michel's aggressive stance. "René is now a free man, is he not? And why should you be embarrassed? Are you concerned your political ambitions might be tainted by your sister's confession?"

"There will be consequences to your actions, Felice."

Despite his cutting words, she managed a casual shrug. "Not to worry. I shall soon leave town. No longer will you be burdened by association with me. And once I have gone elsewhere, *dear* brother, I intend to do whatever suits me without you forever hounding me."

Had she blinked just then, she might have missed the flaring of Michel's pupils. He stared at her for a long moment, as if digesting her words, then fisted his hands on his hips. "Oh, for pity's sake, Felice. You cannot run hither and yon, doing as you please with no accountability. No matter where you end up, there will always be rules. You also have others to consider besides yourself."

There went her insides, falling apart again. She slipped her hand into the crook of her father's arm and made to step away from Michel. "I do regard others. In fact, I placed René's freedom above my own reputation. In case you've failed to notice, I have been and will always be a willful and independent thinker."

And here I thought I wouldn't argue with him.

She gave her father's arm a tug. "If you'll excuse us,

dear brother, I am on my way home, where I shall practice being perfect like you."

"Humph," Michel retorted.

Directing her father to the side door exit, she passed the young guard. Without breaking stride, Felice slipped her garnet earrings into his jacket pocket, then snapped open her parasol.

Her father cocked a brow. "Heaven forbid I should inquire as to what you just presented to that young fellow."

"Heaven forbid indeed." A secret half smile tugged at her mouth. "You've the patience of Job when it comes to your squabbling children. Do accept my apologies for our unbecoming behavior, but kindly take note that Michel started it."

Papa huffed a breath. "If you didn't care so deeply for each other, you'd not bother exchanging those ridiculous barbs. I'll speak with Michel this evening about any further attempts to control you. Do have patience with him. He and I were mightily concerned about your being present when Ainsworth took the stand. Aside from what would be revealed, we were certain he'd be found guilty. We wanted to save you the grief of learning of his crime in such a public setting."

A landslide of emotions swept over her, nearly toppling her. "You knew of those photographs beforehand?"

He nodded.

"How?"

"René and Bastien discovered Ainsworth's wicked pastime prior to Mrs. Worth's murder. Naturally, we thought him to be the killer."

How much had transpired unbeknownst to her? Feeling dizzy, she paused to press her fingertips against her temples.

"Are you all right?"

"Yes, yes." She squeezed her father's arm and started

forward again. "It seems I have extremely poor taste in regard to men. Perhaps I should join a convent and forget about that gender altogether."

"Humph. Try doing as you please in a place like that, dear girl. In under a month, those devout sisters would toss you out, lock the gate behind you, and hide the key."

She sighed. "You're right. I'd make a miserable shut-in. Nonetheless, avoiding men does hold merit."

"Don't go judging all men because of Ainsworth's misdeeds. He used his cultured upbringing and charm to deceive you into thinking he was a decent person. He's like a snake eating its own tail, busy destroying himself without anyone's help."

"Were you ashamed of my behavior in court as well, Papa?"

"Never, my dear. I applaud the courage it took to speak your truth. No telling what would've taken place had you followed my directive and remained at home. You've got your mother's backbone, which suits me just fine. Do you really intend to leave town?"

At the thought of abandoning her aging father, of never again crossing paths with René, another sharp pain sliced through her. "I should like to stay in our home upriver for a while, Papa. I'm suddenly yearning for some peace and quiet, with only you for company."

"I cannot leave until Abbott's estate is settled."

"I see." She chewed at her bottom lip. "Perhaps I might go on alone. You could join me later."

Her father paused, grasped her by the shoulders, and peered deep into her eyes. "Is what you revealed on the stand your reason for wanting to flee? To avoid the town gossips? Or is it because you are in love with René and you assume your feelings are one-sided?"

She froze in her tracks, unable to speak. Shrugging off

her father's hold on her, she focused on the empty streets, nearly devoid of people in the sultry afternoon heat. A single carriage drove by, pulled by a slow-moving draft horse clip-clopping along, chains and tack jangling.

"Answer me, Felice."

Suddenly aware of the thin layer of humidity coating her skin, she gave her parasol a twirl and managed a bit of a breeze. "I do wish to hurry home, Papa. I'm in need of a cool bath, and then my bed for a lie-down."

"Answer me."

"Oh, fiddlesticks. René and I had a brief affair, nothing more. Neither of us had any intention of marrying, nor of carrying on any further. We are both adults. We knew exactly what we were doing. Love had nothing to do with it."

Her father took to walking again. "You might be fooling yourself, but you do not fool me. When René walked into the courtroom alongside his attorney, you jolted in your seat as if struck by lightning. That and the expression on your face were all I needed to know. You, my dear, are in love with him, and that changes everything."

A soft noise escaped her throat as those blasted tears threatened to fall again. She swiped at one corner of her eye. "I confess, I do love him. But I must be practical. He will soon leave town, as will I. We shan't cross paths again. And he does not share my feelings."

Her father waved a hand through the air, dismissing her comment. "Why not board the same ship? Preferably one to China. See what transpires once you've been thrown together for so long."

"Papa!" she choked out. "Are you saying you are in favor of a rascally Thibodeaux insinuating himself into your daughter's life? Have you forgotten Michel sacked René

today? Intends to have him banned from the shipping
industry worldwide? And all because of me."

"Your brother was completely out of line. He needs to
concern himself with his own daughters, who will soon
enough become young ladies with suitors coming to call."

At last, they reached the town house. While her father
fished in his pockets for a key, he said, "Have you informed René of your feelings for him?"

"Oh, please, Papa. What good would that do when we
are about to go our separate ways? I told you, he does not
share my sentiments."

Her father turned the key in the lock, then paused. "Oh,
we men can be such odd creatures. We like to act big and
strong and courageous for the world to see, but when it
comes to telling women we love them, we become pitifully weak. The idea of being rejected by the one we care
most for in the world frightens us half to death."

He gave a nod to his left. "He's only two doors over.
Perhaps he could use a friendly visit from you about now."

Her heart did a flip. "Don't be absurd. He stormed out
of the courtroom not two feet from where I sat with nary
a glance my way. I'm the last person he'd want to see."

"Try to remember what he's been through all week, and
the devil of a time Michel gave him after the trial. Don't
end up regretting the good you might have done him were
you to march over there right now and tell him that you
love him."

Her bones turned to jelly and her insides threatened to
crumble. "Don't, Papa. I . . . I cannot take any more of this
kind of talk just now. I need to lie down. I need to think."

"As you wish." He pushed open the gate for her to
enter, then stepped aside. "I am off to the shipping office.
From there, I shall join Michel and his very large, very
noisy family for dinner. Care to come along?"

"No. I'd rather swim with the alligators."

"I thought not." He blew her a kiss on each cheek, then strolled off.

Felice watched him disappear before making her way up the stairs to the main living quarters, where she sought out Marie and requested a tepid bath, along with a simple, cool cotton dress with a front opening, one she could manage on her own. And no petticoats. She'd not be going anywhere in this miserable heat.

Once the bath was ready, she shed her clothing and lowered herself into the tub. Using a thick sea sponge, she drenched her skin so the water's soothing coolness washed over her body, then leaned back and closed her eyes with a deep sigh. Her father's words buzzed in her head like a hive of bees.

Marie returned with a sprigged cotton day gown and an equally thin chemise, along with a tall glass of lemonade. "Henri brought ice a while ago, so's I made you some nice lemonade."

"Thank you. It sounds heavenly." Felice stepped out of the tub, dried herself, and donned the lightweight clothing.

After Marie brushed Felice's hair until it shone, she made her way to her room and took to her bed, where she ended up staring at the ceiling, pondering her father's words. What if he were right—what if René truly needed someone? Needed her?

The ache that gripped her every time she thought of their intense time together rolled through her once again, setting every nerve alight. Curling onto her side, she slid her hands under her cheek, closed her eyes, and tried to think of something besides René.

When she opened her eyes again, it was near dusk. How long had she dozed? Once more, her father's words rattled around in her restless mind. What if René was truly

hurting and no one was there to console him? Surely
Bastien must be there. But was his brother enough to as-
suage the hurt?

What did she have to lose by going to René? If he ordered her from his home, she'd leave without hesitation.
At least she could let him know that someone besides his
brother cared for him.

Donning a pair of slippers, she made her way downstairs to the street. Heart pounding in her throat, she
approached the gate to René's home just as Monique
exited her quarters.

Her pulse quickened. "Good evening, Monique. I am
here to see René. Would you mind letting me in?"

Monique shook her head, her expression sad. "*Non,
mam'selle. Monsieur* gave me strict orders not to let
anyone in. Not even his brother."

"Oh, dear. Could you at least let him know I am here?
Perhaps he'll change his mind and decide to see me."

Monique shook her head again and began wringing
her hands. "Won't be doing any good. He be in an ever-
so-dark mood such as I never seen before."

A sense of urgency—or was it desperation?—gripped
Felice. "Please, Monique. Do tell him I'm here."

"All right, but it won't be doing no good." Monique
turned to do as she'd been bidden. She took a few steps,
then paused and moved back to the gate, looking even
more miserable. "Oh, *mam'selle*, Monsieur Thibodeaux,
he be hurtin' something fierce, and it be mighty worrisome to me. I've never seen him so downtrodden."

It's worse than I imagined. Felice struggled to speak.
"That's why I'm here."

Monique swung open the gate. "You'll be findin' him
in the mews. He been mucking the stalls, shining up tack,
washin' horse and dog. Now he be busy refilling the water

trough he cleaned out. Been at it since he got home from the courthouse, so mayhap he could use a friend. I'll be takin' me a nice long walk around Jackson Square, free as I please now that Lucien can't get to me. Close the gate quietlike behind me so *monsieur* doesn't hear and chase you off, *s'il vous plaît*."

The moment Felice shut the gate, the sense of being an intruder set her nerves jangling. She could've been standing at the edge of a cliff about to topple over for the blood roaring in her ears. She made her way into the cobbled courtyard and paused beside the bubbling fountain. Facing the covered mews in the waning light, she spied Miz Sassy curled on a pile of hay in front of the fancy carriage parked at the rear of the mews. Commander's big head hung over the door to his stall as he watched his master.

Shirtless, barefoot, and clad in a pair of lightweight linen trousers slung low on his hips, René stood with his back to her, pumping water into the horse trough. Transfixed, she watched the muscles along his back and arms ripple as he raised and lowered the pump's handle. Even his simple movements were beauty in motion.

God, she loved this man.

He bent to dip his head and shoulders under the pump as a final burst of water cascaded over him. He straightened and tossed his head, spewing water droplets in the air around him like a wet dog shaking himself dry.

Easing closer, she paused once again to remind herself that she'd come to offer comfort. What was he feeling? What was he thinking?

He reached over and grabbed a drying cloth off a brass hook hanging between a saddle and a harness on the tack wall opposite Commander's stall. Swiping the towel over his face and hair, he began to dry his upper body.

A flash of summer lightning cracked overhead, startling her. In the distance, thunder rumbled.

He stilled, holding the towel against his chest.

Her breath left her lungs.

He knows I'm here.

A strange and sudden awareness of someone standing behind him rippled over René's skin. Instinctively, he knew it had to be her.

He turned.

She stood not ten feet away in a gown so thin he could see the outline of her lush body. Her lips parted, and her dark, luminous eyes grew wide.

An exhilarating rush like no other flooded his veins. She was the last person he wanted to see. But she just might be the one person he needed most to soothe his wounded heart.

He couldn't explain it, but suddenly, he understood the glorious highs and the plunging lows his emotions took whenever he was around her. How many nights had he spent of late with no chance of sleep, replaying her every touch?

Her presence in his home wouldn't do.

Not at all.

He had to get rid of her before he did something he'd be sorry for. Blood roaring in his head, he growled, "Go home."

She gave him a furtive smile, but said nothing and took a step closer, her expressive eyes fixed on him. "Seems I've heard those words coming from you quite a bit of late."

The velvet in her voice, the touch of her gaze stole his breath. He managed to bring enough of it back into his lungs to issue another warning. "I don't want you here, Felice. I don't want anyone here. Leave me be."

She took another step forward. The top of her thin gown slipped, exposing the soft skin of her shoulders— shoulders he'd once spent hours kissing. A raw, naked edge of desire shot through him.

He bit back a groan.

She stepped closer until they stood mere inches apart. Her delicate nostrils flared, as if catching his scent. Her eyelids quivered, then lowered as her gaze ran the length of him and back up.

"I would like to touch you," she said. "And I would like you to touch me. I want to relive all the caresses that gave us both so much pleasure."

"Christ," he muttered. For the life of him, he doubted he had the strength to resist her.

She reached out for him.

He attempted to take a step back but failed.

The moment she touched his chest, hot need violently welled up in him, and a groan left his throat. He grasped her shoulders and backed her against the wall where the tack and saddles hung.

She gasped and grew still for a moment, questions in her eyes.

He buried his face in the smooth contour of her neck, tasted her sweet, silken skin. "Tell me to stop," he rasped.

A shudder ran through her. "I cannot. I will not."

His hands moved all over her now. He knew her, knew the caresses that drove her mad, knew which touch turned her bones to gel and left her mindless. It was his last conscious thought before his craving for her took over completely. Grasping her hips, he drew her to the length of him. He shifted her higher against the wall and bunched up her skirts. Lowering his trousers, he fitted himself inside her, easing the ache in his heart.

Instead of resisting him, she slid her arms around his neck and, with a soft moan, wrapped her legs around his hips and settled herself upon him. His craving for her turned into a pounding need. Suddenly, nothing existed but the two of them. His desire for her was so strong, he buried his face in the sweet curve of her neck once again and moved inside her, lost to another world.

She matched his rhythm in a mating that went deeper than their heated act. It was the beautiful meshing of two souls, and it tore out his heart. Her ragged breaths matched his as he searched the intimate places of her body with desperate hands while he suckled her breasts, nipped at a shoulder, then settled his lips onto hers, his mouth desperately clinging.

She moved with him, harder and faster, undulating her hips as he explored her lushness. He was drowning in her, in the heat of her. With a hard thrust of his hips, he drove deeper. She clutched his shoulders, bit into one of them and dug her heels into his hips, then cried out as ecstasy rolled through her.

Feeling her release, he unleashed himself, attacking her mouth, pumping his hips as his climax crashed into him.

They stilled, clinging to each other, gulping air.

And then guilt washed over him. He eased her legs from around his hips and set her feet on the ground, brushing her gown around her legs. He had to work his throat to get his words out. "Forgive me. I took advantage of you, and that was the wrong thing to do."

"No. We both needed this." She pressed her hands to his cheeks and forced him to look at her. "When we were together those two wonderful days, it was as if nothing else in the world existed but you and me. Time didn't exist. We made love in every way possible, and it was glorious. We shared ourselves, and it was wondrous. But most of all, I felt cherished, something I'd been needing for a long, long while. The memory of our short time together will live with me forever, and this equally astonishing moment will remain with me as well."

He pulled away from her, adjusted his trousers and shoved a hand through his still-damp hair. "About those days, *chère*. Let them disappear into our past. You deserve more than what I could ever offer you."

She stepped away from him as a great sadness washed over her features. "Do you remember the day you followed me into the sweet shop on Rue Dauphine, where I was busy consuming ice cream?"

"*Oui.*"

"During our conversation, you said you liked me and you were pretty sure that I liked you as well. Do you remember?"

He nodded, watching her as she took another step away from him and lifted her chin.

"Well, things have moved on since then," she said. "Because now I can say the same, but with a change of one word."

She paused, and an expression crossed her features that he'd not seen before. "I love you, René. And I am pretty sure you love me. But just because it is so doesn't mean we are meant to be together. Like you, I have come to realize it is best if we go our separate ways."

Stunned, he took a step to her, but she waved him off and backed away, toward the gate.

"You will go your way and I shall go mine," she said. "I hope we will both have a deep and abiding memory of what we shared together, short as the time was. And with that memory I will have the knowledge that I loved a man very much, and it was wonderful. Wherever you end up, whatever life hands you from now on, don't let the awful things that occurred this past week destroy you. Don't let your soul die, René. It is far too beautiful."

Her gaze locked with his, she backed toward the gate, opened it, and slipped out into the night.

René staggered back against the wall. His legs gave out and he slid to the damp floor, the agony coursing through him too painful to bear. At the terrible sound that left his throat, Miz Sassy whimpered, crawled into his lap, and licked René's cheek.

With a moan, he swept the dog into his arms, buried his head in her fur, and wept.

Chapter Thirty

Felice stood on the third-floor veranda in slippers and a robe, dolefully watching the drip, drip, dripping remnants of a storm that had raged unabated ever since the night she'd walked away from René. Perhaps a little sunshine this morning might chase away her melancholy. Forcing herself to ignore the powerful urge to glance over at his veranda, she returned to her bedroom.

Once inside, she stood in front of the full-length cheval glass. Bending her head to the side, she exposed the curve of her neck and the love bites René had left on her skin—faint now, but still visible. At the thought of him, at the vivid memory of their erotic encounter two nights before, another ache cut deep into her heart.

"Everything all right, *mam'selle*?" Marie eyed her through the mirror, concern etching her face.

"I'm fine. Truly I am. Fetch me a colorful dress today. Something with a high collar."

"Mmm-hmm. Done got that figured out already."

She helped Felice into a pastel yellow traveling gown with a bit of white lace peeking out of the top of the garment's high collar. Felice twirled in front of the mirror. Butterflies randomly embroidered around the hemline appeared to come to life, fluttering about.

"Perfect." Her mood lifting, Felice seated herself at the boudoir table while Marie styled her hair into a fashionable chignon at her nape. "You've a fine way with hair. Whatever will I do without you?"

Marie gave a start. "I thought I was going with you, *mam'selle*."

"Upriver, of course. I shan't remain there long, however. I've decided to sail to Liverpool. Visit with Trevor and his family. Once I make up my mind as to where I want to—"

"Did you hear that?" Marie cocked her head. "Someone's ringing the bell at the front gate."

"If Michel is still with Papa, he can see who's come to call."

"This early, it must be my kitchen delivery." Marie hurried out the door.

Felice followed her down the stairs to the parlor, where Michel and her father were discussing business. "Good morning, you two."

A wide-eyed Marie scurried back into the room. "It's Lord Ainsworth come to call."

"What?" Felice looked from Marie to her father and brother. "Of all the nerve. And here I thought him long gone." She turned back to Marie. "Leave him be. He'll get the message he's been refused soon enough."

Her father stood. "Actually, I would like to speak to him."

Papa's stern countenance said there'd be no arguing the matter. "Go ahead and fetch him, Marie."

Michel looked at Felice with a glint in his eye. "Care to join me in the library while our father attends to . . . whatever he has in mind?"

"Gladly. Ainsworth is the last person I would ever wish to see again." Moving into the book-lined room, Michel gave her a sly wink and left the door open a crack.

"Felice is not receiving visitors," her father said.

Ainsworth cleared his throat with an abrupt cough. "I had hoped to speak with her before I leave town. Unfinished business and all."

"I'm afraid that won't be possible. However, there is something I would like to share with you."

Felice looked at Michel in question.

He shrugged, moved closer to where she stood and, propping his chin atop her head, peered through the opening with her. She would've laughed at the absurdity of the situation were their silence not vital.

Papa moved to a side table, retrieved the packet he'd brought along from upriver, and handed the contents to Ainsworth. "When I learned my daughter had notions of wedding you, I had you investigated."

"You don't say?" Mayhew paged through the documents, his face turning crimson.

"As you can see, Lord Ainsworth, I am well aware that not only is your family flat broke, but your debts are rapidly mounting. This, and what transpired in the courtroom, brings me to the conclusion that you cared not a whit for my daughter other than what her inheritance and investments might provide you."

Her father paused, looking down his nose at a faltering Ainsworth. "Perhaps you should thank me for arranging your transport back to England on one of our company ships; I doubt you could afford passage on your own. Now if you'll excuse me—"

"Why, you old tosspot," Mayhew snarled. "You act as if your daughter is some kind of a prize catch. Whyever would a man of my ilk want such a tart-mouthed, low-heeled termagant, if not for her wealth?"

Felice gasped.

Michel clasped a hand over her mouth. "Shh."

"Truth be told," Mayhew continued, "you've done me a favor. I doubt I could've stomached her physical presence long enough to produce an heir and a spare."

"Get out," her father growled. "You are a disgrace to the world."

Ainsworth laughed. "What are you going to do, old man, box my ears? The only reason I came to call was to reclaim a necklace I'd given her, so if you will collect it for me, I shall be on my way."

"Fine." Her father moved to the stairway. Instead of going up, he lifted his cane from the banister, retrieved a sword hidden within, and pointed it Ainsworth's way. "If you think I am too old, or I do not know how to use this, give it a try, why don't you?"

"Stay here," Michel whispered to Felice. "But do continue eavesdropping."

He stepped from the library and sauntered into the parlor. "I'd ask if you needed any help ousting the bastard, Father, but I see you have things magnificently under control."

Felice stifled a giggle.

Ainsworth sputtered as he backed out the door with her father in pursuit. "I want the necklace, old man. I won't leave town until I get it."

Once the two exited the room, Felice rushed in. "Marie, run get that horrid necklace from my jewelry case. You know the one. Take it to my father before Lord Ainsworth departs."

She turned to Michel, who'd lifted a brow in question. "I want nothing of his to sully my person." She paused for a brief moment, then burst into laughter. "I had no idea Papa had it in him."

Michel chuckled. "Neither did I. And here I thought I'd waltz in and save the day."

Marie scurried down the stairs and out the door with

a black velvet box in hand. In moments, Felice's father returned to the parlor, sheathed the sword, then took a seat on the divan as if nothing had occurred.

"Oh my," Felice said. "I had no idea you carried a hidden weapon."

"Most gentlemen do once they reach my age. When I was a young buck, my fists were my weapon of choice, but no longer."

She plopped down beside him with an exaggerated exhale. "How could I not have seen through that awful man's facade at the outset? He is the embodiment of my worst, most humiliating mistake."

Her words hung heavy in the air, renewing her melancholy. "Am I truly considered flawed and low-bred because I form my own opinions and have the courage to express them?"

Michel scooted a chair beside her and, in a rare act of comfort, took her hand in his. "Pay no attention to the toad's shallow, ill-mannered words. He may be a titled lord, but beneath the layers of his so-called noble breeding, he is nothing but pond scum. The man's essence pales in comparison to the bright light that always shines forth from you."

Felice blinked back a rush of emotion at her brother's unusual show of affection. "My, aren't you being kind. What is it you want?"

Michel grinned and sat back. "Breakfast would do."

Marie poked her head through the door. "I'm about to get to it now the excitement's done with."

Felice's stomach rumbled. "I'm suddenly so famished, those flowers over there look appetizing." She frowned at the huge arrangement atop a side table. "Where did those come from?"

"They was delivered late yesterday," Marie said. "After you was abed. There's a note attached."

"Oh, for heaven's sake." Felice marched over to the grand floral display, which included at least a couple dozen pink roses. She snatched the attached card, scattering petals over the table and floor. "A pox on you, Ainswor . . . oh my. They are not from him after all."

"Then from whom, pray tell?" her father said.

"Émile Vennard. He's invited me to dinner, the cur." She waved the card at him. "To the convent, Papa. Seeing as how I attract the worst kind of men, I shall henceforth lead a cloistered life."

"That'll be the day." Michel swiped the note from her. "What do you intend to do about him?"

"Oh, I'm about to make my intentions perfectly clear to Monsieur Vennard. Marie, please return this monstrosity to the florist at once. Inform whoever is in charge that there's been a mistake, that the arrangement was meant for Madame Vennard, and it is to be delivered to her immediately."

"Yes, *mam'selle*. Should I return the card as well?"

"No. Let Vennard try to explain to his wife why he sent them to her. Poor thing, she deserves something nice for what he's put her through all these years."

Felice eyed her father's odd expression. "What? You disagree with my decision?"

He swiped a hand over his face, then chuckled. "Not at all. Oh, this is rich. Quite rich. Coffee first, Marie."

Marie scowled. "That Vennard is up to something, I'll tell you. He done had his agent call on Monsieur Thibodeaux yesterday and offer a princely sum for that beautiful home."

"What?" Shock hit Felice like a lightning bolt. "Where did you hear this?"

"From Monique. She's beside herself. Don't know what's gonna happen to her and her son if that no-good worm buys the place."

Felice's head spun and her knees threatened to give way. She took to the sofa. *Then it must be true. René is leaving for good.*

Something shriveled inside her.

Chapter Thirty-One

Empty of feeling, René stood on the veranda watching Michel's eldest son load several steamer trunks onto an open wagon.

Felice, she be leaving town.

To where, he could not guess. Nor did he care to know. He'd soon be gone himself, so what did it matter?

She appeared in the street below, dressed in a flowing yellow frock. Her father followed on her heels. She hugged him, and although René couldn't make out her words, the lilting sound of her voice made his gut clench. Her father helped her onto the wagon's seat. As the wagon rumbled down the street, she turned and waved to her father without glancing René's way.

But her father did.

As René turned to go back inside, Justin paused and looked upward, straight at René. He waved.

Christ. René gave a nod in return and strode inside. The hell with its not being yet noon—he helped himself to a couple of fingers of Armagnac. Settling into his oversize chair, he patted his thigh. Miz Sassy's ears perked up. She bounded from her bed on the floor and into his lap, waited for a pet, then promptly curled up and went back to snoozing.

René continued sweeping a hand over the dog's head. He'd be taking her with him when he left next week—wouldn't think of leaving her behind. The last thing he'd expected when he'd arrived at the shipping office to collect his final pay yesterday was an apology from Michel. Nor had he expected an offer to not only return to the workplace, but to take on Michel's position after all.

The offer came too late. René needed to leave New Orleans, needed to begin anew elsewhere. After René had refused the proposal, Michel then presented him with the management position in the Jamaican office—exactly what René had wanted in the first place. He'd accepted. A good offer, to be sure, but a hollow one now.

"*Monsieur?*"

René looked up to find a worried-looking Monique coming toward him. "Are we back to formalities with names now? What be the matter?"

"I'm sorry to bother you, but Monsieur Andrews, the elder one, he be at the gate asking for you."

What the hell could he want?

"Show him in." René had become better acquainted with Justin when he'd started delivering documents upriver that required the man's signature. René ended up staying the night on more than one occasion, something he found he enjoyed. Justin had taught him to play chess, and had spent hours going over the finer points of horsemanship. In the end, René had purchased Commander, the horse he'd trained on and one of Justin's prized geldings.

René stood. He lifted a sleeping Miz Sassy off his lap and onto her bed, raked his fingers through his hair, and tucked in his shirt. Not bothering with shoes, he sipped his drink and waited.

Despite carrying a walking stick, Justin Andrews walked into the parlor in long, purposeful strides. René had met men who, in the brief time it took them to enter a room, immediately commanded respect and took control. Here stood one of them.

Justin didn't utter a word. He simply leaned on his cane and looked at René with a silent message that said, *you will be the first to speak.*

With a wave of his hand, René indicated the divan. "Would you care to take a seat here or on the veranda, *monsieur*?"

"The veranda."

René gave a nod toward the glass he held. "Join me in some Armagnac?"

"Thank you, no."

Miz Sassy followed them outside and curled up in one corner while Justin helped himself to the settee. "I heard a rumor that Vennard made an offer on your place. Ordinarily, it would be none of my concern, but as you happen to reside two doors down from our family town house, I'd hate like hell to have a man I dislike as a neighbor. Thus, I am concerned. I am also concerned that should the sale take place, Monique and Henri will have no home."

René took a moment to assess Justin's words and decided to be forthright in return. "Bastien, he'll be taking up residence here. If I were to sell to anyone, which I will not, it would only be to my brother. As for Vennard, he can go to the devil. *Oui?*"

"Indeed." Justin found René's gaze and held it. "I'll get right to the other reason I came to call—it's about my daughter."

What the hell?

René didn't reply—couldn't trust his own voice. Rude as it was, he turned his back on Justin and, shoving his hands in his pockets, made his way to the wrought-iron railing, where he stared at the street below as a slew of emotions ricocheted through him. Damn, he needed to stay focused.

"What do you want of me?"

"Tell me, René. Do you love her?"

A deep stab of pain hit him in a rush, leaving him bleeding inside. He stood there looking at nothing in particular for a long while as memory after memory rolled through him, slicing him to ribbons. He remembered the first time he'd laid eyes on her, when he'd walked into the shipping office three years ago to negotiate his employment. There she stood, a vision in blue, her eyes sparking fire, daring him to engage her. From back then to this last time he was with her, and everything in between, memories of her threatened to take him under.

"Answer me," Justin said. "And turn around. I don't like staring at your back."

René stood in place for a moment longer while he drew a barrier around his emotions. He didn't dare let Justin's words penetrate his skin again. He turned and, removing his hands from his pockets, leaned against the wrought-iron railing and set the flat of his hands on it for support. He found Justin's gaze still locked on him.

Taking a deep breath, he dove in. "I have loved your daughter since the first time I met her, some three years ago. Even after she'd run off—which had something to do with me—I never stopped loving her. But I managed to carry on because I knew she was forbidden fruit. Had she stayed, nothing good would've come of us."

"All those years, and you never forgot her?"

"*Non.*" He swiped a hand over his face. "Her return tore up my life. I had every intention of ignoring her. But *mon Dieu*, try as I might, I couldn't help it. I ended up falling even harder."

Justin studied René with a penetrating gaze. "As I suspected."

René gave his shoulder a shrug. "What good does my

loving her do, *monsieur*? I am a Cajun bastard brought up in a shack in the bayou by a voodoo witch. Thanks to my thieving ways when I was young, I can still describe the inside of every jail in town. Hell, last week I even managed to get locked up in one newly built."

"I fail to see the problem."

Justin's response caught René off guard. He paused to let the words sink in. "You cannot be serious. The absurdity of the gulf between us is laughable."

Their eyes met, and something passed through Justin's. "I think not. I could use that Armagnac you offered a bit ago. Preferably over ice, if you have it."

René made his way inside to the table holding the liquor, his fingers shaking so much he could hardly pour them each a drink. When he returned, he saw that Justin had moved to one end of the settee.

"Come, sit with me," he said.

Reluctantly, René did the man's bidding. *Merde. I should've poured myself a full glass instead of two fingers.*

Justin took a sip of his drink and, with a satisfied sigh, said, "I always enjoyed our visits whenever you came to me on business. I never found it particularly difficult to talk you into remaining a few days, if only to patronize a lonely old man."

René frowned. "Don't be thinking your living alone was my reason for staying. You're an interesting man. I liked your home. I liked the peaceful surroundings. A couple of days upriver was a good break from city life, don'cha know."

Justin nodded. "I found your conversation thought-provoking as well. What I also found was an inquisitive, intelligent, and driven man with a remarkable strength of character. Despite what you went through growing up, you remained filled with hope and a passion for living, which

I admired. Dare I mention how many times I was struck by what a good match you'd make for my willful, independent, and unconventional daughter?"

René took a hard swallow of his drink. For a brief moment, he wanted to dive back into the morass and retrieve the numbness that had gripped him these past two days. "I would never give her the Thibodeaux name. Could never do that to her."

Justin let go a soft snort. "Do you actually think my daughter would give a damn about what name she carries? Get hold of yourself, René. After all that has transpired, I am even more convinced there is no one better suited for her than you."

He paused for a moment, then turned and shifted on the settee to face René. "I would be proud to call you my son."

"Jesus Christ!" The emotional blows just kept on coming. René had been trying to ride them out, but his insides imploded at Justin's words, then shattered into a thousand little pieces. He groped for the settee's arm, managed to prop his elbow on it for support, then covered his eyes with his hand, as if doing so would shut out his misery.

Justin reached out and gripped René's shoulder. "I know I'm being a meddler, but I don't give a damn, because the two of you are about to go your separate ways, which I think is a mistake. Felice is a beautiful woman both inside and out. I'm convinced you've made her all the more beautiful by loving her."

René fought to string two sentences together. "I don't know how to . . . I . . . failed her in so many ways."

"Humph. Haven't we all thought we failed time and again over the course of our lives? It's how we go about overcoming the perceived failure that reminds us of our strengths and level of integrity."

Justin stood. "Now that I've had my say, I shall take my leave. Mark my words, she won't give a damn if the man she marries happens to be an illegitimate Cajun from the bayou named Thibodeaux whose mother is a voodoo witch. She's smart enough to know she'll not only be with the man she loves, but one who will cherish her in return. Believe me, your love will not diminish her."

René made to rise. "I'll see you out."

Justin waved him off. "Monique can escort me to the gate. I have one last question—what are you going to do about the two of you now that I've said all I can to shake up your world?"

René shook his head and flipped a hand through the air in defeat. "I don't know what to do. I've made such a mess of things that—"

"Since you've admitted how much you care for Felice, would you like to hear my solution to your quandary?"

The only thought René could manage at the moment was that he needed to be alone. The only action he could manage was a shrug.

"It's simple. Try loving her even more." Justin started off, then paused. "By the way, she's with Brenna and my grandchildren until her departure at four o'clock. In case you've a mind to go after her."

With Justin gone, René closed his eyes. Leaning his head against the back of the settee's upholstered frame, he let his thoughts wander. His life had been one long lesson in how to take care of himself. The results hadn't always been pretty, but one way or another, they were usually effective . . . even the way he'd managed to get Bastien and himself hired with the shipping company. But whenever an emotional crisis struck his life, he sought solace in isolation. He'd found answers in being alone. But right now, isolation wasn't feeling so good.

A nearby church bell pealed out the noon hour. *Mon Dieu*, the man had been here less than an hour, yet he'd managed to shake up René's life like a tornado.

I'd be proud to call you son . . .
Your love will not diminish her . . .
No one is better suited for her than you . . .
You've made her more beautiful by loving her . . .
Try loving her even more . . .

What would life be like if he never saw Felice again? He tried to picture the future. All he saw was a dark tunnel with no light at the end of it. The words that struck him were abject loneliness. He had every material thing he could possibly want, but without her, there was no light at the end of that tunnel. The clearer his thoughts became, the more his heart and mind agreed as to the future.

He scrambled off the settee, then headed to his bedchamber for a fresh change of clothing. He knew what he wanted for the rest of his life now, and he was damn well going after it.

Years of heartbreak and loneliness were about to end.

Felice seated herself at the table nearest the front window inside *Les Deux Bonbons*' crowded sweet shop. In moments, the waiter placed before her a fluted glass filled with three kinds of iced cream.

"Thank you," she said, taking note of the other patrons watching her, albeit none too discreetly. Had they all attended the courtroom folly, and were they hoping for more entertainment?

What did she care? She'd be gone from here in little over an hour. Ignoring the whispers around her, she slipped a spoonful of the sweet confection into her mouth, expecting a blissful reaction.

Nothing.

Blast it all. Was everything out of sorts today—even her sense of taste? Surely leaving town would lift her spirits. Eventually.

The bell over the front door jingled. A hush fell over the room. She glanced up to see who'd entered.

René!

A buzzing filled her head.

He came straight toward her, moving with the fluid grace of a predator, his dark eyes filled with purpose. Despite the shock of seeing him, she was mesmerized. Was there ever created a more beautiful man?

A familiar yearning swept through her.

Without a word, he lowered himself into the chair opposite her, ensnaring her with a steady gaze.

Had he come to say goodbye? Oh, she wished he hadn't. His closeness, the very essence of him, sent the buzzing in her head through her entire body. "What are you doing here?"

"I came for you."

A jolt shot through her. *He came for me?* That sensuous mouth of his tipped up at one corner into an almost smile, but the deepening color of his eyes sent a more serious message. What in heaven's name was he up to? She struggled to find words. "How did you find me?"

"Your father said you were with Brenna. I was on my way to find you when I passed by and, voilà, here you are."

Find me? "My father told you where I was?"

"*Oui.* He gives his blessing, by the way."

"Blessing for what?"

He reached over and, with a gentle grace one would hardly expect from a man his size, he took the spoon from her hand, dipped it into the glass, and brought a mouthful of the ice cream to her lips. "Open, *chère*."

Startled, she complied. The collective gasps all around her sounded like a small whirlwind. "You're creating a scandal, you know."

"Then leave with me so we can have our discussion in private."

"What discussion? As you can see, I have not finished what I ordered. I have no intention of going anywhere until it's time to leave town entirely."

He lifted a brow. "Then I will have my say here."

She didn't know what he was up to, but he was making her nervous. Very nervous. "If you've come to say goodbye and wish me well, get on with it."

Slowly, he shook his head. "That's not why I'm here. I've done some thinking, *chère*."

"And?"

He leaned over, his words a throaty whisper. "*Veux-tu être ma femme?*"

"Marry you?" she blurted out. "Oh!" She clasped a hand over her mouth.

He grinned.

"You cannot mean this?"

"*Oui*. I do. Since you are leaving town, as am I, come away with me."

The breath left her lungs. She raised a hand. "Stop."

"*Non*. Hear me out, *s'il vous plaît*."

She splayed her hand across her forehead, as if doing so might clear the wild thoughts ricocheting in her brain. *The man I love wants to marry me. Then why am I not racing out the door with him and to the church?* She knew why. She'd not make a good wife to anyone, and she loved him too much to selfishly agree to his proposal.

She'd get up and walk away, but she doubted her legs

would carry her. "Look around you, René. There isn't an eligible lady present who, if you went on bended knee right this moment, wouldn't say yes."

"Oh, but it is not them I want, *chère*. It is you. I always have."

She managed to shake her head. "I would make no man a good wife. I shall not be owned. Nor can I become a dutiful wife who does whatever she is told. You've worked alongside me. You know full well I can take care of myself. I don't need you, René."

A flicker of a shadow crossed his face, but it was gone before she could name the emotion. He dipped into the glass and brought another spoonful of the sweet concoction to her mouth. "I know you don't need me," he said. "But you want me, and that is even better."

Lord, he was actually carrying on like this in front of everyone. She could've heard a pin drop. And heaven help her, she was so disoriented, if the world were to turn upside down right now, she wouldn't know if she stood upright or on her head.

He held her gaze and leaned over, murmuring low. "I love you, Felice. And I know you love me, so why don't I take you home, where we can finish this conversation with me deep inside you?"

She choked on her ice cream. Covering her mouth with her serviette, she discreetly glanced around the room. "Someone could have heard you."

He chuckled.

"You are being purposely and scandalously wicked. What went on between us those two days we were together in your home was mere lust."

"*Non*. Lust would be me wanting to sleep with you for the thrill of it and nothing more. Love is me wanting to wake up next to you every day for the rest of my life. Once

I got you into my bed, I could not bear to let you go. At the time, I was convinced there was no future for the two of us, so I selfishly held you captive for as long as I dared. My only regret about our time together is that I cannot turn back the clock, because if doing so were possible, I could've loved you sooner."

A pulsing urge to run built inside her.

"You're scared, aren't you?" The light in his eyes changed, deepened. "Find out what you're afraid of, *chère*. Maybe start with how it will really feel to be alone when we could've been together."

He took her hand, laced his fingers with hers, then turned it palm up and caressed the center with his thumb. "I love your wild heart and your feisty spirit. I even love the chaos you create. Come away with me."

The air around her hummed with delirious expectation. She bent her head, kept her eyes on her now-empty glass for a long, blank moment, unable to think, aware of nothing but the solid warmth of his thumb caressing the palm of her hand. *He wants to marry me—the very man who swore never to wed.*

"I'm not going to drag you out of here like some ruffian, *chère*. I want you to come with me of your own free will. I want you to be aware of the same rare opportunity that lies before us. Here's a chance for the two of us to share happiness in a place where no one will give a damn what we do. Marry me and we can cherish every moment of the rest of our lives. God knows such happiness can be fragile as spun glass."

Slowly, he withdrew his hand from hers. The space separating them suddenly felt empty. "Do me a favor, *chère*."

"If I can."

"Let go of your thoughts," he said softly. "Clear your mind long enough to let your heart speak to you. Get a sense of what it would be like if we never saw each other again."

Never see him again? She closed her eyes against the thought, and the awful pain it produced. Her heart stumbled in her chest. She swallowed a sob. Her hand went to her chest, as if doing so might ease her breathing.

She loved him.

She'd told him so.

And now he was telling her that he loved her and wanted to spend the rest of his life with her. She didn't have to ponder long. She knew exactly what she wanted. Oh Lord, she knew it without a doubt. When had her eyes grown damp? She opened them and saw in his more than desire—she saw a depth of conviction. And abiding love.

He slid his hand over hers. "You've made up your mind, *oui*?"

She sniffed, and brushed at a corner of her eye. "Do you know what you're getting yourself in to, René? I am not a person whose ways are easily understood. Truth be told, there are times I don't understand them myself."

He grinned. "If I am to have the choice of either understanding you or loving you, I'll take the chance of loving you."

He paused, his gaze steady. "So, will you come away with me?"

"God, yes!"

"*Bon.*" Pleasure shimmered in his eyes. He reached out and slowly ran the back of his hand over her cheek, his words leaving his throat in a husky whisper. "Can you promise me forever, *chère*?"

She could only manage a nod.

They sat there for a long moment, gazes locked, the air between them electric. Then he slipped from his chair and stood before her. He held out his hand, assisting her to her feet. With a bend of his head, ever so gently, he placed a tender kiss upon the backs of her fingers. "*Je t'aime tellement.* I love you very much."

She looked down to keep from laughing. "You are intent on creating even more scandal, aren't you?"

"*Oui.* I wouldn't want this moment to be easily forgotten."

She looked back up at him, at the deep satisfaction on his countenance. "Well then," she announced for all the gawking onlookers to hear. "I love you very much as well."

He sent her a silent message that what was about to come when they reached his home would turn into yet another night she'd not forget. Then he tucked her hand through the crook of his arm. "Shall we take our leave, *mon amour*?"

"Indeed, we shall."

A collective sigh swept through the room. The enchanted murmurs as they made their exit would become yet another sweet memory to tuck away in her heart, something to savor during her winter years.

Epilogue

Jamaica, four months later

Felice lay alongside René in the new hammock he'd fashioned from fishing net and hung between two palm trees. A soft breeze blew over her skin and set the bed swaying. Nestled into his shoulder, she rested her cheek against his warm, bare chest, and slid her leg across his thighs. Lulled into a lethargic torpor, she thought speaking seemed almost too much of a bother. "Will we be able to get ourselves out of this thing with any sort of grace, do you suppose?"

When he failed to answer, mischief whispered in her ear. She ran a finger ever so lightly down the center of his splendid chest, then circled his navel. When she still got no response, she continued downward, tracing the fine line of dark hair that disappeared below his linen trousers. Teasingly, she slid her fingers beneath the waistband, then paused. Still no response. "Are you asleep?"

"*Oui.*"

"If you are asleep, how can you be talking?"

"My eyes are closed."

She lifted her head just enough to see his lips twitch, then snuggled closer. She remained quiet for a long while before deciding to speak again. "Did you read the letter from Papa I left on the table?"

"It be Sunday, *chère*," he drawled, soft and low. "I do not work on Sunday."

"Reading a letter is work?"

"*Oui.*"

She smiled to herself. "You want me to tell you what's in it, right?"

"*Oui.*"

"Lazybones. Why is it, whenever a letter arrives, you insist I inform you of its contents, then you turn around and read it anyway?"

"Because, *mon amour*, your telling it is different from my reading it, so I get two letters in one, which amuses me. What be in the letter?"

She went back to circling his navel with her fingertips. "Papa writes that Michel has been elected mayor, his children are running wild, and the shipping company is much busier than when you left, so he has no time to sleep. Also, Brenna is with child again, her eighth."

"He should've slept instead of working on number eight." A long pause ensued before René spoke again. "Your brother, he be wanting me to return, *non*?"

"So it would seem. What do you want to do, René? You've been content living here, and you've done a fine job running the shipping office."

"*Oui.* I've been missing home, though. What about you, *chère*?"

"A little," she admitted, continuing to toy with his marvelous upper torso.

"Jamaica being a British holding doesn't sit right with me," he said. "They did abolish slavery here, so there's that. Trouble, she be a brewin' back in the States on that particular matter. Makes me think it might be good to have two homes, *oui*? Most of all, I want our children born in America."

"As do I." She propped her chin on his chest and watched Miz Sassy sitting at the water's edge, waiting for the next sand crab to appear. Life in Jamaica had been good. Better than good. And living in a lovely home with the sea nearly at their front door had been a little piece of paradise. But of late, she'd sensed a growing restlessness in her husband. Even his Cajun accent had thickened. Truth be told, she was beginning to feel some kind of change in the air as well.

"What do you want to do, *chère*?"

"You know I'll go wherever you go, but I shall miss our life here, especially my freedom to dress as I please. The thought of all those layers of petticoats and tightly laced shoes fair tires me out."

"*Oui.* I am especially fond of these frocks when you have nothing beneath them but my hands." Slowly, he ran his fingers up her arm, then slid them beneath the short, wide sleeve of her thin, cotton dress. Tenderly, he caressed her breast. "You could wear them in the privacy of our home in N'awlins, *non*?"

"Mmm. That feels so very, very good." Contented, she lay against him and let her heart lead the way. There'd be talk when they returned, but the subject wasn't even worth bringing up. She never cared what the gossips stirred up, and René was now well established; he no longer cared so much what others thought of him. "If we do decide to go back, I'd like to take the bookkeeping position. Work alongside you."

"Hush, *mon amour*." He continued to leisurely caress her breast. "No discussing work on Sunday."

Odd how such a delicate play of fingers could be so soothing, while at other times, the same action drove her mad with want. "You're right." She sighed. As the sway of the hammock and the slow, steady beat of his heart lulled her into oblivion, her eyes drifted shut. "We don't discuss work on Sunday."

ACKNOWLEDGMENTS
&
AUTHOR NOTES

Most Americans today are unfamiliar with the history of how the Cajuns of southeastern Louisiana came to exist. In 1755, British troops embarked on what is now referred to as *Le Grand Derangement*. Over 18,000 French-speaking Acadians were expelled from their Canadian homeland for refusing to swear unconditional allegiance to the British Crown. Thousands were killed, innumerable families were torn apart, and property was plundered. While a great many of the Acadians were relocated to British colonies, some of them sought refuge in what was then the French colony of Louisiana. These displaced people became the ancestors of our modern-day Cajuns— an independent and proud people with their own French dialect, amazing food, and unique culture. Although the term Cajun was not formally recognized until 1868, the word had been tossed about for years in various forms by those who either kept shortening Acadian or mispronounced it. Because *Felice* is a novel, I've taken the liberty of moving the usage of the word Cajun to 1859, the time period of my story. For the French spoken in my story, I used both a Cajun dictionary, and a bilingual French-Canadian friend as reference, which is why some of the words vary from that spoken in France.

   In the middle of creating this story, a series of mishaps took place (a broken arm for one thing) that stalled my writing process. Many thanks to my wonderful and talented critique partners Tara Kingston, Averil Reisman, Barbara Bettis, and Tess St. John, who became my best support group. Without them cheering me on, I doubt René and Felice would've reached their happy ending in that hammock in Jamaica.

   To my beta readers, Barbara Bettis and Kathi Valdizan, your precious input and catching those little typos and sentences that didn't make sense saved me on more than one occasion.

   Jill Marsal, you are my super-agent who never fails to amaze me with your quick response and solution to any questions I might have, despite the huge time difference in our locales.

   To the Kensington crew working diligently behind the scenes, you are all beyond wonderful. To my editor, Alicia Condon, there is an inherent grace about you that elevates how I perceive myself as a writer. I thank you for believing in me.

   And thank you, dear reader, for picking up this book. Without you, I'd be writing for my own entertainment. I love hearing from readers. You can contact me on Facebook, Goodreads, Twitter, or through my website at www.kathleenbittnerroth.com.

   Authors appreciate and need reviews so if you'd care to leave one, I'd be ever so grateful.

Don't miss Kathleen Bittner Roth's next novel,

LILY,

coming soon!

"Like hell we'll be taking on passengers!" Clad in nothing but a pair of low-hanging linen trousers, Bastien Thibodeaux barreled down the gangplank, bare feet slapping wood, sweat beading his arms and chest. He landed on the shipping company's dock with such force, it trembled. "In case you failed to notice, Monsieur Fellowes, my crew and I are loading bananas and coconuts, not people."

Fellowes, the Englishman he'd hired as his replacement, stood before Bastien, unruffled. "A mere two persons—an English gentleman and his wife."

Bastien shoved a hand through his hair and huffed. "Why did you not consult me before booking passage, *s'il vous plaît*?"

Fellowes shrugged. "Mr. Talbot has urgent business in New Orleans and is eager to be on his way. They arrived from England late yesterday."

Bastien shot Fellowes a hard glare. "They are traveling from England to N'awlins via Jamaica? *Vous n'avez pas trouvé l'itinéraire inhabituel?*"

"Indeed, I did find the route unusual, so naturally, I inquired. According to Talbot, the crucial timing of his aforesaid business matter caused him to take passage on the first available ship. And in case *you* haven't noticed, Mr. Thibodeaux, you are near to shouting. And once again, you've slipped into that lazy Cajun parlance of yours, which I find most irritating."

Bastien cursed under his breath. "You do not have my permission to use the word Cajun, *Monsieur Britanique*. To you, I speak *Français Acadien*."

His accent grew thicker with each degree of irritation. He knew it. He didn't care. "As if I haven't had a belly full of those *hautain* Englishmen lording over everything and everyone on this damn island . . . not you, Fellowes. You be the only decent Brit I've dealt with in my three months here."

A corner of Fellowes's mouth twitched. "Mayhap that's because you're the one who hired me?"

"Humph." Employing Fellowes had been a brilliant move. Despite his glib tongue, he was intelligent and well-bred, and easily interacted with the high and mighty controlling the island. Come the morrow, Bastien would sail back to New Orleans and leave the management of the Andrews Shipping Company's Caribbean offices in good hands.

"You know the only reason I sought to captain the *Aria* back home was for the sheer pleasure of seeing the expression on my brother's face when I sail this fine lady into port. I am of no mind to take on the added responsibility of passengers. Especially a couple of *rigide* Brits expecting to be catered to. You should've consulted me, damn it."

"And have you turn them down?" Unperturbed, Fellowes stood his ground. "Talbot also mentioned he's an old school chum of the man who founded this shipping company."

"A schoolmate of Monsieur Justin Andrews? *Mon Dieu*. Andrews departed England some forty years ago. How damn old you figure this Talbot to be?"

"Late sixties, perhaps."

Bastien moved to the edge of the dock and peered into turquoise waters so clear, it seemed as if he could reach out and touch the white, sandy bottom. A sea bottom that actually lay some thirty feet below the surface. A quick dip would be just the thing to cool off both body and temper. He reached for the top button of his trousers. A school of barracuda, their silver backs flashing in the sun, darted out from beneath the dock. Never mind. He'd take his final swim later, in the isolated cove he favored.

He whistled to his assistant, who stood near the *Aria*'s stern. At the signal to join him, Henri scampered off the ship, raven hair tangling in the breeze, a wide grin splitting his face. Son of Bastien's no-good cousin, Henri had been the errand boy for their N'awlins shipping offices until this trip. Barely sixteen, he'd taken to seafaring life as if he'd been born a sailor. "You looking forward to heading home?"

"*Oui*," Henri replied. "I had me a mighty good time here, but I have me a powerful yearning for some of *Maman*'s filé gumbo, don'cha know."

Bastien chuckled.

Fellowes cleared his throat. "There's something else you should be made aware of before your departure."

Bastien released a litany of Cajun curses. "What the devil now?"

"Mr. Talbot wishes to board the *Aria* later this evening. Preferably after midnight."

The hair on the back of Bastien's neck stood on end. "Why the odd hour?"

"The gentleman indicated his wife has been ill and has a sensitivity to the sun—"

"*Mon Dieu!* I will not risk bringing a disease-ridden passenger on board."

Fellowes shook his head. "Talbot says it's a weak heart, not a sickness."

Some intuitive sense prickled Bastien's gut. "Did you check his papers? Make sure the man is who he says he is?"

"But of course, thorough man that I am."

When Fellowes grew silent, Bastien settled another hard scowl on him. "What you be leaving out?"

"He would like separate lodgings for him and Mrs. Talbot."

"*Sacrebleu.* Next you'll be telling me to bunk below with the crew because he wishes the captain's quarters for himself."

Fellowes grinned. "Can I offer you a brandy to celebrate your last night here?"

Bastien snorted. "You mean from my own supply?"

Fellowes glanced over Bastien's shoulder. "Looks like your crew's finished loading the fruit. Come, join me. A few good swallows of your fine liquor and you'll get a better night's sleep."

Bastien waved him off. "*Non.* I shall meet with the Talbots before taking to my bed. If it's her heart and nothing infectious, I will allow them to board. But only because he claims to know the company owner. As it is, I've a mind to set sail early in hopes of leaving them behind."

Fellowes cocked a brow. "An ill woman you'd leave behind? Tch, tch, tch. I got the impression Talbot doesn't care for Jamaica any more than you do. The heat and all, he said."

"What the devil does he think the weather in N'awlins be like, Northern England?" Bastien turned to leave, then paused to glance over his shoulder at Fellowes. "If I agree to the Talbots' taking passage, you'd better have a personal maid lined up for the lady. One who speaks English and is willing to travel to N'awlins and back."

Fellowes folded his arms over his chest and smirked. "Already seen to."

"Humph. Come along, Henri. Time for our last swim in this beautiful water. There won't be any bayou swimming back home. Not unless you want those gators making a meal of you." Bastien strolled into the shipping office, donned his shirt, snatched up his shoes, and, with Henri by his side, headed for the isolated cove he favored.

As they made their way through town in silence, thoughts of Louisiana overwhelmed Bastien's mind. He'd be glad to get back to N'awlins. Five months on this island with the British and their rigid rule over Jamaica had been about four months and one day too long. When he'd offered to act as temporary manager for the island offices, he'd not given thought as to how controlling the British might be, or how much he would resent their self-important hierarchy. One would never know slavery had been abolished here years ago for the way those louts treated hired hands.

When Bastien and Henri reached the isolated cove with its white sand backed by a stand of palm trees and waist-high ferns, Henri stripped and hurried into the water. Bastien paused to watch the sun dip to the horizon, sending swaths of orange and pink across the waters. His breath caught at the splendor of it all. Despite his constant clashing with those in authority, the beauty of this lush island had turned out to be a soothing tonic for Bastien's thirsty soul. But now, it was more than time to head home.

✳ ✳ ✳

With every bump and rattle of the carriage, pain shot through Lily's head. Despite her efforts to control herself, she moaned aloud.

"Hold steady, dear. We're nearly there; then all you need do is manage the few steps from the carriage into the shipping company's office while the ship's captain makes a few inquiries as to your health."

"The captain . . . I . . . I cannot," Lily managed, barely above a whisper.

"You can, and you must. Soon, you'll be aboard ship and in your own stateroom. Then you can take to your bed for the duration."

It took all the energy she possessed to form her words. "Oh, Uncle, I simply do not have the strength."

The arm he held around her shoulders tightened. "Listen carefully to me, Lily. No longer can you call me Uncle. What is my new name? Tell me who I am."

All she could manage was a sigh.

"Oh, this simply will not do." He gave her shoulders a shake. "Stay awake, Lily. You must forget your pet name for me. Who am I now? What is my new name?"

At her godfather's words, she sighed. She couldn't think. "Yes . . . no . . . Charles . . ."

"Bloody hell," he muttered. "My name is now Percival Talbot. You must never again speak my given name."

His words echoed through her head in a jumble. No matter how hard she tried, she could not string them together to make any sense.

"Do you hear me?" He shook her again. "Lily, buck up. Your life depends on this short interview with the captain."

"Can't think. I . . . I'll remember when the time comes." She collapsed into the crook of her beloved godfather's arm, wanting desperately to drift away, to not have to think. "Why can we not go to our staterooms directly?"

"The captain is concerned you might have an infectious disease. He insists on examining you before he'll grant us leave to board the ship. I told Mr. Fellowes it was your heart making you weak, not some disease that would be of concern to others. Of all the dratted luck. Fellowes claims this Captain Thibodeaux is some kind of Cajun healer out of a bayou near New Orleans. You *must* make it to the shipping office and cooperate, Lily."

The carriage pulled to a stop. One side dipped as the driver scrambled off his perch. Lily was able to make out the wavering image of a ship afloat in the harbor. Her blurred vision made it look as though the vessel was wrapped in a gossamer mist. The thought of sailing on rough waters yet again sent a wave of nausea washing through her.

The door to the carriage opened, and a footman lowered the steps. Her godfather slipped out ahead of her. Leaning back inside, he fitted the hood of her cape over her head, obscuring her face within its folds. Straightening her spine, and with all the strength she could muster, she stepped from the vehicle and into her godfather's arms.

"Good girl," he whispered. As they moved toward the shipping office, he raised his voice. "Shall we, my dear?"

With gas lanterns lighting the way, she kept her head down, her hazy vision focused on the wooden planks beneath her feet lest she stumble. As she stepped inside the office, her befogged gaze landed on what appeared to be large, booted feet, then traveled upward, past the tops of leather boots to long legs clad in tight breeches. And from what little she could make out, a trim belly and broad shoulders.

"*Bonsoir*," came a deep and resonant voice.

She jolted. The captain was French? Weren't they supposed to be going to America? Confusion engulfed her once again.

"And a good evening to you as well, Captain Thibodeaux," her godfather replied.

Heart pounding, Lily kept her head down. She'd let Uncle . . . no . . . she must forever wipe that word from her mind. In vain, she tried to remember to call him . . . to call him . . . what? She'd simply call him husband until—or if—her mental faculties ever fully returned.

"If you wish to make this journey with us, I must insist on examining your wife," said the captain.

Was he truly a Frenchman? What an odd accent. Nonetheless, she found his deep voice with its melodic cadence soothing.

The sound of a chair scraping across the wooden floor caught her attention. And then, thank heavens, someone eased her onto its hard seat. Conversation between this captain and her . . . her husband ensued, but the words escaped her muddled mind. Someone slid back the hood of her cape, then fingers, gentle but firm, touched beneath her chin, nudging it upward. Eyes closed, she drifted off again into sweet oblivion.

"Madame Talbot," came that same lyrical voice. A feathering of breath landed upon her lips. "Open your eyes, *s'il vous plaît*."

Startled out of her reverie, she did as she was told and found herself staring into the captain's face, fuzzy though it appeared.

"I need you to tell me how well you can see. Can you make out my face?"

How did he know? Had he guessed it was not her heart distressing her?

Oh dear.

"A bit," she managed.

Were his eyes really so blue? Was he truly so handsome? Oh, what did she know when everything was such a blur? No man could be so striking. She was tired, so very tired. Her eyelids, excruciatingly heavy, refused to remain open. She held out her gloved hand, desperate to find her godfather's . . . no . . . her husband's. She felt his steady grip and relaxed. She needed a moment, just a moment to rest. Leaning her head on his shoulder, her nose and mouth settled against his throat. So comforting. So very comforting.

You smell so good, she thought.

"*Merci.*"

That magical, deep voice rumbled through her. She sat up straight. Had it not been her godfather's hand she'd clutched? His shoulder she'd leaned on? Had she actually spoken aloud? No, she couldn't have. Hallucinating again, that's what this was about. She'd only imagined he'd spoken, as well. She went back to leaning on her godfather's shoulder.

"Madame Talbot," came that deep voice again.

Fingers, firm but ever so tender, slipped under her chin again and lifted her head away from . . . oh Lord, it had been the captain's shoulder she'd leaned on. "Please," she said. "I must rest. It's my heart . . ."

"Look at me." He tilted her head upward again. "Open your eyes and look at me once again. Henri, hold the lantern closer."

She flinched and used her hand to shield her eyes from the painful light.

"Take a breath and exhale, *madame*, then tell me your name."

She breathed out as he'd instructed. Had he actually sniffed the air? "My name's Lily."

Books by Bestselling Author
Fern Michaels